ANTICIPATION

"Have you ever drunk brandy while a Saquinnish Indian washed your back."

"Not lately."

"Then here, hold this." He gave her back the brandy while he unbuttoned his shirt.

When his last remark sank in, she straightened. "Wait a minute. What do you mean a Saquinnish Indian? You're Saquinnish?"

"I think so." He stepped out of his jeans and peeled off his socks. Arielle watched him, so caught up in the conversation that she forgot to be nervous at the prospect of viewing Carter naked for the first time. She liked what she saw. He followed the line of her sight and then glanced at her with a smile.

"He has a mind of his own," Carter explained.

"And what has he been thinking about?" she teased as he stepped into the water.

"The same thing I've been thinking about for the last few weeks," he replied.

She noticed that his eyes had yet to stray from her. "And what is that exactly."

"You."

Books by Patricia Simpson

Whisper of Midnight
The Legacy
Raven in Amber
The Night Orchid
The Lost Goddess
Lord of Forever
Mystic Moon

By Debbie Macomber, Linda Lael Miller,
and Patricia Simpson

Purrfect Love

Published by HarperPaperbacks

Harper
Monogram

MYSTIC
MOON

Patricia Simpson

HarperPaperbacks
A Division of HarperCollins*Publishers*

This is a work of fiction. The characters, incidents, and dialogues are products of the author's imagination and are not to be construed as real. Any resemblance to actual events or persons, living or dead, is entirely coincidental.

HarperPaperbacks   *A Division of* HarperCollins*Publishers*
10 East 53rd Street, New York, N.Y. 10022

Cover illustration by Jon Paul

First printing: May 1996

Printed in the United States of America

HarperPaperbacks, HarperMonogram, and colophon are trademarks of HarperCollins*Publishers*

❖ 10 9 8 7 6 5 4 3 2 1

For cloudseeders.

MYSTIC MOON

Prologue

Saquinnish Indian Reservation

Just after midnight, Reuven Jaye crawled out of his old Ford and trudged up the muddy flagstone path to his front door. The wind howled in the cedars above his head, flinging branches across the yard and drive, and spattering him with hard points of rain. Reuven was too worried to be bothered by the storm, for in the space of one day, his future and the future of the tribe had taken a sudden turn for the worse.

Arielle Scott was back.

Reuven thought he'd seen the last of Arielle ten years ago and believed the lie he'd told her would keep her away from the reservation and out of his affairs forever. But no. She had returned as a volunteer at the health clinic and was sure to ask questions. He'd thought most of his troubles were over and had never expected a ghost from his past to reappear. He'd have to do something soon. Something drastic. Something final.

Earlier in the day at a council meeting, he almost choked when informed of the name of the new volunteer physician. He quickly recovered his composure and looked around to see if any of the other elders detected his alarm, but no one seemed to have noticed his expression. All afternoon he carried on an internal debate, knowing he would have to deal with the problem soon but hating the thought that violence was the only solution.

Drunk, Reuven staggered up to the front door of his house. He'd tried to drown his worries in a pitcher of beer at the Rainbow Bar, but no matter how many glasses he downed, he couldn't douse the burning in his gut. It was the same feeling he'd suffered eleven years ago when all this had started.

That night he'd come home late in a storm just like this, only that time he'd staggered from the effects of grief and exhaustion, not alcohol. He had spent the day at Children's Hospital in Seattle, struggling to be brave for his twelve-year-old daughter Evaline, to contain his tears the entire day—the longest day of his life—but his endurance had cracked once he reached the reservation.

Weeping, he fumbled with his clutch of keys, his hands shaking, feeling for the house key, while he looked at the black windows of the tiny ranch-style home he'd bought when his daughter was born. He'd never been in the house alone. Ever since he could remember, Evaline had always been there waiting for him, always turning on the porch light if he were late, banking the fire to keep the place warm, making his breakfast in the morning before she went to school. Not until that night, when she lay in a hospital in Seattle, her face and arms swathed in bandages, did he realize how much her presence in his life meant to him. Now that he approached the vacant house, he realized how truly alone he was. The truth ran through him like an electric shock. What if Evaline didn't recover?

He slid the key into the lock and it made a grating noise, triggering the vision he'd been holding back all day. He tried to shut down the sound and the sight, but he hadn't the will left to fight his own guilt. The sounds rushed in on him full force—the frenetic snarling of the wolf, Evaline's shrill screams, the gun shots that killed the beast, and then the silence—the awful, awful silence when he'd dropped his gun in the grass and reached down for his Evaline, the child of his twilight years, his dearest possession, her face and torso covered with blood.

He pushed his way into the house and closed the door behind him, shutting off the tears and the wailing wind. Instantly, he noticed an unfamiliar silhouette sitting in a chair by the fireplace, the same chair Evaline sat in when she practiced her basketmaking. Reuven blinked, wondering if he were seeing things, wondering if his mind were playing tricks on him because he wanted so fervently for Evaline to be there for him as always. He wished with all his heart that today had been just a bad dream. But he knew this was no dream. And when the figure rose, stooped and round, all visions of Evaline vanished.

"Who's there?" he called, reaching for the light switch on the wall beside the front door. He flipped on the switch, but nothing happened. The living room remained dark, full of shadows. The wind must have knocked out the electricity.

"Reuven Jaye," a quavering female voice called out.

"Who are you?" He fumbled for the lighter in his pocket and reached for the candle he kept on the corner of the counter. The lights went out all the time and he was accustomed to working by candlelight. He lit the wick and the flame caught and held. Shadows jumped onto the walls, startling him. He got ahold of himself and glared at the old woman hobbling toward him in a faded dress and tattered white tennis shoes. He'd never seen her before. "What are you doing in my house?"

"I have been waiting for you, Tree-Falling-Down."

Another shock passed through him. Tree-Falling-Down was his spirit-quest name, a secret name that no one but him and his uncle knew. He hadn't spoken the name in years, and his uncle and mentor was long since dead and buried. Who was this old woman, who defiled him by speaking his secret name? Her voice wasn't familiar and her squat figure, a body shape all too prevalent among the elderly women of his community, gave him no clue as to her identity.

He crossed his arms over his chest. "You speak a name that is not yours to speak, Old Woman."

"And you take that which is not yours to take."

Reuven swallowed. Surely she didn't know. No one had seen him at the Wolf House. No one had been at the old village, that desolate place of rotting plank houses and dilapidated mortuary poles miles from town. He was sure they'd been alone—just him and those guys from Seattle. Everyone else had bought his story about who had really stolen the house post, or so he'd thought. Besides, that was old news. Year-old news long-forgotten by everyone.

"What are you talking about, Old Woman?"

"You know very well, Tree-Falling-Down. You have violated the Wolf Clan. You have taken that which is sacred." Her words popped in a strange way, as if many of her teeth were missing, and her ancient tongue was slapping against smooth gum. But when she stepped closer, he noticed that her lower lip sagged down in a loose flap of flesh. He'd seen sepia prints of his people from the turn of the century, when a few of the old women still wore labrets, the wooden or bone disks pushed into a slit in the lower lip. Labrets were a symbol of prestige and beauty, and the larger the disk and the more ornate, the greater the woman's social standing. But they permanently disfigured a woman's mouth, making it hard to eat and speak, especially if the labret was removed. No one wore labrets anymore. The practice had ceased with the coming of white men in the early–1800s. And surely no one pictured in the old photographs could still be alive.

Reuven felt a trickle of sweat roll down his forehead and into his eyebrow.

"Return that which belongs to the Wolf Clan," the woman warned. "This must be done."

"I don't know what you're talking about, Old Woman." He flung his keys on the counter which separated the living room from the kitchen. "And I want you out of my house."

She ignored him. "Do you think the wolf attack was a random act?"

Her question startled him, for he had thought the attack had been nothing but a senseless tragedy. Did she know something he didn't? Reuven studied her wrinkled face in the gloom. He didn't recognize her, which was odd because he thought he knew everyone on the reservation. Her black eyes, nearly concealed by her sagging lids and milky cataracts, glinted at him. "What do you mean?" he responded at last.

"Isn't it unusual for a wolf to attack a human?"

"I don't know. Maybe." Reuven knew very well that wolves never attacked men. In fact, there hadn't been a report of so much as a wolf sighting in the area for as long as he'd been alive. Just like the members of his clan, the wolf population had dwindled on the Washington coast. Soon there would be nothing left of either of them, man or beast. If Evaline died of her wounds, there would be no hope of the Wolf Clan sustaining itself, and no grandchildren for Reuven. Evaline was the last of the Wolf Clan, except for him and Mack Shoalwater, the man who bore the blame of the theft and who had consequently been banished to Lost Island. It was highly unlikely now that either man would father any children. Reuven was too old to take another wife, and Mack would be trapped on Lost Island until he died of exposure or old age.

All the other clans in the village thrived—the raven, bear, eagle, and beaver. Only the Wolf Clan was in danger of dying out, a victim of alcohol abuse, poverty, broken marriages, and heartbreaking infant mortality.

Reuven ran a hand through his hair. "Animals act strange these days, Old Woman."

"No. There is always a reason for what an animal does," she retorted. "Unlike human beings, animals do not kill for sport or pleasure. They follow the laws of the Great One."

"I can see no reason for attacking a twelve-year-old girl," Reuven said, his voice husky with suppressed outrage. "No reason at all."

"Perhaps the attack was meant for someone else."

"Someone else?" He felt another bead of sweat roll down his neck. Reuven thought back to the time leading up to the attack. He usually got home from the casino at three o'clock in the morning, after closing up and having a nightcap with the bartender. But that morning, he had stayed up later than usual, going over the contractor fees for the new construction, and had fallen asleep at his desk. Evaline, finding him gone when she awoke, had made him breakfast and was carrying it to him when she'd been attacked. Reuven cleared his throat. "No, they said it might have been the smell of meat that drew the wolf. The smell of bacon."

"The smell of betrayal drew the wolf," the old woman said. "The stench of dishonor brought him from the hills. The attack was meant for you."

Thunder rolled through the sky, rattling the panes of glass in the window and shaking the bones in Reuven's legs. He thought he'd faint. The attack had been meant for him? He had been the target, not his twelve-year-old daughter, who lay unconscious, her face ripped beyond recognition and perhaps repair? The attack had been meant for *him*?

"Get out!" he bellowed.

"You are cursed!" she hissed. "It is the time of the Wolf Moon, Tree-Falling-Down, a time when the spirits seek balance."

"Get out, Old Woman!" He grabbed the door and flung it open. A flurry of dead leaves blew in and stuck to his pants.

"You are cursed by the Wolf Spirit—you who call himself a son of the people. But you are no son! You are damned, Reuven Jaye!"

He couldn't speak. Anger, guilt, shock, and disbelief swirled around him, snatching his thoughts away like an eagle swooping down for a salmon, snaring the fish in its talons, and flapping back into the clouds.

The woman teetered on her swollen misshapen feet, coming toward him, her strange bluish eyes boring into him. Reuven stepped back, out of her way, afraid that she might touch him. He couldn't look at her distorted mouth any longer.

She paused in the doorway. "Return what belongs to the Wolf!" She pointed a gnarled finger at him, bent by arthritis into a knobbed claw. "Or there will be more sorrow for you, Tree-Falling-Down."

"Get out!" he cried and slammed the door after her. He ran a shaking hand across the side of his head. His thick gray hair was drenched in sweat.

Reuven shut off the memory and opened the door. He switched on the lights and quietly shut the door behind him, hoping Evaline hadn't waited up for him. He had no wish to explain his unusual drunkenness to his sensitive twenty-three-year-old daughter. With an unsteady hand, he brushed back his hair. It was white now, snow white. He was eleven years older and broken by worry and guilt. But he couldn't let his sacrifices count for nothing or allow everything he'd built to be destroyed by one well-meaning white woman.

Arielle Scott had to be silenced. Either that or Reuven would have to get rid of Mack Shoalwater—not just by extending his banishment indefinitely, but by really getting rid of him this time. The more Reuven thought about it, the more it made sense to eliminate Mack.

Reuven frowned and sighed heavily as he reached for a water glass. Accidents happened every day, especially out in the dangerous waters of Puget Sound. He filled his glass with the sulfur-laced water from his well and leaned on the counter as he gulped down the odoriferous drink. Yes, an accident. Perhaps by drowning. That way, no body would ever be found. And without a body there could be no autopsy.

1

Seattle

  As soon as the ambulance team from Harborview Medical Center left the clinic, Dr. Arielle Scott rushed into her private office and headed for the wastebasket. Overcome by nausea, she sank to her knees by the trash can, shaking and panting, trying to blot out the vision of what she'd just seen—a human abdomen partially consumed by *necrotizing fasciitus*, the much-feared flesh-eating bacteria. The bacteria was so rare that she'd seen it only in pictures in her medical journals and texts, and fortunately didn't expect to see it in a patient again. Now that she had viewed *necrotizing fasciitus* firsthand, she had to say the textbook pictures with their neat sterile frames and tidy captions were a far cry from the real thing—like the difference between discussing a fracture and seeing actual shards of bone sticking out of torn flesh.

Another wave of nausea surged through her but she choked it back and fumbled for a tissue in a box on the desktop above her. Trembling, Arielle wiped her face and swallowed, thankful that she'd managed to retain her control until she was apart from others who could witness her breakdown.

A few minutes earlier, she'd snipped away the bloody, fetid shirt of an elderly transient, thinking the man was drunk on fortified wine and had been involved in a back-alley brawl. But he hadn't been a victim of alcohol or violence. He'd been delirious with pain, burning with fever, and his emaciated body had nearly shut down due to the poison leaching from the festering mass above his left hip.

Normally she wasn't squeamish. She was calm, cool, collected Arielle Scott, whose hands and head were legendary at Johns Hopkins where she'd graduated with honors four years ago. She could operate through any crisis, diagnose at a glance, and work a full shift on an hour of sleep. As a doctor, she thought she'd seen everything. But this—this had knocked her for a loop. Arielle bunched the tissue and let it drop into the trash can. She would rather turn in her stethoscope than allow her new coworkers to see her now, leaning over the trash can, shaking like a baby.

No class in medical school had prepared her for the sight of the gaping hole ringed with rotting flesh. She'd never seen anything like it. And she wasn't sure she'd ever be able to put it out of her mind.

Suddenly Arielle heard approaching footsteps in the hall outside her office. She rose to her feet, swaying but determined to put on a good front to hide her unusual lapse. Someone rapped on her door.

"Dr. Scott!" a woman called. She recognized the voice of the receptionist, Katie McDowell. "Doctor, are you in there?"

"Just a moment." Arielle smoothed back her chin-length chestnut hair and took a deep breath, wondering if she could feign composure long enough to endure Katie's scrutiny. Then she took a stance by the window, pretending to gaze out at the rooftops of the historic farmers' market on the bluff below. She cleared her throat. "Come in."

"There you are, Dr. Scott," Katie said behind her, her voice filled with relief. "I was wondering where you ran off to. Are you all right?"

"Of course." Arielle was reluctant to turn and face the woman, afraid she'd give herself away.

"You were looking mighty pale when the Harborview guys were here." She stepped closer.

"I'm fine." Arielle made a point of studying the huge, red neon letters of the market sign set against the steel-gray water of Seattle's Elliott Bay. PUBLIC MARKET CENTER. The sign glowed in the darkness of late afternoon, lighting up the line of old wooden buildings constructed in 1907. Crowds of people were down at the market selecting Christmas presents for their loved ones, buying salmon and octopus, raspberry-apple cider and handcrafted wind chimes, listening to the street performers, eating dinner at Place Pigalle Restaurant—

Eating. Arielle put her closed fist to her mouth and fought back another wave of nausea.

"You sure you're okay?" Katie said, craning her neck to study the side of Arielle's face. "I heard that was *some* mess you took care of."

"All in the line of duty." Arielle forced a soft laugh, taken from her repertoire of physician-in-control mannerisms. "But I'm fine, Katie. Really."

"I was thinking of stopping in at the The Kells pub to have a brandy. Want to join me?"

"Sure," she managed to squeeze out. "That would be nice."

"I've got to clear off my desk. Meet you out front in five?"

"Okay." She waited until Katie left before she turned around. A brandy would be good. It would settle her nerves, warm her frozen hands, and put the color back into her cheeks. The more she thought about it, the better a nice smooth cognac sounded.

Arielle straightened her desk and stuffed a file of articles inside her briefcase. Then she pulled on her dark green trench coat, closed the door to her cramped office, and walked down the deserted hallway toward the clinic waiting room. All the other staff members had left except for her and Katie, who had stayed late to see to the discharge of the elderly man.

Without the hustle and bustle of patients and other health care workers as a distraction, the place seemed more dingy and tattered than ever. Over the past few weeks since she'd moved to Seattle, Arielle questioned the wisdom of choosing this clinic as her first practice. Then she remembered Mack and her vow to give of herself, and the dreariness of her surroundings no longer seemed important. Good work could be performed anywhere. And there was plenty of work to do in the heart of this city.

By the time Arielle reached Katie's desk, she was feeling much more like her old self.

"Let's blow this sheep camp!" Katie exclaimed as she locked the clinic door behind her.

"My sentiments exactly." Arielle dropped the blood work in the aluminum box near the door where it would be picked up by the lab later on that evening. The driver usually ran behind schedule and tonight he was later than usual, probably because of the weather. Traffic on I–5 and the downtown exits was always hell during heavy rains. If the temperature dropped to freezing as the weathermen were predicting, the roads would be even more of a mess. Above her head, rain poured off the faded orange awning that covered the doorway of the Pike Place Medical Clinic, and near the toes of her new and expensive black pumps, rivulets coursed down the gutter of the brick alley toward the steep grade of Virginia Street behind her.

"Hungry?" Katie asked, pulling an umbrella out of her purse. Beneath her short waves of blond hair was a round face which was perpetually smiling, seemingly undaunted by the plight of the patients she saw. Katie was one of the few women who could wear pink lipstick and not look like a baby doll. She was older than Arielle, almost forty, and seemed to be the confidante of everyone at the clinic, including many of the patients. "I don't have to get right home tonight. And I'm starving."

"Let's have the brandy first, " Arielle replied, hoping her appetite would eventually return so she wouldn't have to explain her weak stomach. She wasn't accustomed to sharing her problems with others and wasn't going to start with Katie. "And go from there, okay?"

"Fine with me!"

Arielle had grown up in Phoenix, Arizona and still wasn't accustomed to the rain and fog of Seattle. Sometimes the dampness seeped into her bones and stayed there until she took a hot bath or put on two pairs of socks and crawled into bed. She hugged her trench coat around her as they headed toward the welcoming lights of The Kells pub, decorated with fir boughs and tiny white twinkling Christmas lights. She wished she hadn't left her wool blazer behind in her office.

They hadn't gone more than a few yards when Arielle spotted something unusual in the courtyard next to the clinic building.

"Hold on!" she exclaimed, stopping abruptly. Katie took a few steps beyond her, and then paused as the command sank in. "There's someone in the courtyard."

A man sat hunched in an odd position on the stairs climbing from the courtyard to apartments and shops a block up the hill. Arielle had walked by the courtyard many times since joining the staff at the clinic, but she'd never seen anyone in that spot before. Not that it was completely repellent. She'd seen transients gathered in much worse places—near Dumpsters behind the Merchant's Cafe in Pioneer Square, in newspaper-strewn doorways on First Avenue, or squatting in the powdery soil beneath the highway overpass by the ferry terminal. But never in the courtyard.

She wondered if the courtyard was too near the medical clinic, and the odds were too high that patients could be caught backsliding by the doctors and nurses who had helped them days or hours before. Arielle knew how easily promises were made to quit drinking and to quit taking drugs, but how difficult it was for patients to follow through.

Arielle put a hand to her forehead to block the downpour so she could get a better look at the man. "I think he's in trouble."

"Oh, he's probably just another drunk sleeping it off," Katie commented. "We could call Detox and have them take care of him."

Arielle didn't answer and peered into the darkness. The figure writhed on the stairs. He could be wounded, drunk, overcome by drugs, or suffering from a score of other problems. But he was not simply sleeping; she could tell by the taut lines of his body, where his thigh curved up to meet his elbow, and in the rigid curl of his back and head, as if hugging his misery like a precious possession. All thought of brandy vanished from her mind, and she took a step toward the man, only to be held back by Katie's cautioning hand on the sleeve of her coat.

"Wait, Ari, he might be dangerous."

"He's in pain," she replied, to explain the risk she'd decided to take. She pulled her arm out of Katie's grip and darted into the courtyard.

"Arielle!"

Her sixth sense kicked in as she ran toward the figure on the stairs, just as it had first kicked in ten years ago when a man's life depended on her courage and clear-thinking. No matter the danger, no matter how hungry she was, how tired or worried about something in her personal life, Arielle could eliminate everything from her mind except for the medical situation at hand. While in school and during her internship and residency, she had been called brilliant, talented, and a natural-born physician—but she thought of herself simply as a person who could focus her mind much better than others. And she hadn't always possessed the ability to focus. That skill had been learned when she was nineteen and marooned on—

"No!" the man gasped, holding his hands over his ears and curling into himself. He writhed as if overwhelmed by a loud noise. He was a young man, dressed in a fairly new brown leather jacket, jeans, and shirt, not the typical person they saw lying on the streets.

"Sir!" Arielle called, setting her briefcase on the stair below him, "I'm a doctor. What's wrong?"

"Aaaa!" The man pushed his shoulder against the cement wall at the edge of the stairs, while the heel of his shoe ground into the step. His entire body went rigid.

"Sir!" Arielle bent over him and put a hand on the shoulder of his leather jacket. The material was buttery soft beneath her palm. "Are you injured?"

"Stop them!" he gasped. "They've got to be stopped!"

"Who?"

"They're getting closer! Louder!"

Who was getting closer? Aliens? Elvis and Jimi Hendrix? The SeaFair Pirates? He must be hallucinating or delirious. Arielle touched his forehead to check for a fever. His skin was wet with sweat or rain but not overly warm. No elevated temperature. At her touch he relaxed slightly and sagged against the wall, his hands still over his ears. Arielle could see no sign of injury or wound. The dark points of his damp bangs swept across the back of her hand as she drew away.

"What's with him?" Katie asked, hovering behind her.

"He's hallucinating."

"Drugs?"

"Hard to say." Arielle straightened. "He seems to be hearing something we can't." She sighed. "Let's get him out of the rain and call Detox."

"You mean take him back to the clinic?"

"It's just a few steps away."

"It's half a block. You think we can carry this guy?"

Before Arielle could reply, the man groaned loudly.

She looked back down at him and watched his hands slowly slide down from the sides of his head. He moaned again and tipped his face to the sky, as if bathed in sudden relief. His Adam's apple poked out of his lean neck where his shirt collar made a small V-shape. For the first time Arielle caught a good look at his profile.

"Mack!" she gasped. Her heart leaped in her chest.

The man turned toward her voice and his eyelids fluttered open. In the darkness of the courtyard, Arielle could just make out his features—his pale skin against the sooty black of his hair, brows, and eyes, the sharp bridge of his nose and stark cheekbones. He was around thirty, not much older than she was, which made it impossible for him to be Mack. Mack Shoalwater would be fifty years old had he lived, and he certainly wouldn't be glaring at her in barely-concealed anger—the way this person was staring at her.

"You know him?" Katie asked.

"No." She felt a sinking sense of disappointment and bent closer, ignoring the man's hostile expression. "Are you feeling better, sir?"

"Yeah." He raked his fingers through his short hair, sweeping the dark strands back from his forehead. Though his eyes were open, he still seemed disoriented and rummy.

"We're from the medical clinic. Come on, and we'll get you dried off."

She reached for his arm. He was too weak to resist. She helped him to his feet by wedging her shoulder against his armpit and wrapping her arm around his back. Katie rushed forward, handed Arielle's briefcase to her, and then slung the man's other arm up and over her shoulders. His hand flapped loosely near Katie's neck.

"Easy now," Arielle said.

"I'll be fine in a—"

"We'll just make sure." Arielle urged him down the few steps to the flagstones of the courtyard. At first their progress was an ungainly dance, but soon Arielle and Katie formed a rhythm in their walk as they retraced their path to the clinic doorway. Rain pelted them but Arielle ignored it.

"I'll hold him up while you get the door," Arielle said when they reached the bottom of the short flight of stairs. Katie located her keys and opened the metal gate and the entry door. Together they guided the man inside and down the hall to the nearest examination room. He shuffled up to the examination table and sank down, and the tissue covering crackled beneath him. Arielle noticed for the first time that he had a small cut just above his eyebrow.

"I'll call Detox," Katie said in the doorway, shooting a look at Arielle to make sure she felt safe being alone with the stranger.

"Just see if they're in the neighborhood, Katie. I don't know if we'll really need them or not." Arielle shrugged out of her long coat and hung it on the hook near the door. Then she stepped to the sink and carefully washed her hands, keeping the man behind her in the range of her vision in case he tried anything rash. In the short few weeks she had worked at the clinic, Arielle had learned to be wary at all times. She had discovered that most of the street people who came to the clinic were surprisingly soft-spoken and agreeable, but once in a while a hostile one would lash out or try to attack her.

Arielle turned to him as she dried her hands and slipped on a pair of gloves. He watched her movements, and no trace of his earlier disorientation remained in his black, glinting eyes. In the harsh light of the examination room, he looked even more like Mack Shoalwater than he had on the steps of the courtyard. The resemblance was uncanny. Unnerving. Who was he? And what had he been doing lying on a sidewalk while dressed in an expensive leather jacket? She regarded his handsome face, severe in its beauty, whose strong sculpted planes hadn't yet been aged by heartache or hard times. Mack's face had been careworn and full of gentle wisdom—the face of a philosopher. This man's eyes burned with fight and fire, and a good deal of unfriendliness—the face of a warrior.

"What are you planning to do with those gloves?" he demanded.

"Bandage that cut on your brow."

He reached up and touched the small wound with his fingertip, and then brought his hand back down to look at it. He smirked at the spot of blood on his finger. "Come off it, lady, it's not like I'm going to bleed to death."

"There's always the danger of infection."

"Infection, my ass." He slid off the table and landed on his feet in a supple, well-controlled movement. "I don't need your help, Miss Nightingale."

She glared at him as he yanked up the zipper of his jacket. Tough guys and their flip speech weren't things she suffered gladly. As far as she was concerned there was enough trouble and pain in the world without having to make matters worse with a bad attitude. "The name isn't Nightingale," she said in a firm and professional tone. "It's Scott. Dr. Arielle Scott."

He studied her through the glossy fringe of black hair that had fallen over his brow. His glittering eyes narrowed, and she was certain he'd caught the pointed meaning of her words—that she didn't appreciate his flip nickname for her, and that not all female health care professionals were nurses.

Seconds ticked by as they faced each other, and she considered dashing out and locking the door behind her to trap him. A vision of a wild animal pacing the examination room came to mind—a huge, black wolf with golden eyes padding back and forth, back and forth, confined and uneasy. She ignored the vision, wondering why her imagination had suddenly burst to life to take her off track. It wasn't like her to get off track.

Breaking out of her unusual lapse, she pulled out a drawer and selected a small Band-Aid and a tube of anti-septic salve. "This will only take a moment, Mister—" She paused, waiting for him to provide his name. She was curious if he was any relation to Mack Shoalwater. "Mister—"

"The name's Mac," he replied sardonically. "Injun Mac to you."

She glanced sharply at him. He'd not only caught the subtle meaning of her cool reproof a moment before, he'd given her a taste of her own medicine. In the court-yard she'd called him Mack. He must have thought the name a derogatory term. She flushed, insulted by his view of her as an insensitive white female, and pulled apart the wrapper of the bandage with far more force than necessary.

"All right, Mac," she said, biting back her anger. "You want to put this on, or do you want me to do it for you?"

"I said I didn't need your help." He stepped to the door. "And I'm not sticking around for the paddy wagon, either."

"Sir, I don't think you're in any condition to—"

He glanced over his shoulder at her, his eyes blazing, and she didn't finish her sentence. There was no doubt in her mind that the man in front of her was entirely in command of his faculties, and quite determined to leave.

Arielle watched him open the door and walk out. A few seconds later she heard Katie's voice calling out in surprise. Arielle rushed down the hall after him, only to hear the front door slam. Katie hurried around the reception desk and put her hands on her ample hips as she stared at the door.

"Well, that's gratitude for you."

"He seemed to be fully recovered."

"The Detox boys said they'd be right over. I'll see if I can head them off." Katie reached over the counter for the phone.

"Good." Arielle brushed back her damp hair while she stared at the door where her patient had stormed out of the clinic. Her body still buzzed with irritation caused by his grating personality. Then she shrugged off the incident. Medical school had left her little time to brood over problems or people who annoyed her. She had trained herself early on to look at a situation, analyze it quickly, and then do what had to be done. If the situation was not in her control she set it aside and continued with her work. Such matter-of-fact training, once a survival technique, was an integral part of her now.

She turned and briskly walked to her office to get her blazer. One positive thing had come of the last fifteen minutes at least—she'd be a whole lot warmer when she left the clinic this time, wearing her wool blazer under her coat.

2

Listen to me, spirit of my spirit, *blood of my blood. Your brothers are calling to you. Can't you hear them? They will bring you to me, to our people. Don't deny them. Don't delay. There is much to do, much to tell. It is the time of the Wolf Moon, the time to set all things right. I am the one who can tell you the story, the one in whom all stories of the Wolf reside. Come to me. You must come to me now. I am the shaman, but you are the war chief. And the time has come for battle.*

Carter Greyson woke up from another disturbing dream, only to hear the sound of wolves again. He reached for his alarm clock, knocking it to the floor.

"Shit!" he mumbled, feeling for the plastic cube on the carpet, and finding it after a few frustrating seconds on top of a large piece of paper. He squinted at the digital numbers glaring in the darkness as he raised up in his bed. Four A.M. Three hours until he had to get up for work, and he hadn't slept for more than a half-hour at a stretch.

Then he reached down and picked up the paper. Without turning on the light, he knew what he'd see on the sheet—a strange design of a creature with large teeth and pointed ears, done in a pattern of flowing lines and symmetrical shapes. He knew he had drawn the design, just like all the other times when the howls came upon him and put him in a trancelike state. The trouble was, he'd never seen such designs before, and didn't know why he had begun to draw them.

Exhausted, Carter collapsed on the pillows and tried to block out the unbearable wailing of the wolves, but there was no way to check the haunting sound. He was sure the sound was made by wolves. He'd heard dogs wailing at sirens, but their lone yodels were nothing like the noise in his head. The sound he heard was like wind moaning in the rafters of a house, an eerie chorus of discordant voices that curled and wrapped around each other, veering away from each other one moment, and joining in a swelling crescendo the next. The noise stayed with him, persistent and tortuous, until the vibration made him want to jump out of his skin.

What was happening to him? No one else seemed to hear the wolves. He'd watched people's faces in the street when an attack hit him, and had seen nothing to indicate they heard anything out of the ordinary. Yet the sound was so powerful it had knocked him to his knees on two occasions, and it was getting louder with each incident. The howling had been so loud in the courtyard that he thought his skull would split.

Carter dropped the drawing to the floor and stumbled out of bed, his hands clamped over his ears as he ran for the bathroom. He yanked open the door of the medicine cabinet and grabbed a packet of earplugs, knocking a bottle of pills and his razor into the sink. He was becoming unusually clumsy as the howling took a toll on his self-control. He fumbled with the paper packet and managed to pick out two yellow foam earplugs, which he stuffed in his ears. For a moment he leaned over the sink, his hands braced on the cool porcelain, praying for relief. But the howling continued, stronger than ever. It originated inside his head, not outside.

"Shit!" Carter said again, louder this time, and pulled out the useless earplugs. He scooped the bottle of pills out of the sink and put it back on the glass shelf, and then picked up his razor. The familiar weight of it in his hand made him hesitate. He stared at the implement, realizing for the first time that he hadn't shaved since Monday. Four days ago. Shocked, Carter stroked his cheek with his left hand, expecting to find a ragged crop of stubble, but felt nothing but smooth skin. Undeniably, unsettlingly smooth skin.

What in the hell was happening to him?

He shut the medicine cabinet and turned on the water. Thrusting his shaking hands under the faucet, he bent and splashed water over his perspiring face and sweat-damp hair. He grabbed a towel and sank his head into it, and when he raised up and dragged the towel down his face, he caught a glimpse of himself in the mirror. *War Chief.* The phrase came echoing out of his nightmare like a voice reading an epithet. Carter paused.

For the past few weeks, his reflection had been looking odd to him. At first he had been sure that it was simply due to his new hair. He'd just have to get accustomed to seeing himself with glossy black hair—the result of his bone marrow transplant a year ago—instead of the curly, dark brown hair he had been born with. But something was different lately. Something else was going on. He turned to get dressed.

Throughout his illness, Carter had learned to accept a variety of reflections in the mirror without getting too upset. Treatment for his aplastic anemia had bloated him into a grotesque caricature—Blimp Man, he'd called himself—and then sucked him dry, until he had been nothing but a living scarecrow. Chemotherapy had robbed him of his hair and the last of his vanity.

Months later during his bone marrow transplant, he lay in a hospital bed, an empty shell drained of all ability to sustain itself, robbed of energy and life. He'd lost his sense of being a man then, and had nearly lost his will to go on. He'd felt like a pupae of some insect, a helpless grub in the dirt, unable to run or survive on his own, at the mercy of sterile strangers and plastic tubing. He'd been no more than a blind and vulnerable chrysalis hanging from a fragile thread in the wind, his hope for life in a marrow transplant bag dangling above his head and dripping down a line into his arm.

Now, through the miracle of science and the life-giving marrow of an anonymous donor, Carter was a man again. But what kind of man? His mutating reflection alarmed him. Not only the color and texture of his hair had changed, something in his eyes was different. They were a shade darker, he was certain of it. His eyes had always been brown, but now it was harder to discern the line between the black of his pupil and the darkness of his iris. Even his skin tone had shifted to a more golden color. But more troubling and insidious was the subtle changes taking place beneath his skin—the planes of his face seemed sharper, more defined, and his hands no longer seemed familiar to him. The bones appeared to be longer, stronger. It could be the result of his new-found health. He had gained weight since the transplant and his body was bound to change because of it. But Carter hadn't expected to see a stranger looking back at him in the mirror. He wasn't a man easily frightened. But this scared him. And so did the wolves.

Sleep was out of the question with the howling surrounding him, compelling him to walk the streets, as if pushing him toward some unknown goal. The howling had sent him down the stairs of the ivy-covered courtyard the night before last, where that icicle of a woman, Dr. Scott, had found him. During his hospital stays he'd met many such men and women—caregivers who used their heads and hands with great skill, but rarely gave of their hearts. Perhaps they withheld themselves in self-defense, fearful of getting too close to patients who were likely to die. He could see in their eyes how they distanced themselves, and Dr. Scott's hazel eyes had been more distant than most.

Carter pulled on a pair of jeans and a black T-shirt. Why in the hell should the look in some woman's eyes bother him? Ever since he was a child he'd known such looks, even expected them. He'd always felt something was wrong with him. Why else had his mother rejected him with long silences and closed doors? Why else had his grandmother ignored him as if his presence disturbed her immaculate home? His teachers and classmates had treated him differently enough to make sure he knew they knew he didn't belong. Was it his appearance—his muddy skin, prominent nose, and curly hair—or some terrible character flaw that branded him as unacceptable?

He didn't know what it was that set him apart, and no one would ever tell him to his face. It was just there, an undefined barrier between him and the rest of the world. The black kids called him an ugly honky and the white kids called him a nigger. He didn't know what to call himself, other than Carter, and he suffered from an acute sense of disassociation. He thought sometimes that his unacceptability was linked to his father, because no one would speak of the man. And certainly the absence of a father only compounded his undesirability in the eyes of the other kids, but mostly in himself.

As a child, he had no inkling that he was a bitter old man in the making. But now that he was an adult, he realized the childhood skills he'd learned to close himself off from the world were both a blessing and a curse. He'd found a steady calmness in his solitary life, but at times the calm was pierced by sharp corners of despairing loneliness.

Carter shoved his feet into his shoes and reached for his leather jacket in the closet by the door. Once he had worn his difference like a cross, which had made him vulnerable to scars and painful blows to his self-esteem. But now he wore it like a shield, letting no one in and nothing of himself out.

Trembling and sweating, he left his apartment and stumbled down the stairs, driven by the wolves to go west, to take the same route toward the clinic he'd taken before. He hoped he wouldn't collapse this time, because at four o'clock in the morning there wouldn't be anyone around to help him if his condition deteriorated. Carter would have done anything to resist the voices in his head, and play it safe by remaining at home, but he knew instinctively that the howling wouldn't cease until he discovered the reason for the noise.

"Damn schizophrenic shit," he muttered.

He opened the outside door of his building and stepped into the sharp chill of the December night.

Most of the Christmas lights had been turned off, leaving the streets more desolate than ever. He put his hands in his jacket pockets, hunched his shoulders, and took off down the sidewalk.

A movement near the doorway of the deli on the ground floor caught his eye. He peered into the darkness, sure his mind was playing tricks on him. He could have sworn he saw a wolf slink around the corner. To prove himself wrong, Carter ran down the sidewalk, streaked past the deli, and turned the corner to follow the animal. He was startled to see a dark shape lope across the deserted street and duck into a shadowed alley. Carter followed the vision, which wasn't much more substantial than a silhouette.

He trailed the elusive wolf for three blocks in the direction of the clinic building. With each step, the wolf howls increased. He grimaced and continued to run, stumbling down the stairs of the familiar courtyard and staggering across the flagstone plaza until the noise swelled so loudly he had to pause at the edge of the courtyard where it met Post Alley. As he stood there, panting and sweating, he caught sight of a flat-bed truck parked outside the parking garage of a tall building across the street from the clinic. The howling swept over him in waves of pain as four men struggled with a large crate on the truck bed. The wooden container was about twelve-feet long and four- feet high, and was heavy judging by the way the men grunted as they slid it to the edge of the bed and very carefully guided it down the ramp to the ground.

Carter wiped the sweat out of his bleary eyes and watched as the men hoisted the crate onto their shoulders and slowly carried it down the slope into the parking garage. The howls seemed to follow the movement of the crate, and grew fainter as the box disappeared from his view. Carter trotted down the brick alley, wondering why the wolf howls would be connected to a wooden box. He walked down the driveway opening of the garage, through the ticket gate, and around the corner, just in time to see the men and box approach a doorway on the east side of the building, which was set against the hill. One of them called out and the door was opened by a fifth man, taller than the rest, and with a large round head topped with long, wiry blond hair. He held the door open as the box was carried into a room.

As soon as the box was safely inside, the tall man glanced around. Carter pressed against the cold cement wall behind him, hoping he hadn't been seen. He stayed there until he heard the door close. Then he inched forward and peered around the corner. The parking lot was empty, except for a green Miata parked between the door and the elevator. The wolf howls had grown much fainter, allowing Carter to catch his breath and consider what he'd just seen. The tall man's surreptitious glance was enough to raise his own suspicions about what had been carried into the room in the basement. What could be in the box—contraband, guns, a body?

He crept forward, his ears ringing from the abuse they'd suffered the past few days, until he was a few feet from the door. Just as he was about to try the latch, he heard someone approaching from the other side. Carter whipped around, looking for a place to hide, but knew he'd be seen before he could make it to the nearest pillar. Instead, he dashed to the little green sports car and grabbed the passenger handle, hoping it might be unlocked. It wasn't.

The basement door burst open and the four men who had carried the box filed out.

"Hey!" one of them yelled.

Carter swore under his breath and turned around. He slumped against the side of the Miata. "Locked myself out," he commented, shaking his head and crossing his arms to heighten his appearance of disgust. "Shit!"

The shortest of the four stepped forward. "That your car, buddy?"

"Of course it's my car," he lied, hoping his fashionable leather jacket lent him the appearance of a sports car owner. "Do me a favor, will you?"

"What?"

"Call a tow truck."

The short man squinted one of his eyes and regarded him, as if to judge whether or not he was lying.

"Listen," Carter went on. "You got to help me out here. If I'm not in the house by the time the wife wakes up, she'll start to put two and two together. Know what I mean?"

The other men snickered.

"At least tell me where the nearest phone booth is." He took a step toward them.

"Stay put," the short man finally said, waving him off. "We got a phone in the truck for stupid assholes like you. We'll call one for you."

"Thanks." Carter ran a hand through his hair and sank back against the car.

"Don't mention it, Pretty Boy," the short guy replied. "'Cause I'm not doing it for you. I'm doing it for Brownie points so I can trade 'em in for a bigger dick."

The other men roared and clapped their companion on the back while they all turned and walked up the slope to their waiting truck. Carter remained by the car, relieved that they'd bought his story. He watched them go, while a doubtful grimace pulled up one corner of his mouth. He'd been called a lot of names in his life, but never Pretty Boy. The guy must be blind. He waited until he heard the truck roll down the alley and grind its way up Virginia Street. Then he straightened, just as the elevator door opened behind him.

Carter turned slowly around and was surprised to see Dr. Scott just outside the elevator, with her foot propped against the door so it wouldn't slide shut. Smart woman. But not someone to whom he looked forward to making explanations.

"Florence Nightingale!" he called out in a voice rough with sarcasm. "Fancy meeting you in a place like this."

She tilted her head and studied him. "What are you doing here, Mac?"

Dr. Scott had the frostiest voice. She had the kind of voice that could form icicles on palm trees, the kind of voice his third-grade teacher had used every time she'd ridiculed him in front of the class. "This, children, is the way a snowflake should be cut," she'd said, holding up a neatly-designed paper, all frills and lace. "And *this*," she continued, holding up his tattered attempt and shaking it in front of his face as if he were blind as well as stupid, "is how one should *not* cut a snowflake." Of course his snowflake looked awful. He was left-handed and forced to use right-handed scissors. He wanted to scream at her, to tell her he wasn't stupid, to tell her that she was an ugly, dried-up old hag, that he'd once seen a bobby pin stuck in her hose and she hadn't even known it was there. But he said nothing. He'd learned two things that year. Not to talk back or he'd pay dearly, and that a well-executed art project was more important than the pride of an ugly little boy.

"I said, what are you doing here?" Dr. Scott repeated, glancing at the vehicle.

"Getting some air."

"Right. Move away from the car, please."

Carter walked around the rear of the Miata and came to a halt when he saw her slip something from her coat pocket into the palm of her hand. A gun? Pepper spray? Did she think she had to defend herself against him? Carter felt the old familiar heat rising in his throat. It was obvious the color of his skin branded him a criminal in her eyes, and before she even knew him she had judged his character according to his newly-defined race.

Resentment swept over him in a cool wind that tightened his throat and gut. He tried to stare her into submission, to the point where she might stammer an excuse and retreat. He wanted her to back down, wanted to see her turn tail.

She surprised him by standing her ground. In fact, she let the elevator close. Then she glanced at the car again and he watched her quickly inspect the wheels and interior. His anger rose another notch. What did she think he'd done? Stolen the hubcaps? The car had to be hers. In fact, the neat little Miata, with its rounded lines and pert design, was the perfect vehicle for a yuppie like Dr. Arielle Scott. He could imagine her speeding up I–5 with the top down and a tennis visor encircling her sleek brown hair, on her way to a doubles match with her well-polished friends. To fit the picture perfectly she should have been a blonde, but Carter knew better than anyone that life wasn't always a perfect vision.

"Leave quietly," she said, "and I won't call the guard."

"Won't call the guard? What for?"

"You tell me."

He held out his hands and kept a tight grip on his temper. "You think I'm down here stealing stuff?"

"I don't know what you're doing down here, but at five o'clock in the morning, it can't be legitimate."

He paused. His presence in the garage at such an early hour must look pretty suspicious. Perhaps he'd been harsh in accusing her of bigotry. Yet he wasn't about to apologize to the snooty doctor.

"So what are *you* doing down here?" He crossed his arms. "Looking for your shipment of goodies?"

"My shipment of what?"

"Goodies. Transported in a suspicious-looking crate I just saw carried through that door." He poked his thumb in the direction of the door behind him.

She glanced at the door and then leveled her gaze on him. "I don't know what you're talking about."

"Sure you don't."

Dr. Scott shifted her weight impatiently. "Look, either I go back upstairs and call the guard, or you take yourself out of here now. Do I make myself clear?"

"Clear as a bell, Florence." He was sure that if he held out his hand, she'd produce a ruler and thwack it across his palm, to punish him for trespassing and for detaining her. He slipped his hands in the pocket of his jacket. "See you around, Doc."

She didn't answer him.

Carter turned on his heel and walked out of the parking garage, his footsteps ringing in the cement cavern. He could feel her wary regard on his back until he turned the corner and walked up the ramp to the alley. Soon afterward, he heard the engine of the Miata start up. He retraced his steps past the clinic to the courtyard and headed for his apartment as he heard the sports car drive away in the opposite direction. A moment later, he saw a tow truck rolling down the alley toward the garage. Ah well. The tow truck would find an empty parking lot and no customer. Carter yawned and ascended the cement stairs flanked by a wall covered with graffiti in two-foot tall, green letters: LEAVE MY DICK ALONE, YOU NAZI BITCHES.

"Exactly," Carter muttered, still burning from his terse conversation with Dr. Scott. He was, however, grateful for his clear head. The wolf howls had completely ceased, leaving him relieved but exhausted. The thought of falling into a warm bed was highly seductive, but in two short hours, he'd have to get up and go to work. He might as well take a shower, find an espresso bar for a strong cup to jump-start his system, and begin his Friday early.

"Hey, Greyson!"

Carter swiveled in his chair, surprised to see the pert young receptionist of Northwest Navigational Systems poking her head around the edge of his doorway, her spiked hair like a starburst around her pale face.

"Hey," he replied as the rest of her petite figure slipped into view. What was the occasion? JoJo Sperry hardly ever left her headset and her computer terminal to travel the long hall to his office. The conversations they'd had since he'd come aboard had taken place at the front desk where he signed in and out, and a few times in the elevator. She was a friendly young brunette with a pierced nose, always eager to chat about her real work—songwriting. She'd dropped numerous suggestions that they meet casually after work sometime, check out some local bands or have a drink. But she was a bit young for him, and he was cautious about fraternizing with females with whom he worked. So he always put her off with good-natured teasing.

JoJo waved a letter in the air and grinned at him over the manila packet.

"Here's that letter you've been waiting for, Greyson." Her blue eyes danced as she watched him stand up.

"From the National Marrow Donor Program?" He'd waited an entire year for information regarding his donor, and had listed his office as his mailing address since he'd moved many times in the last year. It was standard procedure to withhold all information from both the donor and the recipient for the year following the transplant, and then not until both parties agreed in writing to allow an exchange of names and addresses. Usually the one with cancer waited until the transplant was considered a relative success, and more often than not that good news never came. But a year had passed for Carter, and now he hoped to discover the name of the person who had given him a second chance at life, and perhaps an address where the donor could be found and properly thanked. Carter might be bitter about a lot of things in his life, but not toward this selfless stranger, whoever he or she might be.

"It's from the NMDP all right." JoJo glanced down at the front of the envelope. "But it'll cost you."

"That sounds like extortion, Miss Sperry."

She grinned and tilted her head. "You know, Greyson, did anyone ever tell you that if you curled your lip a teeny bit more and grew some sideburns, you could be Elvis?"

"Not lately." Carter held out his hand. "Give it."

"But you have that look. You know, that sultry kind of look, that kind of kiss-my-ass look."

"Sperry, you're nuts. Now give it up."

She whipped the envelope behind her back. "Not until you say blue suede shoes."

He'd been dying of curiosity to learn more about his donor, especially since he'd been told marrow recipients could take on appearance characteristics of their donors. He wondered if the Native American part of him—which he'd never known he possessed until a year ago—had been given a boost by the transplant. He also wondered if his donor was physically and mentally similar to him, for he secretly hoped that somewhere on the planet was a person who might be a kindred spirit. Carter had spent thirty-one years in his own apartheid hell, and longed for just one person to count as a family, as a friend, as a confidante.

"Say it, Greyson."

"Blue suede shoes."

She rolled her eyes. "Say it with feeling!"

"It was with feeling, dammit." He crossed his arms and grimaced. "Now hand it over."

JoJo pouted and reluctantly swept the envelope in a wide arc, holding it to the side. "Promise to tell me what it's all about?"

"It's just about a bone marrow donation program, that's all." He didn't share his medical history with anyone and wasn't going to start with her.

"You're going to donate marrow?"

· "Maybe." He took the envelope out of her hands. "Don't I hear the phone ringing?"

She paused and listened, not aware that he was only teasing her. Then she caught herself and rolled her eyes again. "You're nasty, Greyson."

"Thank you, darlin'," he replied in his best Elvis impersonation voice. "Thank you verra much."

JoJo grinned and regarded him from the side, in a sly expression she probably thought was provocative, but actually she reminded him of an opossum. Carter remained unaffected, waiting to open the letter. Finally she realized he wasn't going to make a move on either her or the flap of the envelope until she left.

Sighing, she walked back to the hall. "See you later," she said.

"Yeah," he replied. "And thanks for bringing this to me, JoJo."

"Anything for you, Elvis," she retorted.

As soon as she was gone, he carefully opened the envelope while his heart thundered a drumbeat in his chest.

3

Carter pulled out the contents of the envelope and sank to his chair. He knew better than to get his hopes up, but he couldn't control the hammering of his heart. He thumbed through the papers, brochures, and forms, and then pulled out a letter.

"Dear Mr. Greyson: Here is the donor information you requested," the letter began. Carter skimmed the text, culling the important phrases.

Donor has withheld name and gender. Age at the time of donation: forty-nine years. Address not indicated. City unlisted. Phone number not available.

Carter's shoulders slumped. He had expected more. A city at least. All he had gained from his inquiry was the information that his donor was a middle-aged adult. Disappointed, Carter stuffed the papers back in the envelope. Maybe it wasn't meant to be. Maybe a person didn't exist who could be his kindred spirit, or at the very least impart to him a long-denied sense of belonging.

What would Carter say to someone like that anyway? He wasn't good at expressing himself. His words had turned more people away than he cared to admit. How did he expect to thank his donor, to say what the transplant had meant to him, to speak the words that were stuffed in his heart, when he was sure he'd make a mess of it? What he longed to say couldn't be couched in sarcasm, and that was the only language he knew.

Regardless, Carter couldn't let the selfless donation go unrecognized. He had never been in anyone's debt before and chafed under the heavy obligation to say thanks. No matter how difficult the search or how uncomfortable he might feel upon meeting his donor, he still intended to track him or her down. At this point all he knew was the age of the donor and that his blood type was rare, found only in certain tribes of the Northwest Coastal Indians. After work, he'd get a list of all the Indian reservations in the area and begin his search by the process of elimination. An inexplicable sense of urgency pushed him forward.

Just after nine on Saturday morning, Arielle turned into the parking lot of the Saquinnish Indian Health Clinic, run by the Bureau of Indian Affairs but staffed by tribal aides and a rotating corps of doctors and nurse practitioners from nearby Everett and Bellingham. She parked her Miata at the end of the lot, grabbed her bag, and got out. As she stood in the parking lot, brushing away the wrinkles that had collected during the hour drive from Seattle, she surveyed the small but modern building of silvering wood siding and cedar shakes.

She had expected more. In her memory, the reservation had acquired mythical proportions of swaying cedars, sparkling bays, and simple houses filled with noble fishermen. The last ten years had either weathered the reservation or altered her perceptions, for the place seemed muddy and run-down now, badly in need of paint and prosperity. She'd seen only one sign of life, the casino near the freeway, which she'd heard had brought newfound economic development for the tribe. Gambling proceeds had funded this medical facility and the school nearby. But she could see little else in the way of improvement.

Arielle locked the car and then walked briskly up the gravel path to the front door. Attempts at landscaping had been made with rhododendron bushes and juniper shrubs planted along the walkway. But lack of maintenance over the summer had taken its toll, resulting in rust-colored leaves and gaping dead spots in the shrubbery. Arielle opened the door and passed from the drizzling rain into the warm waiting room.

She looked around, nonplussed by the shabbiness of the clinic with its tattered orange and brown couches and extensively thumbed magazines, since it was no worse than the Market Clinic in downtown Seattle. At first she had been appalled by the ripped chairs and dingy paint of the Pike Place Medical Clinic, but concern for her patients soon outweighed the grim atmosphere of her new post, and she had learned to overcome the dreariness of her surrounds. She expected she would settle into this place just as easily, with its cracked picture window and crooked drapes, a room bereft of the comforting fish tank and greenery so often a requisite of more well-appointed facilities. Arielle shut the door behind her.

"May I help you?" a low voice asked in a tone so musical and soothing that Arielle turned at the sound.

Instantly she tried to swallow her shock. The young woman who had spoken from behind the front desk was startling with her scarred features. Arielle glanced at her face, quickly taking in the crooked nose, droopy eye and oddly canted mouth, and then she looked away, hoping she hadn't stared too long. All she wanted to do was openly inspect the receptionist's face, wondering how human features could be so artlessly arranged. In her years of medicine, she'd seen many victims of the cruel whims of nature, but never one so unexpectedly twisted.

"Hello," she stammered, stepping closer. When she approached the desk, she saw that nature hadn't created the woman's face. Something else had intervened, something that had left a shocking legacy of scars from scalp to chin, dragging the woman's features down in a ruinous slant. "I'm Dr. Scott."

"Hi. I'm Evaline Jaye." The woman looked down and briefly touched her cheek, obviously sensitive to the scalding stares of strangers. Arielle felt a twinge of guilt and wished she had been able to hide her initial reaction more artfully. Then quite suddenly Evaline looked up, startling Arielle again with eyes of such compassion and intelligence they shone like polished onyx in the harrowed field of her face. Hers were the eyes of a true healer, the kind of person who gave of herself totally and completely to the welfare of others. Arielle had always admired such people, for she aspired to be worthy of her calling. But she was aware that some innate selfishness, perhaps a product of her pampered youth, would forever hold her back from giving one-hundred percent of herself to her patients.

Stiffly, almost clumsily, Arielle stuck out her hand. "I'm pleased to meet you, Ms. Jaye," she said.

"Oh, just call me Evaline," the young lady said, smiling, which drew her crooked lip up on the left to reveal a line of white, even teeth. She shook Arielle's hand. "We're not formal around here, you'll notice that right away."

"Then call me Ari," Arielle replied, feeling immediately at ease with the other woman's spirit but woefully uncomfortable with her physical presence. She wished she could say something to get the subject of Evaline's unusual appearance out of the way, but didn't quite know what. Instead, she turned back around again, motioning toward the waiting room.

"Where is everyone?" she asked. "Nobody sick today?"

"Oh, there's plenty sick all right. Flu is going around. But they don't come in, not most of them."

"Why not?"

"They want the doctors to come to them."

"You mean they expect home visits?"

"Yes. Why should they come here when they're sick? Why leave their homes, their beds?"

Arielle raised her eyebrows and glanced back at Evaline. "Good point."

"And there are many women who don't want to see Dr. Thom. He's the doctor who comes in most Saturdays."

"Why don't they want to see him?"

"Because they are too modest. They aren't comfortable with a male doctor. And most doctors ask nosy questions, much too nosy for us."

"I see." Arielle unzipped her coat. "So what does Dr. Thom do when he's here?"

"He waits until the patients give up and come in. He says he isn't paid to go driving around Hell's Half-Acre. That's what he calls the reservation."

"A comedian," Arielle commented in a wry tone, fully aware that Evaline didn't find the nickname amusing, and probably the rest of the folks didn't think it was funny either.

"So many comedians, so little cleverness," Evaline replied with a dour smile.

Arielle met her eyes and knew in that instant she was going to like working with Evaline Jaye.

She leaned over the counter. "So do I get a tour of the clinic and a list of patients to visit?"

Evaline blinked, as though surprised. "I'll make a list right now." She turned to a notebook and ran her finger down the page. Her forearms bore long white scars also. Had she fallen through a glass window? Had she been mangled by farm machinery? Arielle had never seen anything like Evaline's scars and couldn't make an educated guess as to the source of her disfigurement.

"One thing to remember when you make your visits, Dr. Scott, is to pay your respects to the elder of the house first. That's very important."

"Okay."

"And some women will not speak to you of their problems, especially the older ladies."

"Sounds like a challenge. Diagnosis through extrasensory perception."

Evaline let out a soft giggle, but almost immediately put her hand up to her mouth to suppress the sound. She bent back down to attend to her task.

"I've heard of you," Evaline commented a moment later while reaching for a blank piece of paper upon which she copied names and addresses. "You were the girl who got shipwrecked years ago, weren't you?"

"Yes."

"I was a teenager then. Around thirteen, I think."

"I was a little older. Nineteen." Arielle studied Evaline's shining black hair, which she wore pulled back and fastened with a tooled leather barrette. Evaline's tresses were thick and lustrous, like the hair of a ballerina or Iberian countess, and her figure was small and willowy in the jeans and sweater she wore. Her hands beneath the scars were slender and graceful.

"I remember thinking you were the strangest creature I'd ever seen," Evaline continued, "with your ragged clothes and sunburn, and your hair all wild."

Arielle laughed. "After three months without conditioner and a good brush I must have been a sight."

"Your hair was more red then."

Arielle was amazed at the young woman's accurate memory. "As I recall, the wind and sun devastated my perm. My hair was a wreck for months afterward. So I cut it and never grew it long again."

"I thought you were beautiful."

Arielle was surprised by her soft genuine words. For a moment she surveyed Evaline's quiet black eyes. "There are many forms of beauty, Evaline," she replied. "Many forms."

"Yes, inner beauty." Evaline handed her the piece of paper. "I've heard a lot about it." She grimaced and rolled her eyes. "Obviously."

"You know—" Arielle began and then stopped. But she was never one to pussyfoot around issues and wasn't about to start. "You know, Evaline, there have been incredible advances in plastic surgery in the last few years."

"I've had my share of operations. Hard to believe, huh?" Coming from most people, the words would have been filled with bitterness, but Evaline's voice was touched with wistfulness and resignation.

"Have you seen any specialists?"

"Many. But something always goes wrong. An infection or an unforeseen problem with scar tissue. Always something."

"I can't believe it."

"I was meant to have this face. I have accepted it as my fate."

"Nonsense. Something can be done." Arielle had never held much stock in the concept of fate, and such statements always filled her with indignation. Fate had no scientific basis and therefore could not be accepted as truth, especially not when she was certain something could be done to change this poor woman's appearance. "If you don't mind me asking, how did it happen?"

"I was mauled by a wolf when I was twelve."

"Mauled by a wolf?"

"Yes. My dad has its skin on the wall of our living room. It was a huge animal. The largest anyone has ever seen."

Arielle couldn't think of a more cruel reminder of Evaline's trauma than viewing the skin of her attacker every day of her life.

"If you like I could get phone numbers of some surgeons I know," Arielle said. "I'm sure they could help you."

Evaline looked down. "Thanks for the thought, Dr. Scott, but I really don't want to undergo any more operations. It's too much for me to take—all the hoping and dreaming, and then finding out it's no better than before when the bandages come off."

"Are you sure?" Arielle inquired.

"Yes." Evaline nodded and pointed to the list, obviously wanting to change the subject. "Those are the names and addresses of people who have called in. I'll give you directions later. But first, let me show you around."

"Great." Arielle put the list in the pocket of her parka and followed Evaline down the hall. "By the way," she said. "Since you remember me, you probably remember the man who was on the island with me—Mack Shoalwater?"

"Mack?" Evaline stared straight ahead.

"Yes. Do you know what happened to him?"

"He is as one dead to us."

"Yes, but how?"

Evaline opened the door of an examination room on her left. "We do not speak of him. He is in banishment."

"No, he's dead."

Evaline glanced at her over her shoulder. "Who told you that?"

"I got a letter years ago in reply to one I wrote, inquiring about Mack. I was told he had died."

"There must have been some confusion. Perhaps you misunderstood the meaning in the letter. Mack might as well be dead, that is what the letter probably indicated."

"No, I remember it distinctly. The letter informed me that Mack Shoalwater had died."

"That is very curious."

"Yes, it is." Arielle felt a sharp twinge of unease. For ten years she had believed Mack Shoalwater was dead and that there was no use in pursuing her vow to exonerate him. Was it possible that he was still alive, trapped on the island and being punished for crimes she was sure he'd never committed? "And I'm going to get to the bottom of it. Who can I talk to that might know what really happened to Mack?"

"My father might."

"Is your father around?"

"He's at home right now, but you can probably catch him later at the casino. He's got an office there."

"Good. I'll go see him when I finish up here."

o   o   o

Later that afternoon, Evaline did her end-of-the-day-filing. Dr. Scott had already left for the casino to talk to her father, and Evaline was nearly ready to leave herself. She went over the list of patients Dr. Scott had managed to see that day and had to admit the woman's progress was impressive. She'd only failed to visit two of the members on the list.

She sighed and opened the appointment book to begin scheduling follow-up visits as indicated by the notes on the patient charts. As she flipped through the pages she thought back to the words she'd shared with Ari Scott. Evaline had expected the doctor to be cold, judging by her elegant looks and assured manner, when instead she'd been casual and friendly. Evaline had felt an instant sense of camaraderie with her, which was surprising, for most people were too put off by her scars to be genuinely friendly. Dr. Scott had plowed through the initial unpleasantness in a matter of minutes and Evaline had the distinct feeling Ari saw past her crooked features to the human being beneath. Not many people got that far.

For the first time in her life, Evaline noticed the oppressive aspect of the stillness in the clinic after Ari had left. She had never minded the silence before. In fact, the clean vacant rooms and shrouded windows had been Evaline's private sanctuary from the world—far away from the busy casino down the road where gamblers from the surrounding cities openly stared at her, their faces lengthening with incredulity.

She had learned long ago that her ugliness brought out the ugliness in others, and she had no wish to subject herself to that any longer. Once she had prided herself for her ability to forgive those who hurt her with their cruel remarks and their averted gazes. But after countless run-ins with insensitive people, Evaline soon found the well of forgiveness in her heart had run dry. Instead of succumbing to bitterness and resentment, she chose to remain in the shadows, giving what she could, but only to those of her community.

The bell on the door tinkled and Evaline looked up from her work, expecting to see Dr. Scott coming back. But instead, an unfamiliar man closed the door behind him and straightened as he turned toward her.

Evaline froze, one hand on the appointment book, the other at her throat. The man at the door was the most handsome Indian male she'd ever seen—from his raven hair swept back over his ears and falling across his forehead, to his tight athletic frame, the kind of body possessed by wide receivers she'd seen streaking across the television screen during one of her father's numerous football programs. He was a man of straight shoulders, long lean legs, and a glow of vitality which streamed from him when he walked toward her, brushing back his hair in an absent gesture.

Evaline flushed, painfully conscious of the contrast between his good-looking face and her grotesque one.

A shadow crossed his features when he glanced at her, and then the usual forced smile appeared on his mouth. But the smile didn't hide the sadness in his eyes, and his pity struck her like a slap. Evaline raised her chin, refusing to absorb his sympathy, for accepting his pity was more wounding than a blow.

"May I help you?" she asked, feeling the heat of another blush searing her cheeks.

"I hope so." He flashed a quick smile at her.

The smile was fleeting, edgy, but thoroughly masculine. Evaline felt something melting inside her. Before her was the kind of man she'd dreamed about coming to the reservation, his car broken down and she the only person available to help him, the kind of man whom she could rescue from the sea and breathe life into, the kind of man she wished would become beholden to her for an act of heroism, enough to garner a moment of his appreciation. She'd never gain affection from a man any other way, and certainly not from a man who possessed as much beauty as the one who stood on the other side of the counter.

"I'm looking for someone," he continued, stuffing his hands into the front pockets of his jeans. He was so potently attractive, Evaline could barely stand to look at him. "I was hoping you might be able to help."

"Maybe. Who are you trying to find?"

"Someone from the reservation who might have donated bone marrow about a year ago."

"A bone marrow donor?"

"Yeah. I don't know the name. Just that the person was a Native American from this area. I know it's a long shot, but I was hoping you could help."

She wanted to help him. She longed to help him and transform his sympathy to gratitude. But having worked at the clinic for the past six years, she was well aware of the rules concerning access to patient records. Evaline swallowed. "I'm afraid such information is confidential, sir."

His eyes darkened and he looked up at the ceiling. "Damn," he said. Then he looked back down at her and tilted his head. "You sure?" he asked. "I just want to find out who the person is so I can thank them. It would mean a lot to me."

"Really, I can't." Evaline closed the appointment book. "I'm sorry." She watched him expectantly, waiting to see what he would do.

"Could you at least give me a list of people who donated bone marrow during a certain time period?"

"I'm afraid not. I am not aware of any such list. But even if I were, I still couldn't let you have it."

The man sighed. He stood silently for a moment and then glanced back at her. "Does the name Elizabeth Greyson mean anything to you?"

"Elizabeth Greyson? No."

He reached into a pocket on the inside of his jacket and pulled out a photograph. He turned it so Evaline could see the likeness of a young woman with a dark brown bouffant hairdo and frosted lipstick, a portrait of an attractive Caucasian coed straight out of the sixties. "Does this woman look at all familiar?"

Evaline regarded the photo and shook her head. "Sorry. No."

He returned the photograph to his pocket and glanced around the clinic. "Is there anyone else around here who might remember a bone marrow donation, someone not bound by medical legalities?"

"I'm afraid I can't think of anyone offhand."

"Could I at least leave my name with you, in case you think of anyone?"

"Of course."

He reached in his jacket pocket and drew out a business card, which he gave to her.

"Carter Greyson?" she read.

"Yeah. I'm from Seattle. Feel free to call me collect."

"All right." She would love to talk to him on the phone but knew she never would. Still, she would keep the information, on the chance that a miracle might occur to throw him across her path again.

"My work phone and my home phone are listed there." He pointed at the card. "Call me day or night."

Evaline smiled softly. "You're really serious about finding this person."

"Yes, I am."

"I'll tell you what, Mr. Greyson, the physician in charge today will be back soon. Perhaps she can help you in some way that I can't. Would you like to wait?"

"Sure."

"Have a seat then." Evaline gestured toward the couches across the room. "She shouldn't be long. Would you like any coffee or tea?"

"No thanks." He ambled toward the sitting area and sank onto the couch. Most people would have reached for a magazine, but Mr. Greyson stared out the window. For a moment, Evaline regarded his lean figure, wishing he had asked for her name or looked at her twice, and not because of her injury. That, however, was far too much to ask of anyone.

After a moment he turned. "Does someone own a pet wolf around here?" he asked.

Evaline felt her throat constrict with fear. She couldn't think of wolves without revisiting the trauma she'd suffered years ago. "Pet wolf?" she stuttered.

"Yes. I saw a wolf run through the parking lot when I got here."

"No. No wolves, Mr. Greyson. They don't tame easily."

"But are there any around here?"

"No. Not for many years. Not even wild ones. Maybe you saw a dog."

"I don't think so." He looked out the window again.

Evaline returned to the appointment book and forced her thoughts away from wolves and back to Dr. Scott. She wondered what kind of information her father would disclose about Mack Shoalwater. Her father wasn't the type of man to gossip about tribal members, especially to strangers on the reservation.

At the casino, *Arielle walked* behind a short man with a beefy set of shoulders and narrow hips who took her to meet Reuven Jaye. The man's brown polyester knit slacks sagged so far down on his hips that Arielle wondered how he could keep his shirt tucked in. He knocked on a door at the end of the hall.

"Reuven," he called, "somebody to see you."

Then her escort glanced over his shoulder at her. "The place is about to open, lady. I got to get back."

"Thanks," she said.

He left her standing in the hall. Arielle heard footsteps approaching the closed door from the other side. She vaguely remembered what Reuven Jaye looked like and waited for the door to open, expecting to see the gray-haired man who'd found her on the island with Mack so many years ago. She was surprised when a man with snow-white hair appeared in the doorway. He had a square face with heavy jowls and deep lines around his wide mouth, and was probably in his mid-seventies. For a moment he regarded her without greeting and then he pushed up the heavy black frame of his glasses and said, "What can I do for you?"

"I don't know if you remember me or not, but I'm Arielle Scott, the new physician at the clinic." She held out her hand. He shook it but inspected her with doubt and suspicion gleaming through the lenses of his glasses.

"I remember you all right," he mumbled. "Want to step into my office?"

"Thanks." His cool reception filled her with unease. She walked in past him and glanced around at the room which was orderly, lined with metal filing cabinets, and decorated with beautiful watercolors. They were coastal scenes whose delicacy of line and wash showed the hand of a sensitive artist and lover of nature. She tried to see the signature of the painter, but couldn't make it out without stepping closer and appearing overly nosy. She'd learned one thing on her first day at the reservation and that was to remain polite and reserved.

"Please, sit down, Dr. Scott."

"Thank you." She lowered herself into a straight-back chair, the kind that could be stacked one on top of the other at big hotels and conference facilities, while Reuven settled in behind his massive desk.

"So you've come back," he said, pursing his lips. His features were as big and coarse as his daughter's were delicate. He hadn't yet smiled at her and Arielle didn't know whether it was because he was unfriendly in general or annoyed at her in particular. "You haven't changed that much in ten years."

"The reservation certainly has. There's some new construction."

Reuven nodded, looking like a contented frog with his glasses and thick neck. "This casino has made it all possible. We've seen good profits for the last seven years."

"I'm glad to hear that."

"And that's why we don't need your services, Dr. Scott. We don't ask no favors from outsiders."

"It's something I want to give. As repayment of a debt."

"You don't owe us nothin'."

"On the contrary, Mr. Jaye, I believe I do owe something. But since Mack Shoalwater isn't around, I can't very well repay him. The next best thing is offering my skills to his people."

"*His* people?" Reuven snorted, his upper lip curling. "Mack Shoalwater didn't care diddly-squat about his people."

"Oh?" Surprised by the comment, Arielle almost leaned forward, propelled by her burning curiosity about Mack. She didn't want to appear too inquisitive, however, for she was well aware that curiosity was considered a violation of privacy. Instead, she concealed her reaction and casually sank back in the chair. "Why do you say that?"

"He spent most of his life as far away as he could get from the Res. Then he comes back—who in the hell knows why—and what does he do? He steals from his own family and my clan, the Wolf Clan."

"He claimed he was innocent."

The corners of Reuven's mouth turned down in disgust. "That's what they all say."

"I believed him."

"Sure you did. You were a young thing. Mack saved your life, like a hero in the movies. But he was no hero, Dr. Scott. He was a thief. A good-for-nothing thief. And a murderer, too. It never was proved in court, but he was a murderer. We all know it."

Arielle tried to hide her shock. Mack had killed someone? She couldn't believe it. Not soft-spoken Mack Shoalwater with his intense dark eyes and infinite patience.

"Didn't you know about that, Dr. Scott?" Reuven chided her with a wry, unpleasant laugh that seemed to originate deep within his nasal passages. "Didn't he ever mention bashing in the skull of another man? A poor old fisherman who never hurt nobody?"

"No."

"Hmph." Reuven shrugged. "A liar, too."

Arielle felt the heat of anger flare inside as she listened to Reuven's slander of a man whose memory she had cherished for ten years. Yet she remained silent, knowing words of protest and loyalty wouldn't change Reuven's opinion. She struggled to contain her outrage and smiled quietly.

"I see that you have no respect for Mack. But I was hoping you might tell me how he died."

"How he died?"

"Yes. You wrote to me many years ago, telling me that he died."

Reuven pushed up his glasses again. She thought she saw his thick fingers slip nervously.

"I'm a bit confused," Arielle put in. "I've been told that Mack is dead. However, your daughter Evaline seems to believe that he's alive, but still banished on the island."

"Discussing those who are banished is not our way, whether they're dead or alive."

Arielle bit back the demand to know what they'd just been doing, if not talking about the dead, and in a derogatory manner at that. She forced her voice down to a relaxed tone, one she used with particularly frustrating patients. "If he is dead, Mr. Jaye, I'd like to visit his grave."

"That isn't possible." Reuven glanced at his watch. "Listen, Dr. Scott," he said, coming around the edge of his desk, "the casino opens in five minutes. Sorry, but I don't have any more time to talk."

Sure. He was bursting with regret. Arielle suspected he couldn't wait to get rid of her. She rose to her feet and zipped up her parka, more unsettled than ever about Mack's death, and unconvinced he was a murderer. He hadn't been the type of man to kill another human being, not even in the heat of passion. Arielle knew it with unflappable certainty. She couldn't have misjudged him that thoroughly even in her naiveté at age nineteen.

"Thank you," she murmured, frustrated by the Saquinnish customs and by Reuven's far from genial hospitality.

As though he read her mind, he reached into his pocket and held out a handful of chips. "Here. Have a few games on the house. You might get lucky. Win big."

"Thanks." Arielle accepted the gold tokens but had no intention of playing. What she prized more was the truth about Mack Shoalwater, and something told her that she had received anything *but* the truth from Reuven Jaye. She walked out of the casino, the clatter of the roulette wheels and country-western music already filling the cavernous building behind her.

Still seething, she drove out of the casino parking lot and headed down the road toward the clinic. However upset she was, she still wanted to say good-bye to Evaline before she left for Seattle. With angry movements, she pulled into the clinic lot, jumped out of her car, and slammed the door. Reuven Jaye had ruffled her feathers and she was having a difficult time setting aside her anger as easily as she did in similar situations, which upset her even more.

Arielle strode to the clinic door and burst into the waiting room.

"Dr. Scott!" Evaline greeted. Then after a moment's pause, she asked, "Is something wrong?"

"Yes. Your father—"

Arielle broke off, surprised to see a familiar face turned her way, and one she had never expected to see in the reservation clinic. Startled, she watched the man slowly rise from his seat and smile his mocking grin at her.

"Florence," he called. "What a surprise."

"Mac." She glared at him, sure that her expression was dour, but she was unwilling to soften it. She wasn't in the mood to cross swords with him, or anyone else for that matter. "What are you doing here?"

"Well, I was in the neighborhood," He crossed his arms. "And I thought I'd steal a few hubcaps."

Evaline hurried around the counter. "This is Mr. Greyson," she put in, flustered and blushing. "He's been waiting to talk with our new doctor."

"Oh?" Arielle swept him with a calculating glance, unable to fathom what she and he had to discuss.

"You're the doctor in charge?" he asked.

"Yes." She resented the skepticism in his voice. "You sound surprised."

"I am. Don't they keep you busy enough in Seattle?"

"This is my day off."

"Which you spend up here?"

"Yes." She saw disbelief narrow his eyes and decided not to explain herself further. His continual analysis of her character aggravated her, as well as the inaccurate conclusions he must assuredly be jumping to. She stuffed her hands in the pocket of her jacket while she saw Evaline staring at her and Carter, perplexed by their rapid-fire discourse.

Evaline stepped closer and motioned toward the black-haired man. "Mr. Greyson wants to know if we could look up names of bone marrow donors for him."

"I'm afraid not. It would violate patient confidentiality."

"Come off it!" Greyson shoved his hands in the pockets of his jeans. "It's not like I'm going to harass anybody."

"Mr. Greyson, you are harassing me right now." She regarded him, wondering why he would be searching for donors anyway. He didn't seem like the type of man to be interested in the medical records of strangers.

"Sorry." Greyson frowned. "I'm just trying to find a certain donor and all I know is that they're a Northwest Indian."

"We can't help you."

"It's frustrating as hell."

"Perhaps, but rules are rules." She nodded briefly to him. "Good day, Mr. Greyson." She didn't wait for his response and turned to the receptionist, lowering her voice. "Evaline, I need to do some quick research of my own. Where are the records kept?"

"In those brown file cases." She nodded to a bank of files on the wall behind the front desk.

Arielle walked across the tile floor, intent on looking up Mack Shoalwater's medical history before she left for the evening. Greyson trailed behind her, showing little regard for which spaces in the clinic were off-limits to patients and visitors, or that he had been dismissed.

Evaline didn't set him straight, either, when he sauntered behind the counter with her.

Arielle pulled out a drawer marked P through T.

"Come on, Florence," he said behind her. "You
wouldn't have to tell me exactly who donated, just give
me a group of names that I might investigate on my
own."

"We can't." She glanced up at him. "And I'd appreciate it if you'd stop asking me to violate the legal rights of
our patients."

Arielle turned back to the file and flipped through the
manila folders, hoping Greyson would leave her alone
and leave the clinic as well, but he stood behind her like
a wall in his dark leather jacket and stone-washed jeans.
She searched through the S's without finding Mack's
file, and then looked cursorily through the R's and T's,
thinking the file might have been misplaced.

Evaline sidled closer. "Are you looking for anyone in
particular?" she asked.

"Yes. Mack Shoalwater," Arielle continued in a
hushed tone, hoping Greyson couldn't hear.

"He should be in there."

"He's not. Do you have his file out for some reason?"

"No." Evaline straightened and frowned. "Why would
I? He's been out of circulation for years."

"His file isn't here." Arielle shut the drawer and rose
up, her hands on her hips. "Why is that?"

"I don't know."

"Is there anywhere else a file might be kept? Do you
have archives somewhere?"

"Not that I know of."

"Surely he was seen by the medical staff at some
time."

Evaline shrugged. "I couldn't say."

Arielle frowned and glanced at Greyson, whom she caught studying her intently, with no sign of his usual flip attitude in evidence. Immediately he broke eye contact, and Arielle felt a cool chill race down her back. The flip attitude was just a front which he had let slip for an instant, just long enough for her to glimpse the man beneath the sarcasm and slick words. What kind of person forced himself to hide behind such a hard exterior?

She shifted her thoughts from him and brushed her hands together. "Well, that's all for today, Evaline. I'm heading back."

"We'll see you in a couple of weeks, Dr. Scott." Evaline held out her hand.

Arielle shook it. "It was nice to meet you, Evaline."

She nodded and smiled shyly, engagingly.

"Well, bye." Arielle turned for the front door, where she found Mr. Greyson staring out the window.

"Mr. Greyson, we're closing."

He ignored the hint. "Looks like you got some company out there," he commented, stepping away to allow her to pass.

Arielle glanced out the window, surprised to see five young men in a ring around her small car. Something about their slouched figures and surly glances at the clinic set off her alarms. If she had any choice, she would have delayed confronting them, in hopes they would drift away after a few minutes. But she had no intention of appearing a coward in front of Mr. Greyson, and no alternative but to leave the clinic.

"Take care, Evaline," Arielle said.

"You too, Dr. Scott. Bye."

"Bye-bye, Doc," Greyson added sarcastically, opening the door for her.

"Thanks." She took out her car keys as she walked briskly to her Miata, sure that a fearless front would be the best weapon against the group of teenagers. She'd had some experience dealing with street kids in Seattle, but not enough to allow her to feel totally confident about handling these boys.

"Good afternoon," she said, looking them over cursorily. She pushed the key in the door.

"Hey, lady, you're not goin' anywhere," the tallest boy stated in a husky voice. The other boys snickered.

Arielle shot a glance at him, her pulse rate beating a bit faster than normal. Was he threatening her? He crossed his arms and gazed at her with belligerence and mockery shining in his eyes. He wore a large plaid shirt over a white T-shirt and baggy jeans, and a ball cap set backward over his black hair, just like his four companions. Arielle felt a moment of indecision, wondering what she would do if they didn't step away and allow her to leave.

She forced herself to remain calm and opened the car door.

"Didn't you hear me?" the tall boy asked, moving closer until he loomed at her shoulder.

"I heard you," she replied. "Now would you mind stepping away from my car?"

"You shouldn't be driving a pretty little thing like that on the Res," the boy warned, without complying to her demand to move back. "Pretty things don't last around here."

Arielle felt another wave of alarm, not sure whether he referred to the Miata or to her. She didn't trust five young males standing in a volatile cloud of testosterone. One on one, she was sure she could handle them, but not as a unit, when they might surrender their individual good sense to pack mentality. When boys succumbed to pack mentality, they invariably did something stupid, and she had no wish to be the object of their game.

"Thanks for the advice." She stared into the boy's eyes, never once letting him see fear. "I'll keep it in mind."

The boys burst into uncontrollable spasms of tittering.

"The thing is, the roads around here are nasty," the boy continued, sliding his hand along the top of the car. "Real nasty. You know what I mean?"

Arielle felt beads of sweat breaking out under her parka. She should just get in the car and back out of the parking lot, or return to the safety of the clinic. Before she could decide what to do, Arielle heard footsteps approaching but didn't dare look over her shoulder to see who was coming. Apparently recognizing the arrival of a greater force, the youths retreated a few paces.

"Party time's over," a dry voice said behind her. "See you, boys."

The tall kid glared at Arielle and then at Greyson, who stepped off the sidewalk and onto the gravel lot. Though Greyson wasn't an overly tall man, there was something serious and intent about him that made him seem formidable and in charge. Even so, the leader of the boys had to show his fearlessness, to prove that he couldn't be ordered around. Heaving a grunt, the boy kicked the rear tire and sauntered off to join his friends. They slowly left the parking lot, laughing and slapping each other. Relief swept over Arielle.

"Thanks," she said, grateful for his appearance this time.

"No problem." Greyson bent down. "Your tire's flat," he declared. "Did they do it?"

"I don't know."

He put his hand on the rubber treads. "Looks like there's a nail here."

"I could have picked something up in the casino parking lot. They're building an addition over there."

Greyson stood up and pulled off his leather jacket, which he handed to her. "Got a jack and a spare?"

"Yes." She clutched the coat, still warm with his heat and fragrant with his scent. "But you don't have to—"

"Hey, I'm a professional," he said, interrupting her. "I used to work at a garage. That's where I learned everything I know about hubcaps."

"Right." His wry sense of humor wasn't lost on her. She reached for the keys and moved past him to open the trunk. Then she stood aside, holding his jacket while he efficiently exchanged the spare for the flat tire and stowed it in the trunk. He worked quickly and quietly, his hands deft and strong, as serious about his task as she was when suturing a wound.

When he was finished, he brushed off his hands and reached for his coat. "You shouldn't drive too far on that spare, Doc. Certainly not all the way to Seattle."

"There's probably a place in Everett where I can stop."

"I saw a tire place right off the freeway on the way here."

"You did? Where?"

"I don't know the street. I haven't been in the area long enough to get familiar."

"Maybe Evaline will know."

Greyson glanced at the clinic and then back to Arielle. "I've got a proposition for you, Florence." He pushed his left hand into his coat sleeve. "How about I show you the tire store and you give me a lift back to Seattle?"

"You don't have a car?"

"No. I came up here on the bus."

Arielle regarded him, not anxious to extend any favors to him. She didn't particularly like the man or trust him. But she couldn't deny the fact that she owed him for coming to her rescue and changing the tire.

"All right," she replied finally. "It's a deal."

She got into the car and reached across to unlock the passenger side, but found it was already open. Arielle stared at it for an instant, knowing it had been locked when she left the car. She always made certain her car doors were locked; it was a habit she'd formed ever since she learned to drive. Uneasy, she sat back and watched as Greyson slipped into the car. His wide shoulders seemed to fill up the car, and his long legs barely had enough room. He glanced around at the tan leather interior of the vehicle.

"Nice little car," he commented.

"Perhaps I should get an old beater pickup so those boys will leave me alone."

"If you think those boys were attracted to your car, you didn't study hormones long enough at med school."

She flashed a dark look at him.

"The name's Carter," he said simply. "And you owe me one."

"Not after I give you a ride."

"The ride's in exchange for the tire." He sat back against the leather seat and smiled. "You still owe me for running off the slavering hoards."

"You're a regular knight in shining armor, aren't you?" she declared, her suspicions tempered by the ring of sarcasm in his voice. "What do you have in mind?"

"Well now, with a woman like you a man has to consider his options carefully, Florence."

Still concerned about her unlocked car, Arielle reached under her seat and pulled out the handbag she'd shoved in the dark space. She never worried about leaving it in the car, because all she kept in it was a change purse, a makeup bag, a few toiletries, and a brush. Just to make sure that the boys hadn't taken anything, she opened the bag to inspect the contents.

"What's eating you?" Carter asked.

"I think those boys broke into my car."

"It doesn't look like they hurt anything."

"I'm just checking." She sorted through the contents of her purse while Carter watched.

"Anything gone?" he asked.

She nodded. "Funny. They left the money and took my brush."

"Your what?"

"My hairbrush."

"That *is* strange."

"Oh well," Arielle said, sliding the purse back under the seat. "I can easily replace it. Let's get out of here."

He looked out the window as she pulled out of the parking lot. Arielle studied him from the side, not knowing what to expect from Carter Greyson. He looked so much like Mack Shoalwater and yet was so unlike him in temperament. Most of the other adult men she'd known or dated had been in the field of medicine, a haven for conservative types and rigid-thinking members of a caste system. She had a sneaking suspicion Carter was neither conservative nor a team player. She would bet he was a man who preferred to work alone, a man who made his own rules. His unpredictability intrigued her, simply for its novelty. But she was still a long way from being comfortable with him in her car.

Her first time back to the reservation had run her through a gamut of emotions, from suspicion to rage to fear. And now, sitting in her car trading banter with

Carter Greyson, she felt the stress of the day still fraying the edges of her equanimity.

"Do you always frown like that?" he asked.

Arielle hadn't been aware her thoughts showed so plainly on her face. She tightened her grip on the wheel. "No. I just don't relish the idea of being in your debt, Injun Mac."

"It might be a good change of pace for you, Flo."

"I doubt it." She shifted into third and raced toward the freeway. "Somehow I doubt it."

5

Carter's recollection of the tire place was accurate, and within a half hour, they were standing in the waiting room while mechanics patched and remounted the Miata's tire. Arielle took one look at the opaque brew in the crusty coffee pot on a small table in the corner and decided to pass. She glanced back at Carter, who seemed to have made the same decision. He put his hands in his pockets and turned away, but not before Arielle caught a glimpse of a lopsided smile on his sharply-defined mouth.

Their thirty-minute drive had been a terse string of unconnected observations about teenage boys, traffic, and the scenery. The rounded humps of the coastal mountains were strange to Carter and Arielle, since they had both come from interior cities in the southern part of the United States. Arielle regarded Carter's back, where his glossy black hair brushed the collar of his leather jacket. Strange, how they had spent a half hour together and neither of them had volunteered personal details, except for the fact that Arielle had been raised in Phoenix and Carter in Atlanta.

He was a man of potent silences, and Arielle guessed that very little got past the dark eyes, which continually scanned his surroundings. More than a few times she had felt his gaze burn across her, but she had stared straight ahead, wondering what he thought of her. He probably disdained her conventional life. Well, he didn't exactly fit her definition of a successful man either. He didn't even own a car. Maybe he was an itinerant artist, or a construction worker who barely scraped by on his seasonal earnings.

A Jeep with muddy wheels and wings of dirt sprayed across its doors pulled into the lot. Arielle ambled across the floor to the corner of the waiting room where Carter stood and joined him at the window.

"There's the kind of vehicle I need," she commented.

"What—that Jeep?" he asked.

"I've always wanted one, ever since I was a little girl."

He glanced down at her in surprise. "You're kidding."

"No. And it would come in handy around here, especially on the reservation."

"Then why in the hell do you drive that cheerleader car?"

"It was a graduation gift."

"From your parents?"

"Yes. My mother checked out what everyone else was giving their daughters and convinced my dad that a sports car was the perfect present for their perfect little girl."

"And you couldn't return it if you were perfect."

She nodded. "They would have been crushed if I had. I thanked them and pretended I had never wanted anything else."

Carter shook his head and stared out the window. His thoughtful silence encouraged her to say more.

"My parents never really knew who I was. Probably still don't. But I don't blame them for it." She paused for a moment. In the bare waiting room, her words echoed loudly, sounding oddly final. Once she had worried about her superficial and unsatisfying relationship with her parents, but she had ceased to be concerned about something she could never change. Mack had taught her to accept and release those things over which she had no control. One day she would have her own family, one of her choosing and design, and she would have no need to look back.

Seeing the Miata being backed out of the garage bay, Arielle reached into her briefcase and took out her wallet. "The Miata's grown on me, though. It's a fun little car to drive. And I get a lot of whistles and honks from guys at stoplights."

"Certainly my idea of a good time," Carter replied sarcastically.

When the mechanic came into the room with her keys, Arielle paid the bill with a credit card. Then she and Carter drove back onto the freeway, heading south to Seattle, another thirty-minute stretch. Not wanting to spend a half-hour in uncomfortable silence, she searched for a topic to discuss and finally decided to ask Carter about his business on the reservation.

"If you don't mind me asking," she began, "why were you inquiring about medical records at the reservation clinic?"

He crossed his arms. Was she prying into information he didn't wish to discuss? "I'm doing a research project."

"A medical study?"

"More of a historical approach."

"Are you a tribal member?"

"Not judging by the bum's rush reception they gave me at the casino and the tribal center."

His expression was an impassive mask. He could evade questions and close himself off more adeptly than anyone she'd ever met. Arielle didn't question him further, and for a few miles they drove without speaking. Then she tried again.

"You know that night Katie and I found you in the courtyard? You seemed to be hearing loud noises. What was going on?"

"I had some ringing in my ears."

"Your reaction seemed to be awfully severe for simple tinnitus. You seemed to be in incredible pain."

"I was. But it's all right now."

"Did you see a doctor?"

"Yeah."

"What was the prognosis?"

"Tinnitus, just as you said. He gave me some pills, but I don't like taking stuff like that. I took a few, but then I got over it."

"What did you hear? Loud tones, roaring? And what kind of medication was prescribed, exactly?"

"Nothing worth talking about, Florence."

"I was just trying to make conversation."

"You don't have to. I can do without chatter."

"I've noticed."

"I don't think you like to chat any more than I do, Doc. So let's cut the charade."

"All right." She flushed at his frank words but was relieved by them all the same. He was right. She had no desire to carry on idle prattle with a person with whom she had nothing in common. For the rest of the drive, she sank into the comfort of her own thoughts, reviewing a few of the questions she had about cases from the reservation. Sometimes her job was more like a detective novel than a medical practice, and she enjoyed the challenge of an accurate diagnosis, made even more difficult by her close-mouthed Native American patients. Much of her free time was spent mulling over details of her patients' problems and searching for answers to her questions regarding their care.

Night had fallen when Arielle dropped Carter off in front of his apartment building. She was surprised to discover he lived only a few blocks from her more fashionable condominium complex. He thanked her for the ride and jokingly promised he'd try to quit lying around the stairs of the clinic courtyard. Arielle watched him stride up the steps to his building. Though she didn't look forward to another solitary dinner at home, she knew better than to ask Carter to share a bite with her. Not only would he make a miserable dining partner with his blunt and recalcitrant nature, he wasn't the type of man she would normally choose for friendship. What her type *was* exactly, she wasn't really sure, not having had much experience with men in the relationship department. She knew more about the male physical structure than she did about their emotional makeup.

Arielle drove to her condo, parked her car, and hurried up to her apartment on the top floor. She didn't own the place but was subletting it through a friend from school, who was in Africa on an extended medical mission. Though Arielle had been in Seattle for a month, she still hadn't unpacked much, and piles of boxes lined the hallways and were stacked in the living room and kitchen. She kept such long hours at the clinic that she was always too tired to attack the boxes when she got home at night. She would eventually have to find a place of her own anyway and didn't see the sense of putting everything away.

Most nights Arielle grabbed a light meal of fruit and cheese, took a cup of tea to the bathroom and read medical journals and case histories while soaking in a tub of bubbles. She'd never spent much time in her dorm rooms or apartments and had never developed a knack for decorating. As long as she had a chair to sit in, a table and a bed, she was satisfied. Though her parents would have given her anything she needed, she never made any requests. She wasn't one to ask for favors and her wants were few. She didn't even own a stereo or television.

As usual, the apartment was chilly. Arielle rubbed her arms and walked to the bank of windows at the other end of the living room. Before her was a gorgeous view of Elliott Bay, a dark field dotted with twinkling lights of ferries and slow-moving freighters. High in the sky, jets sailed by, red and white beacon lights flashing, as they banked southward to the airport. Far across the bay she could see the lights of houses on Bainbridge Island and behind them, the sharp zigzag shapes of the Olympic Mountains. A slice of yellow moon hung over the bay, throwing a wedge of cool glitter from shore to shore. Arielle breathed in and smiled, knowing the splendor of the Seattle scenery would always fill her with awe. There was something to be said for living in a city that could so magically renew her spirit.

Since it was Saturday night and she didn't have to work the next day, Arielle decided to have a glass of the pinot noir she'd bought at the market a week ago. She looked around, unable to remember which box contained her corkscrew. She opened a few of the cartons in the kitchen and found a stack of framed photographs.

Arielle lifted a frame, the kind that had multiple windows, and gazed down at scenes from her past, all collected by her mother. There were shots of her with her perpetually blond mother and others with her lean, handsome father, but never with both parents at once.

Her parents had been miserable with each other and were still putting on a good front for their well-heeled friends, the neighborhood, and their church. They'd given her everything money could buy but had been far too preoccupied with their problems to offer any emotional support. She'd spent a lonely childhood shuttled from one private lesson to another, from ballet to soccer, and then to riding classes and tennis. What she would have preferred was spending the evenings in the circle of her mother's arms, reading a book, or learning to play golf with her father—simple things warm with the attention and love she had so desperately wanted. But they never offered and she never asked.

As the years flew by, the subjects had changed to group shots of friends and cheerleading outfits. But the tone of the photographs altered drastically after the summer of 1984, when she spent three months alone on an island with Mack Shoalwater and had returned to Phoenix a different person.

Gone were the designer clothes and pleasure-pursuing friends. In their place were intense students more concerned with grade points than coiffures.

Her gaze drifted down to the picture in the corner of the frame, a snapshot of her and a boyfriend from college. In the photo, she and Steve were dressed in Halloween costumes and appeared very happy with each other. Arielle grimaced as she studied the lovesick smile on her young face. The happiness hadn't lasted more than a year. Steve had insisted upon moving in with her during finals, disregarding her need to study and sleep. His insensitivity had been the last straw and she'd told him to get lost. He left and she never spoke to him again. Now he was a neurosurgeon in New York, married to a child psychologist, and the father of twin girls. Sighing, Arielle put the picture frame back in the box.

Steve had been her last serious boyfriend. Her life had become far too busy after that relationship to afford her any time for regular dating. When had that been? Her senior year in college. Eight years ago? She hadn't had a relationship for eight years? God, she hated it when she started counting the years and reviewing her personal life.

Arielle uncorked the wine, poured a goblet full and let it breathe while she drew a bath.

She undressed and looked at her tall, slim figure in the mirror on the closet door as she thought of her nonexistent love life. Now that she was on her way in her profession, she yearned to complete her life with a significant other. Yet she would never settle for just any relationship simply to be in one. When she decided to get serious about a man, she would demand emotional satisfaction above all else. No facades for her, no compromises, no settling for second best, no matter how many Saturday nights she had to spend alone. She had learned from her parents that nothing was as sad and futile as spending a lifetime with someone you didn't love.

Arielle went back to the kitchen and took a sip of her red wine. Then she selected the latest issue of *New England Medical Journal* and returned to the bathroom. She sank into the hot water and leaned back, opening the journal to an article about an AIDS study, which discussed the results of using baboon bone marrow to rebuild ravaged immune systems in humans. Previous efforts had failed but the discovery of tissue called facilitating cells had given doctors new hope for successful transplants. She finished the first page and then turned to the next to continue the article, but realized her thoughts were wandering to the scene in Reuven Jaye's office when he'd told her Mack had died.

"He's lying," she said to herself. "I know the bastard is lying."

The lined face of Reuven slowly faded and gave way to a vision of Mack Shoalwater. She could see his dark eyes and his long black hair blowing in the breeze from the sea. She could almost hear the deep rumble of his voice.

"Watch a man's eyes when he speaks to you," Mack had once advised her. "If he tells you something and looks away, he is telling a lie."

Reuven had looked away all right. He had lied through his teeth to her.

"Oh, Mack!" Arielle cried softly, praying that he wasn't dead and yet wasn't still trapped on the island either. No man deserved to be in solitary exile for ten years. But if not dead or on the island, where could he be? What had really happened to him?

Mack had claimed that distance was not a barrier between people, and that if a person's spirit was strong enough, they could connect with someone through the power of concentration. Shamans were known to possess such a skill, especially with those of their own clan.

Arielle needed to connect with Mack now more than ever before. She closed her eyes and tried to conjure up a vision of him, to learn his whereabouts. His face loomed before her, and she focused every shred of her being on that vision, trying to seek him out.

o   o   o

Arielle was nineteen years old when she first saw Mack
Shoalwater. The sight of him was burned into her mind,
more vivid than any of the snapshots her mother had
painstakingly framed for her. Arielle had awakened from
a long sleep after having been pulled from the frigid
waters of Puget Sound. On vacation for the summer,
she'd been on a boat ride with some friends of hers who
assured her that they knew how to sail. Being young,
she'd trusted them, not realizing that they would drink
countless beers during the afternoon voyage. The older
of the boys had laughed when warned about the strong
currents surrounding the islands in the Sound, claiming
he'd lived in the area all his life and knew the waters like
the back of his hand. But he'd been wrong, or too
impaired to handle the sudden storm, the strong wind,
and the fierce tides. The boat had capsized, throwing
the five young people in the water. All the others were
too drunk to swim, and flailed helplessly in the waves.
Arielle threw them a life ring, an empty ice chest, and
had tried to swim to the closest person, but he slipped
away, leaving her screaming in terrified disbelief when
he disappeared into the depths. One by one, the others
sank beneath the waves. She clung to the small boat
until it, too, slipped beneath the surface. Then, frightened and chilled to the bone, she struck out toward the
distant shore, knowing she would have to save herself.

Half-dead with exhaustion and hypothermia, she'd
managed to swim close to the island on which Mack was
banished. He'd seen her in the water, jumped from the
rocky bank, and had somehow dragged her to shore,
even though his right arm was so twisted from an old
fracture that it was nearly unusable. She'd lapsed into

unconsciousness soon after the rescue and fell asleep by his fire on the beach.

Early in the morning she awoke to the grating squawk of a raven and raised up, not recognizing where she was. Dawn had just arrived and a mist still hung over the water, a fuzzy white curtain suspended a few feet off the surface. Across the sand walked a naked man—tall, straight, and muscular—holding a small branch of spruce in his left hand. His long black hair brushed his shoulder blades, and his supple buttocks rose and fell as he strode to the water. Against the wild backdrop of the deserted beach where nothing linked him to modern civilization or time, his nakedness seemed primal, disturbingly raw in its masculinity, yet beautiful beyond words. She was more than a little surprised to learn later that the magnificent figure belonged to a forty-year-old man.

Arielle raised up on one elbow and pushed back her salt-caked mop of brown curls. She'd seen some naked guys before, but always in the darkness of a dorm room, and never someone so strikingly well-developed. He seemed part of the wilderness around him. She couldn't imagine any of the boys she knew being able to walk naked down the beach like that with such dignity of purpose.

Without testing the temperature of the water and apparently immune to the chill, the man entered the sea, continuing forward until he was chest-deep. Then he began to bathe, washing his body and his hair with slow, relaxed strokes. Afterward, he softly flailed his back, chest, and arms with the frond of spruce while he sang a song to the rising sun. Snatches of his strong voice carried across the sand. Arielle had never seen or heard anything like it.

When she saw him turn to walk back to the beach, she immediately pretended to be asleep, wondering where in the hell she was.

That had been her first glimpse of Mack Shoalwater. At the time she had no idea he would become her friend, her mentor, and the father she'd never really had.

What had happened to the fine man who had taught her to value herself in the ways that were important, who had taught her the lessons to be learned from listening instead of speaking, and who had helped her find the courageous spirit inside her that she'd never known existed? How had Mack died? Where were his medical records? Arielle knew she had to find out before she could lay his memory to rest.

On Monday morning, she walked into the Pike Place Clinic, surprised to see Dan Williams, the owner of the building, leaning on the counter, talking with Katie. He was a tall man with a round, open face and blond hair that he wore long and loose. Whenever she saw him she was struck by his resemblance to old-fashioned drawings of the sun, because of his jolly demeanor and corona of golden hair. He was in his mid-forties, and though he wore expensive suits and shoes, there was a sense of sloppiness about him that disturbed her. He never buttoned his suit jacket and his pants hung too low on his hips. As soon as he saw her, Dan straightened and focused his smile on her.

"Dr. Scott!" he greeted. "How are you?"

"Hello." Arielle smiled briefly. She'd never been much of a morning person and hadn't consumed a cup of coffee yet, the necessary evil which took the edge off her crankiness. "Hi, Katie."

"Hi, Ari." Katie already knew Arielle's habits, and slid a steaming mug of coffee across the counter.

"Thanks. You're a saint." Arielle wrapped her chilled hands around the cup and took a sip.

Katie smiled and sat down in her chair. "We've got someone in number three waiting for you."

"Okay. And will you call Harborview and get an update on that elderly man with necrotizing fasciitus?"

"Sure."

Arielle unbuttoned her coat while Dan held out an envelope. "I'm having a Christmas party this Friday night. The whole building is invited."

"Oh?" Arielle replied, looking down at the expensive linen envelope he thrust in her hands.

"I hope you'll come. Feel free to bring a date. I always put on quite a spread—just ask Katie here."

"He does," Katie put in, nodding and smiling as she waited for her phone call to go through. "Dan's parties are the best."

"Sounds great." Arielle slipped the invitation in the pocket of her briefcase. "But you'll have to excuse me, Mr. Williams. I have a patient to see."

"Of course!" He beamed at her and she could feel the heat of his eyes slip down to her torso. She disliked men who let their gazes drop to women's breasts. "See you Friday, Doc."

"Bye."

Arielle walked to her office, thinking about the invitation. Then and there she decided to go to the party. She was new in town and it was time she met some people. But she'd only attend for a few hours and wouldn't stay up late. She had a full week of paperwork to catch up on at the clinic, plus an Alcoholics Anonymous meeting she'd promised Katie she would hang around for to open and close the conference room. Then on Sunday, she planned to go back to the Saquinnish Indian Reservation and find out just what had happened to Mack.

6

Carter glanced at his watch and frowned. He should shut down his computer and leave to get ready for the party that night, but he hated to stop. Five more minutes, he promised himself. Just five.

All week he'd been working on a particularly knotty problem in the development of his global positioning system, a directional device for use on seagoing vessels. The problem was centered around his attempts to merge GPS data with oceanographic chart data that came from differently formatted computer systems. For the entire week, a glitch had kept him occupied and challenged—a state in which he found much satisfaction—and also with no time to think of his frustrating search for his bone marrow donor. He'd spent the last five days sequestered in his office, working at his computer, and also with the men who were manufacturing the prototype. They rarely took a break, and always stayed until late at night. Now that Friday had arrived, however, he had to quit on time to get ready for a party his boss insisted he attend.

Five minutes went by like a second. Carter grimaced and turned off his machine, wishing he could get out of the Christmas party. Dan Williams, a prominent Seattle businessman, and one of the main backers of the fledgling Northwest Navigational Systems, had invited the entire staff to his annual bash. Attendance was mandatory and everyone had been instructed to have a wonderful time. Carter closed the door to his office. He had yet to attend a party and deem it a wonderful time.

JoJo waved as he walked past her desk.

"See you later, Greyson," she called, wiggling her eyebrows.

He stepped closer. "Isn't there any way I can get out of this party?"

"None." She beamed. She was probably looking forward to spending the entire evening at his side.

He, on the other hand, wasn't thrilled at the prospect of a party. He'd never liked small talk, didn't care to dance with strangers, and even before his illness had avoided alcohol completely. There were many devils inside him, and he'd found out in college that booze brought out the worst of them.

"A piano might fall on me when I walk home."

"Sure," she laughed. "And the dog might eat my homework."

"Tell me, JoJo, how formal is this gig?"

"It's kind of formal. Definitely no jeans. Wear a suit, if you have one."

"Sounds awful."

She giggled and smiled, showing a wad of gum pressed between her teeth. "Oh, it'll be fun!" She took off her headset. "You bringing a date?"

"Nope."

"Neither am I." She paused, waiting for him to offer to serve as her escort. He couldn't bring himself to do it.

"I'll see you there, JoJo." He gave her a wink and strode out the door without looking back to see her expression. He knew she'd be disappointed, but he wasn't about to start anything with her. She was the type of woman who attached herself like a second skin to a guy. He hadn't the time or patience for such a relationship.

Three hours later, Carter stepped off the elevator into the swank top-floor suite of Dan Williams's Company. People were everywhere—in the hall, doorways, and reception area. Carter eased his way through the throng, looking for familiar faces from his office, and found himself in a huge meeting room with a band at one end and food and drink at the other. Tables ringed the room, where couples could sit and gaze out at the glittering city fifty stories below. Carter knew that Dan owned several properties around town in addition to his other business interests, for the man's name was always in the papers when big real estate deals were featured. This office tower was only a few blocks from Carter's apartment, but it was worlds apart from the restored brick structure where Carter lived, two floors above Wally's Deli and the tattered parade of street people on Second Avenue.

For a moment Carter stood at the edge of the room near the door, conscious of faces turning his way, aware that many of the women gave him lingering glances. He wasn't accustomed to such attention. Before his marrow transplant, women rarely looked at him twice. But now, with his slowly changing appearance, he garnered stares he'd never received before. He was sure if he answered one of those come-hither looks, he could catch himself a beauty. But the idea of women responding to him for his dark hair and new face tarnished the glow of the attention. He didn't want to be appreciated just for his looks, especially when they weren't even his. Besides that, he'd made a vow to stay clear of entanglements until he was in complete remission. He'd lost one girlfriend to his illness, and would be a fool to go through that devastating experience again.

Carter ran a finger along the inside edge of his collar, cursing the constricting noose of his tie, and ambled to the buffet to check out the food. He glanced at his wristwatch, telling himself he would give the party an hour and then leave.

Just as he predicted, JoJo soon showed up at his elbow, gushing about the food and what some of the women were wearing. She had come in a black leather skirt, metallic silver blouse, and large silver earrings in the shape of snowflakes. Carter listened with one ear to her running commentary on the people who walked by—who they were, who they were sleeping with, who they wanted to stab in the back—displaying a surprising knowledge of the crowd. She must gossip with everyone she met. Then she begged Carter to dance. Reluctantly he agreed, if only to have a moment's respite from her chatter.

Unfortunately, she even talked when she danced. When the song was over, he excused himself for the men's room.

On his return, hoping to avoid JoJo, he took an alternate route. The hallway took him past a different bank of elevators located near some secluded offices, and probably used only by Dan Williams and his upper-level managers. Carter heard a faint hum as he approached the elevators, and thought at first he was hearing the workings of the motor up above. Soon, however, the hum turned into howling.

"Damn!" Carter swore. The wolves were back. He thought he'd gotten over that problem through the sheer force of his will. But here they were again. If the howling got as bad as the other times, he might collapse and cause a scene. So far, he'd concealed his affliction from his coworkers, and he certainly didn't want his boss to see him huddled and sweating, unable to speak or move. Carter stood in the hallway, his hands and knees shaking, when the doors to the private elevator opened.

Three impeccably-dressed men walked out, chuckling and talking, sipping their scotch-and-waters as they strolled toward the main party. The howling noise followed them like a cloud, growing fainter as the men drifted away. Puzzled, Carter watched them merge into the crowd while the howls faded to a bearable pitch. The trembling in his limbs dissipated. What was going on?

He waited a few moments and then walked to the elevator and pushed the button. There were no numbers anywhere to tell him what floors the elevator served. After a long wait, the car arrived and the doors slid open. Carter stepped forward, only to be denied entrance by a tall man with slicked-back hair and a pin-striped suit. Another man, similar in height and choice of tailors, stood at the rear of the car, his arms crossed over a massive chest.

"See your card, sir?" the man asked.

"What card?"

The elevator attendant exchanged a sneer with his companion. Then he turned back to Carter. "No card, no ride, buddy." The man grinned.

"Where does this elevator go?" Carter asked.

The man's grin grew wider. "It goes up and down, buddy. Up and down—without you." Then he pressed a button and the doors closed, shutting off the vision of his leering face.

Carter moved back to avoid getting caught by the gleaming silver doors, more than a little flustered by the noise in his head. Then he heard the deep male voice of his dreams speaking over the wolf howls.

Listen to me, spirit of my spirit, blood of my blood. You must not ignore the cry of your brothers. They speak to you for a reason, they come to you for a reason. When you see them, you will know that you are close to me. They will bring you closer. But you have to see them, follow them. It is the time of the Wolf Moon, a time of seeking balance. You must act. You are the war chief, and the fate of a people is in your hands.

Carter staggered backward, trying to escape the voice, and almost bumped into a man who had come up beside him.

"Enjoying the party?" the man asked in a nasal voice that grated on Carter's already tender ears. The intensity of the howling picked up again.

He glanced at the man, surprised to see the tall blond guy from the crate incident in the parking garage a week ago.

"Yeah," he answered, quickly regaining his self control. "It's great."

"I don't believe we've met." The blond man held out a hand with a huge ring glinting on it. "I'm Dan Williams."

"Carter Greyson. From Northwest Navigational Systems."

"Ah, NNS," Williams said. They shook hands and Williams gave him a quick but intense survey with his small twinkling eyes. Carter wasn't fooled by the eyes. They twinkled with cunning, not amusement. "Great little company, great product. Gary's a genius. He'll go far and take you with him, if you play your cards right."

"Maybe."

"Well, you have yourself a good time, Greyson." He slapped him on the back. "Get yourself a drink."

"Thanks."

With Williams standing at the elevator, there was no chance for further investigation of the wolf howls or to find out why an elevator was operated by tough guys demanding proof of membership for admittance to a private party. Carter could only guess that drugs were involved, but he had no idea why wolf howls were connected to any of it or why he still seemed to be the only person capable of hearing them.

Still disturbed, he walked back to the party and mingled in the crowd, talking to his boss and a few women who pressed themselves upon him. Out of the corner of his eye, he glimpsed JoJo coming his way. Carter sipped his mineral water, trying to think up an excuse for ignoring her. He didn't want to be mean, but he had no desire to spend the rest of the party with her. Annoyed, he looked across the room and froze, the glass of Perrier pressed to his lips, while his annoyance gave way to bald admiration.

Forty feet away stood Arielle Scott, tall and slender in a plain black sleeveless dress that scooped down in the front and hung just above her knees. She wore black stockings and black high heels, and her shapely legs went on forever. He might have guessed that Arielle Scott would know how to dress for the evening by playing up her svelte figure with understated elegance, but he never would have guessed her matter-of-fact good looks could transform to such distinctive beauty. She had swept her dark brown hair behind one ear, where an earring sparkled and matched the glints of color in her hazel eyes. She surveyed the dancers, appearing at ease while standing there alone. Could she have come without a date?

In any other situation, Carter would have backed away and melted into the crowd to regard her from a distance. But JoJo barreled toward him, intent on his company. And Arielle seemed to be alone across the floor. Without glancing to the side, Carter set down his glass on a nearby table and walked around the edge of the dancers toward Arielle. She saw him coming and gave him a small but not overly friendly smile. He appreciated her honesty. He could tell she didn't like him much, but at least she didn't make a pretense of friendship. He would rather deal with frank people like Arielle than play senseless games with the others.

"Care to dance, Doc?" he asked, dispensing with the usual small talk.

She looked down, uncharacteristically unsure of herself. Did she want to refuse him and wasn't sure how to do so politely? Carter stood his ground. Then she gave him a little smile, the first personable expression she'd ever bestowed upon him. "I don't dance, Greyson," she replied.

"Neither do I, but I'm trying to escape the attention of a coworker, so do me a favor and just come onto the dance floor with me."

Arielle glanced around, apparently took notice of JoJo behind him, and decided to have pity on him.

"If I go out there and make a fool of myself," she said, "then we'll be even."

"What do you mean?"

"I owe you one, remember? Getting me to dance will settle the debt."

"Fine." He held out his hand, just as the music changed from a rock number to a ballad.

Carter paused, clutching her slender fingers in his, and for an instant wasn't sure it would be wise to carry out his plan, not if they had to dance a slow song together. He hadn't danced in years and apparently neither had the doctor. They might spend the next few minutes stepping on each other's toes, adding frostbite to their already chilly acquaintance. His alternative, however, was JoJo Sperry with her chewing gum and sweet perfume. He decided to take his chances with Arielle and guided her to the center of the floor, where their fumbling attempts at dancing would be hidden from most of the crowd.

"I like the piano in this song," Arielle commented as she turned to face him.

Her remark somewhat eased his misgivings and he pretended to listen to the music as he slipped his arm around her waist. He'd never had a woman like Arielle in his arms before, never one so elegant and self-assured. In heels, she was almost as tall as he was, and when they drew close together, he was surprised at the precise way her breasts and hips fit against him. Her scent floated up to him, an intoxicating mixture of clean skin and powder. When he began the first steps to the slow romantic rhythm, she effortlessly followed his lead. He'd assumed they'd be stiff in each other's arms, clumsy and forced to crack jokes throughout the dance. Instead, he was pleasantly surprised at the ease in which they moved, as though they'd been partners for years. Her companionable silence relieved him of the pressure to make comments or small talk, allowing him to enjoy the music and her closeness.

She felt comfortable in his arms, wonderfully feminine and willowy, so different from his first impression of her. One of her hands rested on his shoulder, and the other was captured in his. As the song went on, Carter gradually moved their hands closer to his body, until her wrist touched his chest. She didn't protest, and never once did she retreat from the intimate press of their torsos. They didn't speak a word, and Carter closed his eyes and bent toward her, listening to her breathing as their cheeks touched slightly. His own breathing was deep and appreciative as his chest rose and fell against the fullness of her breasts. He thought for a moment how nice it would be to always have someone near like this. But Arielle would never be that person—no matter how wonderful she felt in his arms—for he had already done his usual fine job of showing her what an asshole he could be.

Then a couple passed by them and he heard the sharp howls of the wolves. Startled, he paused and Arielle stumbled against him.

"What's wrong?" she asked.

"What?" Carter replied, disoriented. "Nothing, I—"

"Are you all right?" Arielle disengaged, taking her wonderful softness and warmth from him.

Carter silently damned the wolves for breaking the spell that had bound them together for the last few minutes.

"Are you all right?" she asked again.

The howling flowed past him as an elderly gentleman with white hair and mustache walked by. Carter stared at the man, wondering if he'd been in the elevator like the others.

"Do you know that person?" Arielle asked.

"No. It's nothing." He urged her back to him. She allowed herself to be drawn against him once more, but the magic was gone, and the song soon ended.

Before he could ask her for another dance, they were interrupted by Dan Williams's obnoxious voice.

"Dr. Scott!" he exclaimed. "There you are, my dear. How lovely you look!"

Arielle smiled. "Thank you."

Carter noticed that her smile for Williams wasn't any friendlier than the one she had bestowed upon him a few minutes ago. Apparently, she wasn't a sucker for flattery.

Williams held out his hand. "Dance with me, pretty lady."

"All right." Arielle turned to Carter. "Excuse me," she said and then allowed Williams to lead her into the crowd.

Carter watched them disappear into the mob on the dance floor, sure that he'd blown the opportunity to spend more time with Arielle, thanks to the damn wolves. But Arielle Scott was out of his league anyway. They might have hit if off on the dance floor, but that didn't mean she was his type. And he knew he definitely wasn't hers. She needed a country-club guy, a rich, well-connected man who zipped around Seattle in a Mercedes or Jaguar. Carter didn't even own a car, and didn't expect to buy one until the medical bills were paid. He had no business thinking about getting to know Arielle Scott. To get to know her better would involve her probing around his dark soul, an examination he didn't care to undergo.

As the band played, Carter slowly paced around the dance floor to position himself at the doorway nearest the mysterious elevator, while his body still hummed from holding Arielle in his arms. He hadn't been with a woman for over two years, and he couldn't deny the fact that he hungered for comforting embraces. That Arielle had been the one to press against him was simply a random occurrence. But heat and hunger had flared inside him at her touch. What man wouldn't react to such a beautiful woman in that way?

Scowling, Carter watched the dancers as he kept track of a constant stream of men going down the elevator and then reappearing not long afterward, the curious wolf howls trailing in their wake. The sound kept him edgy and uncomfortable, and soon his head began to pound.

"Just about pumpkin time," Carter muttered to himself, knowing he couldn't predict what might happen if the howling got any worse. He turned to leave just as Williams and Arielle danced close to the edge of the crowd. A flush of jealousy washed over him, startling him. Williams laughed and talked as much as JoJo had, and Carter wondered if Arielle found Dan as amusing as he seemed to find himself. The music slowed to another ballad, and Williams pulled her close, in a swift possessive gesture that Carter intuitively knew wouldn't suit Arielle. Trying to ignore the burgeoning pain in his ears and the burning resentment in his gut, Carter watched them dance, realizing he was paying more attention to Dan and Arielle than he was to the elevator behind him, especially when he saw Dan's thick hands stroke Arielle's back as they danced. Was it his imagination, or did Arielle seem to be holding herself more rigid than when she danced with him a few minutes ago? Then he saw her say something, and move her hand down from Dan's shoulder to his forearm, as though to distance herself.

For a few moments they danced without incident, but soon Dan's hands roamed freely once again, this time to Arielle's trim backside. He squeezed her rump in both of his hands. Dan's callous treatment of the doctor made something in Carter snap. He strode forward, waging an internal battle with the anger and jealousy flaming inside him. He wasn't accustomed to such sharp slices of jealousy, and Arielle's reputation and safety were none of his business.

"I'm cutting in," Carter declared, thrusting his elbow between Arielle and Williams. "If you don't mind, Doctor Scott."

"I mind," Williams answered for her. "Arielle and I were talking."

"That's not what it looked like to me." Carter reached for Arielle's arm. "Come on, Dr. Scott."

"She's not going anywhere," Dan countered.

"Don't go feeling ladies up on the dance floor, Williams. It's rude. They don't like it."

"Says who?"

Carter glared at him and tried to keep steady on his feet, but his ears pulsed with the wolf howls, which whined and swirled, nearly shattering his eardrums. He blinked, while the round face of Dan Williams doubled and then overlapped.

"What I'd *like* is a glass of champagne," Arielle put in, fanning herself with her free hand. "Would you be a sport, Dan, and get one for me?"

Dan switched his glowering glance from Carter to Arielle and then seemed to change gears. He smiled. "Certainly. You stay right here, Ari. I'll be back in a second."

"Thank you." She beamed at him and Carter marveled at her ability to defuse the situation.

But a second later all he could think about was escaping the howling noise. As soon as Williams turned to leave, Carter pulled Arielle toward the door.

"What do you think you're doing!" she gasped, trying

not to alert the attention of the other dancers.

"I've got to get out of here." He held tightly to her arm, refusing to let her remain behind. Dan Williams's turf wasn't a safe place for either of them.

Fortunately Arielle didn't wrestle out of his grip and reluctantly kept up with his hurried pace as he charged down the hall to the nearest vacant office. He pulled her through the doorway and slammed the door. Instantly, she wrenched out of his grip.

She backed away, her clothing in disarray. "Don't you ever, *ever,* manhandle me like that again!"

"I was only trying to protect you!"

"From what? Dancing with Dan Williams?" She glared at him and pulled up the strap of her cocktail dress with a jerk.

"The man's hands were all over you."

"I'll fight my own battles, thank you."

"It didn't seem like it—not with Williams or those kids on the reservation the other day."

"That's because you butted in before I had a chance to do anything."

Carter's anger bubbled and broke just below his skin. He couldn't have stood aside and let Arielle handle Dan Williams, no matter how good she was at defusing difficult situations. The sight of Williams's thick hands stroking her back and shoulders and touching her ass had been too much to bear, but he'd never admit it to her. She'd laugh in his face. No—worse—she'd give him that look, the look of incredulity at the idea he might lay claim to her in any way, be it as a friend or potential lover. His jealousy of Dan Williams suddenly seemed a mockery, even to him. He had no claim on this woman. None whatsoever.

"Now open that door," she demanded.

At his glowering silence, Arielle rolled her eyes and

stepped toward the door. Her silk dress clung to the sinuous curves of her tall, slender figure, and the drape of fabric at her back revealed her upper shoulders and the seductive fragility of her neck below the soft curve of hair. Carter sucked in a breath and hung back, sweeping aside his damp bangs with a trembling hand.

She put her fingers on the doorknob. "What's wrong with you anyway? You've been acting strange tonight."

"I'm fine."

"You look terrible. Your ears are ringing again, aren't they?"

"Listen, Flo," Carter said, ignoring her accurate diagnosis. "There's something going on here. Didn't you see those people going down the elevator, a few at a time?"

"What people?"

"Men in expensive suits and satisfied faces."

Arielle paused and regarded him over her shoulder. "You don't trust people with satisfied faces?"

"No. Smugness is a sign of a rotten heart."

"Smugness?" Her stiff posture eased and she leaned her shoulder against the door, smiling a faint lopsided smile which was her most genuine expression yet. "Where do you get such stuff from, Greyson?"

"Life 101," he replied. "A self-study course."

For the first time since they'd met, he felt her full and honest regard, as if she were viewing him with all her shields down. A strange feeling of exhilaration passed over him, which was quickly drowned by dread. Those sharp, hazel eyes might see far too much of him if he let her stare at him too long.

"So what do you think they're doing, those men?"

Carter shrugged and glanced away. "I don't know."

"But you think I should be careful of Dan, because of them."

"Yeah."

"Maybe it's just a private party. Maybe they've got better hors d'oeuvres on some other floor. Better mind-altering substances perhaps."

"Yeah, and I'll bet the party's in the basement."

She shook her head and frowned. "What's with the basement and you, anyway?"

"I know there's something down there, in the parking garage." He stepped toward her, intent on making her believe in him, but only succeeded in making her wary and putting the shields back in place. She straightened and stared at him, her eyes flashing a warning not to come any closer.

"You need to see someone about your ears," she said, slipping back into doctor mode. "A specialist. Do yourself a favor, Carter, and have yourself examined."

"My ears or my head?" The biting reply came out before he could stop himself. He regretted his words the instant they slipped out, but his regret couldn't wipe away the harsh effect his sarcasm had upon her.

Arielle's expression cooled immediately and her eyes leveled on him.

"It's up to you, Carter." She opened the door. "You know yourself better than anyone. Good night."

He watched her go, aching to apologize for his behavior that evening and all the times before. But he didn't know how.

7

Late Saturday afternoon, Arielle reached for
her second cup of bitter coffee. Her office was gloomy
and rain pounded incessantly against the window behind
her desk. In another hour, the clinic's weekly AA meeting would be finished and she could lock up and go
home. Then in the morning she'd drive up to the reservation to ask a few questions about Mack Shoalwater.
Instead of wasting her time staring out the clinic window
into clouds of drizzle that offered no answers, she'd go
directly to the source—the Saquinnish people themselves. Somehow, somewhere, she'd find someone who
would tell her the truth.

Arielle turned back to her desk and picked up her pen
just as an unfamiliar knock rapped upon the frosted
glass window of her door. She looked up.

"Yes?" she called, wondering if the AA meeting had
ended early.

The door opened to reveal Carter Greyson standing in the dim light of the corridor.

"Hi," he said. He was dressed in his leather jacket, a dark blue shirt, and faded jeans, a much more casual outfit than when she'd seen him last at the party. In either type of clothing—jeans or a suit and tie—she couldn't deny the man had a definite presence. Some might have called it charisma. In Carter's case, she had to call it attitude.

"Hello." She rose, keeping the desk between them. "Come in."

"I saw the lights on in the clinic," he explained, stepping into her office. He shoved his hands into the pockets of his jacket. "I thought you might be here, slaving away."

"I just can't get enough of this paperwork."

He smiled at her wry comment and glanced around her office, in no hurry to continue the conversation. He was one of those people who could appear amused and restless at the same time. She waited for him to speak, more curious by the minute as to the reason for his visit.

"I thought doctors made piles of money."

"Some do."

"Well, you could sure spend a few bucks on a decorator."

"This clinic could use a lot of things." Then she smiled. "Have you brought some wallpaper swatches to show me?"

He returned her smile with a fleeting one of his own. Then he grew serious. "No, I—" He cleared his throat and turned to face her head-on. "I came to tell you that I—" He broke off.

She regarded him steadily, wondering why it seemed so difficult for him to speak. He didn't strike her as a shy man, or someone who didn't know his own mind. "What are you getting at, Carter?"

"The hell with it," he blurted, whipping his hands out of his pockets. "I came here to tell you I'm sorry."

"Sorry?"

"For last night. At the party." Carter pivoted and strode to the door. He stopped at the threshold and turned around slightly, not quite looking at her. "I'm sorry I dragged you off like that."

"I'm glad to hear it. And I accept your apology."

"I don't usually manhandle women. I don't know what got into me."

"Perhaps your ear problem?"

"My what?"

"Your ears seemed to be causing you some distress last night."

"I can't blame my rudeness on them. It was me, plain and simple, Flo."

He brushed his coal black hair away from his forehead. She admired his truthfulness and his thoughtfulness in seeking her out to apologize. Not many men had the guts or gallantry to apologize when they were wrong.

"Why don't you let me have a look?" she asked, reaching for the keys on the top of her desk.

"At what?"

"Your ears." She didn't wait for his consent. "Come on. I'll open up your favorite examination room across the hall."

She didn't give him time to react, afraid that he'd refuse. Instead, she unlocked the room and briskly washed up.

"Sit down," she said, drying her hands.

"What's your fee, Doc?" he asked, lowering himself to the examination table. "I'm in between insurance companies right now."

"An espresso."

"A bit steep, wouldn't you say?"

"Not for an expert opinion." She smiled, once again amused by his dry sense of humor, so similar to hers. She picked up the otoscope and flicked on the light. "Now hold still a minute."

He held his breath as she stepped close to him and studied the inside of his left ear. His shoulder nearly grazed her chest, and she tried not to remember the way it had felt to dance with him. His arms had been strong and steady, and she'd felt an instant assurance from him that allowed her to relax and enjoy the music—something she had found quite surprising about him.

Arielle gently pulled at his earlobe to get a better view of his ear, ignoring the silky blackness of his hair as it brushed her knuckles, and the light scent of his body— leather and soap and musk combined.

"I don't see anything unusual," she murmured. "Let's have a look at the other one."

He rotated his head and she examined his right ear. "Perfectly normal," she said, after a long moment.

"I thought so."

"Let's check your glands." She stepped in front of him and reached for his neck, but was immediately struck by the prospect of touching the taut flesh beneath his sharp masculine jaw. Arielle had never been affected by the attractiveness of her male patients before, not until this moment when Carter presented himself for her inspection. As her fingertips lightly pressed the warm flesh of his throat, she steeled herself to treat him in a professional capacity and nothing more.

Gently she palpated his neck and looked at a spot on the wall above his head, to avoid meeting his dark gaze and to ignore the proximity of his head to her torso. She could feel the cool breeze of his breath at the top of her blouse, which had a startling effect on her breasts. As if turning traitor to her cool professionalism, her nipples tightened and hardened. She prayed Carter couldn't detect the sudden transformation through her bra and blouse.

"Your glands are fine," she finally said, stepping away quickly. "How long have you been experiencing the tinnitus?"

"Just a few weeks."

"Can you attribute it to any unusual occurrence? An infection? A loud noise? Have you gone to any heavy metal concerts lately?"

"No. Nothing unusual."

"What about at your job?"

"I work with computers."

Arielle frowned and studied him, intent on solving the mystery of his malaise. "And you hear ringing noises?"

"Not exactly."

"What *do* you hear?"

Carter's attitude abruptly changed. He slid to his feet. "Noises, that's all. I can handle it."

"I'm sure you can." Arielle sighed, aware that his cooperative mood had ended. What was he so touchy about? She'd never met anyone so prickly. Frustrated, she pulled the sanitary tip off the otoscope and put the instrument away.

She heard Carter zip up his jacket and guessed he was preparing to leave.

"Are you taking any medications?" she inquired, still intrigued by his medical problem.

"Not for my ears."

"What are you taking?"

"Some anti-rejection drugs," he replied.

She turned in surprise. "You've had a transplant?"

"Yeah. But it has nothing to do with this."

"What kind of transplant?"

"Listen, Flo." He pulled up the collar of his jacket. "I'm not real keen on telling you my life story."

"But it might have some bearing on your—"

"It might. But I don't think so." He stepped to the door. "Thanks anyway."

She quickly evaluated their last few minutes of conversation and decided to act on instinct. "Not so fast." Her voice stopped him. "What about my fee?"

He looked back at her in mild surprise. "Are you serious?"

"Yes. I could use a decent cup of coffee. I swear they brew it with formaldehyde here."

Carter shifted his weight, apparently uncomfortable with the prospect of spending time with her.

"I promise I won't ask any questions you don't care to answer," she put in.

"Okay."

"There's a place across the street that might be open. I'll just grab my purse."

A few minutes later they hurried through the rain to a restaurant bordered by iron grillwork that opened into its own small courtyard. Ahead of them walked a man in a white coat, who slipped through the gate and into the front door.

"Looks like the cook," Carter commented, opening the iron gate for her. "They're probably closed."

"Let's just see."

When they pulled open the door, a waitress behind the counter looked up. "Sorry," she said. "We don't open until five."

Arielle glanced at her watch. It was four-forty. She felt Carter's reluctance behind her, but decided to press their case regardless. She smiled graciously. "We're hoping for a glass of wine," she began. "Would that be possible?"

"Well—" the young waitress shot a glance toward the kitchen where the cook was just firing up his ovens for the dinner crowd.

"You wouldn't turn us out into the cold, cruel world, would you?" Arielle added, tilting her head. "It's raining like crazy out there."

The waitress looked at Carter and then back at Arielle. "Well, I guess we don't have to cook the wine," the waitress said with a smile. "Go ahead and sit down. I'll be right with you."

"Thanks." Arielle turned and winked at Carter. For a moment their eyes locked and held, and Arielle felt the energy change between them, just as it had during his examination a few minutes ago. Surprised, she broke eye contact with him and walked to a small table by the window.

"I thought you wanted an espresso," he said, taking off his jacket and hanging it on the back of a nearby chair.

"I changed my mind."

"Just like a doctor to increase the fee without notice."

"If it's a problem—"

"No, forget it." He sat down and briefly inspected the small room. "This isn't a bad little place."

"It was nice of the waitress to let us in when she didn't have to."

"Nice nothing. You bulldozed her with charm." His dark gaze traveled over her face and into her hair. "I bet you could charm your way into anything."

"And you couldn't?"

He sat back. "I'm different. You've got looks and good breeding written all over you."

"And you don't?"

Carter appeared surprised. "You must be kidding."

She shook her head. "You are a very attractive man, Carter. And don't tell me you don't know it."

She could see him trying to fight back a slight flush of pleasure, but it flared in his eyes. "Not to change the subject or anything, Doc, but why did you call me Mac the night we first met?"

"You took it as an insult, didn't you?"

He paused and she worried that he was about to close up on her again.

"Did you think the name was derogatory?"

"Yes."

"Why?"

"I thought it was a term people around here used for a drunken Indian."

"Well, you were wrong."

At that moment the waitress appeared. "The wine list, sir?" she said, handing the menu to him.

"Thanks," he answered, and immediately gave it to Arielle. "Here," he said. "I don't drink."

"Very well." Arielle perused the wine-by-the-glass selections and settled on a local merlot. Carter ordered a glass of soda. "And thanks again for letting us in early," Arielle added. "I promise to come back for dinner sometime when you're really open."

When the waitress left them alone, Carter leaned forward. "So, why did you call me Mac?"

"You remind me of a person I knew once. His name was Mack Shoalwater."

"The guy whose records you were looking for at the reservation clinic?"

"Yes. You look so much like him, it's quite remarkable."

"Hmm." Carter glanced down at the table, as if he didn't care to reveal his reaction to her observation.

"Are you related to him by any chance?"

"Not that I know of." Carter sat back. "So who was he to you?"

"Mack is hard to describe." She smiled at the prospect of telling Carter about Mack. No one else in the past ten years had been the right kind of audience to hear more than just the adventurous aspects of her tale. She longed to go beyond the rescue and survival story and tell the underlying tale of her transformation, in the hopes that some of Mack's wisdom might rub off on edgy, bitter Carter Greyson. If she could help Carter concentrate on the positives in life as Mack had taught her to do, then she would have passed on Mack's legacy, which would be the finest tribute she could give him. Just thinking about Mack turned the rain on the window beside her to a comforting rhythm instead of a dreary splatter.

Carter watched Arielle take a sip of her wine and carefully put the goblet back on the table. She was silent for a long moment as she gazed out of the window, collecting her thoughts. Gradually a peaceful expression eased through her features, an expression of such joy and love that Carter felt another sharp stab of jealousy, like the one he had suffered at the party.

"You know how sometimes you meet someone who changes your life forever," she began, returning her hazel regard to his face, "—a friend, a lover, or a mentor?"

Of course Carter had never experienced such a thing, but he gave a noncommittal nod to encourage her to continue. He was eager to hear about a Saquinnish man who looked enough like him to arouse comment. Perhaps Mack was the connection he had been searching for.

"That was the type of person Mack was to me."

"Was he a Saquinnish Indian?"

"Yes. Tall, strong, and good-looking. But also gentle, wise, and well-grounded—probably the most spiritually-centered person I've ever known."

"How did you meet this paragon of virtue?"

Arielle's peaceful smile faded. "You know, if you don't wish to hear this, Carter, just say so."

Carter flushed. "Sorry, Doc. Go on." He took a drink of soda, reminding himself to curb his sarcastic remarks. She kept her clear gaze leveled on him and he had no idea what she thought of him, whether she planned to continue her story or throw her wine in his face. "Come on, Arielle," he said. "I do want to know. How did you meet this Mack character?"

"I was involved in a shipwreck. He saved my life."

"Sounds like he made a good first impression."

"I sure didn't, though." She threw back her head and laughed softly. The sound poured over Carter like an aphrodisiac. He'd love to make beautiful Arielle Scott laugh like that, so natural and free, the kind of laugh he'd never known himself. He was wound much too tightly to give more than a constricted chuckle at best.

"Why?" he asked. "What did you do?"

"It wasn't what I did, it was who I was." She shook her head and smiled. "I was nineteen. I was more horrified that I'd broken a nail than I was about the predicament of a crippled man who had been banished to a remote island and left to fend for himself."

"What do you mean—banished?"

"Mack was accused of a crime, and his punishment was to be marooned on a remote island for an indefinite period of time."

So much for Mack being a connection. A banished man couldn't possibly have been his bone marrow donor. Still, Carter wanted to hear more. "So Mack was crippled. In what way?"

"Right before he was banished, his arm was broken and went untreated. No one set it or gave him medicine for the pain. It healed badly, leaving his arm nearly useless."

"And there was no one else on this island but you and Mack?"

"No one. We were out in the middle of nowhere. I learned later that the currents were so dangerous around his island, only a few people knew how to navigate well enough to get there. To this day, the route is a clan secret of the Saquinnish. Mack told me later that it was a miracle I didn't drown in the rip tide." She paused, her eyes clouding for a moment, as she apparently recollected a dark memory, and then she continued. "At first I sat on the beach and felt sorry for myself. I couldn't believe I was stuck on an island with a moody middle-aged man who wouldn't respond to my expert eyelash batting. I was pretty awful to him the first few days, refusing to eat the weird stuff he gathered from the sea and cooked over an open fire. He ate things like sea slugs and fish oil, seaweed and geoducks. Have you ever seen a geoduck?"

Carter smiled and nodded, recalling the strange sight of the large mollusks he'd seen in the farmer's market—fleshy wrinkled gray tubes stuffed in a too small shell, an unlikely and unappetizing source of nutrition.

"Until the island, the only meat I ever came in contact with was the kind plastic wrapped on Styrofoam trays—neat and tidy and so far from the real thing you could forget it was once alive." She shook her head. "I thought Mack was the most barbaric person I'd ever met. Disgusting. He pulled those blue mussels right off the rocks and ate them. I thought I'd throw up."

"What changed your mind?"

"Extreme hunger." She chuckled again. "After I finally gave in and tried one of his meals—which wasn't half-bad, by the way—he showed me his cache of canned food left for him by the tribal elders of the reservation. After all the hunger I went through, I could have had an ordinary can of soup or plate of beans. He had a good laugh at my expense, but I was so angry I didn't speak to him for days."

Carter took another sip of soda. "So what happened?"

"He let me pout until I was weary of my own silence and self-pity. He let me go hungry until I had to beg for food. When he gave me food the second time, he said he expected me to learn to get my own."

Arielle paused and fingered the stem of her wineglass. "I thought he was the most selfish boor I'd ever met. I'd never had to work a day in my life, much less scratch for my own dinner. He just smiled at me and walked away. I wanted to run after him, jump on him and pound away at him for all I was worth."

"Did you?"

"No. But in the true spirit of a selfish teenager, I vowed I would never ask him for help. The next day I decided to follow him, watch what he did, and try to copy him."

8

July, 1985—Coastal Islands—Saquinnish Reservation

Arielle bided her time while Mack watched the tide go out. Then using a shovel, he dug holes in the sand down by the water. Guessing that he was after clams, Arielle rooted around in a pile of driftwood until she found a weathered board to serve as a digging tool. She returned to the shoreline, trying not to step in wet spots. So far that day she'd managed to keep her sneakers dry, which was a top priority in staying warm. For all her care, however, she accidentally traversed a bed of horse clams buried in the sand, and they shot sprays of water at her. In a matter of seconds, her canvas shoes were damp.

She stayed a good thirty yards away from Mack, and a bit farther up the beach so the waves wouldn't surprise her and completely soak her shoes. Mack had left his boots above him on the bank, and worked in his bare feet and a pair of jeans cut off above the knee. He wore a red shirt with the sleeves rolled up, and his hair in braids to keep it from hanging in his eyes while he dug.

The perpetual wind from the sea whipped Arielle's long hair around her face and plastered her T-shirt against her slender frame. Though the sun shone down through the low clouds, she was still cold and wondered if she'd ever grow accustomed to the incessant wind. Shaking off the chill, she thrust the board into the sand. The soil was a jumble of little rocks, broken shells, gray sand, and to her disgust, once she dug far enough, oozing gray sludge filled with marine worms and all kinds of creepy-crawlers she had never seen. She could barely bring herself to look at the mess. And the smell! The brackish odor of rotting life and sea water was enough to make her sick to her stomach. Worse yet, as soon as she scooped out a portion of the sludge, murky water rushed in to fill up the hole. At this rate, she'd never find any clams floating around.

Arielle continued to dig without seeing a single mollusk, while a burning sense of futility ate at her empty stomach. She glanced down the beach at Mack and could see him dropping a handful of clams into a plastic bucket beside him. Every once in a while he'd move farther down the beach, digging, bending down, and depositing his catch in the bucket.

How did he do it, and with only one fully functional arm? Arielle straightened and rubbed her gritty hands on her shorts. Then she pushed the hair out of her eyes. After a week on the island with no shampoo or conditioner and exposed to the constant wind, her hair had become a greasy, snarled mess, and she didn't even have a brush or comb to use to untangle it. If anyone important saw her in this condition, she'd be mortified. She hated being trapped on the island. She hated the wind, the sand, the sound of the ocean, and especially Mack Shoalwater.

Swearing out loud, Arielle kicked a pile of the sand she'd dug. Much to her surprise, she saw the flash of a white shell edged in maroon zigzags. All of a sudden it dawned on her: she'd been looking for clams in the wrong place. All the time she'd thought they'd be floating in the water, never dreaming they'd be lodged in the sand. What an idiot she'd been.

Forgetting her hair and disregarding the fact that she had to touch the disgusting sludge, Arielle reached down and picked up the shell—the first clam she'd found in two hours. It was fairly big, about two inches across. She held the prize in her cold hands, grinning with satisfaction, and glared at the dark figure down the beach.

"Eat dirt and die, Mack Shoalwater!" she shouted into the wind, even though she knew he couldn't hear her.

Intent on finding more mollusks, Arielle dropped the clam onto the ground. It struck the sand and opened on impact. To her dismay, she saw that her prize clam had been merely an empty shell filled with sand, whose weight had completely fooled her. Arielle grimaced, her pride stinging, and was glad Mack hadn't been able to hear her shout of victory. Next time she found something resembling a clam, she wouldn't be so quick to gloat.

Too angry to care about her nails, Arielle clawed through the rest of the pile of sand she'd dug. There had to be live clams somewhere, along with the empty shells. After a few minutes, her efforts were rewarded with the discovery of two clams the size of half-dollars.

The small success encouraged her, and Arielle dug a few more holes, pushing through the sand with the end of her board. But after another hour, she had collected only a handful of clams. Discouragement descended as time rushed by, for her findings were too meager to make a decent meal, and the sun was quickly going down. Soon Mack would be sitting at his fire, cooking something in his black pot while the fragrant steam drifted her way, driving her mad with hunger. But she wouldn't ask any favors of him. She'd rather die first.

After another half hour, she heard the crunch of Mack's footsteps on the barnacle-encrusted rocks behind her. Arielle kept digging, refusing to acknowledge his presence. She had no intention of looking up to see the disdainful expression that would surely glitter in his black eyes once he glimpsed the paltry results of her entire afternoon of work.

"You're too far from the tide line," he commented, walking past in his dry leather boots. "And look for little holes in the sand. Air holes."

Arielle kept her gaze focused on his boots and didn't say anything. He made no mention of her pitifully small pile of clams, but just kept walking toward his plywood shack. Soon she couldn't hear his footsteps any longer.

She wanted to yell at him and say something mean about his clam-digging outfit of shorts and boots. But she was too hungry to waste her time on revengeful remarks. Instead, Arielle took his advice and scooted closer to the water. There she saw many telltale air holes, marking the presence of clams. Racing against the encroaching darkness, she began to dig once more. This time when she dumped a pile of sludge onto the sand, she immediately saw the white edges of mollusk shells. She bent over and picked them out of the sand. Six this time! Heartened, Arielle pressed on. A strong wave surged up and over her shoes. She hardly felt it. Four holes later, and in less than twenty minutes, she had found two dozen clams.

Dusk surrounded her as she trudged up to the fire, her clams wrapped in a rag she'd found on the beach, and her soggy sneakers making squishing noises with every step she took. She was cold and miserable, dirty and unkempt, a far cry from the homecoming queen she'd been when she'd set out on her summer vacation two weeks ago. Never in her wildest dreams would Arielle have pictured herself in such a bedraggled condition, much less forced to dig her dinner out of the dirt.

Mack looked up from the pot where he was watching his clams boil. Nearby in a skillet, four pancake-like breads sizzled to a golden brown. The smell brought saliva springing into Arielle's mouth, but she swallowed it back, well aware that the food cooking on the fire was not for her. She might have enough clams for a meal now, but she had no idea how to prepare them, and her long day suddenly seemed to have gotten the better of her. She stood near the heat of the fire, her hands hanging at her sides, and wished she could have a pizza delivered. Pepperoni and black olives with extra cheese. She could almost taste it. But no, she was stuck on this damned island with Mr. Personality. Why was Mack Shoalwater so mean? She closed her eyes and fought down the urge to cry.

"Sit," Mack said. He reached for her sack of clams and she relinquished them without a protest. Then she sank to the weathered log that served as a bench and slipped out of her shoes. Wet sand had grated away the flesh at her heels and ankles, leaving them red and raw. Arielle said nothing about the pain and placed her feet on the warm rocks bordering the fire. She'd sit a few minutes and rest, and then cook her own damn clams. How hard could it be?—if Mack didn't begrudge her the use of his pots, that is.

Arielle was surprised when Mack thrust a dented metal plate into her hands, piled high with steamed clams and two pieces of warm fry bread. Startled, she glanced up at him.

"Thanks," she said through her cracked, weather-beaten lips, too hungry to refuse on the grounds of obstinacy and pride. She took the plate.

He nodded. "We'll eat your clams tomorrow." Then without a smile or a word of praise for a job well done, he sat down and ate his simple dinner in silence.

Arielle quickly consumed her meal, marveling that bread and clams could taste so good. She looked out at the water as she ate. In the absence of conversation, she became aware of a surprising array of noises—coots calling good night to each other, the wind rattling dried blackberry canes in the woods behind her, fish jumping in the bay, and the fire crackling near her warm toes. She watched the sun sink behind the islands in the Sound, her belly full of food and her soul full of a strange glow of contentment. Regardless of Mack's failure to recognize her accomplishment, she was proud of herself for having gathered enough clams for a meal, for learning a skill that could actually mean her survival. She had to admit the lesson she'd learned that day had opened her eyes to an entirely different world.

Soon afterward, Mack took the dishes down to the water and washed them. Then, as was his custom, he ambled off to a huge rock overlooking the bay where he meditated.

Arielle remained by the fire, seeking the warmth and company of the dancing flames. Her thoughts drifted to her family and friends and how they must be thinking she was dead. She wished there was some way to contact them, some way to tell them she was reasonably all right. But Mack had told her the first day she spent with him in exile, that no one ever came to the island except a self-appointed tribal elder from the Saquinnish Indian Reservation, and he wasn't due for another three months at the earliest. Judging by Mack's tone of voice when he spoke of the man, Arielle deduced that the elder was not respected by Mack, and that his arrival wasn't something Mack looked forward to.

Arielle leaned her elbows on her knees and hunched forward, wondering which of her friends would really miss her. And whom did she miss? With a stab of guilt, she realized that for the entire week, she hadn't thought once of her boyfriend back in Phoenix. Hadn't she been madly in love with him? Perhaps not. Arielle frowned, disappointed at her lack of feeling for him. She didn't like to think of herself as callous. She knew she should miss her parents, too, but didn't really, for they had never spent much time with her, and certainly none to speak of since she'd left home for college. When it came down to it, when she pared away all the time spent at parties, classes, and chatting on the phone, to search for a single meaningful moment of connection to another human being, she came up with nothing.

Arielle flushed with shame and disappointment and let her gaze travel up to the silhouette of the man on the rock. In all his silence, Mack Shoalwater seemed to be peculiarly content. Did he possess a secret that filled his life with meaning?

She grimaced and leaned her cheek on the back of her hand, enervated by the hard work and fresh air. She was going to be stuck with Mack for three long months. Perhaps she would have to break down and get to know the man.

The next day shortly after dawn, Mack struck out for the interior of the island, catching Arielle by surprise. She jumped to her feet, grabbed her sand-encrusted shoes where she'd left them by the fire the night before, and took off after him, mincing across the rocky beach on her tender feet. She'd never gone barefoot outdoors and felt every sharp surface of rock and barnacle. But her fear of being left alone was far stronger than the pain she felt.

"Hey!" she called, slapping her sneakers together to dislodge the sand. "Hey! Where are you going?"

He turned, glanced at her, and then continued up a steep path that rose from the beach through a tangle of vine maples. She watched him disappear up the embankment, swallowed by the curtain of dense vegetation, until all she could see of him was the flash of a tin can he carried.

She plopped down on a large rock at the base of the bank and stuffed her feet into the stiff canvas of her shoes, wincing as her chafed skin was sandpapered anew. Every step she took was bound to be painful, but she had no choice. She could either run after him and ignore her feet, or stay behind and fend for herself. She knew better than to consider herself capable of surviving entirely on her own.

"Mack!" she called frantically. "Mr. Shoalwater, wait for me!"

She tied her shoes and scrambled to her feet, swearing and gasping her way up the bumpy path. The trail was barely visible, crossed by fallen trees and clumps of ferns, and she was afraid she'd get lost. She pushed her way through the overhanging branches of alder and cedar, ignored the scrape of blackberry shoots and the sting of nettles, and crashed through the forest, totally unaware of its pristine beauty in her effort to catch up with Mack. He walked quickly but silently, and she caught only glimpses of him, first his shining black hair, then the glint of the can. She was terrified that she might lose sight of him altogether, and kept up a grueling pace, more taxing than any physical education course she'd ever taken.

At about ten o'clock, as far as she could guess, she caught up with Mack as he stood in a clearing near a bank of shrubs, picking some kind of berry. At the far edge of the clearing, she glimpsed a stream babbling its sparkling way toward the sea. Arielle paused for a moment, drinking in the pleasant sound of the brook and basking in the warm rays of sunlight. She hadn't been truly warm since she'd landed on the island seven days ago.

The clearing was carpeted with long, tender blades of grass. Arielle slipped off her shoes and breathed a soft sigh of relief. Then, knowing she'd eventually have to walk back to camp, she had the presence of mind to rinse all the sand out of her sneakers and leave them to dry in the sun. Afterward, she dipped her hand in the stream and drank the sweet water until her thirst was slaked.

Arielle patted the cool water over her face, refreshed by the stream, and then leaned over and rinsed her matted hair, hoping to get out most of the salt and sand. She squatted on the bank, squeezing the water from her hair, and then combed through her tangles with her fingers. She was glad there were no mirrors around to show her what she looked like, because she was sure she must look like a cave woman.

Afterward, she rose and minced across the grass toward Mack.

"What are you picking?" she asked, watching him pluck an orange berry from the shoulder-high thicket.

"Salmonberries."

"Can you eat them?" she inquired.

He snorted in contempt at the silliness of her question.

She blushed. Of course they were edible. Why else would he be gathering them? She would have to learn not to ask the obvious.

Gingerly, she pulled one of the berries off a stem and inspected it. It looked like a juicy raspberry but was orange in color. Tentatively she touched it with her tongue. The flesh was only mildly sweet, but after a week of nothing but fish and bread, the bland berry tasted like a fine dessert. She picked another one and another, and shoved them in her mouth. Out of the corner of her eye she saw Mack glance at her and shake his head.

Chagrined, Arielle swallowed her mouthful of berries, and realized how childish she must appear to him. When stripped of her designer clothes, her flawless makeup, her fashionable friends, and her well-orchestrated schedule of classes and dates, she realized she was nothing but a child.

"What are you going to do with the berries?" she asked, picking a few and reaching over to drop them in his can. "Something special?"

"Make a sweet syrup for the pan bread."

"That sounds good. May I help?"

Mack looked down his sharp nose at her. He was the type of person she would usually avoid in order to protect her reputation. She might have spoken briefly to him just to be polite, but would never have given him a second glance or thought. He was too old, too rough-edged, and a Native American, an ethnic group her parents frequently disparaged by carefully sculpted remarks that showed their tolerance of differing lifestyles while keeping the caste system intact.

The tall, self-contained man standing beside her was far from her parents' vision of Native Americans as second-rate human beings. In a raw sort of way, Mack could even be considered handsome, had she considered it proper to be attracted to older men.

"Pick only the soft berries," he instructed. "The ripe ones pull off easily."

"All right."

They gathered berries in silence until the can was brimming with the orange fruit and the sun had climbed directly overhead. Mack carried the can to the stream and set it in the shallows where the cold water would keep the berries chilled. Then he returned to the clearing and stretched out in the grass, rubbing his crooked arm as if the joint pained him from holding the can of berries. He tipped his face to the sun and closed his eyes. Arielle sat on a rock near the stream and watched him relax, wondering how long he would rest, but sensing she shouldn't ask. For a while she sat in the shade and then she wandered around the periphery of the clearing, hot and drowsy, but uneasy with the idea of joining him in the grass.

Since her arrival on the island, she had spent the nights wrapped in a blanket near the fire while Mack slept in his small wooden shack, separated from her by distance and wooden walls. Lying in the grass with him seemed far too intimate, especially out in the middle of nowhere. When she realized Mack was obviously going to sleep for a while, she paced the glade, dangled her feet in the stream, and then finally gave in to the peace and quiet of the afternoon by taking a nap.

Arielle found a soft patch of grass and sank back onto the ground. For a few minutes she enjoyed the warm light beating down and the rich sweet smell of the earth enveloping her in a fragrant cloud. She closed her eyes, and slowly her senses of hearing and touch took over. They had become much more acute in the last few days, being used considerably more often than just her sight.

Gradually she became aware of the hidden world around her. The grass and air were full of buzzing and scuttling things, as full of foreign creatures as the beach sludge had been the day before. Arielle felt an ant crawl over her hand. She jerked up, flinging the insect off in disgust, and worried how many bugs might have already crawled into her hair. Then she shook her head and frantically brushed off her shoulders. A turquoise-colored dragonfly buzzed past her, circled back, and hovered close to her face.

"Get away from me!" she exclaimed, swatting the air.

The dragonfly zipped away just as she saw Mack turn slightly and shade his eyes with the edge of his hand to look at her.

He was probably smiling. The damn man seemed to derive pleasure from her misery, as though she had been sent to the island for his entertainment. Arielle glowered. She had never been the source of anyone's amusement and wasn't about to lose the last shreds of her dignity in front of this man. Steeling herself for another onslaught of bugs, she plopped back down to the grass, this time on her side, with her head resting on her elbow. Perhaps if she braided her hair, she would provide less of a haven for insects to crawl into. She'd do that tomorrow.

Arielle tried to nap, but was too upset to relax. Each day with Mack Shoalwater was like a prison sentence. What had she done to deserve such punishment? She looked back on her well-ordered life and couldn't see where she had taken a turn so wrong as to throw her in the path of such an exasperating individual.

She clenched her teeth and ignored the little gnat that landed on her arm and got tangled in her fine blond hair. From now on, things would be different. Starting tomorrow, she wouldn't let him see her flinch, not at anything, no matter how slimy, how scaly, how dirty and creepy-crawly. If he could take it, so could she. She would show him that she was just as tough as he was.

"Things are going to be different tomorrow, Mack Shoalwater," she said under her breath. "Just you wait and see."

9

Things were *different between them* after that, and a quiet truce settled over the camp at the beach. Routines established themselves as they learned to accommodate each other's company. In the mornings, Arielle remained at her bedside fire until Mack finished his morning bathing ceremony in the bay, and she never peeked as he walked naked in and out of the water. In return, Mack made himself scarce each evening when Arielle slipped away to the small stream that emptied into the sea north of the camp. She had discovered a protected glen where the creek poured into a waist-deep pool. There, she bathed and washed out her underclothes every evening, and spread them out to dry on warm rocks taken from the fire.

They usually ate the evening meal together in silence. A few times Arielle attempted to make conversation with him, curious about the reason Mack was stuck on the island. But his answers were curt and never very informative, and she finally gave up the futile investigation into his past. Most of the evenings Arielle sat near the fire, watching the sun go down while Mack meditated. Once in a while he didn't climb up to his perch on the rock. Those nights, he went to his shack and came back with a cigarette, which he slowly smoked as he sat by the fire, warming his twisted arm. She guessed the damp weather and hard work caused him pain, especially at the end of the day. Though they never spoke, she liked those evenings more than the others, for she felt a tiny glimmer of companionship between them.

One morning some three weeks after her arrival, Mack finished his coffee, rinsed his cup, and told her to come with him. He set off southward down the beach, carrying two sharp sticks as long as broom handles, and a net in his ever-present plastic bucket. From what she could tell, Mack's right arm had been broken and never fixed, for the lower portion from elbow to wrist was nearly unusable except for his hand. Still, he seemed to get along fairly well.

Arielle stood up and dashed after him. In the old days she would have demanded to know where they were going, but now she knew better than to expect an answer to a demand.

Arielle's spirits were high as she joined Mack on his walk along the shoreline. The day was bright and diamonds of light danced on the water, dazzling her. For all the dirt and bugs and strange food, she had begun to wake up at dawn the last few mornings, curiously rested and ready for the day. Though she spent the nights lying in the chilly sand in her blanket cocoon, she awoke with more energy than she ever remembered having. Even her mind seemed clearer, perhaps because it was less cluttered with the rampaging images of television commercials and city traffic.

"Look," Mack said, pointing upward. "An eagle."

Arielle shaded her eyes and peered into the sky. Against the periwinkle blue backdrop soared a huge brown bird with something hanging from its talons.

"It's got a fish!" Arielle exclaimed.

Mack nodded and smiled. "It appears my brother the eagle has found my fishing spot."

"Or you've found his."

Mack glanced at her in surprise and then chuckled. She'd never heard him chuckle before. The sound was rich and real, as though it bubbled up from his belly and coursed through his heart. That he had laughed at her remark was unusually satisfying to her. She walked at his side, grinning and swinging her arms, scanning the sand for shells. She'd started a collection of shells and looked for additions to it everywhere she went. The challenge was finding perfect specimens of good color and without chips or holes.

Mack's fishing spot was over an hour's walk from the camp, and by the time they'd reached the wide curve of sandy beach, Arielle was hot and sweaty. Mack handed the bucket to her.

"Fill it half-full," he instructed, "and bring it back."

The beach was unusually free of rocks and vegetation, a smooth expanse of gray well-packed sand. Arielle slipped off her shoes, placed them above the tide line, which she had learned was beyond the border of dried seaweed and rubble, and then ran down to the water. Arielle waded in to her knees and scooped up the water, wondering what they'd catch this time.

She hoisted up the heavy bucket and struggled to bring it back to Mack, who stood staring out at the calm inlet.

At the end of the curving beach was a line of black rocks that spilled out into the water like the tail of a huge beast.

When she put the bucket on the sand, he handed one of the pointed sticks to her.

"Go to those rocks," he said, pointing to the dragon tail with the handle of the net. "Then get in the water up to here," he indicated his waist, "and walk toward me, swishing your stick in the water, like this."

He swept the sand with the tip of his stick.

She raised her eyebrows, doubtful as to the object of the exercise.

"When you walk, don't go too fast," he added. "I'll stand on the rocks there," he pointed at a smaller pile of barnacle-encrusted boulders nearby, "and wait where they can't catch my scent."

"They? What are we hunting for?"

"Flounder. They sit on the sandy bottom nearly unseen unless disturbed."

"You mean those weird fish with both eyes on one side of their body?"

"Yes."

"I've never tasted flounder."

"They're ugly as hell, but good eating." He waved the air. "Now go on. Herd them my way."

She did as requested and splashed into the bay. The water was so clear she could see every detail on the bottom, even when she waded in up to the waistband of her shorts.

Arielle swept forward, churning the bottom in front of her. Sand and silt swirled upward, blocking her view, but she continued her slow advance. The first pass produced nothing, but the second time when she got close to the rock where Mack stood bare-chested, he held up his hand to stop her. Then he tensed and hurled his sharpened stick into the water. With a yell, he jumped into the sea, grabbed the stick, and scooped the net below the surface, all in one smooth movement. He straightened, and held the net up, while water dripped down his muscular chest and arms, displaying the captured flounder.

She wrinkled her nose. "You're right," she said, inspecting the fish. "They *are* ugly."

Mack looked into the net. "Thank you, my brother, for giving yourself to us, so that we may eat."

Arielle glanced at Mack's serious face, surprised by words that sounded very much like a prayer. "Do you always thank fish when you catch them?"

"Of course." He began to walk toward the shore. "We always thank the animals. Otherwise they wouldn't think we appreciated their sacrifice."

"Animals don't know anything about sacrifice!"

"Oh? What do you know of animals?" he retorted. His manner grew distant again, and she realized she had said the wrong thing. During the return trip to camp, Arielle trailed after her silent companion, miserable, homesick, and hating the island more than ever. Three months with Mack Shoalwater was going to be like three years.

That night they feasted on flounder which Mack cooked slowly over the fire, supported on a framework of alder branches. The flesh of the fish was tender, white, and delicate in flavor. Along with the fish, they had fry bread with some of the salmonberry syrup, plus a savory mixture of young nettles steamed with wild onions that Mack had gathered on the bluff. Arielle caught herself licking her fingers in appreciation of the dinner, and blushed at her lack of manners. Her mother would have died had she seen her use anything but a napkin.

The thought made Arielle smile, but she said nothing in deference to Mack's desire for quiet. Besides, her comment that afternoon had obviously insulted him. To make up for it, she rose soon after the meal ended and took the dishes down to the water.

When she returned, she found Mack sitting on a log not far from the fire, smoking a cigarette. She walked past him and put the dishes away on a shelf in his shack and stepped back out into the dusk-softened light of the beach. Cool air wafted off the water, blowing tendrils of her hair against her cheeks. For a few moments she watched the smoke from Mack's cigarette float away in the breeze, and then she walked up to him.

"Look, I'm sorry about what I said earlier," she blurted. "It just sounded peculiar, that's all, about fish having sensibilities."

He took a long drag on his cigarette and let the smoke swirl out through his nostrils. "Everyone has a right to their own beliefs," he answered finally.

Arielle waited for him to continue, but he just kept staring out at the water, until she realized that was all he was going to say on the matter.

"I don't know much about Native American culture," she ventured. "I never took any classes in it."

"Neither did I."

She wasn't sure if he were being sarcastic or sincere, and felt frustrated by his strange notion of conversation. When she tried to chat with him she never received a response that encouraged her to continue.

"But you've lived on the reservation all your life."

"That's an assumption."

"You're a Saquinnish Indian, aren't you?"

"That isn't all I am."

Arielle frowned and stuffed her hands in the front

pocket of her shorts. Mack's answers confounded her more than his silences. She'd never met anyone who was so puzzling and yet so reluctant to talk about himself.

"What do you think about on that rock up there?" she asked, nodding toward his meditation spot.

"Many things."

"Like what?" She pressed him, hoping he wouldn't lapse into his trademark silence. "What did you think about yesterday when you were sitting up there, for instance?"

"Yesterday?" Mack stubbed the cigarette out on the log beside him. He flicked the filter into the fire and then turned back to face the water. "Yesterday. Let's see." He pursed his lips while Arielle waited, anxious to hear what Native American philosophy afforded him such acceptance in the face of unending banishment.

"Ah, yes," Mack nodded. His hair glinted at his shoulders with the movement of his head. "Yesterday I was looking out at the bay and thinking about that TV show, *Gilligan's Island.*"

"You're not serious!"

He glanced at her, as if offended by the incredulity in her voice. "Sure I am. I was thinking about all the stuff that used to float into their little lagoon. Like trunks full of costumes or electronic equipment. And I was wondering why nothing like that ever shows up on my beach."

"You don't mean to tell me that you sit up there and think about television programs!"

"What do you *think* I think about?"

"Life." She paced the sand in front of him, highly disturbed that her preconceived ideas of Mack might be entirely off base. "The reason we're on this earth. How myths explain the relationship of man to animal. That kind of thing."

"Deep Native American thoughts."

"Well—yes!"

He snorted and shook his head. "You are one bigoted mademoiselle, you know that?"

"Bigoted?" She stopped in her tracks. "I am not!"

"Yes, you are. You see my hair and my skin and you think to yourself, he's a Native American. Then you slap a label on me and believe everything else that comes with the stereotype."

"I'm *not* a bigot! I try not to discriminate against anyone."

"Just seeing me as a Native American and not as a man is discrimination." He picked up a small branch at his feet. "You see me as a noble savage, don't you? Some goddamn Hiawatha type living in the wilderness."

She stared at him, realizing how close to the truth his words were, and how preposterous her initial view of him suddenly seemed.

He held up the branch and shook it in the air. "See this?"

"Yes."

"What is it?"

"A stick."

"What kind of stick?"

"I don't know." She leaned over for a closer look. "Some kind of pine tree branch?"

"Western red cedar."

She stared at the gray branch. The only cedar she could readily identify was the pink aromatic wood that lined her hope chest back home in Phoenix.

Mack lifted a strip of the stringy bark and pulled it off in one piece. "See how it peels away? No other tree has bark like this. In the old days, my people used cedar bark for making baskets, clothing, mats, things like that. Red cedar. *Thuja plicata*. Grows to be six feet in diameter sometimes. Know where a noble savage like me learned about trees like this?"

"From your parents?"

"Nope. My dad was a drunk and my mom died when I was six."

Arielle flushed at the devastating personal information he dropped into the conversation as though it was a casual remark. "Your grandparents?"

He shook his head. "Botany 105, Harvard College."

She gasped and fell back a step. She couldn't help it. Her shock was too intense to contain. "You went to Harvard?"

"I rest my case." He tossed the branch with a flick of his wrist and it sailed all the way to the water, where it landed with a soft splash.

"What do you mean, you rest your case?"

Mack rose to his feet. "You are surprised, Leaf-on-the-Water, because you are a raging, dyed in the wool, complete with blinders, all-American bigot."

"Why you!" Arielle blurted, angry and ashamed at the same time, and belittled by his strange nickname for her. Leaf-on-the-Water sounded like a candle-in-the-wind type of person, not a nineteen-year-old woman. "And why are you calling me such a stupid name?"

"Because you are like a hapless leaf, caught in a current, twirling helplessly."

"How dare you!"

He waved her off, seemingly immune to her outrage. "I've dealt with plenty of young women like you." Calmly, he rolled down the sleeve of his red shirt over his crooked arm. "And you know what I learned over the years?"

"What?"

"That I don't have the energy to educate everyone about who or what I am. I know who I am and that's enough."

"If you ever said more than two words at a time, Mack, a person might see that you aren't like all the others."

"All what others?"

Arielle blushed, realizing she was guilty of lumping people together as stereotypes again, just as he had accused her of doing.

"Generalizations are for people with mediocre imaginations," Mack said. "And I doubt you like to think of yourself as mediocre."

"Not usually." She crossed her arms over the resentment inside her.

"So how do you like to think of yourself?"

She tossed her hair and stared at him. "Not as a bigot, that's for sure."

"You're telling me what you aren't. Tell me what you are."

"I think I'm a decent person." She tried to come up with a few phrases to describe herself in ways that carried meaning. "I have a great sense of color. I'm a fair tennis player. I have a lot of friends—"

"Those are external things. Who are you in here?" He pointed to the side of his head. "And here?" He thumped his chest over his heart.

She shrugged and gave a short laugh, hiding in humor. "Maybe I don't want to know!"

"Well," he said softly, "maybe you *don't* know." He raised his dark eyebrows and let his words drift into the evening air.

"You're saying I don't know myself?"

"That's right." His regard swept over her. "You are

like a cookie, stamped from a mold just like a thousand others. And though you are attractive in a symmetrical sort of way, there is nothing about you that stands out. That's because you're camouflaged by the safe and conventional labels you have taken on to describe yourself." He stood up. "You see, Leaf-on-the-Water, your bigotry applies not only to people like myself, but to your own personality as well."

"You're wrong. I know who I am. I know where I'm going."

"Do you?"

"Yes!"

"And where is that, exactly?"

"I'm going to finish college, get a great job, and make lots of money."

"Why?"

"So I can buy what I want and travel, and—you know—have a secure life."

"Like the one you have now?"

"Yes, I guess so."

"That kind of life will make you happy?"

"I think so."

"And are you happy now?"

"You mean on this island, or in general?"

"In general."

Arielle paused. She couldn't claim to be happy, not when she'd spent most of her life waiting to find someone to love her and give her the emotional sustenance she craved and had never received from her parents. She had spent the last few years keeping distracted and busy, so the flatness of her life wouldn't overwhelm her.

Mack folded his arms. "You're silent. Is the question too difficult?"

"No. It's just that I wonder if anyone can ever be truly happy."

"We are not discussing rhetoric or philosophy here. We're talking about you. Just you. Are you happy or not?"

"I guess I am."

"You guess?"

She threw him a sheepish glance. "Yeah."

"You don't sound sure. What's keeping you from being really happy?"

"I don't know. I guess I want more than I have."

"More money?"

"No. Not that." Arielle frowned, trying to come up with a phrase to describe the peculiar lack she'd always felt inside. "More like a connection."

A light flickered in Mack's eyes. "A connection to what?"

"I don't know!" She turned away from him, suddenly unable to meet his direct gaze. "If I knew, I'd find it!"

"Perhaps if you knew yourself and were at peace with who and what you are, you wouldn't seek connection outside of yourself."

She stood silently, glaring at the bay.

"Many people don't know themselves." He paused and stood behind her. She could hear his steady breathing, but didn't move, and waited for him to continue. "That's to be expected. You're young. But there are ways to correct this," he said.

"How?" She glared at him from the side.

"Through meditation and reflection. By taking the time to consider what has true value to you and pursuing those things above all else."

"Meditation? I don't know. I've never been one to sit still very long."

"Because you are not comfortable with yourself." He

hooked his thumbs in his belt. "Try something and see what happens."

"What?"

"Find your place on the beach."

"What do you mean?"

"Walk around until you find a spot where you feel comfortable."

"That would be the fire," Arielle replied, trying to joke her way out of the serious discussion.

"Come on, Leaf. Try it."

"You mean now?"

He nodded. "This is a good time of day to open yourself to peace." He tilted his head in the direction of the stream where she bathed. "Walk around, cleanse your mind of doubt, and see what happens."

Arielle stared at him. Was he crazy? He expected her to stumble around the beach in the dusk, looking for her special spot? What about the mosquitoes, the crabs, and the bats? All kinds of night creatures were out there on the periphery of the fire.

"Go ahead," he urged.

She knew he wouldn't let up, not unless she said something to insult him. Rather than offend him again, she rolled her eyes and took off across the sand. Inner peace. Who could find inner peace in frayed shoes and soiled clothes, walking around the middle of nowhere?

10

Arielle stumbled across the beach, worried that a bat would fly into her hair, or that a crab would skitter across her shoe and crawl up her leg. Inner peace. The only thing she expected to gain from the evening exercise was a string of bug bites. She glared at a rock surrounded by piles of driftwood, then at a log swept by delicate branches of alder. No single spot called to her, nothing jumped out at her as a meditation site. She glanced over her shoulder, hoping to find Mack had left for his rock down the beach. But he hadn't moved from the fire and was watching her progress. Arielle frowned and huffed north toward the stream.

She didn't find her special place that night, but hated to admit it to Mack. Failure meant that he was correct in assuming she didn't know herself. Obstinate as ever, she continued her evening search for inner peace for the next few weeks, much to Mack's apparent amusement.

One night in mid-August, Arielle set off as usual. Gradually she forgot to be worried about the creatures of the night, and soon the soft sounds of evening blossomed around her. Cool sea air surrounded her with a mellow musky scent, and deep in the woods, bullfrogs throated a rusty *a cappella*. Gradually Arielle's step quieted and slowed, as she slipped through the deepening shadows, visualizing herself first as a doe and then as a she-wolf, her paws soundlessly padding across the sand. She had to smile, for until she came to the island, she never would have succumbed to such a foolish fantasy. Her friends would have laughed themselves silly. But here in the wilderness where there was no one to see her but Mack, she felt free at last to be whatever she wanted to be.

Arielle paused where the stream in which she bathed emptied into the bay, fanning out in a wide shallow delta. Huge logs clogged the stream, thrown upon the beach by winter storms to form a primitive bridge. Arielle stepped up on the nearest log, unafraid in the dim light, for her eyes had adjusted to the dark. She walked the silvery column until she came to the next log, pushed at an angle into the first. She stepped onto the second log and walked its length, all the while listening to the gurgle of water below, like the happy chatter of a good friend. When she got to the halfway point, she heard the mournful lowing of a fog horn, far beyond the humps of the coastal islands that surrounded the bay and comprised Mack's prison walls. Arielle stopped and listened for the horn to sound again, the only clue that civilization still remained outside her little sphere. As she stood there, she noticed another log behind her which formed a convenient seat. She lowered herself to it, and leaned back, drinking in the quiet song of the stream, and the push and drag of the waves across pebbles which echoed the rise and fall of her own breathing. Not far above her, a nighthawk dipped and soared, feasting on insects with acrobatic grace, her only visible companion at the water's edge.

Arielle sighed and let her gaze slowly rake the beach and water. She stretched her long legs out in front of her and wiggled the toes of her soiled white sneakers. Her skin was darkening to a rich tan from days spent outdoors—better than any salon tan she'd ever had—and the muscles on her legs and arms seemed to have more definition lately, a result of hard work and constant activity. Physically she felt great. Mentally, she felt great, too, which was a surprise.

During the first few weeks on the island, she thought she'd die of boredom. But she'd been wrong. Television had been replaced by the constantly changing face of nature. And reading had been replaced by a steady stream of knowledge regarding the flora and fauna on the island, about which Mack knew plenty. He taught her the names of every wild flower in bloom, every tree, each mineral, and all the mosses. She learned to identify an incredible array of sea life, from jellyfish to mud sharks, from kelp to algae. He was also showing her how to carve the intricately beautiful Saquinnish animal designs, all of which had stories associated with them.

Whenever she asked to be taught to perform a task, he never once refused instruction. He seemed to have confidence in her abilities and her intelligence, and never once assigned a role to a task on the basis of gender. He cooked more often than she did because he was better at it, and she chopped most of the wood to spare him suffering from his twisted arm, which aggravated

him for days after wielding an ax. Arielle appreciated
Mack's trust in her, for his trust gave her the chance to
grow, an opportunity she'd never had in the rigid society
and insidiously-defined roles prescribed by her father
and mother.

Mack became her professor, her survival instructor,
and her friend. All the bedtime stories she'd missed in
the curve of her mother's arm were compensated for by
the fascinating tales Mack told in the dark by the dying
fire, his deep voice lulling her into an unexpected state
of contentment. Often Arielle went to sleep in the lean-
to she'd built from driftwood and cedar boughs, rolled
up in her blanket all snug and warm, dreaming of the
wolves, bears, and whales of the Saquinnish myths.

Sitting on the log in the stream, Arielle closed her
eyes and tried to visualize her parents. To be honest, she
didn't miss her family or friends very much. Certainly, it
would be nice to see them and assure them that she was
all right, and to continue her studies at college, but for
now she was content to spend her time on the island
with Mack. She had grown to appreciate him, to value
her daily instruction. And she had learned to be content
with her own company.

A grin spread over Arielle's face. *Damn*. She was content with her own company, with where she was for the
moment. She was sitting in the middle of nowhere in
tattered clothes and chipped nails, and she was actually
happy. In spite of herself, in spite of her bigotry and
stubbornness, she'd found her place on the beach. She'd
discovered inner peace.

"Damn you, Mack Shoalwater," she said. Then she
laughed out loud.

*   *   *

Early in September, Arielle found Mack staring across the water, toward the small dip in the hills of the outlying islands where a narrow passage led into their bay. It was the same passage through which she'd been swept by the storm over two months before. Mack stared, shading his eyes, while a grim expression pulled down the corners of his wide mouth.

"What are you looking at?" Arielle asked, coming up behind him with her latest cedar carving, a mask of a raven, hanging from her hand.

"I thought I heard something," Mack answered. He lowered his arm to his side. "I thought it might be Reuven Jaye coming with supplies."

"The elder?" Arielle's heart surged and fell nearly simultaneously. Ultimately she wanted to be rescued from the island, but it seemed far too soon. "The guy from the reservation?"

"Yeah."

"Didn't you say he came every three months?"

Mack looked down at her and his black eyes glinted with amusement. "It's *been* three months, Leaf-on-the-Water."

"Really?"

"You surprise me." He tilted his head slightly. "I thought you'd be counting the days until you could have a hot shower again."

"It's not a shower I want so much," she retorted. "It's getting away from your cooking that I look forward to."

"My cooking!" He snorted. "I'm a five-star chef compared to you."

"It's not how you cook," she continued their good-natured bantering, "it's what you cook."

"I haven't noticed you refusing anything."

"That's because I don't want to starve!"

"Admit it," he said, turning back toward his plywood shelter. "You're going to miss my alder-smoked oysters like crazy."

"No, I'm not." She trailed up the beach with him. "Once I get off this damn island, I'm never going to eat fish again, just you watch."

Arielle meant for her words to playfully insult him, but as soon as they left her lips, she heard them as Mack probably heard them. She was going to get off the island and he wasn't. She flushed with regret at her lack of thoughtfulness in choosing her words.

"Mack," she stammered. "Sorry, I didn't think—"

"No need to be sorry." He stooped down and picked up the rattle he was carving out of a burl.

"But what are you going to do when I'm not here?"

"What I've always done." He pulled out his pocketknife from his jeans and sat down on the flat-edged log where he carved. The ground around his feet was a jumble of wood chips, sand, and pebbles.

Arielle watched Mack for a long moment as he positioned the rattle in the hand of his crippled arm and carefully whittled away at the shape of a bird, whose tail served as a handle and whose belly formed the rattle. When he was done, he'd find a handful of round, perfectly formed stones all of the same color, to enclose inside.

Mack didn't look at her and she couldn't detect from his tone whether he was sad or accepting. Yet how could he not be frustrated? How could he just sit there, knowing he was to be marooned alone again, and not go absolutely crazy?

She shifted her weight and crossed her arms over her chest. "Doesn't it bother you?" she asked.

"Doesn't what bother me?"

"To be out here. All alone."

"No." He paused and studied the bird. "I have been alone most of my life."

"Not like out here!"

He shrugged. "To live among strangers, or to spend your days among people who don't understand you, is not far from living in banishment. In some ways, I prefer to be here."

"But you're a prisoner!"

He chuckled and shook his head. "Reuven Jaye and his like can keep my body out here for as long as they want," he commented. "But they have no chains strong enough to imprison my soul."

"Don't you miss the rest of the world, though?"

"Nope."

"What about your family, your friends on the reservation?"

"You think I had friends on the reservation?"

"Didn't you?"

He shook his head again. "I was an outsider from the day I was born. I never fit in."

"Why?"

"Because I was driven to follow my own path. I was determined to make something of myself beyond a tribal member. I left the tribal school when I was in eighth grade and enrolled myself in a public school in Everett. I lived with a white buddy of mine and went to school with the white kids."

"What was so wrong about that?"

"To be a Saquinnish and to be an individual is not possible. To the Saquinnish, all things are done to bring honor and recognition to the group, not to yourself. Personal attainment is frowned upon."

"What made you so different? Your upbringing?"

"No." He gave a short laugh. "I didn't have much in that department. I think it was something I was born with. I never thought of myself purely as an Indian, and I was too determined for people to tell me any differently."

Arielle nodded and sat down on a nearby log, where she had left her carving implement—an old paring knife that Mack had shown her how to slide over a whetstone until it was razor sharp.

"What did you do after high school?" she asked. "You mentioned you went to Harvard. But how did you end up here?"

"I was searching for something when I went to Harvard—for my place on the beach." He cocked an eyebrow at her in a knowing expression. "I didn't realize it at the time but I was trying hard to find out who I really was." He brushed a chip off the rattle. "Well, I didn't find anything in Boston. And I didn't fare any better in New York. So I came back to the Res, thinking I hadn't given my roots a fair shake."

"And what happened?"

"Some people resented me for leaving. And some resented me for coming back. I was accused of a crime and banished."

"What kind of a crime?"

Mack snorted in contempt. "The crime is immaterial. It's the reason I'm really here that matters. And that reason is because I caused trouble for some of the powerful elders." He studied his rattle. "The ironic part is, that in being banished, I literally found my place on the beach."

"I still can't believe you can be satisfied here."

"There isn't much on the mainland that is better than the world you have discovered here."

"But what about other people?"

"I don't need the contact of many people." Mack smoothed the cedar with his broad thumb. "I once thought there must be something wrong with me. But not anymore. Now I believe it has to do with my clan heritage."

"What do you mean?"

"Many of my ancestors were shamans. A shaman always underwent a spiritual transformation of some kind, and then lived apart from the tribe. Shamans were healers, but also magicians, and thought to be a bit crazy."

"I don't think *you're* crazy."

"That's because I've put a spell on you."

Arielle chuckled, but looked down at the sand. She knew his words were said in jest, but suddenly she wasn't quite sure he hadn't put her under some sort of spell.

"Most of the people respected shamans but feared them, too," Mack continued, "which always set the shamans apart. I have the blood of many great shamans in my veins, which is why I must feel at home here in this remote place."

Silence drifted over them as Mack lapsed into his usual quiet and continued to carve. Arielle did likewise. She was intensely aware of the sounds of their blades chipping at the wood. She was surprised when Mack broke the silence again.

"Sometimes you remind me of myself as a young person," he commented.

Arielle looked at him in surprise. "You've got to be kidding."

Mack's gaze settled upon her. "You have a spark inside you that is different from most people."

"I don't know what it could be!" She gave a nervous laugh, to hide the warm feeling that coursed through

her. To be compared to Mack was a compliment.
"Shaman craziness, maybe."

"No. A thirst."

"For what?"

"Life."

She tried to avoid his gaze, but her eyes locked with
his as the curve of her smile faded from her mouth.

"You have a heart and a mind that should not be
wasted, Leaf-on-the-Water. And if you leave here having learned one thing from the past three months, it is
that."

Arielle didn't know what to say.

Mack blew a few wood chips from his rattle. "When
you first washed up on my beach," he continued, "I
thought my true punishment had arrived. I thought you
were a spoiled brat, a nightmare come true. But you
came around."

"I had to or I would have starved!"

He shook his head. "I could have fed you for three
months. But I was pretty sure you'd learn something if I
didn't. And I wanted to see what you were made of."

"Bully."

He smiled and resumed carving.

When he didn't speak, Arielle stopped whittling and
looked at him from under her lashes, so he wouldn't feel
her staring at him. She let her gaze travel over his jet
black hair, his strong rugged face, and his broad shoulders. A lump formed in her throat at the thought of leaving this man behind. Mack might find peace alone on the
island after she was gone, and most likely he would forget
all about her in a few days. But peace would come harder
for her, for she knew it was going to be a difficult task to
grow accustomed to life without Mack Shoalwater
in it.

*   *   *

A few days later, Arielle woke to rain pattering on the roof of her shelter. Though the ground was wet all around her, the blanket she lay upon was still dry, for the cedar boughs she'd used to construct her roof didn't let a drop of rain through. She was cold, though, and shivered as she slipped on her tennis shoes. Afterward, she crawled out of her lean-to, hoping Mack had risen before her and started a fire already. Her muscles and bones complained from the sudden movement, for the damp weather had seeped into her body, leaving her stiff.

Arielle stood up and hugged her arms as rain pounded around her. Heavy gray clouds hung upon the distant islands, creating a muted, claustrophobic world she had never seen before. She glanced around while a sense of foreboding settled around her like the clouds on the hills. Something didn't seem right. The bay was far too silent in the rain, especially without Mack's familiar figure nearby.

Much to Arielle's disappointment, she saw only the blackened remains of the previous night's blaze and not a morning fire. She glanced at the plywood shack, wondering if Mack was up. It seemed late for him to be sleeping, but the sky was so dark he might have misjudged the time. Arielle scampered to the woodpile covered by a plastic tarp, and pulled out an armful of cedar which she had split herself. She tossed a few pieces of kindling on top and returned to the fire. The rich, pleasant smell of cedar rose up in the rain as she deposited the wood in the sand and then bent to poke around for live coals. She didn't have a match, but usually she could start the fire by carefully arranging wood on top of coals and kindling, and then blowing on them the way Mack had taught her.

As she worked, she listened for the sound of Mack's presence—his step, a cough, or the clink of his bucket. But he didn't make an appearance. She blew on the fire, shielding the side of her face from the rain, and concentrated on the task. She'd never awakened without seeing Mack on the beach, bathing or brewing the morning coffee.

When the fire caught, Arielle ran back to her shelter and retrieved her blanket, which she wrapped around her shoulders to protect her from the downpour. Then she sat by the fire, hunched toward the meager heat, while she scanned the south beach and then the north, expecting Mack to appear any moment. Still, he didn't show.

After what felt like a half-hour, she rose and walked to the plywood shack filled with his tools and canned goods that he would use only in an emergency. She'd been in the shelter before, but never when Mack was sleeping. Arielle knocked on the side of the crude door. No sounds emitted from inside. She knocked harder.

"Mack?" she called. "Are you up?"

She waited a moment and then cautiously opened the door, allowing her eyes to adjust to the darkness inside the windowless room. The shack smelled of tobacco, smoke, and wet plywood. "Mack?" she called into the darkness. Gradually the looming shapes of crates stacked on the floor and clothing hung on pegs materialized, as did the ledge of Mack's bed at the far end. The bed was empty.

Arielle's uneasiness intensified. She backed out of the shack and closed the door.

"Mack!" she shouted.

No one answered.

She let the blanket fall, cupped her hands around her mouth, and yelled his name as loudly as she could. Still nothing. A sharp sense of panic rose into her throat, choking her. She hadn't spent more than a few hours alone on the island and Mack's unexpected absence frightened her. What if something had happened to him?

She ran down the beach, calling his name. Where could he be? Why would he have left so early in the morning? Arielle sprinted to the end of the beach, where it narrowed to make way for a jutting cliff of clay topped by madrona trees. Mack was nowhere in sight.

Arielle turned around and headed back to the camp, out of breath, her concern mounting with every step. She passed the fire and continued to trot northward toward the stream. Every few minutes she'd stop to catch her breath and call out Mack's name. By the time she reached the stream, she was exhausted and heartsick. What could have happened to Mack? An hour must have elapsed since she'd first awakened. Mack rarely disappeared that long without telling her where he was going.

Panting, Arielle glanced up the stream, where the green water cut a small canyon through the wall of cedar and fir. In the overcast and rain, the woods looked dank and gloomy—not the sun-dappled haven to which she had grown accustomed. She didn't relish the idea of slogging through the wet ferns and tramping through the muddy paths to look for Mack. But she might have to, if he didn't show up soon.

She stood in the drizzle, too overheated from running to need the blanket any more, but holding it around her shoulders nevertheless. The blanket was much too valuable to leave behind. The pungent odor of the damp wool around her shoulders mingled with the sharp scent rising from the patch of camomile she had trampled underfoot. Arielle rubbed her nose and then pushed back a tendril of wet hair that had escaped from her braid.

"Where are you, Mack?" she muttered. No one responded. Not a single peep came from the trees around her. All the birds and small animals seemed to have taken cover from the downpour and were silently waiting out the storm.

After Arielle caught her breath, she trudged back to the camp, her stomach growling with hunger and her throat parched. She grabbed a cup of water when she got back to the shack, and then stashed her discarded blanket in her lean-to. She looked up at the bluff above camp. Mack might be up there gathering herbs. He might know of a plant that should be harvested during a rainstorm. There was probably a perfectly reasonable explanation for his absence, and he would laugh at her when he discovered how she had worked herself into a frenzy over his disappearance. But she would rather be laughed at and know he was safe than sit back at camp and do nothing.

The path up the side of the bluff was treacherous in the rain. Arielle stepped carefully, holding on to roots and shrubs as she struggled up the slope. Much of the soil was made of clay, which grew slippery in the rain, and in some places the trail was inches deep in muck. Once or twice she almost lost a sneaker in the ooze.

At least in the trees the rain wasn't nearly as driving. Arielle was grateful for that. She inched her way up the bluff and stopped to rest at the top. Ahead of her was a tangle of dripping lush foliage, as thick as any Central American jungle.

She took the berry-picking route and checked the side trail where they had gathered wild garlic. There was no sign of him. She pressed onward, pushing branches out of her way, unmindful of the gritty slog of her shoes and the rain pooling at the tip of her nose.

"Mack!" she called.

She listened and thought she heard something above the hiss of the rain.

"Mack?" she called again.

There, up and ahead and to the right—she was sure she heard something.

"Mack!"

Arielle stumbled forward, dashing toward a large cedar. And then she saw a flash of red at its base.

11

"Leaf—" Mack's voice sounded unusually weak and raspy.

Alarmed, Arielle rushed toward the source of his voice and soon spotted the crimson color of his wet red shirt where he lay on the ground behind the tree. One glance at his powerful body lying in a clump of ferns and the way his left leg twisted to the side in an unnatural position, and she knew something was wrong.

"Mack!" she gasped, running to his side. "What happened?"

"I broke my leg," he said with a grimace.

She glanced at his leg, then at his ashen face, and felt the color drain from her own. "How?" she croaked.

"I surprised a she-bear with a cub. She ran me up the tree. I fell getting down."

"How can I help?"

"You're going to have to splint my leg."

"Me? I don't know how!"

"You're going to have to try."

Mack looked up at her with an exhausted expression and then licked his lips. His breathing was shallow and strident, and she noticed his eyes held a peculiar metallic gleam, probably the result of withstanding hours of intense pain. She was surprised he hadn't lapsed into unconsciousness from shock.

As she stared at him, his eyelids fluttered and closed.

"Mack!" she cried, dropping to her knees beside him. Her entire body trembled with fright. "Wake up!"

Slowly he opened his eyes.

"Don't go falling asleep on me," she pleaded.

"Leaf, you've got to splint my leg and get me back to camp."

"But I told you—I don't know how!"

"There's no other choice."

"Mack, I—"

"You can do it."

She wished she felt the same confidence she heard in his voice. She'd never been tested like this, had never been the one responsible in a life and death situation. Yet she had no choice but to help him. She couldn't very well dial 911 and request a medic.

"All right. I'll try." Arielle tried to sound reassuring, but her arms and legs shook so much she had trouble getting to her feet. For Mack's sake, she had to get hold of herself. Arielle glanced around and forced her heart to quit pounding. She had to think, she had to plan, and forget her own terror of the situation.

From watching emergency shows on television, she knew a splint required two straight supports which were tied around the broken limb to hold it in place. Cedar branches would have to do. She scrambled around in the underbrush until she found two sturdy branches almost as long as Mack's leg. Then she pulled off her T-shirt, disregarding the fact that she wore only a bra underneath, and ripped the fabric into three strips with her teeth.

Once she set to work, she noticed her trembling gradually dissipated. She set the splint materials to one side and then reached for Mack's belt.

"I'll have to cut away your pants," she said.

He managed a slight nod. His eyes were closed and his chest rose and fell with his labored breathing.

Arielle found the knife he always wore on the left side of his belt. Deftly she cut through his jeans with the razor-sharp blade. At any other time she would have died of embarrassment to touch a man so intimately, but under the circumstances she gave neither her modesty nor Mack's a second thought. Gently, she draped the denim to either side of his leg and examined the sight before her.

For a moment, nausea nearly overcame her, but she wiped it away as she wiped away the sweat and rain mingled upon her forehead. The bone hadn't broken through his skin, which she was pretty certain was a good sign. Still, the flesh below his knee had swollen to a purple lump. Arielle knew she'd have to pull his ankle and try to coax the fractured ends of his shin bone in place. She couldn't remember if the tibia or the fibula was the larger bone in the lower leg, but it didn't matter at this point. The larger bone was the one that was broken. And if she pulled at it, she had to have some kind of resistance so Mack wouldn't simply slide in the same direction. His body mass would help somewhat in weighing him down, but she thought there should be more to resist her tugging, or she would cause him additional agony.

Arielle glanced up and saw a small tree behind Mack. She jumped to her feet and gently guided his hands above his head.

"Can you hang on to this sapling while I try to set your leg?" she asked.

"Yeah." He wrapped his big hands around the small trunk.

Arielle ran back to her position at his feet. "All right. I'm going to pull your foot now. Ready?"

"Yeah."

Clenching her jaw and praying she wouldn't hurt him too much, she slowly pulled his foot toward her.

Mack sucked in a breath and his features contorted with pain, but he didn't make a sound. Arielle studied the shape of his leg as she pulled, and slightly turned his foot, thinking of the line his shin would normally take. She'd seen him often in his clam-digging shorts and tried to recreate the same shape, but it was difficult because of the swelling.

With excruciating care, she slowly lessened the tension. Suddenly, something seemed to catch, to fall into place. Mack let out his breath in a relieved burst and Arielle realized the bone must have set properly. She wedged his ankle between her knees so his leg couldn't move. Then she reached for the ties and slipped them under his leg, one above the knee and two below. Quickly she positioned the branches on either side of his leg and tied them firmly in place.

Mack's hands slipped from the trunk of the sapling and his body wilted into the ferns.

"How are you doing, Mack?" she asked.

"Better," he gasped.

"Just take it easy."

"We've got to get out of here."

"No, you need to rest. Do you have some pain relievers at the camp? Aspirin or something? I can go and get them."

"No, we need to clear out in case that she-bear comes back."

"You think she will?"

"She might."

"Can you make it?"

"I'll have to."

Arielle stood up and reached down for him. Mack raised his hand and grasped hers. She pulled hard, throwing her weight back to help him rise to his feet. Mack lumbered upward, swayed, and then sank against her shoulder. She almost collapsed under his heavy frame, but managed to keep both of them upright. Then, with him in his tattered jeans and her in her bra, they slowly staggered back to camp.

Mack slept most of the day and night. Late the next morning, he stirred and Arielle looked up from her seat near his bed. Relief swept over her as his eyes opened and he squinted at her.

"How are you doing?" she asked.

"I'm hungry," he answered.

"That's a good sign." She rose, wearing his cast-off shirt and her well-worn shorts. "I'll make you some soup." She turned toward the cache of canned goods. "Do you want an aspirin?"

"How about four?" He winced. "My leg hurts like a son of a bitch."

She nodded and shook four aspirin out of a small plastic bottle. She'd been giving them to him off and on for the last twenty-four hours. Sitting on the side of his bed, she urged him to sit up. She held a cup of water as she watched him toss the pills into his mouth. Then he took a long drink and gave the cup back to her.

"Thanks," he said.

"Don't mention it," Arielle replied. She placed the cup on a crude plywood table near the bed and rose to get his lunch.

"What'll it be, Mr. Shoalwater?" she asked, holding up two cans of the same variety, the only type of soup in his larder. "Chicken noodle or chicken noodle?"

"Chicken noodle. I hear chicken's good for invalids."

She grinned, relieved to see his humor was still intact. "Only if prepared by your mother."

He smiled. "You kind of look like my mother."

"Thanks!" She made a face and reached for the can opener.

"Leaf?"

She turned and glanced at him. He leaned on his elbow and gazed at her earnestly, all traces of humor gone.

"Yes?"

"You did good," he said. "In fact, you did more than good. And I'm grateful. Thanks."

"You're welcome." She beamed at him as her heart swelled. She *had* done well. In fact, she'd surprised herself. Three months ago she wouldn't have thought herself capable of splinting someone's leg with her own two hands. But helping Mack had come naturally to her, and during the traumatic situation she had found a reservoir of calm and strength in herself that she hadn't even known existed. Nothing in her life had given her a deeper sense of satisfaction than in successfully assisting Mack—not her tennis, not her homecoming queen crown, and not her designer wardrobe. Could she have found her true calling at last—in medicine?

"I'll be right back," she said, heading for the fire outside the shack.

Arielle poured the chicken noodle soup into a pan, added water, and waited for the concoction to heat. Just as the soup came to a boil on the fire, a glint in the bay caught her eye. She looked up to see a black and white boat chugging toward the shore.

Within the half hour, the expected tribal elder, Reuven Jaye, dropped anchor offshore and rowed to the beach in a scarred aluminum dinghy packed with a few cardboard boxes and some sacks of vegetables. Arielle waited for him near the fire, curious to learn why Mack vehemently disliked the tribal elder, and determined to convince the man to take Mack to the nearest hospital.

Puffing and blowing, Reuven pulled his dinghy past the tide line and then straightened. He wore a black ball cap, a red windbreaker that advertised a bowling alley, and a pair of baggy, worn jeans. His short hair was well peppered with gray, but the mustache over his full wide mouth was still a solid black. He pushed up his glasses, and they glinted in the midday sun.

"Who are you?" he demanded as his eyes raked her up and down.

"Arielle Scott," she replied, stepping forward and holding out her hand. They shook briefly. "I was in a boating accident a few months ago and washed up on Mack's beach."

"Where is he?"

"In there." She nodded toward the shack, somewhat taken aback by Reuven's lack of manners in not introducing himself. "He broke his leg yesterday."

"Broke his leg?"

"Yes."

Reuven grimaced at the plywood shanty, showing his set of large flat teeth. "Damn fool," he said and spit.

"It was an accident."

"Well, if he thinks I'm going to cart his supplies for him, he's got another think coming."

"I'll do it."

"You?" He glanced at her doubtfully.

"Yes, me. Mack's in no condition to do anything."

Reuven shrugged and shuffled up the beach toward the shack while Arielle hoisted a carton of groceries out of the boat. Anger flared inside her. The least Reuven could do was take a sack of vegetables with him.

She struggled with the heavy carton as Reuven pounded on the side of the shack.

"Shoalwater, you in there?"

"Get lost, Jaye," Mack's voice boomed, sounding much stronger than the previous day. For that, Arielle was grateful.

Reuven ignored the command and opened the door, just in time for Arielle to duck into the shack with her load. The elder trailed after her, stuffing his hands into the pockets of his shiny red jacket.

"Looks like you got yourself into some trouble," Reuven commented without a trace of sympathy.

Mack didn't bother to answer.

"The terms of your banishment specifically state no unauthorized visitors, Shoalwater."

"As if I had a choice."

"The way I see it, you've violated the conditions of your sentence. We just might have to extend your little vacation here on the island."

"Wait a minute," Arielle said, stepping next to Mack's bed. "That's not fair!"

"Fair don't apply to Mack Shoalwater, Miss Scott. He lost his rights when he became a criminal."

"He's no criminal!"

"Yeah?" Reuven snorted. "Ain't he told you what he done?"

"He didn't have to. I know a decent man when I see one!"

Reuven ignored her. "What'd you do, Mack, have one of your high-powered friends back east drop her off here?"

"For Chrissake," Mack growled. "She's just a kid."

"Yeah, but I heard white bitches always went for you." Reuven shot a sidelong glance at Arielle.

"I don't care what you heard. I want you to take Miss Scott back to the reservation and call her folks. They must be worried sick about her."

"They should, her being stuck here with the likes of you."

"He never touched me!" Arielle interjected, her cheeks flushing. "He's been like a father to me."

"Sure he has."

"And I'm not leaving without him."

Reuven laughed outright then. "He's not going anywhere."

"What do you mean? He needs to see a doctor."

"Why? That leg'll heal."

Arielle stared at him in disbelief. Surely he didn't expect Mack to mend without medical attention and to fend for himself until his leg was better. How would he manage? Arielle glared at Reuven. He must have been the one to maroon Mack with an untended broken arm. "He needs a cast, mister," Arielle said, barely suppressing her outrage. "And he needs to see a doctor."

"He's not leaving the island, miss. Not after what he done."

"I don't care what he did! Even a murderer deserves medical treatment for an injury. And if you don't take him to the nearest hospital, I'm going to speak to the authorities about this!"

Reuven regarded her with a stolid expression in his dark eyes, obviously not cowed by the threats of a nineteen-year-old.

"My father is an attorney," she added. "I'm sure he'll have plenty to say about the violation of Mack's rights."

"This isn't federal property, miss, it's Saquinnish. Different laws, different jurisdiction."

Arielle refused to back down. "Human rights have no ethnic or geographic boundaries, Mr. Jaye. I'm sure the local media would love to make an issue of it once they hear about Mack's treatment. And believe me, if something isn't done with Mack's leg, I'll tell every reporter in Seattle about it."

Reuven's face flushed but he made no response.

Arielle used his hesitation to plead her case further. "Besides, I should think out of plain human decency you would see to Mack's injury."

Reuven rubbed his nose and glanced at Mack, who had been characteristically silent during the last few minutes. Then he turned back to Arielle and cleared his throat.

"You want to spend four hours on a boat ride with a dangerous criminal?"

"I'll take my chances." Arielle crossed her arms and regarded Reuven with a steady glare.

"Then get that boat unloaded. We have to catch the outgoing tide."

o   o   o

Later that day, Arielle heard the familiar, high-pitched laugh of her mother in the hallway of the hospital, and glanced at the clock on the wall. Seven o'clock! Her parents had arrived already to take her home. It was too soon. She wasn't ready to say good-bye to Mack yet, but knew she'd have to say something before her mother and father knocked on the door. Once they burst into the room, she would lose all hope of meaningful conversation. Her father would dominate the scene with his jokes and shallow goodwill, and her mother would bombard her with questions about her adventure, and she'd never have an opportunity to say the things she wanted to say to Mack.

"They're here," Arielle said, rising.

"You don't sound too happy."

"It just seems so quick."

Mack lay in a bed in the small Bellingham hospital where he'd been taken after a long and restless ride aboard Reuven's fishing boat. Arielle insisted upon accompanying them to the health care facility. Since she had to wait for her folks to fly up from Arizona and had nowhere to go until their arrival early that evening, she convinced Reuven to let her go with Mack. The doctor had examined Mack's leg, took x-rays, complimented Arielle on her splinting job, and then put a cast on Mack's leg.

He also insisted that Mack spend a few days in the hospital to recover from the traumatic experience and give his leg a chance to heal before he went back to the island.

Arielle gazed down at Mack, whose healthy color had returned. She only hoped he would be treated decently once she left.

"How will you manage without me?" she asked.

Mack rolled his head toward her. His black hair was stark against the white pillowcase. "As I managed before."

"But you didn't have a broken leg then."

"I'll be all right. Don't you worry, Leaf-on-the-Water. It's time for you to float down another stream."

"But how will you fish? You can't get that cast wet, you know."

Mack glanced at the large white cylinder of his leg lying atop the gold blanket. "As much as I hate the thought, I'll just have to eat pork and beans for a while."

Arielle lowered her voice. "And what if that Reuven Jaye character never lets you see a doctor again?"

"I can take the cast off myself if I have to."

Arielle heard her mother's laugh again, much closer this time. She glanced over her shoulder at the door and then back at the tall man lying on the bed. He meant so much to her. How could she say all that she felt for him in the few moments she had left?

"Mack?" she began, wishing she had the guts to reach for his hand or touch his face. Instead she stood near him, suddenly awkward and shy, while the precious moments ticked away. "I just want to say—"

The door burst open. "Arielle!" her father called.

"My baby!" Her mother's mouth fell open in surprise at the altered version of her daughter, with her wild hair and tattered clothes. Arielle derived a twisted sense of satisfaction at the look of horror in her mother's eyes. Then her mother rushed forward, high heels clicking on the tile floor and her purse flopping around her elbow, as she propelled herself into Arielle's arms. Arielle was almost surprised at the rush of happiness she felt in seeing her parents.

"Ari," her father asked, quickly joining them. "Are you okay?"

"Yes."

"Oh, my poor baby!" her mother wailed, "What have they done to you? What have they done?"

"Mom, I'm fine." Arielle caught Mack's eye over the top of her mother's head. He gave her an amused smile and sank back on the pillows.

"Oh my precious!" her mother squeezed her tightly. "We thought you were dead! It's been a nightmare. An absolute nightmare!"

Her mother's exclamations and tears merged into a drone of sound. All Arielle could think about was Mack. Her time with him was over. Yet he would always be with her, as a part of her. Having known him had changed her forever. She had found herself, had found a sense of confidence, and had found a place in the world where she knew she could make a worthwhile contribution to mankind—all because of a wrongly-convicted shaman lying in a hospital bed in a small town in Washington.

She gazed at him and he looked at her, and between them flowed all the words they would never say to each other.

12

"*So whatever happened* to Mack Shoalwater?" Carter asked, finishing the last of his soda.

"I'm not certain."

"What do you mean?"

"When I got home after being rescued, I wrote to the Saquinnish Tribal Center, hoping to do something about Mack's banishment, especially since he had broken his leg. I was told that he had died."

"Died?" Carter barely suppressed a gasp. He couldn't imagine the vibrant wise man of Arielle's story dying so unexpectedly.

"Yes, but when I was at the clinic last week, Evaline Jaye made a comment that made me think he might still be alive on the island."

"Why would anyone tell you Mack was dead if he really wasn't?"

"I don't know." Arielle put her wineglass down. "All I do know is that Reuven's been my only contact since my rescue, and personally I don't trust the man. Mack didn't trust him either."

"Didn't you speak with him when you were up at the clinic?"

"Yes, and he wouldn't talk about Mack."

Carter studied her face. During her stories of the island, her clear hazel eyes had come alive with joy. Now, however, Arielle's eyes flashed with anger and her dark brows knitted together in concern. "You suspect foul play," he commented.

"Yes. Mack was healthy and strong. There was no reason for him to die of complications from a broken leg. Reuven Jaye hardly gave me the time of day when I asked him about Mack. I think he was hiding something. Plus the fact, Mack's medical records are now missing. Don't you think that's a bit suspicious?"

Carter nodded and glanced at his watch. He was shocked to discover two hours had passed like two minutes, and all around them sat patrons eating dinner. He had been so entranced by her tale he hadn't been aware of people coming into the restaurant. He couldn't remember the last time he'd spent two hours talking nonstop with a woman, or with anyone for that matter.

Arielle sighed. "I can't bear the thought that Mack might still be out there, that I have spent the last ten years doing nothing to rescue him or clear his name."

"But you thought he was dead."

"He doesn't know what I've been told. What if he's alive and thinks I left the island and never looked back?" She gazed at him, and her stricken expression twisted something in Carter's gut.

"Arielle—" The depth of her care for Mack struck Carter like a blow. He had thought of her as a cool, self-absorbed woman, bent on furthering her career and garnering satisfaction in healing the poor while buying herself expensive toys with her doctor's salary. He'd been wrong. There was more to Arielle Scott than her elegant exterior. She was deeper than most people he'd met, and far too deep for him to get involved with her. His sarcasm and distrust could puncture and deflate someone as sincere and giving as Arielle. Yet he thirsted for the friendship of such a person. He knew that seeds of sincerity and trust were the parts of himself he longed to nurture. But those ungerminated grains had never lived in an environment where they could flourish. The few times he'd ventured toward the world of light and warmth, he'd suffered immeasurable loss. He was better off to remain closed and aloof.

Carter longed to tenderly brush back Arielle's shining hair, to caress the side of her face, and tell her that Mack was the type of guy who would understand no matter what she did. He wanted to kiss away the self-doubt in her beautiful eyes. But he didn't make a move. To reach for Arielle would involve lowering his own barriers, something he wasn't prepared to do.

"Don't blame yourself," he said at last. "You did everything you could with the information you had."

"I never should have believed Reuven Jaye. Not then, not now."

"What other choice did you have? You were nineteen and a stranger to the reservation. What else could you have done?" He reached for the check and saw Arielle bite the side of her lip and glance out the window.

"I'm not a child now," she said, her gaze slicing back to him. "And I'm going to find out one way or another what happened to Mack, even if I have to take a boat out to the island myself. I'm going to start by searching for his records on the reservation."

"That sounds like a dangerous proposition. What if someone doesn't want you poking around?"

"I'm going to anyway. I have to."

Carter placed a crisp ten-dollar bill on the tray and looked up at her. "You saw how those boys acted toward you the other day, ruining your tire. I don't think it's a good idea for you to go traipsing around by yourself."

"You have a better idea?"

"Yeah. Take some muscle with you."

Her eyes leveled on him. "Got anyone in mind?"

"Yeah. Me."

"I can't ask you to get embroiled in this."

"You didn't ask. I volunteered."

He expected her to roll her eyes or gracefully refuse his offer. Instead, she surprised him by reaching for her coat.

"Okay. I'm going up to the reservation tomorrow. Shall I pick you up?"

"When?"

She pulled her coat across her lap and paused. "I hadn't given it much thought. I hoped to get into Reuven's office unnoticed and have a look around."

"In the middle of the day?"

"You have a better idea?"

"How about right after the casino closes tonight?" Carter suggested. "We could hang around a back room somewhere and wait until everyone leaves. That way we wouldn't have to break in."

Arielle raised her brows as she considered the merits of his plan. Carter sank back in his chair across the table from her, trying to appear nonchalant. He surprised himself by realizing how much he wanted to help her. He'd already discovered that she fiercely protected her independence and took pride in her ability to manage her own problems. But in this situation, Carter thought it would be too dangerous for her to act alone. He would worry too much about her safety. Besides, after hearing Arielle's tales about the island, he felt as if he had come to know Mack Shoalwater and shared Arielle's outrage at the way Mack had been treated. "Well?" he asked.

"That sounds like a good plan," she replied. "Should I pick you up around eleven? That will get us to the casino about midnight."

"I think it closes at two." He stood up. "Why don't you come to my place at eleven and we'll grab a snack before we go. As long as we get to the casino by one, we should have plenty of time."

"Eleven?" Arielle turned her wrist and glanced at her watch. "That's about four hours from now."

"Go home and try to get some sleep. It could be a long night."

She rose and Carter helped her on with her coat. He left her to lock up the clinic and drive to her condo.

Tired from her busy schedule and relaxed by the glass of merlot, Arielle managed to sleep for three hours. She rose at ten, took a shower, and dressed in jeans and a brown plaid shirt. Then, thinking she should contribute something toward the snack with Carter, she ducked into a nearby deli and bought a pint of pistachio ice cream, hoping Carter might like her favorite flavor, too. She parked near his building and found the number of his apartment, which she buzzed so he could let her in. The lock clicked and she pushed open the lobby door. Carter appeared at the top of a wide set of stairs with a spoon in his hand.

"Hi," Arielle said, feeling a sudden attack of apprehension at entering Carter's private world.

"Hi. Come on up."

He lived on the second floor of a restored brick building, which he explained had been built at the turn of the century after the big Seattle fire. Many of the original brass hardware and porcelain light fixtures had been retained, as well as the ornate moldings and brickwork. Arielle surveyed the building, which was much more interesting than the modern steel and glass building in which she lived.

Carter opened his door and the delicious aroma of spices and warm bread met her as she entered his apartment. She glanced around as Carter took her parka. The place was small, but had high ceilings and a large bank of windows. He'd furnished it with navy blue leather furniture set off by rust and blue accents which contrasted nicely with the red brick walls. A guitar stood in a stand near the end of the couch, a laptop computer and a sheaf of papers took up most of the coffee table, and a cheerful blaze crackled in the fireplace across from the couch. His cozy, well-lived in apartment was vastly different from the cold, austere rooms of her condo.

"Try to ignore the mess," Carter said. "I've had to bring my work home a lot this week."

"This isn't bad," Arielle chuckled, following him out to the kitchen. "You should see my place. I still have boxes sitting around." She held up the bag containing the ice cream. "Can I put this in the freezer?"

"Sure."

She opened the freezer, surprised to see neat stacks of plastic containers and small bags of vegetables, a far cry from her clutter of frozen entrees and half-empty bags of coffee beans. Arielle stowed the ice cream in the top of his refrigerator while Carter stirred something on the stove. She glanced at his back. He was dressed in black jeans that hugged his lean hips and a black sweater with the sleeves pushed up on his forearms. His shoulders looked strong and wide in the sweater, and his newly washed hair, still a bit damp, brushed the collar of his shirt.

Arielle felt a surge of attraction toward him and had a crazy urge to step up behind him, wrap her arms around him, and tell him that he was the sexiest guy she'd met in years. She vividly remembered the warm and solid feeling of his chest as they'd danced and wanted to enjoy such closeness again. But he'd never made a move to indicate he was interested in her that way, and she wasn't about to foist herself on a man unless she was sure her attentions were desired.

She smiled bitterly to herself. That was exactly why she felt comfortable with Carter—he'd never made a move on her. She'd grown weary of men who didn't make the effort to get to know her before they hit on her, and she had no patience for those who were too shy or insecure to talk to her on an adult level. Where Carter fit in was still a mystery. He certainly wasn't shy, and he seemed willing to get to know her. But why wouldn't he flirt with her, just a little?

"Can I do anything to help?" Arielle asked, stepping away from the refrigerator and pushing thoughts of other men from her mind.

"You could put silverware on the table," Carter said, replacing the lid on the large pot.

"Okay. Where is it?"

"On your right, first drawer."

Arielle placed the flatware on either side of his plain stoneware plates, noticing that he'd put down place mats and had arranged two candles on the table. Many years had passed since she'd eaten by candlelight at home. She was pleased by the thoughtful touch.

"It'll be a few minutes," Carter said. "Can I get you something to drink?"

"Will you join me?" she asked.

He shook his head. "I avoid alcohol."

"Has it been a problem for you?"

Carter reached for the lid of the pot. "You're off duty now, Flo, so you can cut the medical questions, all right?"

"Sorry."

He peeked in the oven and then turned to the refrigerator, obviously too busy to talk, or wanting to make it appear that way. Arielle wandered back to his living room, idly perusing the walls. A stack of drawings on his entertainment center caught her eye and she reached for them.

"Mind if I look at these?" she asked, glancing over her shoulder at him.

He came to the doorway with a bowl of salad in his hand. "No. Go ahead."

Arielle studied the drawings, which were pencil sketches remarkably similar to the animal shapes Mack had often carved. The designs had the unmistakable stamp of talent and sensitivity. "Did you draw these?" she asked.

"Yeah."

She ambled back to the kitchen, perusing the masterful lines of the designs. "Have you taken classes in Native American art?"

"Nope."

"Really? These are very good."

"They're just abstract scribbles."

"Scribbles? Don't you know what you've drawn here?"

"Rorschach test patterns?"

"Hardly!"

"So tell me. You're the doctor."

Surprised, Arielle looked up at Carter to find him staring at her, his dark eyes glinting and intense. She tipped the pile of drawings toward him. "These are Wolf Clan designs."

"Wolf Clan?"

"Yes. Mack explained to me how Saquinnish designs were first developed from the actual animal. The artists divided the creature right down the middle, flattened out the two halves, and formed the resulting shapes into graphically pleasing curves and spaces." She bisected his drawing with the edge of her hand, showing one-half of the wolf face. "See?"

Carter nodded silently, but she could sense that the conversation upset him. He didn't say a word and his glare could have burned a hole in the paper.

Arielle forced a smile, hoping to lighten his mood. "The designs are really quite advanced for what some consider a primitive culture."

"So these are all drawings of wolves?"

Arielle nodded and watched him as he studied the papers. The muscles of his jaw flinched as he clenched his teeth together and then frowned.

"Some are representations of heads," she said. "Some are the entire body. See?"

"Yeah."

"Mack was a member of the Wolf Clan. He was always carving these particular designs. That's why I recognize them."

At that moment, the oven timer buzzed and Carter hurried back into the kitchen, leaving Arielle puzzled and worried. Why would Carter draw designs he knew nothing about? Why had he been upset to discover what the designs meant? He was a man of many secrets and obviously didn't trust her enough to discuss any of them with her.

Disappointed, Arielle put the papers on top of the stereo cabinet and walked back to the kitchen.

"Dinner's ready," Carter said, unwrapping a long loaf of fresh bread that he'd been warming in the oven.

"Want me to light the candles?" she asked.

"Sure." Carter nodded toward the lower cabinets. "There're matches in the drawer under the silverware."

While Arielle lit the candles, Carter set out two bowls of some kind of stew which gave off an aroma that made her stomach growl audibly. She grimaced, hoping comic relief would dispel the tension of the last few minutes. "Pardon me!" she exclaimed.

Carter met her eyes and smiled.

"That smells absolutely wonderful!" she added, looking down at the stew.

"It's jambalaya, a southern dish I thought you might like to try."

Arielle couldn't help but be impressed. "You made this?"

"Surprised?" He pulled out a chair for her. "Thought I'd cook something that starts with a K and comes out of a little blue and orange box?"

Arielle chuckled in response but paused as she reached for her napkin. Carter's choice of words and tone of voice made him sound just like Mack. If she closed her eyes and forgot where she was, she could easily imagine herself back on the island with Mack, instead of sharing a late meal with this younger, more troubled version of him.

Carter brought the warm sliced bread to the table, turned off the lights, and sat down. They filled their plates with the rustic peasant bread and salad and then Arielle dipped her spoon into the jambalaya. The mouthful burst with flavors—seafood, sausage, ham, rice, red peppers, okra, and a rich tomato and chicken broth. She could see Carter watching her reaction out of the corner of his eye.

"This is delicious!" she said. "Where did you learn to cook?"

"From a cookbook."

"Your mother didn't teach you?"

"My mother barely ate, let alone cooked," Carter replied, the warmth in his eyes fading.

"Why? Was she an invalid?"

"She was an alcoholic." Carter shot her a hard glance and then looked down at his food. She was sure it had taken a lot for him to reveal that particular piece of information.

Arielle flushed. So that was why Carter avoided alcohol. His mother had abused it and he was probably afraid the potential for addiction had passed on to him. She wished she had been more sensitive in questioning him about his drinking habits earlier.

"She *was* an invalid in some respects," Arielle put in. "Alcoholism is a disease, you know."

"Not in her case. She chose to drink. It helped her forget."

"Forget what?"

"That she was wasting her life waiting for something that would never happen, for a man who would never show up."

Arielle studied Carter's hard expression. "Your father?"

"Yeah." He pulled off a piece of bread. "She'd stay in her room for weeks at a time, crying, drinking, and sleeping off the booze."

"Sounds like clinical depression."

"Oh, she was depressed all right. No doubt about it. She was a beautiful woman at one time. Could have asked for the world and gotten it. But she was from a southern town. And southern girls didn't go off to college and come home pregnant. And if they did, the daddy of their baby had better be a white boy."

"And your father wasn't?"

"Nope. And no Greyson woman was going to marry a prairie nigger, no matter how much she loved him."

"Marry a *what*?"

"A prairie nigger," Carter repeated through clenched teeth.

"What on earth is that?"

"What my mannered southern grandmother called an American Indian."

Arielle sat back in her chair, stunned anew by the cruelty of labels and stereotypes with which people continued to punish each other.

"So your father was a Native American?"

"Yeah, but I didn't know it until last year, when a doctor told me I belonged to a rare blood group found only among some coastal Indians."

"You never knew your father at all?"

"Nope. My grandmother vowed to disown my mother if she ever spoke to the guy again, much less married him. My mother was an obedient southern girl, the kind who wouldn't think of defying her folks, the kind of person who hadn't the guts to strike out on her own. So she drank to drown her loneliness and her bad luck, and waited for years for her boyfriend to rescue her."

"And he never did."

"If he ever made the effort, my grandmother probably ran him off with a broom. But who knows—maybe he just didn't care enough to come after my mother. That's probably closer to the truth."

The rough edge in Carter's voice was ample evidence that he had suffered plenty because of the absence of his father. Arielle felt a stab of sympathy for him and slipped her hand over his forearm. He glanced down at her hand in surprise.

Arielle wished she could tell him that having a father who was uninvolved and insensitive was almost as bad as growing up with no father at all, but guessed he would consider her opinion invalid. Many people made the mistake of assuming she'd had a perfect childhood.

"It must have been tough," she said softly, giving his arm a squeeze.

"Yeah, but I got over it."

Had he? Arielle heard the bitterness in his voice and wasn't certain Carter had put his past behind him.

"Mack told me something once," she said, sliding her hand away from his warm arm. "And I'll never forget it."

"What was that?"

"That we have a choice every day regarding the way we will look at the world. We can't change the past. We can't change the way people will act. We can't change the inevitable. All we can change is our own attitude. Attitude can bring us peace or anguish. And every day we wake up, we have the power to choose what kind of world we want to create for ourselves."

Carter nodded slowly and his hard expression gradually softened.

Sensing progress, Arielle decided to continue. "And he said one more thing."

"What?"

"That if the world is cold to you, it's up to you to build fires."

Carter gave a tight chuckle and looked over at Arielle. "This Mack of yours was quite a guy."

"I think so."

Carter's gaze roamed over her face and then slipped down her torso and landed on her hand. He reached for her fingers and slowly drew her hand to his mouth. Arielle watched, spellbound, as he closed his eyes and tenderly kissed the back of her hand in a gesture full of gallantry and heart. Then, just as gently, he returned her hand to the side of her plate.

"Thanks," he said gruffly, glancing into her eyes.

Arielle thought her heart would explode with appreciation for the intense and intelligent man across from her. Mack's words hadn't been lost on Carter. Somehow she had known all along the seeds of Mack's wisdom would fall on fertile ground with Carter. "Anytime," she replied.

A fleeting smile pulled up the corners of his mouth and then vanished. "Got any more advice for a guy with twisted dials?"

"That depends." She cocked an eyebrow at him. "Got any more jambalaya?"

13

Just before the casino closed for the night, Evaline Jaye stacked the receipts in a bag and headed for her father's office down the hall. She'd get started on the deposit and would almost be finished by the time the doors closed. Normally she didn't spend much time at the casino, but her father had been ill for the last few days and she had taken it upon herself to assume his duties while he lay in bed. She knew the routine of going through the money and checks, sorting the bills and change, making out a deposit slip, and dropping off the money in the bank's night deposit box. She'd had a busy day at the clinic and was tired, but knew her father's peace of mind was worth the extra effort. He trusted few people enough to manage the money at the casino, and trusted no one as thoroughly as his own daughter.

Evaline frowned. Her father claimed to be ill, but she'd smelled the booze in the house. She hadn't said anything and made up excuses to the other tribal members to hide her father's condition from the rest of the reservation. He rarely drank, and she'd seen him drunk only a few times in her life. It wasn't like her father to drown himself in alcohol. Something must be bothering him so much he couldn't face it, and until he confided his problems to her, she'd wait patiently and do what she could to help. Reuven was getting old and she didn't want anything to jeopardize his health, for he was all she had in the world. In time he would tell her, she was sure of it. He had always told her everything.

Deep in thought, Evaline passed by the rest rooms and continued her walk down the dimly lighted hallway. Not until she reached for the door of her father's office did she realize a man had stepped out of the shadows on her right.

"Hey, babe," an unfamiliar voice said, barely audible over the din of the casino behind her.

Startled, Evaline turned around. No one called her babe. And no one had any business hanging around in the shadows near the back rooms of the casino.

"Hold on, there." The man laughed softly and held up his hands. He was a short, stocky man, not much taller than herself, with light brown hair, and dressed in jeans and a blue T-shirt that stretched across a wide chest. "Don't go gettin' all riled up."

"What do you want?" she demanded, reaching for the cold doorknob.

"I want to talk to you."

Evaline looked him up and down, trying not to appear too derisive. Men never wanted to talk to her. He must be after the money.

"It's nearly closing time, sir," she said. "If you want to talk, come back some other time."

"Well now, sweetie, that's why I'm here. To catch you when you aren't too busy. I've been keeping my eye on you, and you are one busy little lady."

His gaze slid from her face to her breasts and Evaline felt a flush of unease. If the guy was interested in the money, why was he looking at her like this?

"Please," she said, trying to keep her voice level. "I have a lot to do. If you want to talk, come back tomorrow."

"I want to talk now," he replied, planting his left palm on the door and trapping her between his body and the door.

Evaline scooted sideways, but he reached for the doorknob and flung open the door, pushing her into the dark room with the force of his body.

"Hey!" Evaline exclaimed, but her voice was swallowed up by the noise in the main room down the hall.

He grabbed her arm and kicked the door shut with his foot. "There's no need to shout," he said, threading his other hand into her thick hair. "I just want to talk to you for a minute. I've been watching you these past few nights and aching to get to know you. I've been aching real bad."

"Let me go!" She struggled, but the movement painfully wrenched the hair in which he'd entwined his fingers.

"God, you make me hot!" he exclaimed, nuzzling her neck. His breath reeked of beer. "Put a bag over your head, and you've got a body that just won't quit."

He tried to kiss her, but Evaline wriggled backward. He didn't lose his grip, however, and they careened across the floor, slamming up against her father's desk. Evaline dropped the bag of money and screamed, but his mouth smothered her cry for help and one of his hands fumbled with the buttons of her blouse.

"In the dark you are something else!" he panted, grinding against her. "Come on, sweetheart. You know you want it!"

"No!" she cried.

"You're not going to get this chance every day," he retorted, crudely squeezing the crotch of her jeans. "And you're gonna like what I'm going to give you!"

"No!" Frantic, she pushed against him. He caught her arms and wrestled her onto the top of the desk as she kicked and thrashed her head back and forth, trying to avoid his insistent mouth. He grabbed her face in a vice-like grip and forced her to kiss him, squeezing her jaw so hard she whimpered in pain. Her foot knocked an ash-tray to the floor and her father's in/out basket fell a second later, scattering papers. The man held her down at the throat and grabbed the front of her jeans, pulling at the snap as his breath came hard and fast. He was going to rape her and no one would even know it was happening. With all the noise in the casino, no one could hear her screams.

The pressure of his hand on her neck cut off her air supply and her vision darkened. Blobs of black swam before her eyes as she scratched and clawed his face and neck, trying to inflict enough damage to make him stop. But her efforts had little effect, and soon he was wrenching down her jeans. Tears of terror and outrage sprang up in her eyes. How could he do this to her—to take without asking, without decency, without care? The room began to swirl and the strength in her arms and legs drained away as Evaline felt herself being sucked into a world of darkness and violence. The man's loud breathing merged with the snarl of a wolf, his hands became claws, slashing at her, and his mouth grew full of sharp teeth, ripping her neck.

"No!" she cried, and heard the voice of her twelve-year-old self, the voice of the child inside her head who ran through her nightmares, screaming. "No! No!"

A swarm of noise and color swept down upon Evaline as the assault merged with her nightmare, man becoming wolf, tearing at her, ruining her, terrifying her. Fear galvanized her, freezing her limbs and shredding her thoughts until her senses shut off entirely to blot out the snarling creature on top of her. Evaline tried to scream but nothing came out, and then she was falling, falling, falling into the blackness of oblivion.

Arielle's heart lurched when she heard a scream, and she lunged for Reuven's office door, completely disregarding the fact she and Carter had been lurking in the shadows to break in later. Carter streaked past her, bursting through the door as Evaline screamed again. He dashed to the desk, yanked the man off Evaline, and literally threw him against the wall.

Standing in the doorway, Arielle gaped at Carter, amazed at his strength and the wild look on his face. When the man slid to the floor, scrambling with his pants, Carter picked him up and threw him against the wall a second time, his chest heaving and his eyes glaring with fire.

"Bastard!" he exclaimed. "You bastard!"

"Carter?" Evaline's weak voice floated through the tense air.

Carter turned, and the other man spotted his chance to get away. He bolted for the door. Arielle stepped forward to block the path, but he shoved her against the doorjamb, knocking the wind out of her. She hunched over, trying to catch her breath as Carter leaned over the sprawled figure on the desk.

"Evaline," he said. "Are you okay?"

"Carter?"

Evaline's voice trailed upward in a thin sing-song tone, alerting Arielle to the fact that she was in shock. Arielle stumbled forward, hoping the man hadn't hurt Evaline. She'd been hurt enough for one lifetime. Arielle stumbled to the desk, anxious to help in a medical way, as well as offer her support as a woman.

Then Arielle saw Carter reach for Evaline's face, his movements tender and assured. He gently pushed back the tangle of hair at her temple and looked down at her, his expression full of concern and warmth. That he could change from a bitter closed-off man to this solicitous gentleman in a time of crisis was a surprising revelation to Arielle. She had suspected Carter might be concealing much of his true character behind a tough-guy facade, but his genuine tenderness surprised her.

Evaline's eyes opened and gradually focused, and when she realized who stood above her with care streaming out of his eyes, she reached up and flung her arms around his neck. Carter slipped his arms around her slender frame and drew her to a sitting position, patting her back, and speaking soft words of encouragement to her. Arielle watched them together, their black hair nearly touching, their skin almost the same shade, and felt acutely out of place.

"Are you all right, Evaline?" Carter asked in a husky voice.

She nodded, apparently unwilling to release him until she absolutely had to.

"Did he—"

"No."

"Don't you want me to go after that guy?"

"No." She increased the pressure of her arms. "It will only make trouble for me."

"What if he comes back?"

"I'll be more careful."

Arielle stepped forward. "I'm sure we could catch that man if—"

"That's okay, Ari." Evaline glanced at her and seemed to realize her time in Carter's arms was over. She sat up straight and ran a shaking hand over her hair.

"Are you sure you don't want us to call the police or something?" Arielle continued. "We'll be witnesses, won't we, Carter?"

"I don't want to go to court," Evaline said at last, while Carter stepped back, allowing her space to swing her legs over the side of the desk. "It would be—" she paused and looked down. "—too humiliating."

"But you did nothing wrong," Arielle protested.

"The courts will see it differently. They will take one look at my face and my background, and decide I must be desperate enough to seduce a man."

"That's ridiculous," Carter said.

"It's happened before with women I know."

"Still, if you think you might change your mind later," Arielle put in, "you might want to have a medical examination to back up your claim. We could go to the clinic and take pictures. It looks like you're going to have bruises on your face."

"Thank you, Dr. Scott, but no."

Silence fell among them. Evaline snapped her pants closed and turned away, suddenly awash in shame that a stranger had nearly undressed her and taken from her what she had never given to a man—and fantasized about giving to Carter. Since his appearance at the clinic, she had thought of little else.

A gentle hand touched her shoulder. "Are you sure you're all right?" he asked.

Evaline closed her eyes and let his touch seep into her bones. No man's presence had affected her as deeply as Carter's. She longed to turn back around and ask him to hold her, to reach up and caress his shining black hair, his strong face, and look into his intense black eyes without fear of seeing pity in them. That would never happen, and her heart broke just a little at the realization of the glaring truth. A handsome man like Carter would never look at her with anything but pity in his eyes.

"I'll be fine." She stepped away from his hand and reached for the light switch. They all squinted at the sudden blaze of light.

"Oh, look at the mess," Arielle exclaimed. "Let's get this cleaned up."

While Evaline and Arielle returned the items to the desktop, Carter straightened the chairs that had been knocked aside during the scuffle. He reached for the bag of receipts and plopped it on the desk.

"Practically as good as new," he said.

Evaline smiled. "I'm so grateful you were nearby, Mr. Greyson. And you, too, Ari. I owe you both for this."

Carter exchanged an inscrutable glance with the doctor and Evaline tilted her head, suddenly suspicious. Until that moment she hadn't wondered why Carter and Arielle were at the casino together. "Why *were* you nearby?" she asked. "To see my father?"

Arielle crossed her arms. "As a matter of fact, Evaline, we were here to go through your dad's files."

"Why?"

"To look for Mack Shoalwater's medical records."

"But why would my father have Mack's records?"

"Because he was in charge of Mack's banishment."

Evaline paused. It didn't seem likely that her father would keep Mack's records separate from those at the clinic. What reason would he have to do such a thing? Her father was an upstanding citizen and a good man. He had nothing to hide, and should have no objection to providing information regarding Mack Shoalwater, especially to someone like Dr. Scott.

"Would you mind if we checked his files?" Carter asked.

"I suppose it wouldn't hurt," Evaline replied. "And I do owe you a favor."

"It shouldn't take too long." Arielle unzipped her parka.

"Don't rush." Evaline sat down behind the desk, her knees suddenly weak. Her initial shock had worn off and she found herself shaking uncontrollably as a result of the attack. "I have to do the deposit. And tonight I'd kind of like some company while I sit here."

Carter searched through the left bank of file cabinets while Arielle took the right. No one spoke as they flipped through the messy manila folders labeled in pen and pencil and stuffed haphazardly with sheets of paper. Evaline worked quietly at the desk, sorting the cash into neat piles and keeping track of the amounts on a deposit slip. He noticed that she had to count the stacks more than once and that her hand trembled as she wrote. Carter was amazed she could even function after having been attacked.

After a half hour had passed, someone knocked on the door. Evaline answered it and came back with the rest of the night's take at the gambling tables, which she added to the stacks on the desk.

"Any luck?" she asked.

Carter turned. "No. Does your father have files in his desk?"

"I think so." Evaline pulled at the large drawer by her left knee, but it wouldn't budge. "It's locked," she said.

Carter ambled to the desk. "There's probably a key in the top drawer."

Evaline pulled out the shallow center drawer and Carter spotted a small brass key lodged among the pens. "There it is," he said.

Evaline stuck the key in the lock and the drawer opened. Carter knelt down and thumbed through the files, highly aware of Evaline's leg nearby. His thoughts returned to the way she had flung herself into his arms. She had held him tightly, pressed against him ardently, and he would have thought his long-denied maleness would have surged to the forefront with such an impassioned embrace. Yet he had remained unaroused, not because Evaline was too disfigured to be desirable, but because his body had been keyed up lately for only one person—Arielle. He'd gotten himself in a tough position this time—that of being turned on by a woman he knew damn well he should leave alone.

Carter forced his thoughts back to the matter at hand and was surprised to see the name Shoalwater, M. printed on a tattered file stuck at the back of the drawer.

"Arielle," he said, pulling out the folder. "I've found something."

She stepped behind him just as he rose to his feet and turned toward her. In her haste her outstretched hand knocked the file folder from his grip and sent papers fluttering to the floor.

"Sorry!" Arielle exclaimed, bending down to snatch up the papers. Carter retrieved the documents that had

landed near the wall and stuffed paper after paper back
in the folder. As he did he glimpsed on one letter-sized
page the familiar logo of Fred Hutchinson Cancer
Research Center, the same medical center where he'd
undergone his bone marrow treatment. Carter glanced
at the date of the letter: March 10, 1994. He scanned
the opening line to Mr. Shoalwater, thanking him for his
donation. The date made the hairs stand up on the back
of Carter's neck. He'd undergone his transplant in
March of 1994 at the same facility.

Whatever information the letter contained, Carter
couldn't take time to read it, in case Arielle would notice
and ask what he had found. He didn't know what he
would tell her, or how much he wished to divulge of his
personal life. With curiosity burning through him, he
stuffed the paper in his jacket, hoping that neither
Arielle nor Evaline had seen him. Then he turned back
to the desk, sure that his expression would give him
away, for he felt pale and shaken. Lucky for him, Arielle
had made her own discovery.

"Look at this!" She held a thick sheaf of legal documents stapled at the corner. "It says here that Mack was
accused of stealing a valuable artifact from the tribe."

"That's right," Evaline said. "Didn't you know?"

"Your father mentioned something about stealing.
But Mack wouldn't talk about his past much."

"What did he steal?" Carter asked, still struggling to
regain his composure and almost unable to take his
mind off the paper stuffed between his jacket and his
sweater.

Evaline glanced up at him. "A house post. They're
kind of like interior totem poles used as corner posts in
the old lodges, except shorter and wider than totem
poles."

"How could a person steal something that big without being seen?"

"Easily," Evaline explained, zipping the deposit bag. "The Wolf House where the robbery took place is at the old village, a few miles out of town on Salmon Point. Hardly anyone goes there any more. As I understand it, Mack pretended to be interested in restoring the village as a historical site when in fact, he planned to clean it out of artifacts while no one was watching."

Arielle frowned. "That doesn't sound like the Mack I knew."

"Sometimes money makes people do unlikely things." Evaline rose from her chair. "The house posts are very valuable. The one Mack stole was worth a million dollars. And that was more than ten years ago."

"A million dollars?" Carter gave a low astonished whistle. "No wonder Mack was at peace with the world. The man was a millionaire."

"Sure," Arielle retorted, "And living at Club Banishment, with all the amenities—cold water baths, canned hors d'oeuvres, and all the firewood you could chop."

Carter gave her a wry smile and then turned to Evaline. "Was the house post ever recovered?"

Evaline shook her head. "No. Mack would never admit to the name of the person he sold it to or the people who helped him steal it. No matter how many years of banishment he was threatened with, he would never tell. That's the story we all heard."

Arielle frowned and looked back down at the papers in her hand. She turned to the next page and scanned the text, shocked anew by what she read.

"And here's the charge of homicide your father mentioned."

Evaline nodded. "Yes, Mack Shoalwater killed an old

fisherman who claimed to have seen the thief towing the pole out to sea."

"Mack would never kill anybody!" Arielle smacked the paper with the back of her hand. "These proceedings are ridiculous! He was obviously framed."

Evaline's eyes widened in disbelief. "But who would want to frame him?"

"Probably someone who wanted to conceal the identity of the real murderer." Carter felt a burning sensation flare in his stomach, replacing the thrill of his earlier find.

"The real murderer?" Evaline went on, still unconvinced of Mack's innocence. "But who would that be? Mack was the only loner on the reservation at the time. No one else who lived here would ever have stolen from the tribe, much less have killed one of our own people. We're just not like that here."

"Are you certain?" Carter asked.

"Yes!" Evaline glared at him, her eyes glinting with conviction.

Arielle heaved an exasperated sigh and angrily flipped through the rest of the document. Carter returned to the file in his hand, searching for a death certificate or anything else that might give a clue as to Mack's fate. For Arielle's sake as well as his own burgeoning outrage, he felt compelled to find something that would solve the puzzle.

Just as Carter was about at the end of the file, he turned over a postcard from the Fred Hutchinson Cancer Research Center, scheduling Mack for an upcoming appointment in February 1994, proof that Mack had been alive a year ago. Relief swept over him. The postcard would preclude the necessity of divulging the existence of the letter in his jacket and at the same time give Arielle hope in her search for Mack.

"Arielle." Carter held up the postcard. "Take a look at this."

She looked over his shoulder. "Mack went to the doctor in 1994?"

Evaline glanced up at the question, with disbelief in her dark eyes, but she said nothing.

"Supposedly."

"Then he isn't dead!" She beamed, and Carter felt a flush of pleasure in seeing her joy.

"Apparently he wasn't a year ago."

"There, you see?" Evaline rose. "He's still in banishment."

Arielle's joy deflated to a sigh of frustration. "It seems I have been under a misconception all these years."

"Very likely you misread my father's meaning."

Carter watched Arielle struggle to subdue her dissatisfaction with the explanations she'd received. He knew she wouldn't learn anything more from Evaline, for the young woman obviously respected and trusted her father. The best recourse was to change the subject, before Arielle's persistence hampered their chances of retaining Evaline as their ally.

"Well, that's it for the papers I found." Carter reached for the pad of documents in Arielle's hand and stuck them back in the file. "Did you find anything else?"

"Nothing useful," Arielle replied, once again in command of her cool head. She looked over at Evaline. "Thanks for letting us look around."

"Thanks for coming to my rescue."

Arielle stood aside while Carter bent to replace the file in the drawer. "Can we drop you off at home, Evaline?"

"That would be nice. I'd appreciate it."

They closed up the office and headed for the Miata. Tiny white snowflakes filtered down like glitter onto the

deserted parking lot. Carter shuddered, more from the
shock of his findings than from the cold night air. Arielle
unlocked the passenger side of her car and turned to
Evaline. "You're going to have to sit on Carter's lap. I
hope you don't mind."

Evaline glanced down. "That's okay."

Carter sat down and guided the small woman as she
gracefully sank onto his legs. Flustered, she gave a soft
giggle and ducked closer to him as he struggled to close
the door. Carter didn't know what to do with his hands
as they drove out of the parking lot. Finally he put one
on the arm rest and draped his left arm over the back of
Arielle's seat. They dropped off the deposit at the bank
and then sped down the road to Evaline's house.

The Jaye house was dark, except for a tiny light by the
front door. Evaline hopped out, thanked them again for
their help, and hurried up to the door while Arielle
waited to make sure she got in safely.

As soon as they pulled away from the house, Arielle
heaved a sigh. "At least we know Mack's alive."

"Maybe."

Arielle glanced at him. "You're not much of an opti-
mist."

"I just don't want to see you disappointed." Not any
more than he wanted to be disappointed himself, Carter
thought grimly. He wished he'd had time to read the letter in his jacket. He told himself Mack could have
donated a lot of things—blood, a kidney, plasma,
sperm—not just bone marrow. Still, the possibility was
great that Mack was his donor.

"He's probably still on the island," Arielle continued.
"And if he's out there, I'm going to find him."

"And do what, Flo?" Carter didn't want to dash her
enthusiasm, but he thought it would be best if she were

realistic and faced facts. "He's been found guilty of murder and larceny. If we rescue him, he'll have to go on the run. What kind of life would that be?"

"What if we could prove he was innocent?"

"How? The crime's eleven years old." Carter rubbed the back of his neck, anxious to tell her of his other discovery, but still not certain he wanted to reveal the details of his past. "It's a bit late for dusting for fingerprints, don't you think?"

"So we do what—just leave him there?"

Carter received her frustrated glare and frowned to himself, wishing he knew what he could do to help.

Suddenly Arielle's expression changed and she made a sharp turn.

Carter braced himself against the door of the car. "What are you doing?" he asked.

"While we're here, we're might as well make a little detour," she said.

"Where to?"

"The old village where the crime was committed."

"But how do you know where it is?"

Arielle shifted gears. "Last week when I made some home visits, I went to a house on Salmon Point Road. That has to lead us to the old village on the point, wouldn't you think?"

"Probably. But is the road passable?"

"I'm willing to take the chance for Mack's sake. Are you game?"

"Yeah." Carter nodded and peered into the darkness, lit only by the twin beams of the Miata, and wondered if the sports car could maneuver the bumpy roads. He crossed his arms over his chest, dying for a moment alone with a flashlight and the letter from the medical center.

14

At *three o'clock in the morning,* the reservation lay in eerie silence. No street lights lined the poorly-maintained asphalt roads, and most of the houses stood bathed in gloom behind the light veil of snow coming down. After a few wrong turns, Arielle found the way to Salmon Point Road. They drove until they passed the outskirts of town, until the narrow road changed from blacktop to gravel, and open fields gave way to encroaching stands of cedar. Arielle tightened her grip on the wheel and carefully guided her car along the lane, wishing there was a white line to mark the side of the road. The last thing she wanted was to run into the ditch and get stuck.

They drove for a half hour, until the forest grew less dense and glimpses of the Sound gleamed through the trees. Presently they rolled into a clearing where the road ended. The high-beams illuminated a ghostly line of dilapidated cedar buildings and weathered, canted totem poles rising into the blackness along the beach.

"Looks more like a graveyard than a historical site," Carter remarked.

"It does. Maybe we should have come up here in the daylight."

"Scared?" Carter teased, smiling at her.

"Not with my muscle along." She glanced at him. "You do have muscles, right?"

"Last time I checked." He chuckled in an obvious effort to relieve the tension, but the sound came out overly dry and forced. Carter reached for his door. "Got a flashlight?"

"In the glove compartment."

He grabbed the flashlight and got out while Arielle locked the car. Then, shoulder to shoulder they walked toward the row of abandoned houses that faced the wide bay. A stiff wind blew off the water, sending hard tiny flakes of snow against Arielle's face like stinging pieces of glass.

"Gosh it's cold!" she whispered, crossing her arms over her parka and then wondering why she was keeping her voice low. No one could possibly hear them. Without answering her, Carter took her arm and pulled her closer to his body. Arielle didn't protest, for his nearness provided a welcome feeling of comfort and safety, just as he had afforded her on the dance floor. They crunched through gravel and sand up to the first house and Carter trained the light on the weathered front planks. Both of them paused.

Arielle studied the shadowy crest that decorated the round doorway leading into the huge structure. Most of the paint had faded, but she could still make out basic shapes of the design. "This looks like the Raven Clan house," she said.

"Let's find the Wolf House before I freeze my ass."

"Good idea." She curled her hand around the top of his arm and walked with him toward the next house. Her hair whipped into her eyes and she pushed it behind her ear, wishing she would have brought a pair of gloves with her. Arielle shuddered. Their footsteps sounded inordinately loud in the gravel, and she couldn't shake the feeling they were trespassing on sacred ground.

"Spooked?" Carter asked, pulling her closer.

"No," she replied, raising her chin. "There's nothing here but a bunch of old houses."

"Yeah." He shined the light on a tall pole standing alone in the high dried grass. A rather grotesque series of creatures consuming each other, from a whale to a frog, decorated the towering cedar pole. "What's that?"

"A mortuary pole, erected in honor of someone who died."

"So this *is* a graveyard of sorts."

"I guess you're right. Mack told me that in the old days when an important person died, sometimes one or two slaves were killed and thrown into the hole as a sacrifice before the pole was raised."

"So there might be dead bodies underneath it?"

"Perhaps."

"Great." Carter urged her even closer. "That makes me feel all warm and cozy inside, Flo."

"Sorry."

They arrived at the next lodge and Carter aimed the light at the crest. "This doesn't look like the Wolf Clan, either," he said.

"Right. It's the Beaver."

"With our luck, the Wolf House will be the last one."

"Murphy's law of Clan Houses. The distance to the house you are looking for is inversely proportional to the temperature of your derriere."

Carter regarded her down his sharp nose. "Can you draw me a picture to go along with that string of doctor talk?"

"Am I making it too hard for you?" she teased.

"You can't imagine."

Before she realized what he'd said, Carter turned the light toward the path and they continued to walk. Arielle flushed, glad he couldn't see her face. Apparently she hadn't been the only one whose thoughts had wandered to something other than Mack's whereabouts. Suddenly she didn't mind the wind and the darkness as much, for she found herself enjoying the ongoing banter and the closeness of Carter's body while her arm was linked with his. For once, she felt his guard dropping just a little, and she was enjoying the amusing man behind the recalcitrant facade.

Just as she predicted, the last house in the lineup belonged to the Wolf Clan. Unease sifted through her as the flashlight beam illuminated the gaping snout of the wolf, grinning at them from above.

"That looks just like the stuff I've been drawing!" Carter exclaimed, running the beam across the row of teeth.

"I told you that you were drawing authentic crest designs," Arielle replied. "Shall we look inside?"

"That's what we're here for."

She kept her hold on his arm as they climbed up the rotting cedar stairs to the entry of the lodge. At the top of the stairs was a small level deck that commanded a view of the bay. Carter paused.

"We're going to have to come up here in the daylight sometime," he said. "This place must have a million-dollar view."

She glanced over her shoulder, but hardly saw the dim line of the coast behind them. Her eyes didn't get past the sharp profile of Carter's face, with its ridged nose and firm mouth and chin. She was acutely aware of the strength in his face and of the strength in his arm beneath her fingers. Arielle swallowed, wondering what had come over her. It wasn't like her to be distracted by a man's appearance, but at that moment Carter's good looks and powerful shoulders were the only million-dollar view she cared to survey. Before he turned and caught her staring at him, she urged him toward the door of the Wolf Clan house.

"Let's go on in," she said, forcing herself to return to business.

"I'll go first." Carter stooped and passed through the entry hole, reaching back for her to help her through. They stepped onto a wooden ledge that ringed the perimeter of the lodge and bordered the earthen cooking area below. As their weight settled on the ancient cedar planks, the old wood gave way with a muffled crack.

Arielle felt the floor collapse beneath her. She screamed and flailed her arms, frantically searching for a handhold. But she caught nothing as she fell through the air and landed on her behind with a painful thump in a jumble of broken wood and sand. Carter tumbled down immediately after her, landing beside her in the sand. The flashlight flew out of his hand, plunging them into darkness.

"Ari!" Carter shouted, reaching for her. "Are you okay?"

"Yes! Carter?" She fumbled in the dark, trying to locate his arm. Instead, she found his rock-hard thigh, and nearly drew back in shock, but didn't have time to retract her hand before she felt him brush her shoulder. She sat up and scrambled to her feet, disoriented in the pitch-black lodge, only to find herself face to face with him.

"Ari?"

Arielle felt the puff of his breath on her mouth, as provocative as a kiss.

"Are you all right?" she asked.

"No." He didn't clarify his cryptic remark, and instead slid his hand around the back of her neck and leaned closer to kiss her, sure of the direction even in the darkness.

Arielle made a mewling sound of surprise against his lips as his other hand found the top of her arm. She hadn't been kissed in years, and had never felt quite so warmed by the touch of a man as she did with Carter. Other men had tasted her or had plunged their tongues into her mouth like an enemy invasion. But Carter's kiss was far different than the others. Perhaps it was because she and Carter were outside in the frigid December air that his kiss seemed more welcome and full of heat than the others. Perhaps it was because for the last few days she had wondered what it would be like to feel his touch.

Her first reflex was to stop his advances by gently pushing him away. She put her palms on his chest with every intention of carrying through her initial plan. But soon she found her resistance melting like snowflakes in a fire, and her hands clutched the supple leather of his jacket as she stood with him, heart to heart, thigh to thigh. She knew without seeing his face that his eyes were closed as he kissed her, giving and demanding at the same time, and she closed hers as well, tipping back her head for more. His arms enveloped her, drawing her against his torso in a hard embrace. Arielle wished their jackets were thinner so she could feel the press of his body against hers, for she could imagine that Carter's lean body was intoxicatingly muscular.

"I'm much better now," he whispered hoarsely, trailing kisses down her neck. A thrill shot through her as he inched down the chilled column of her throat, tickling her with the soft ends of his hair. It wasn't just the cold that made her skin quill with pleasure, but something about this particular man that affected her. His wry wit fascinated her, his dark good looks attracted her, and his unyielding reserve challenged her. She bowed into his body, giving herself up to his kiss as his mouth found hers once again. She gasped and opened her lips, and his tongue slipped over hers, exploring her with a driving, sensual hunger as his fingers spread across the back of her head, pinning her to his mouth.

With a moan, she wrapped her arms around his neck and pressed her breasts against the layers of his clothing. She sank her fingers into the silky strands of his hair and felt a delicious ache streaming out from a place deep within her. His hair was as soft as she had imagined, and his arms as strong as she had suspected.

"Arielle!" he said, his voice more strident. He moved her forward, pressing her thighs into the platform planks behind her. She had nowhere to go but closer against him, and was once again frustrated by the insulating thickness of their coats. She wanted to feel her breasts crushed into his chest, her hips to his. She wanted to explore his body with her palms and fingers, and to be explored in return.

As though he read her mind, Carter reached for the zipper of her coat. But the moment he found the pull tab, they were startled by the sudden cry of a wild animal behind them.

Carter jerked to attention and Arielle released him as she glanced toward the door.

"What was that?" she asked, still blind in the darkness. The sound raised goose bumps on her arms.

"You heard it?" Carter seemed surprised.

"Yes. It sounded like a dog or a wolf or something." She slipped away from him, all thoughts of embracing him having vanished at the eerie wail. "Where's the flashlight?"

"Think a flashlight will scare off a wolf?"

"I don't know. But I'm certainly not going to stand around in the dark waiting to find out!"

They stumbled around together, bumping their heads on the collapsed lumber and swearing when their hands brushed through cobwebs. The wolf howl grew louder, closer, and Arielle's hands trembled as she imagined being jumped by a pack of wolves and torn to shreds as Evaline Jaye had been attacked years ago. Had the wolf come back to attack again?

Suddenly her fingers groped across the cold metallic ridges of the flashlight. "Found it!" she whispered.

She grabbed it and pulled it out of the sand where it had lodged, lens down. Light poured out in a narrow column, showing the deserted floor of the cooking level at the center of the lodge. On the north wall of the lodge, the side farthest from the car, she saw a gaping hole where boards had been knocked out and the perimeter platform torn up. But there wasn't time to wonder at the reason for the hole. She aimed the flashlight at the front door, expecting to see yellow eyes peering at them from the darkness. The round opening was empty. Quickly she flicked the light from right to left, startled by the monstrous faces of the totems staring down at her from the corner posts, each at least four-feet wide.

"Look at those!" she said. "The paint is almost like new!"

"Forget them. Come on." Carter clutched her fingers and pulled her toward the rear of the house. "There must be a back door to this place."

"There should be. The Saquinnish would never take their dead out the front, in case the ghost would remember what house it had died in and return to haunt it."

"Must you keep mentioning the dead?" he puffed, as they sprinted across the dirt floor.

"Spooked, Mr. Greyson?"

"You're damned right! I'm not sticking around for another session with my ears!"

His words puzzled her, for she was hearing the wolves just as much as he was. But she had no time to question him. As they ran toward the back wall, the flashlight beam bounced, running a mad pattern over a wooden screen sculpted in cedar. It reached from floor to ceiling and surrounded an opening just large enough for one person to stoop through. Another wolf howl joined the first.

"Hold it!" Arielle gasped, skidding to a stop. Though they didn't have any time to waste, she shot the light from one back corner of the lodge to the other rear corner. Both corners were empty of house posts. "That's funny."

"What's funny? I don't think anything's funny right now."

"Carter, look." She repeated the movement of the light. "There are supposed to be four house posts. But only two are in the lodge—the ones in the front."

Carter paused in the darkness. "Goddamn," he murmured. "And look. Shine the light on the floor over there."

He put his hand over hers and guided the flashlight toward the left section of the room. Arielle was surprised to see marks in the packed dirt near the corner, rough grooves leading all the way to the ragged hole in the north wall.

"The post was dragged across the dirt floor," Carter put in as he took command of the flashlight.

"Somebody has stolen a second post!"

"And recently, by the looks of it."

"And obviously not Mack!"

"Mack didn't steal the first one. We both know that, Ari."

The howls intertwined, forming a bloodcurdling duet that vibrated the air near the door.

"Come on, Doc," Carter said, grabbing her hand again. "We've got to get out of here."

They squeezed through the hole in the screen, ran to the back wall and out the small rear door of the lodge. Dried sea grass, as high as their knees, covered the property at the back of the house. They tore through the vegetation, galloping clumsily toward the Miata while the wolf howls grew closer. Arielle glanced over her shoulder, trying to catch a glimpse of fur or eyes to see just how close the creatures were, but she couldn't make out anything but the silhouettes of some large rocks along the shoreline.

"Faster!" Carter yelled, nearly dragging her. "Where are your keys?"

She stuffed her free hand in the pocket of her jacket as she stumbled through a patch of briars. Carter grabbed the keys and lunged for the car, unlocking the passenger side and then dashing around to the driver's side. Arielle flung herself into the car and slammed the door while Carter started the engine and pulled out of the clearing, with the back of the sports car fishtailing in the slick gravel.

"See anything?" he asked.

Arielle peered into the night, sure she would see wolves running after them. "No. Nothing."

She turned back to face the front while Carter sped down the gravel lane. For a few minutes they drove in silence, both recovering from the dash to the car and their startling discovery at the lodge.

Finally, Carter let out a sigh of relief. "Whew," he said. "That was close."

"It was just a ploy," she put in, smoothing back her hair and trying to regain her composure by joking with him.

"A ploy?"

"To get to drive my car."

He snorted and glanced at her with a half-grin. "If I wanted to drive this cheerleader contraption, I'd ask."

"Don't try to fool me, Carter. You've been lusting after this Miata from the moment you saw it."

He opened his mouth to begin to make a retort, but then closed it again, and Arielle wondered if he had started to make a remark about lusting. She had certainly experienced an undeniable wave of desire for him back at the lodge, and was certain he'd felt the same thing. Perhaps, though, it was better not to bring up the subject again so soon, not until they'd had time to think about the ramifications of what had transpired between them before the wolves had interrupted.

"So who could be stealing artifacts?" Arielle mused, deciding to change the subject.

"Good question."

"And where would the buyer come from?"

"Just about anywhere."

Perplexed, Arielle sank back against the soft leather seat. She'd never ridden in her car as a passenger and was enjoying the change. Warmth from the heater blew out on their hands and feet, thawing her frozen fingers. Arielle rubbed her hands together and was suddenly struck by something Carter had said earlier in the lodge.

"What did you mean back there, Carter, when you said you didn't want to have another session with your ears?" she asked.

She saw Carter tighten his grip on the steering wheel. He didn't answer.

"You seemed surprised that I heard the wolves, too, Carter. Why?"

"I just didn't think you would, that's all."

"But you could hear them." She stared at the side of his face, at the hard set of his jaw and his serious expression. "Tell me, have you heard the sound of the wolves before?"

He shot a dark glance at her and then returned his glare to the road.

"You have, haven't you?"

After a prolonged pause, he finally responded. "Yes."

"That's what's been bothering you, hasn't it? You've been hearing wolf howls. Overpowering wolf howls."

Carter sighed and swallowed. "Bingo, Doc."

"But why wolf howls?"

"How about if we talk about this later?" He turned on the windshield wipers. "I need to concentrate on driving. The road's a mess."

"You wouldn't be putting me off, would you?"

"Me?"

"Yes, you. Master of escape. Mr. Houdini."

She was relieved to see a quick grin flash across his mouth.

"I'll tell you what," she said. "I'll cook breakfast if you promise to tell me what's been going on with you. Deal?"

He glanced at her. "You want to cook breakfast for me?"

"Sure. I do great toast."

"Toast?"

"Yes. But for you, I might go all the way and try scrambling eggs."

Carter gave a tight chuckle. "If that's your idea of going all the way, I don't know—"

"I'll throw in some great coffee. That I can do."

He paused and arched a brow.

"Fresh-squeezed orange juice?" she added in a hopeful voice.

"You're twisting my arm, Flo."

"Good."

She smiled and watched the wall of cedars fly by. Though it was nearly dawn, she wasn't the least bit tired. The thought of taking Carter into her home sent a chill coursing through her that had nothing to do with hearing wolf howls, and everything to do with her enigmatic companion.

15

Carter followed Arielle into her apartment and glanced around at the expansive white living room and the dun-colored boxes stacked against the far wall. The apartment was a sleek combination of sharp angles, plush gray carpeting, chrome accents, and recessed lighting. It looked like the home of an architect or engineer. Did Arielle own the place? He'd be surprised if she did, because the stark geometric lines of the apartment didn't suit her.

"May I take your coat?" Arielle asked, extending her hand.

"No." Carter stepped back and then flushed at his defensive reaction. He'd remembered the piece of paper he'd stuffed in his jacket and couldn't allow Arielle to see it. He softened his tone. "You don't have to wait on me. In fact," he held out his hand, "I'll hang up your coat so you can get into the kitchen where you belong."

The chauvinistic reply would surely distract her from his hasty refusal, but he was also certain his words would annoy her, so he followed them up with a wink.

Arielle smirked. "You wouldn't say that if you knew what kind of cook I am."

"I have limitless faith in you, Doc."

She chuckled and turned her back to him as she slipped out of her parka. Carter reached for it, highly conscious of the fragrance of her body as he stood behind her. Her brown hair glinted like polished walnut above the pale ivory column of her neck. He remembered what it had been like to kiss her at the deserted Indian village, and how she'd wrapped her arms around his neck. A surge of desire washed over him. To be here with her, in her home, chatting easily with her, was an experience he'd never expected. Feeling lucky, but half out of his mind with wanting her, Carter leaned forward to press a kiss on her throat, just below her left ear.

Arielle paused and then sighed, slightly lolling back her head, obviously enjoying his touch and offering herself up for more. A smile pulled at the corners of her mouth, which encouraged him to continue. Carter kissed her upturned cheek and then pressed a lingering trail to her lips, forcing himself to remain gentle even though his body railed against the restraint. He had jumped to full attention the moment he'd watched her walk up the stairs to her apartment building and noticed her slender hips swaying at the hem of her parka. He wanted those hips in his hands, naked and surrendered to him.

Now that he stood behind her, his jeans seemed far too tight, his appetite far too keen, and it was all he could do to keep from crushing her against him.

Carter tasted her lips, full and soft and yielding. She turned a bit more and the kiss deepened, but the angle was all wrong and Carter knew he'd go crazy if he didn't pull her close. To free his hands, he tossed her coat on a nearby chair and then clasped her shoulders to urge her to face him squarely. Before he realized what she was doing, she reached for the zipper of his jacket and eased it down.

"Let me take it off," Carter mumbled, his mouth against hers, while he shouldered out of the leather jacket, careful to grab the letter in the folds so it wouldn't fall to the floor. He tossed his jacket on top of hers and quickly regained possession of her elbows.

Arielle slid her hands up his chest and eased them over his shoulders and then around his neck. He loved the touch of her hands, strong and purposeful and appraising, as if she truly cherished the contours of his body. Then she stepped toward him and he forgot all about her hands as the firm mounds of her breasts pressed into him. A shaft of longing shot through him and he clutched the curves of her lithe waist in his hands, drawing her hips closer. She had the slender hips of a model, and a firm little ass. Carter cupped her rump in his palms and crushed her to him, his intentions as blatant as the rigid erection pressed against her belly.

He tried to be gentle, he wanted to savor each moment with Arielle, but the instant he felt her against the most primal part of him, he knew time and restraint were careening out of control. He stroked her back, pushed a hand into her shining hair, and kissed her as he'd never kissed a woman—hoping he wasn't being a fool to start this, and knowing he didn't care if he was a fool or not, as long as he could have this one time with beautiful, remarkable Arielle Scott. Whatever happened, it would be worth any future heartache to make love to this woman tonight.

Carter undid the buttons of her plaid shirt and slid a hand into the opening. His breath caught in his throat when his hand found her breast, covered by a satin bra. She was warm and firm, and she sighed near his ear when his thumb passed over her nipple, already as hard as a little pebble. A flood of goose bumps spread out on his skin where her soft breath brushed him like the wings of a fragile butterfly. Carter glanced at Arielle and found her eyes closed—a beautiful, rapt expression that affected his heart as well as his cock. He thought he'd burst with wanting her.

A fraction of a moment later, all thoughts of tenderness vanished, and he was pulling her shirt out of her jeans and tossing it somewhere in the direction of their jackets, unmindful where it landed. Then he unfastened her bra and slipped it off. Arielle let out a ragged sigh as he took each of her breasts in his hands and gently squeezed them. Carter glanced down at her, his cheeks hot, as he kneaded her. Her breasts fit perfectly into his hands, like two halves of a succulent grapefruit.

Someone else sighed, and with a start, Carter realized it was his own voice letting out a long moan of pleasure and satisfaction. There was something about Arielle's form that seemed right to him—the texture of her skin seemed as familiar as his own, her height was tailor-made for him, and the way she moved against him was a well-timed slow dance meant to take him over the brink of self-control.

Closing his eyes, he leaned down and sank his mouth over her nipple. He spread his fingers over the width of her back and held her as he sucked at her breast and pulled at the tip until she collapsed against the closet door, her breath coming in strident bursts. Carter kissed her other breast while her fingers clutched the back of his head, urging him to take her harder and more deeply. His mouth went dry as her hips moved against his. All he could think about was plunging into her and making her moan with pleasure.

"Carter!" she whispered. "Ah! That's so nice—"

Her breathless voice intoxicated him. He caressed her with nearly desperate hands and kissed her between her breasts and the base of her throat as she pushed up his sweater and then slipped her hands onto the burning skin of his chest. She gently pinched his nipples, making him crazy with desire.

"Wait!" he gasped. With a quick motion, he yanked off his sweater and threw it aside, and without breaking contact, pulled her against him. Their naked flesh came together with a rush of heat. Carter could hardly catch his breath, he was struggling so hard to hold back. Her hands set him on fire as she caressed his shoulders and back, driving him wild with hard little kisses she sealed upon his jaw and throat. She nipped his earlobe and the sensation shot straight to his cock. He could take no more.

With a low growl, Carter lifted her off her feet, grasping her thighs in his hands and pressed her against the wall. He ground against her, trying not to imagine what it would be like if they were completely naked. If he let that vision blossom, he'd come like a kid in high school having his first girl in the back seat of a car. Such a lack of restraint would not be worthy of Arielle, especially not the first time. But at this rate, he wasn't sure he could hold back another moment.

He reached for the metal button at the top of her jeans.

"Carter!" she gasped, tilting her hips so her blazing heat rubbed over the bulge in his pants. "Oh, God, wait a minute—"

Her words barely broke through the roaring in his head. What was she saying?

She slipped her hands down and gently pushed them against his chest.

"Arielle?" he asked, his voice cracking with desire.

"We can't—" She pulled back, her eyes dark pools of green, her pupils huge.

"Why not?" he croaked.

"Oh, God!" She leaned forward and kissed him fully upon the mouth, clutching his head in both of her hands as she pushed her tongue into him and writhed against him, as driven with need as he was.

Carter thrust against her again, and her breasts skidded across his chest. She hung on to his neck and squirmed against him, just as desperate for more closeness and deeper contact. Carter could feel the blood pounding at his temples, thudding in his neck, throbbing in his loins. How could he stop? If he pulled back now, his bellow of frustration would wake the entire city of Seattle.

Her lips were at his ear again, and each puff of her soft breath was like a chant to him, urging him on. He pushed against her, every inch of his being aching to complete the union they'd begun with their lips.

"Carter, we can't," she said. "Not without protection."

"Ari—"

"It's too risky—"

"Forget the medical stuff for once," he replied, his tongue sticking to the roof of his mouth as the truth hit him. She was drawing the line. She was backing away. He knew she was being sensible, but right now good sense was the furthest thing from his mind.

"I can't forget it, Carter."

He licked his lips. He couldn't talk. He could barely stand up. He closed his eyes and slowly let her slide to the floor, trying to ignore the way her body felt passing down the front of him, trying to ignore the leaden weight of his devastating disappointment.

"We have to be responsible about this," she added. "And I don't have anything."

"Neither do I."

"Carter, it just wouldn't be good for us. These days, it's—"

"I know." He ran a hand through his hair, and hoped she didn't notice the way he was trembling. Had she refused him because he didn't have a condom, or had she suddenly been overwhelmed by second thoughts? She'd acted as if she wanted him, but maybe she was one of those women who liked to tease more than engage in true intimacy. Still, he couldn't imagine Arielle acting or teasing.

The touch of her hand on the side of his jaw made him look up.

"Carter?" she asked, cocking a brow, "I can have a rain check, can't I?"

He gazed down at her, grateful for her ability to defuse the situation with humor and allow him to back down with his pride intact. He suddenly realized he had been selfish for wanting to plow into her without thinking about the consequences. Lucky for the both of them, she'd kept her head.

"A rain check?" Carter said, trying to imbue his voice with a good grace he found nearly impossible to muster. "You just pick the day."

Then he dropped a quick kiss on her mouth before she could make some excuse about being busy all week. She surprised him by wrapping her arms around him again and returning the kiss with ardor. She gradually pulled back, as though it was as difficult for her to draw completely away as it was for him. She smoothed the hair at his temples and let her hands drag down the sides of his face, his neck, and then settle on his shoulders. Slowly, she opened her eyes.

"You make me absolutely crazy," she said.

"Lady," Carter shifted uncomfortably. "You don't know the half of it."

"We'll both feel better if I fix us some breakfast. What do you say?" She took a step away and headed for her discarded garments. Carter watched her, wondering if it would be possible to keep his hands off her. She didn't put on her bra, and the thought of her naked breasts under the flannel shirt was a sure recipe for arousal.

"I should go," he ventured.

"Why?" Arielle glanced up at him as she buttoned her shirt. The sexy vision of her tousled hair and smudged lips was more than he could bear.

"I just should."

"But we have to discuss the game plan."

"What game plan?"

"My plan to get a boat and find the island." Arielle combed back her hair with her fingers.

Carter watched the movement, hardly able to remain where he stood. He wanted to gather her up in his arms and kiss her all over again. Dragging his glance from her, he walked over to the chair and snatched up his sweater, which he yanked over his head. "Didn't Mack tell you the route to the island was a secret?"

"It has to be on a map."

"You mean a chart?" Carter asked. In his line of business, he dealt with navigational charts every day.

"Yes."

"You want to hire a boat to take you out to the island?"

She nodded. "Tomorrow."

Carter carefully picked up his folded jacket and draped it over his arm so the letter wouldn't fall out. "Don't hire a boat until I make some calls." He walked to the door and put his hand on the doorknob. "I'll talk to some people I know, okay?"

"You're sure you have to leave?" Her crestfallen expression made his heart swell in his chest.

"Yeah." He looked at her standing by the white leather chair, her green eyes huge in her pale face. He'd never wanted to stay with a woman more. He wanted to stay all night. The next day even. Perhaps longer. But he knew better than to entertain such a notion. Arielle had refused him, plain and simple, and it would be best that he let her make the first move the next time—if there should be a next time. He certainly wasn't going to allow himself to get all worked up again and make it difficult for them both. "I'll call you in a few hours."

"Okay." She didn't move from her position by the chair.

"Good night." He gave a slight wave and left the apartment, hoping no one would see him walking dejectedly down the stairs.

Arielle watched the door shut behind Carter and then sank to the arm of the chair, her body still humming from his embrace. She'd never felt anything like the fire she'd experienced with him. He'd aroused her so thoroughly she'd almost lost control, something that had never happened to her. She had never engaged in unprotected sex, not with her boyfriend in college or with the intern she'd had a brief affair with during medical school. And neither of those men had left her with shaking legs and a light head, the way she was feeling now. She'd loved every moment and even yet felt bathed in delicious waves of afterglow.

Regret mingled with the glow, however. She had seen Carter's face, his stricken expression. She'd heard the incredulity in his voice when she asked him to stop. Of course he'd taken it personally. What man wouldn't? Arielle scowled and stood up, chiding herself for allowing him to undress her and for encouraging him. She should have made her position clear from the moment he kissed her. But how could she have known what his embrace would do to her, that he would turn her blood to quicksilver and her legs to rubber bands?

Arielle picked up her parka and remembered the kiss in the lodge—how warm he felt, how perfectly his torso molded to hers, how right it seemed to stand in his arms. Yet she hardly knew the man. She'd only met him a couple of weeks before, and he'd barely told her anything about himself. Looking back on the times they'd spent together, she realized she'd done all the talking.

She shoved the hanger into the arms of her parka and hung the coat in the closet. Carter was a touchy man to deal with, but she was fairly sure she could understand him. He had a hard exterior, a tough-guy facade, but underneath she sensed his vulnerability and his fragile view of his place in the world. Would her refusal turn him away forever? Was his male ego so easily wounded? She didn't want to start anything with a man whose confidence was so thin he would permanently retreat after one small setback. Arielle frowned again and stared at the door. Her head told her that Carter had more confidence than most men she knew and that she should have faith in him. Still, her heart remained troubled.

∘   ∘   ∘

The moment Carter flipped on the lights of his apartment and took off his leather jacket, he heard the low moan of a wolf.

"Shit!" he exclaimed. He not only had Arielle's refusal to deal with, and an aching head from the long night of no sleep, now he had to face another session fending off the sounds in his head.

"Leave me alone!" he exclaimed to no one in particular, but to everyone, including himself. He'd had enough. He'd had enough of his own bad company, enough of biting back his feelings because he felt incapable of expressing them, and enough of the wolves that plagued his every move. A man could only take so much until he exploded. Yet he wasn't ready to talk, to blurt out the truth to Arielle about his past and his hope for a possible future with her. What if she turned him down again? Could he face the possibility of being told he was a nice, attractive man, but just not her type? He wanted to be everything to Arielle, not just a warm body, not just a friend.

And the wolves. He'd managed to shut them down lately through the power of his mind and his disbelief in the shadowy shapes and phantom sounds. But they'd returned at the deserted village and now were back in his head. Had he begun to believe in Mack, in the Wolf Clan, in Arielle's stories of the dead? What an idiot! No rational man would succumb to mere tales. He wasn't ready to believe that some indefinable thread connected him to the Wolf Clan and the Saquinnish Indians, or that he might be the medium through which the Wolf Clan could regain its stolen treasures. The wolves had been trying to tell him as much, as had the voice in his head—the strange voice that told him he was the warrior, blood of another, spirit of another, and the last hope of his people.

He had never belonged to a people. He didn't expect to ever have any people, or find true roots, even if he discovered the source of his heritage. For what value lay in a name without a history attached to it? And what was the advantage of genetic similarity if detached from the love and care of a family? Why bother? Why endanger his life and his tenuous sanity for something from which he'd get absolutely nothing?

With a sheer force of his will, he shut out the howling and refused to give in to the compelling sensation to run after the wolves and to seek out the source of the sound.

Carter rubbed the bridge of his nose and sank down on the couch, holding the wrinkled letter in his left hand. He carefully read the typed message which thanked Mack Shoalwater for his donation. Again, Carter's heart pounded as he scanned the text, for his suppositions were supported by the body of the letter. Mack had donated bone marrow for a transplant which had been performed on March 2, 1994, the exact day Carter had received marrow. Too many other facts existed for the dates to be coincidental, especially since Carter knew his antigen types were extremely rare and likely to be found only in the tribes of the Pacific Northwest. The same tribe, the same medical center, the same date, the same transplant. Mack had to be his anonymous donor.

A warm feeling spread over Carter as he leaned back against the couch. The idea that Mack Shoalwater had given him bone marrow pleased him greatly. The island philosopher who had made such a strong impression on Arielle had given them both a second chance at life. He

had half-guessed as much all along. Arielle had told him
he bore an uncanny resemblance to Mack. But he had
never let himself believe it, not until proof hit him
squarely in the face.

He had a sudden urge to pick up the phone and call
Arielle to share his news. He even reached for the
portable phone on the coffee table, but then reconsid-
ered before dialing her pager number. She was probably
already in bed, asleep. Besides, she probably wouldn't
comprehend the depth of gratitude he felt for his donor,
and there was no way in hell he would get it across to
her over a phone that Mack's gesture meant more to
him than anything anyone had ever done for him. Such a
discussion was better saved for another time, when they
were rested and had plenty of time to talk.

Carter put the phone down. He longed to talk to
Arielle, but knew if he continued to talk with her only as
a friend, he'd constantly burn for more and the resulting
frustration would eat him alive. He'd be a fool to expose
himself to such a destructive relationship. Still, he
wanted to explain Mack's connection to them both. And
he wanted to find the man, for himself as well as for
Arielle. After they'd found Mack and helped clear his
name, Carter would step out of her life and get back to
his normal routine.

Another thought rose in the back of Carter's mind—
that Mack Shoalwater was the right age to be his father.
But before the idea could take complete form, Carter
relegated it to a dark corner where he didn't have to
examine it. He'd spent thirty years hating the absent
father who had deserted his own son and the woman he
supposedly loved. Hate was not a legacy he cared to
overlay on the donor who saved his life. Besides, deser-
tion and abandonment didn't jive with Arielle's version

of Mack Shoalwater, and Carter trusted her judgment of the man. So he dismissed the paternity theory. At most, Mack might turn out to be a cousin or some other distant relative. There might be no more connection between them than simple biological construction.

Carefully, Carter folded the letter and slipped it into the back pocket of his jeans. Whatever Mack might be to him, Carter knew he was just as anxious as Arielle to find him. Tomorrow, if they were lucky, he might be shaking his donor's hand.

16

The next morning when Evaline sat up in bed, she was surprised at how stiff she felt. Her body protested as she slid to her feet onto the cold vinyl floor of her bedroom. In fighting off her attacker she had used muscles she didn't know she possessed until now. She pulled on the robe she kept at the end of her bed as extra protection against the night chill, and limped to the door.

Evaline dragged herself into the bathroom, tired and sore, and hoped her father wasn't awake yet. She didn't feel up to making breakfast or facing her dad. If she were lucky, he'd stay in bed all day again.

In the bathroom she splashed water on her cheeks, rubbed them dry with a towel, and straightened up to glance in the mirror. Purple bruises in the shape of fingertips branded each side of her jaw. Gingerly she touched the discolored flesh and stared at her reflection, so similar in appearance to the times she had undergone surgery.

Each painful operation had ended with the same devastating result—a face more swollen and twisted than when she'd entered the hospital. Afterward, infections and complications scarred her skin as well as her spirit, and she learned to expect she'd be uglier than ever when the bandages came off. Each time she'd undergone plastic surgery, she was assured by her father that the operation would work, that the doctor was the finest in the country, that the new techniques would make a difference. But no specialist seemed capable of changing her fate.

Evaline moved her lower jaw back and forth slightly to test the condition of her mouth, but stopped when pain shot up to her cheekbones.

"Bastard!" she whispered vehemently, as a hot flood of shame and outrage poured over her. No one had a right to treat her so brutally, no matter how cruelly she'd been treated by nature and fate. Tears pooled in her eyes, but she quickly blinked them back. Evaline shot a glance at the bathroom door. How could she hide the bruises from her father? He'd surely see them and ask questions, and she would rather die than describe the disgraceful situation she had endured at the casino. She had never discussed sexual subjects with her father and would be mortified just in telling him where she'd been touched, let alone relating the entire incident.

With shaking hands, Evaline reached into the drawer where she kept a small cache of cosmetics. Years ago she had bought makeup, hoping it might enhance what beauty lay in her crooked features. The results of her experiment had only made her disfigurement more obvious. But she still had some foundation, which might cover the purple marks on her face. Evaline smeared a dab on her jaw, gently swirling the thick liquid over her skin. The bruises appeared fainter with the application of the makeup, but were still visible. Evaline turned her head this way and that, trying to see what effect light and shadow had on her swollen jaw. Perhaps she could fool her father, especially if she kept in the shadows.

Her chest felt tight as she walked to the kitchen to make coffee, praying all the while that Reuven was still in bed. She cinched the belt of her robe more securely and turned the corner into the small outdated kitchen, with its avocado appliances and curtains trimmed in rick-rack. There at the small metal table sat her father, with a can of cola in his hand.

Evaline froze and almost put her hand to her face, before she caught herself. Then she noticed Reuven wasn't wearing his glasses. He glanced up at her.

"Dad, I'm surprised to see you up."

"I got things to do." He slurped his pop.

"Are you feeling okay?"

"Good enough."

"Want some breakfast?" She hoped he'd grab something at the cafe next to the casino.

"Yeah. Scramble me up some eggs, Evaline," he replied. "Maybe they'll settle my stomach."

"All right." Evaline put the skillet on the stove and reached into the refrigerator for the eggs and margarine. She felt the heat of her father's stare.

"Everything go okay at the casino last night?"

Evaline turned her back to him and cracked four eggs into a bowl. "Yes."

"Get the deposit done?"

"Yes." She continued to work, keeping her back to him. When the eggs and toast were done, she slid the steaming plate of food onto the table in front of him and tried to duck out of the kitchen.

"You're not eating?" he asked, his words stopping her.

"I'm not hungry."

He looked up at her. She turned away, intent on leaving the kitchen as quickly as she could, but he caught her wrist. "Evaline, what's that on your face?"

She tried to act puzzled. "My face?"

He pulled her closer and shoved his glasses on. "You got marks on your face."

"Marks?"

Reuven peered at her and dabbed the foundation off with the side of his thumb. "What in the hell happened to you?" he demanded, rising to his feet.

"Nothing." She covered one side of her face with the flat of her free hand.

"Nothing? You don't get bruises like that from nothing. Who did that to you?"

"Dad, it's nothing, really." Her face flamed with embarrassment. "Just sit down and eat your eggs before they get cold."

"Eat? You think I can eat when I see your face all bruised up?"

"It isn't that bad."

"Evaline!" He tipped her chin and inspected both sides of her jaw. "Who did this to you?"

"I don't know."

"What do you mean?"

Evaline hung her head, knowing her father wouldn't be satisfied without an explanation. She decided to give him some information but not all. She sighed. "Some guy at the casino was waiting for me near your office."

"Some guy? Who?"

"I don't know. I'd never seen him before."

"Somebody from the Res?"

"No."

"And what did he do?"

"Nothing, Dad. He just got a little rough, that's all, but Mr. Greyson and Dr. Scott stopped him."

"Dr. Scott?"

"Yes. She and Carter Greyson came by."

Her father released her wrist and tilted his head. "Dr. Scott just happened to drop by my office?"

"Yes. She was trying to find Mack Shoalwater's medical file."

Reuven blinked and pushed up his glasses while a deep scowl lined his face. Evaline suddenly wondered if she had betrayed her father by allowing Dr. Scott to search his office. But there was nothing to worry about; he didn't have anything to hide. His privacy might have been invaded, but that was all the harm done.

"Did you tell her to look at the clinic?"

"She already did."

"The woman's too nosy for her own good." Reuven sank down to his chair and lifted his fork, obviously forgetting about Evaline's bruises. He let the fork balance between his fingers as he lapsed into thought.

"I found Mack's file for her," Evaline ventured. "For some reason, it was by itself in your desk."

Reuven's scowl twisted into an expression of alarm. "You let her see it?"

"Yes, but there was—"

"Evaline!"

"She didn't learn anything she didn't know already. Besides, I owed her a favor."

"You don't owe that doctor a damn thing." Reuven stabbed a lump of scrambled egg and shoveled it into his mouth. "You should never have let that woman into my office!"

"But, Dad, there was no harm done."

"No harm done?" Reuven slammed his fist on the table, rattling the plate as well as Evaline, who was startled by his sudden outburst. "How do you know there was no harm done? You should have let me handle that woman!"

"I didn't think—"

"That's right! You didn't think!" Reuven struggled to his feet and grabbed his car keys off the table while Evaline watched in shock. Her father had never yelled at her like this. In fact, she couldn't remember a single instance when he'd raised his voice in anger to her.

"Dad, I'm sorry if—"

"From now on," He cut her off with a hard glance, "you keep out of this Mack Shoalwater business, you hear me?"

"Yes, Dad, but—"

"I'm going out. I might not be back tonight."

"Where are you going?"

He snatched his jacket off a hook near the door. "Fishing."

Reuven slammed the door. Evaline stood in the kitchen, completely unnerved by his strange behavior. She heard his old car fire up and roar down the road. Then she jerked into action, cleaning up his half-eaten food with shaking hands, and replaying the casino debacle over and over again in her mind. She couldn't find fault in her thinking or actions and couldn't find a reason to doubt Arielle Scott's motivation for trying to locate Mack Shoalwater. And yet her father had been angry with her, angrier than she'd ever seen him. What was going on?

•   •   •

Snow fell in huge wet flakes from a yellow gray sky when Arielle and Carter pulled up to the marina at ten o'clock Sunday morning. Carter's business acquaintance met them at the entry gate to the dock in La Conner, a small town on the coast north of Seattle. Carter had personally installed state of the art navigational equipment on Ron Bennett's boat a month ago, and had assured Arielle that Ron would be happy to take them to the island. Ron was a lanky man of sixty-eight with a steel gray crew cut and the weathered red face of a sailor, as if his skin was more leather than flesh. His age and twinkling blue eyes reminded Arielle of her own father, and she was struck by a sudden stab of guilt. Christmas was only a week away, and she hadn't even called her parents to see what the arrangements were for the holidays. Surely it was too late to book a flight for Phoenix, or for them to drive up. Secretly Arielle hoped they'd made alternate plans. She didn't know how long it would take to find Mack and clear his name, and that would be her entire focus for the time being.

"Morning, Ron," Carter said, extending his hand.

"Howdy, Greyson." Ron's lined face cracked into a series of parentheses around his mouth. "And you must be Dr. Scott."

"Nice to meet you," Arielle shook his hand. "And thanks for doing this at such short notice."

"No problem." Ron squinted up at the clouds. "But I have to say, I don't like the looks of this weather."

"I thought it didn't snow much in Seattle."

"It doesn't." He held open the gate for them. "This is unusual."

Their footsteps thumped along the thick wooden planks of the dock as he guided them to his boat, the *Shangri-La*. The craft was clean and well-maintained, but even so Arielle felt a surge of dread as she climbed aboard. Since her boating accident ten years ago, she'd never enjoyed sailing and avoided any kind of boat. But this journey could only be accomplished by sea.

"Did you find the island we're looking for?" Carter asked.

"Yeah," Ron answered. "Watch your step there, Arielle, going down those stairs. Not much head room."

She ducked and stepped down into a cabin off the galley. The smell of coffee brewing filled the small space, and she was grateful for Ron's attempts to make them comfortable. The air coming off the water and her tenseness about sailing had left her chilled to the bone. She looked forward to holding a warm cup in her hands.

"Do you think we can get there by early afternoon?" Carter asked as Ron grabbed three mugs out of the cupboard.

"Probably." Ron poured two cups of coffee. "But like I told you on the phone, that island's in some of the most treacherous water I've ever sailed. If the weather gets any worse, I won't attempt the channel. It'd be way too chancy."

"We understand," Arielle put in. Ron handed her a mug and didn't ask if she'd like cream or sugar. "Thanks."

"You're welcome." He winked at her and then gave Carter a cup. "How come my doctor isn't this pretty?"

"You must go to the wrong clinic."

"Damn right." Ron laughed and poured himself a cup of coffee. He took a gulp, seemingly immune to the scalding temperature and the nearly impenetrable opacity of the brew. "Besides that, my doctor's a man!"

They all chuckled and then Ron left to fire up the engines. Carter raised his eyebrows and stared pointedly at her mug of coffee. She grinned.

"Is this sea-muck or instant crystals?" Carter asked, raising his cup.

"Only your hairdresser knows for sure," Arielle replied. Before Ron had a chance to return, she poured her drink down the sink drain.

"How about yours?" Arielle asked, glancing over her shoulder.

"I'm desperate," Carter replied. "I'm going to drink it."

"Boy, you must be." Arielle smiled at him and knelt on the bench seat so she could stare out of the porthole as Ron maneuvered the *Shangri-La* out of the slip and toward the breakwater. The farther they chugged from land, the more nervous Arielle became. Carter moved to stand behind her. She didn't look back at him, but could sense he was mere inches away. Neither of them had mentioned what had gone on the night before, and she didn't know whether to bring it up. Carter seemed more tightly wound today than ever. She didn't want to make the trip unbearable if he proved unwilling to discuss their changing relationship. Still, she could think of little else, and ached for his strong embrace to warm her and ease her fear of the water.

"Remember that old song," she ventured, singing the first line in a shaky voice. "Your kisses take me . . . to Shangri-La?"

"Nope," Carter replied.

Disappointed in his curt response, Arielle propped her forearms on the windowsill and watched the marina grow smaller and smaller. So much for giving Carter a blatant hint. Obviously, her hot-and-cold friend was running a bit chilly again.

They motored past Everett, cruised along the shore of Whidbey Island, one of the longest islands in the U.S., and continued north toward Bellingham. By the time midafternoon set in, a stiff wind churned the Sound into an angry expanse of dark blue water and white caps. The sky took on a sinister shade of purple, and Arielle grew increasingly uneasy. If Carter had talked to her, she might have kept her mind off accidents at sea and the possibility of capsizing and drowning. But he spent the trip restlessly pacing the boat like a trapped animal and was more silent than ever. Much of the time he stood on the bridge with Ron.

Arielle had never been seasick, but with each surge and dip of the boat, she felt a swell of queasiness. Waves slammed into the ship until it bobbed like a toy in a bathtub. Snow fell so thick and fast that Arielle could barely make out the blue humps of land to the east.

At three-thirty, Carter came below, rubbing his hands and blowing on them.

"It's freezing out there!" he exclaimed.

"I made some coffee," she ventured. "Want some?"

"Yeah, thanks."

She fixed him a cup while he ran a hand over his hair. "Ron's decided to take us in."

"In?" Arielle gave him the coffee. "You mean into the channel?"

"No," Carter frowned. "The weather's too bad. He doesn't want to chance it. He's heading for the Saquinnish marina nearby."

"What'll we do then?"

"Dock until the storm passes."

Arielle nodded but felt her heart sink. She had been so sure she would see Mack today. In fact, she had counted on it. She wondered how much he had changed in ten years. And would he recognize her after all this time? She knew he would remember her name, but her appearance had changed and matured from the nineteen-year-old girl he had known ten years before.

They plowed through the snowstorm until Arielle could discern the rectangular shapes of buildings and the vertical lines of the wharf pilings. Her fears eased a bit, just knowing she was close enough to swim to shore should anything drastic happen to the *Shangri-La*.

A half-hour later, they pulled into a slip, secured the lines, and hurried through the blowing snow toward a lighted cafe sign at the end of the dock. Carter took her elbow, for which she was grateful, and guided her toward their destination.

They opened the cafe door, stamping their feet to knock off the snow, and Arielle glanced around the shabby but cozy restaurant done in red and white gingham. She didn't think any restaurant still used red and white table covers, but there they were. And at the table nearest the door sat Reuven Jaye.

He stared at her, and at his cold expression Arielle's blood chilled momentarily. Then he rose and pushed up his glasses, obviously taking his leave now that she'd shown up at the cafe.

"Hello, Mr. Jaye," Arielle greeted him.

He didn't answer immediately and she realized Reuven was staring at Carter behind her. "Doctor," he finally replied, without looking at her.

"This is Carter Greyson," Arielle explained. "And his friend, Ron Bennett."

"Nice to meet you," Reuven mumbled, shaking their hands but never once taking his eyes off Carter. Was he shocked at Carter's resemblance to Mack? Arielle had nearly forgotten their striking similarity until she saw Reuven's open stare.

"Mr. Greyson," Reuven remarked. "You aren't from around here, are you?"

"No."

Reuven's mouth turned down at the corners in response to Carter's terse answer. For once, Arielle was grateful for Carter's blunt reluctance to offer information about himself. She wanted Reuven to learn as little as possible about her companion.

Reuven turned his attention to Arielle. "What are you doing up here on a day like this?"

"Taking a cruise."

"In a snowstorm?" Reuven's frown deepened. "The waters around here are dangerous. You of all people should know that."

"Technology has improved in the last ten years," she replied. "We can find our way, Mr. Jaye."

He looked at the men and then back to her. "You're wasting your time, Dr. Scott."

"I don't think so."

"And endangering lives." He brushed past her and glanced over his shoulder. "For nothing."

"I don't consider Mack Shoalwater nothing."

"Maybe you should." For a brief but galvanizing moment, Reuven's intense black eyes seared into hers.

Then he slapped some money on the counter by the till and left the cafe. Arielle watched the door close behind him and felt a deeper chill seep into her bones. Had Reuven's last words been a mere warning or a threat?

17

By the time Arielle and her companions finished their dinner, the snowstorm had turned into a blizzard. Gale warnings were reported for the coastal waters, preventing further travel. Ron decided to stay docked at the Saquinnish marina until the weather cleared, but Carter and Arielle took the last bus back to Seattle, since they both had to work in the morning. Due to hazardous driving conditions, the trip took twice as long as the normal one-hour drive. Carter was silent and withdrawn the entire way, so Arielle dozed, hoping to catch up on the hours of lost sleep during the weekend. It was nine P.M. when they rolled into the deserted streets of Seattle. They took a cab from the bus station, and when it dropped her off, Carter didn't even kiss her good-bye. Arielle walked up to the entry of her building, sure that her refusal to make love with him the night before had done irreparable damage.

"So be it," she muttered to herself, as she punched the keypad to open the door. She would be better off anyway to remain uninvolved with a man who was obviously troubled. Arielle waited for the elevator, feeling woefully disappointed, not only for their failure to get to Mack, but for the wall that had risen between her and Carter. *Had* risen? She smiled bitterly. The wall had always been there. She just hadn't seen it for what it was.

The next morning as Arielle climbed the few steps to the clinic, she was surprised when an agitated Katie met her at the door and nearly dragged Arielle into the waiting room. The other doctor, two nurses, a pregnant teenage patient and the landlord Dan Williams stood in the room, and all of them turned at her arrival.

"There's been a break-in!" Katie exclaimed.

"What?"

"Somebody broke a window in the back," Katie replied, painfully squeezing Arielle's forearm and apparently unaware of her strong grip.

Arielle gently pulled away and unbuttoned her coat. "Was anything stolen?"

"Not so much as we can tell," put in one of the nurses, a short plump woman named Marian. "We haven't checked your office yet, though."

"Somebody was probably after drugs," Dan remarked, combing his fingers through his wiry blond hair. His office was across the street, and he often came in for morning coffee to start the day by chatting with Katie and trying to talk with Arielle, but she usually didn't have much time or patience to spare for him. "The police are on their way. I called them."

"Good." Arielle glanced at the pregnant girl, who

couldn't have been more than fifteen. Probably a run-away. Probably alone, with no job and no hope for a better future. "Have you been seen?" she asked. The girl's blue eyes were huge in her pale face and she wrapped her arms around her swollen belly.

"Not yet."

"Well, let's put you in three." Arielle turned to Katie, knowing the best remedy to restore calm was to put everyone to work. "Is Room 3 okay? Where was the break-in?"

"In the coffee room. Three's fine."

Arielle nodded. "Marian, would you do the preliminaries?"

"Sure." Marian stepped toward the girl. "Come this way, miss."

The girl followed Marian down the hall as Arielle draped her coat over her arm. After her tense weekend at the reservation and her floundering friendship with Carter, she felt relieved to be back to the familiar routine of work and the people of the clinic, even if there had been a break-in. She glanced around.

"And just where's my java?" she demanded dramatically. "Don't tell me somebody stole my coffee cup!"

Katie stared at her in astonishment, and then realized she was joking. She burst out laughing. "Oh, you!" Katie giggled.

Arielle smiled at her, satisfied that the levity had relieved Katie's worried expression and defused the strained atmosphere in the room. Then she headed toward her office to hang up her coat before she checked out the break-in site. To her annoyance, she noticed Dan Williams step up behind her.

"This clinic ought to have an alarm system built in," he began. "I can have one installed. Monthly fees would be minimal. What do you think?"

"I think you should talk to the board, not me."

"You could convince them to go for it, Arielle." He reached for the latch of her office door. "You're a very persuasive woman."

She paused in front of her door, hoping she could persuade Dan to leave her alone. But before she could say anything, he continued to speak.

"You're wasting your talents here, you know," he said. "I have some friends who are opening a practice in Bellevue. Very nice place. State of the art. You could do very well for yourself there. Just one word from me and—"

"Thanks, but I like it here." She crossed her arms, hoping her body language and the barrier of her long winter coat hanging over her arm would broadcast her message of personal disinterest in him and any business offer he might make as well.

"You actually like it here?"

"I provide care here for people who really need it. It gives me a sense of satisfaction."

"When you get tired of satisfaction and want to make some real money—and you will, sooner or later—just keep me in mind."

"Don't hold your breath, Dan."

He grinned. "I love tough women! You know, I just love 'em!"

So much for getting her message across.

Dan pushed open her door and kept hold of the doorknob, so that she had to brush by him to enter the room. His grin widened as she passed by him, ignoring his smile.

"Mmm," he said. "Somebody smells awfully nice this morning."

She ignored his juvenile attempt at flattery. She'd take Carter's silence over this man's bullshit any day. At least when Carter said something, if and when he ever did, she'd know he was sincere.

Dan trailed her into the room. "Since Katie didn't have time to make coffee, would you like me to get you a latte?"

"No thanks, Dan."

"Wouldn't mind at all."

"I've got to see my patient in a minute, thanks anyway."

She hung up her coat and grabbed her white clinical jacket. As she was putting it on, she glanced at her desk. An unfamiliar dark shape sprawled across her blotter.

"What's that?" she asked, stepping closer.

"What?" Dan asked.

"That *thing* on my desk!" Arielle leaned over her desk and stared. There on her open calendar lay a huge dead frog with a string tied around one of its back legs. Had the frog been wet, it might have been a glistening moss-green color, but having spent hours exposed to the air, its skin had dried and darkened like the hide of an overripe banana. The black creature with its staring golden eyes was hideous and shocking.

Arielle grabbed the string and raised the frog off the blotter. It stuck to the paper at first, but then broke free and swung toward Dan.

"God!" he exclaimed, jumping back. "Keep it away from me!"

"What do you think it is?" she inquired, holding it up and letting it rotate in front of her as she studied it.

"Some fucking voodoo crap, that's what."

"Who would leave such a thing in my office?" Arielle gaped at the frog and saw that its mouth had been lashed shut with thick black thread.

"Who did you offend lately?" Dan edged out of her way as she moved closer to her physician's bag. "Walk across any graves over the weekend?"

Instantly Arielle thought of the deserted Indian village and just as instantly discarded the notion. She hadn't done anything wrong there. Carefully she let the frog back down to the paper.

"What are you doing?" Dan demanded. His tone of voice displayed a surprising amount of fear.

"I'm going to cut those threads," she replied, opening her physician's bag and retrieving her suturing kit. She opened it and took out a pair of slender scissors. "See where the mouth has been sutured?"

Dan bent closer. "That's disgusting."

"Yes, and why has it been sewn shut?"

"Hell if I know."

Long ago Arielle had lost her squeamishness about dead things or cutting into flesh. She'd learned from Mack that certain jobs had to be done and a person just set aside their distaste or disgust and did them. The frog was hideous and its presence unsettling, but Arielle knew she had to find out why someone had bound its mouth. Was it a hint to shut her up and abandon her search for Mack?

A few snips was all it took to cut the thread. Dan hovered close by as she selected a pair of tweezers and pried open the jaws of the frog.

"Something's in there," she murmured, completely engrossed in the task.

"What is?" Dan said. "Pull it out."

"I am." Carefully she inserted the tweezers, eased out a small bundle, and held it up to the light.

"Hair," Dan said.

A chill raced down Arielle's back when she saw the

color and texture of the balled-up hair. She felt Dan's regard.

"And it's just like yours," he added.

"It looks like mine," she agreed. "But it couldn't be." Arielle said the words as calmly as she could, while at the same time her thoughts raced back to the day the boys had broken into her car on the reservation. She suddenly remembered the missing brush from her purse. If this *was* her hair, someone had taken the hairs from that brush, wadded them up, and stuffed them in this poor creature's mouth. Why?

"What did I tell you?" Dan waved his hand at the frog. "Goddamn voodoo. That's what we have here. Voodoo."

A shudder coursed through her. Someone had gone to a lot of trouble to leave this frog on her desk. They'd even broken into the clinic to do it. Who was behind this? Reuven Jaye? Did he think a dead frog would scare her off? Or did he believe in its power to cause her harm? Whatever the intent, it had succeeded, for she felt unnerved and alarmed, though she refused to reveal any of her fears to Dan Williams.

"What a nice way to start the week," she commented wryly, dropping the hair on the paper beside the frog.

"You're a cool one," Dan said. "Most women I know would be screaming their heads off if this happened to them."

"Screaming wouldn't help." Arielle shook her head and gazed at the frog. "I just can't imagine who would do this."

But she could imagine it. Very easily. Reuven Jaye had left this, or someone who worked for him. She wished she could talk to Carter, but not when Dan was in her office. And she really couldn't leave her patient waiting any longer.

"I have to examine my patient," she said. "Let me see you out."

"You're going to show that frog to the police, aren't you?" Dan followed her to the door.

"Of course."

"I'd be scared if I were you. This is really sick."

"I don't intend to let it get to me. Being frightened of the unknown is the psychological principle on which voodoo is based, Dan. That's why it's sometimes successful."

"Well, I'd be scared, Arielle." He paused on the threshold. "If you need protection, don't you hesitate to call me."

"Thanks."

"I mean it."

She nodded noncommittally. "Thanks."

He waited until she knocked on the door of the examination room, and then she saw him turn and walk down the hall. Arielle kept her composure for the pregnant teenager, for the police, for Katie, and for the rest of the people she met during clinic hours. But inside, she felt on edge and by the end of the day was not looking forward to going home. If a frog had been left in her office, what might be waiting for her at the condo? Did Reuven know where she lived? It might not be wise for her to walk into her apartment alone or unarmed.

Near closing time she had a few minutes to call Carter, and then realized she didn't know where he worked. Instead, she called his home phone and left a message on his answering machine to call the number of her pager. She didn't want to go home until she heard from him, and hoped he would check his messages soon. Even though they might not be on the best of personal terms, she was sure that he'd help her and would want to know what had happened. After the last patient left, Arielle sat down at her desk and attacked her paper-work, hoping Carter would call soon.

At five-thirty the phone rang. Arielle's heart skipped a beat and she answered it, disappointed to hear Dan Williams's voice on the other end.

"Say, good looking," he began. "I've been thinking about you all day."

"Oh?" She cradled the receiver and continued to open mail as he talked.

"I don't like the thought of you walking around down-town tonight when that voodoo crazy still might be in the neighborhood."

Arielle was not completely convinced by his concern.

"Why don't you let me take you to dinner and drop you off at your place so I won't worry about you all night."

"That's nice of you, Dan," she replied, wishing Carter had been the one to make the offer. "Can I get back to you?"

"Instead of calling, why don't you pop over to my office in a half-hour or so? I'll have some figures from the burglar alarm people for you by then. Buzz 1710 and I'll let you in."

"Fine. Bye."

Arielle hung up the phone and sifted through her mail, wishing Carter would call before she left. She could always use a medical emergency as an excuse to get out of dinner with Dan. Once again she tried Carter's house, but the phone rang off to his machine. After forty minutes elapsed, Arielle closed up the clinic and headed for Dan's office tower across the street.

Up on the fiftieth floor, Dan ushered her into his plush office, a den of maroon leather and burgundy carpet that was at least an inch thick. Behind his massive rosewood desk soared a bank of windows that looked out upon Elliott Bay and Queen Anne Hill, a view so breathtaking it seemed more like a huge poster than the real thing. The office was immaculate, without a stray paper or misplaced pen, the office of a man who rarely sat at his desk but rather spent his time in meetings and on the phone.

Arielle walked to the center of the room. "Nice view," she remarked.

"Best view in town." He came up behind her and reached for her shoulders. "Can I take your coat for you? I thought we'd have a glass of wine and relax for a few minutes."

Arielle paused. She'd never encouraged Dan regarding friendship and she didn't wish to foster any misplaced notions with him now. Yet, what was she afraid of? She could handle men. She'd been handling them for years.

"All right," she replied, and allowed him to slip off her coat. For a long moment he stood behind her in complete silence, until the hairs on the back of her neck raised up in warning. She couldn't help but remember the way Carter had stood behind her and kissed her neck, and suddenly worried that Dan was considering the same thing. Arielle stepped away. He draped her coat over the back of a nearby chair.

"What did the police say about the frog?" Dan asked, moving to a bank of built-in cabinets and shelves that housed spotlighted sculptures in black stone.

"Just what you did, that some nut left it to scare us." She surveyed the sculptures, surprised to see foot-high totem poles of exquisite craftsmanship. While she looked at his collection, she thought she detected the faint cry of a wolf, just like the one at the deserted

Indian village. But how could she possibly hear wolves this high above the city? Soon the distant but disconcerting howl was overlaid by the pop of a cork and the sound of Dan pouring the drinks, and she put the howl out of her mind. Once again he sidled up behind her, reaching around to give her the glass of white wine and using it as an excuse to touch his chest to her back. "Thank you," she said, taking the goblet and discreetly moving aside at the same time.

"I've never seen sculptures like these," she ventured to break the sudden tension.

"They're argillite. It's a mineral found up north. Canada mostly."

"They're beautiful. Are they old?"

"No. Contemporary. Most are done by a Haida Indian who's making a name for himself these days. This is my little investment."

"Think they'll be valuable someday?"

"Oh, they already are. My investments always do well." He caught her eye as he took a big sip of his wine. His expression smacked of self-satisfaction, and yet his eyes bore into hers as though he required her approval and was surprised he wasn't finding it immediately. Being the object of his overwhelming stare was like standing in the path of a huge snowplow. Either way, a person would get overwhelmed, whether by the flying snow of his big talk or the looming metal blade of his domineering personality. Arielle couldn't help her negative reaction to Dan. No matter how fine his surroundings or how expensive his wine, there was something unkempt and common about him that she found singularly unattractive.

"Do you know a lot about Native American art?" she asked.

"A little." He took her elbow, "But enough about my collection. I want to talk about another little plan I have in mind."

"Oh?"

He led her to the maroon leather couch and indicated that she sit. She didn't want to spend much more time in his office, but also didn't want to appear rude.

Dan sat down next to her and set his glass on the table at his knee.

"What did you have in mind?" Arielle asked.

His eyes lit up. "Well, now, I've been thinking about a possible merger."

"With whom?"

"With a party I'm sure will go places." He smiled, and his gaze drifted to the top button of her blouse. Arielle almost reached up to cover herself.

"I'm an excellent judge of people," he continued, smiling at her again. "I can tell who's going to make it and who isn't. I can tell who can be bought and who can't. I built this empire of mine on my ability to spot winners. And you, my dear Ms. Scott, are a winner."

Arielle froze. "Why, thank you."

"You've got what it takes to put that special stamp on things," Dan went on. "Class, that's what you've got."

Arielle sipped her wine. Perhaps opposites did attract, at least on Dan's part. She was silent, however, and willing to let him dominate the conversation, as was his habit.

"Picture yourself the head of a medical facility, perhaps a research hospital, making a name for yourself, making a real difference in the world, making history."

"That's a bit out of my league."

"Not if you dream big. Not if you have a backer. A partner."

Arielle leveled her gaze at him. "What are you suggesting, Dan?"

He smiled and reached for her shoulder. "I'm suggesting that two go-getters like us—as partners—could have the world at our feet. I'm talking marriage, Arielle. Wedded bliss."

She slipped away from his attempted caress and rose, skirting the coffee table and eliminating any chance of further contact.

Dan stood up with a chuckle. "Surprised, Arielle?"

"As a matter of fact, I am."

"We'd make a dynamite couple." He straightened his tie over his stomach. "I'm serious."

"What's in it for me?"

"You pull in the real class acts of this town. We're talking old money here, Arielle, the founding-father types who snub their noses at Williams, Inc., even though I could buy them out in a minute. Together, you and I could eat up this town and spit it out. That's living, Arielle. By God, that's living!"

Arielle was silent. His offer held no allure for her, but she didn't quite know how to say it without sounding rude. He was, after all, the owner of the clinic building and she wouldn't be able to avoid seeing him in the future.

"First Seattle, then maybe San Francisco and New York. We could have the world, Arielle!"

"You do dream big, Dan," she commented. Then she put her wine-glass on his desk. "But I'm afraid I'm not the man for the job."

"Thank God for that!" he chuckled. "And don't think I haven't noticed."

He stepped up behind her. Arielle tried to move away, but he clutched both of her shoulders and pressed her against the edge of his desk. Before she could pull out of his grip, he nuzzled her neck. "You're the classiest woman I've ever seen," he said near her ear. "I want to drape you in diamonds. I want to dress you in furs."

"Dan—"

"I want to pour champagne over your breasts," he murmured, squeezing her coarsely, "and lick off the bubbles."

"Dan, let me go," Arielle demanded. His hands dropped and she immediately stepped away, heading for her coat draped over a chair by his desk. She didn't like the turn in the conversation and thought it would be best to leave.

"I could do things for you," Dan continued, following her across the floor. "You wouldn't believe what I could do for you."

"I'm content to make my own way."

"I know your kind," he said. "You're the type that likes a challenge. You don't want some namby-pamby man you can boss around. You need a real man who knows what he wants. Who knows how to take it and give it, too. And that's me."

"Dan, I'm not looking for a man right now." She picked up her coat and straightened, anxious to get away from him.

"Wait!" Dan reached out to grab the coat from her hand, but she whipped it back. She'd had enough of his pushy personality and overly intimate comments. The heavy fabric of her coat brushed the top of his desk and swiped across his Rolodex, knocking it off. The metal box fell to the ground at their feet with a soft clunk, spraying little white cards over the plush carpet.

Dan stared at the cards for a moment and then glanced at her, his blue eyes a steel color. At his sudden cold expression she questioned his true intentions and worried that he might try to detain her against her will.

A shudder of fear and disgust passed through her at the thought of Dan manhandling her.

"Sorry," Arielle exclaimed, backing away and stooping to retrieve the cards.

"Forget it," he replied in a surly tone. "Just leave them, Arielle."

"But—"

"I'll get my secretary to clean them up later."

Arielle reached for a card near the leg of the chair and paused in astonishment when she saw a familiar name and phone number typed in neat block letters on the white rectangle. Before the surprise could register on her face, she choked it back down and slid the card in among the others in her hand and placed them on the desk. Then she shrugged into her coat.

"You don't have to go," Dan said. "I'll behave."

She buttoned her coat in silence.

"I don't like to see you going off by yourself like this."

"I'll be all right," she replied.

"Come on, Arielle." He grabbed the top of her arm. "You don't know what's good for you."

"Oh, yes, I do." Arielle yanked out of his grip and backed toward the door. "Goodnight, Dan."

"I don't take no for an answer." He reached out, grabbed her arm again, and roughly pulled her up to him. "That's one thing you're going to have to learn about me."

She glared at him, struggling to free herself from his grip.

"When I see something I like, I do everything necessary to get it."

Arielle reared back as he bent to kiss her. His eyes gleamed as he bent closer, his full mouth inches from hers. "And I like you, Dr. Scott."

With that, he pressed her lips and tried to wedge his

tongue into her mouth, but Arielle clenched her teeth tightly together. Then, burning with indignation, she raised up and stamped on his instep with the heel of her pump.

"Goddammit!" he howled, staggering backward, and hopping on one foot.

"Bastard!" Arielle lunged to the side, raced across the room, grabbed her purse from the chair by the door, and sprinted away, half-blind with rage and fright. How dare he push himself upon her? She punched the button for the elevator and waited angrily while Dan appeared at the end of the hall.

"Arielle!" he shouted. "Come on back. You forgot the estimates for the alarm system."

"Put them in the mail." She glared at the elevator light, willing the car to arrive.

"Arielle!" Dan yelled, striding toward her. "So I got carried away. Can you blame me? Come on. I'll take you to dinner."

"Porker," Arielle fumed under her breath. The door of the elevator opened and she rushed in, praying that he wouldn't have time to stop it. The doors closed on a red-faced Dan Williams, his expression a mixture of outrage and disbelief. Did he actually expect a woman to respond to his heavy-handed advances? Arielle leaned against the side of the elevator, her heart pounding furiously, and her mouth dry.

As the elevator sped to the ground floor, Arielle remembered the Rolodex card she'd seen on Dan's floor and tried to figure out what connection the two men could have, but couldn't come up with anything. In her mind's eye, however, she could clearly see the name and number:

JAYE, REUVEN
(206) 555–4905

18

Arielle walked briskly but not quickly enough to keep the frosty air or the mounting anger she felt for Dan Williams at bay. She'd never been that close to being assaulted by a man, and felt uncharacteristically rattled. Wind off the Sound cut through her coat, reminding her of the cold rainy days she'd spent on the island with Mack. She knew she could survive the cold, but she wasn't so sure she could face the solitude of her dark and lonely condo. Sometimes it was difficult to be a stranger in a new town, with no relatives or close friends to take the edge off a traumatic day like the one she'd just experienced. Today was the kind of day when she needed a friend. But who else except Carter could she count as a friend? Unnerved and lonely, she turned up Pike Street and stuffed her hands in her pockets as she waited for the light to change. She dreaded going home, and yet there was no alternative.

Just before the light turned green, she felt her pager vibrate at her hip. With numb fingers she reached into her coat and pulled the pager off the belt of her skirt, tipping the little black gadget up to the light so she could see the readout. She was rewarded with a familiar number—Carter's. Arielle glanced around and realized she was closer to his apartment than her condo. With renewed determination, she turned and walked in the direction of his place, happy that he had returned her call at last.

Minutes later, she rang his apartment and he buzzed her in. She burst into the lobby and hurried up the stairs, but he met her on the landing, his face full of concern.

"Ari!" he exclaimed. "What's wrong?"

She paused, suddenly overwhelmed by the day, and watched him come down the stairs, her heart swelling larger and larger the closer he got. She had tried to act casual over the intercom, but he must have noticed the unusual quaver in her voice.

"Ari?" he repeated.

"Hi," she said. "Do you have a moment, Carter?"

"Of course." She saw his eyebrows raise as his gaze swept over her. "Come on up."

He gently took her elbow as was his habit, and guided her up the stairs. She was grateful for his light touch of support and also for the fire that crackled in his living room. She stumbled across the floor to the fireplace while Carter closed the door. Now that the danger was past and Carter was there for her, she felt strangely enervated and painfully vulnerable.

She held her hands out to the heat from the fire and couldn't keep from trembling. She was cold, hungry, angry and scared, and for the first time in a long time, close to tears. Carter came up beside her and she could feel his regard on the side of her face. She didn't look at him, and concentrated on regaining command of her emotions. It wouldn't do either of them any good if she broke down.

"Ari?" he said softly. "Are you all right?"

She glanced at him and saw the dark concern in his eyes, which proved her undoing. "Oh, Carter!"

He reached for her and she turned to him, falling into the haven of his embrace. His arms came around her as she wrapped hers around his neck, hanging on to him with every shred of her being. He squeezed her tightly, doing more to warm her in a matter of seconds than any fire could do in ten minutes. His chest was like a furnace, and his hands made her feel protected and cherished at the same time. She pressed her cheek against the firm space above his shirt pocket and closed her eyes, drinking in his nearness and his strength.

"Ari." His voice rumbled next to her ear. "What happened?"

"Just hold me," she whispered.

He fell silent and did as she requested, without allowing his embrace to go over the line of friendship, and for that Arielle was thankful. He seemed to sense her need to be comforted, not aroused.

Gradually, Arielle felt her calm center returning and the trauma of the last few hours falling away. She eased back, wanting more than anything to wash Dan Williams's handprints off her skin before Carter did so much as kiss her. She wanted his kiss, but not now, not when she felt soiled by another man.

"Thanks," she said, glancing up at him. Carter gazed down at her, his eyes worried and full of questions.

"Are you going to tell me what's happened?"

"Yes. I've got a lot to tell you. But," she paused, knowing her request would sound odd.

"But what?"

"This is going to sound crazy, Carter, but may I take a bath first?"

"Sure." He raised a brow. "And I'll bet you haven't eaten all day, have you?"

"No. Have you had dinner?" she asked.

"Not yet. I just got home. Why don't you hop in the bath and I'll run down to Pike Place Market and get us some supper."

"That would be lovely."

"The bathroom's right down that hall." He pointed to the passage next to the couch. "Clean towels are in the cabinet."

She nodded and brushed back her tangled hair. Carter tilted his head and studied her.

"Are you sure you're all right? You look shook up."

"I'm fine now," She mustered a smile. "Thanks."

"Okay. I'll be right back." He grabbed his leather jacket off a chair by the couch, but paused at the door and turned. "And don't go using all my Mr. Bubble."

She grinned a genuine smile, glad to have Carter for a friend. He might be moody, but he was also the gentleman Dan Williams could never hope to be, the kind of man she could depend upon and trust. She felt happy in his company, at ease with him. His apartment felt like home to her, and she had no desire to leave, not tonight or even tomorrow. Standing there in her coat and watching Carter walk out the door, she suddenly realized that she loved him. She loved his edginess, his dry wit, his mercurial silences, and his care. He truly cared about her, of that she had no doubt.

A few minutes later, she eased into the bath and sighed with pleasure. The hot water purged the rotten day from her spirit as well as her body. She shampooed her hair and washed herself from head to toe. Then she ran a tub of clean water, sat back, and relaxed until she heard Carter return from the market. After a few minutes, she heard his footsteps come up the hall, and to her surprise, he strolled into the bathroom as if his presence during her bath was the most natural thing in the world.

Arielle blushed furiously as he sat down on the side of the tub and held out a goblet of brandy. He gave her a slow smile and kept his eyes locked on hers, until she realized he hadn't come to gawk at her nakedness. The combination of being naked in his presence and yet unmolested by both his hands and eyes was surprisingly erotic.

"Thank you," she said.

"Feeling any better?" he asked.

"Yes. Much." She sipped the brandy and handed it back to him while maintaining eye contact. He surprised her by taking a small drink of it himself.

"Mind if I join you?" he asked, standing up.

Arielle choked on her surprise. "In here? In the water?"

"Why not?" He reached for a white paper bag and put it on the side of the bath. "I've never eaten brie and apples in a bathtub with a beautiful doctor. Thought I'd like to try it."

"I see." She tried to remain nonchalant, but his offer completely astounded her.

"And have you ever drunk brandy while a Saquinnish Indian washed your back?"

"Not lately."

"Then here, hold this." He gave the brandy back to her while he unbuttoned his shirt. She had to smile. She'd envisioned falling into Carter's bed, perhaps making love with him in front of the fire—but not munching a snack in the bathtub with him. She'd never eaten in a bathtub with a man before—or anywhere else without her clothes on for that matter.

Then his last remark sank in, and she straightened. "Wait a minute. What do you mean, a Saquinnish Indian? You're Saquinnish?"

"I think so." He stepped out of his jeans and peeled off his socks. Arielle watched him, so caught up in the conversation that she forgot to be nervous at the prospect of viewing Carter naked for the first time. He rose up and pulled off his briefs, and she was surprised and a bit pleased to see he was fully aroused. He followed the line of her sight and then glanced at her with a smile.

"He has a mind of his own," Carter explained.

"And what has *he* been thinking about?" she teased as he stepped into the water.

Carter glanced at her and she thought she detected a blush flaring on his sharp cheekbones. "The same thing I've been thinking about for the last few weeks," he replied.

She noticed that his eyes had yet to stray from hers. "And what is that exactly?"

"You."

He knelt down in front of her, straddling her legs. "Ah," he sighed as the water rose up around them. "That feels nice." Then he leaned closer to kiss her, cradling her face in one warm hand. His kiss was exquisite in its gentleness, his fingers soft as he pushed his hand into her hair. For a moment she was aware of nothing but his mouth and the sound of their breathing. Then he eased her head to his chest and held her there while he stroked her wet hair.

"You feel even nicer," he added.

She rubbed her cheek against him in answer, loving the firmness of the smooth expanse of his chest.

"Ari," he murmured. "I'm glad you've come to me."

"I'm glad you were here."

Sitting there, Arielle thought her heart would burst with love for him. She held the brandy goblet aloft with one hand and encircled his back with the other, while she listened to his heart thudding beneath her ear. He had a magnificent chest, well-defined and muscular, and his back was straight and wide, just as she had imagined it would be. She felt her breasts immediately tighten as he held her close.

"I haven't been with a woman for two years," he said. "My girlfriend dumped me when I got sick, and after chemotherapy—"

"You don't have to tell me this."

"Yes I do."

"Why?"

"Because I want you to know. I'm clean as a whistle, Doc. They radiated the hell out of me. I've been tested so much with so many needles I practically leak when I take a drink. If I had any immunity problems, I'd be dead."

"That's true."

"The only thing is, I don't know how much control I'm going to have."

"Maybe I don't want you to be in control." She glanced at him, surprised at her brazen words, but knowing them to be true. She wanted to be swept away by a man, and she wanted that man to be Carter.

He continued to stare at her, his black eyes pouring into her. "Another thing, Ari. I have to tell you this. I've been changing since my transplant. I haven't always looked the way I do now."

"What do you mean?"

"I had brown curly hair before. I wasn't very attractive—I was an ugly sonofabitch, actually. Since the transplant, even my face has changed. I don't know what it means, or how I might have changed inside either."

"I've never heard of such a thing. What kind of transplant did you have?"

"Bone marrow. For aplastic anemia."

"God, that's serious, Carter. Are you in remission?"

Carter shook his head. "I won't know for a while yet, but I feel good." He reached for the brandy and took a drink. Then he set the goblet on the side of the tub. "The doctors told me there might be changes. Sometimes a person takes on certain characteristics of his donor. But none of the doctors expected the changes to be so drastic."

"Hold on—you said you took on your donor's attributes?"

"Yeah." He stared at her, as though waiting for a light to come on. And it did come on, like a floodlight, almost blinding her.

Arielle touched his face. "You're saying you've taken on the looks of your donor, a Saquinnish Indian?"

He nodded.

"Mack?" she asked incredulously.

Carter nodded again. "I'm almost sure of it. He was at the same medical center the same time I was. I found a letter in that file in Reuven's office."

"In Mack's file?"

"Yes, but I didn't show you."

"Why?"

"I couldn't. I didn't know what to think. I wasn't sure I could tell you."

"Why not?"

"I didn't want to tell you about myself."

"Why, Carter?"

"Because I don't know who the hell I am."

Carter's words hung on the air like an epithet. He stared at her, and in his troubled eyes Arielle sensed all the heartache and rejection he'd endured for the past thirty years. And in his bruised way, Carter probably thought she'd rejected him, too, for the same reasons everyone else did. He wasn't part of the group, didn't fit in, or lacked the heritage to gain entrance to the gates he might have easily passed through had his skin been a different color. She felt her heart surge with tenderness and love for him. Didn't he know her well enough to realize that she was blind to conventional systems, especially social ones? Didn't Carter realize he was enough for her just the way he was, no bloodlines attached? Didn't he know the most important thing was to define himself by his own merits, regardless of birthright or fortune?

"Carter," she said, reaching up to lay her palm upon his cheek. "If you're a Saquinnish, great. If you're the man in the moon, great. But I don't care about that. Do you know what's important to me?"

"What?" he asked, his eyes never wavering from her face.

"That you are a gentleman, that you are intelligent and kind, and that you can make me laugh. I don't know where you come from, or what your story is, but I know this: you are one of the finest men I've ever met."

For a long moment he stared at her as if he couldn't move, and then he gathered her into his arms and kissed her, desperately, roughly, pulling her up to a kneeling position and wrapping his arms around her. She could feel his shaft between them, and a frisson of desire crackled through her. She thought about the danger of knocking the brandy over or pushing the lunch sack into the water. She thought about the danger of making love to a man without proper precautions. And then he was lifting her up and she was sinking down upon him. And he was pushing into her and sighing in her ear as they moved together, unmindful of the water sloshing up the sides as he pressed her against the wall. Carter was the man who belonged in her arms, inside of her, as part of her, and she realized that nature had intended this to happen, to even the most careful of people, when it was truly meant to be.

Then he was filling her up and she was crying out, astonished at the way his body made her soar. She thought at first it was because she was experiencing him as she had experienced no other man, skin to skin, flesh to flesh, and nothing in between. And then she realized the real reason he transported her far beyond ecstasy had nothing to do with birth control devices or the lack thereof. It was because she loved him. She loved Carter fully and fiercely, as she had never loved anyone in her entire life.

Their lovemaking was hot and furious, as uncontrolled as Carter had predicted. Even so, when it was over, Arielle slid down his torso and into the warm water in a delicious daze, surprisingly sated. Carter settled against the back of the tub and urged her to sink on top of him, and for a long while they lay together, simply growing accustomed to the length and contours of their bodies. Then he sat up and turned her around, so that her back faced him. He washed her, each part of her, his soapy hands exploring every curve of her body. She languished against him, adrift in the slick caress of his soapy hands sliding over her breasts and belly, and the way he would lean forward and kiss her cheek or her shoulder or her neck. No man had savored her in just this way.

Afterward, she lathered his body with her hands, taking time to memorize the long sheaths of his muscles, the way his wet hair curled behind the curve of his ear, the masculine strength in his long straight fingers, and the lean flat bow of his abdomen.

While they bathed, they finished the brandy, cheese, and fruit, lingering in the tub until the water grew cold. Then they toweled each other dry, smiling and caressing, but never once speaking. To speak would have shattered the unfathomable communion passing between them.

Then Carter swept her off her feet and walked with her down the hall to his bedroom. He pushed open the door with his elbow and walked to the bed. Tenderly he lowered her to the comforter and kissed her mouth as he reached for the bedclothes. She moved aside to allow him to pull down the cover and then scooted between the sheets, cool against her warm, glowing body. She stretched her legs and then held out her arms to him. He smiled at her, a smile so genuine and full of awe that her heart flipped in her chest.

He felt the same way she did, she was certain of it, that what they had found in each other was something totally unexpected, something amazingly wonderful and whole. Carter sighed and lowered himself onto her, ready again to make love with her.

"You are so beautiful," he whispered, brushing back the hair at her temple as he studied her face. "I could look at you all night."

"That's not what I had in mind, Mr. Greyson."

"And what did you have in mind?"

"Something slow and southern and earth-shattering."

Carter smiled. "Ah, the pressure's on." He glanced at the clock beside his bed and Arielle did, too. She was shocked to find it was after 1 A.M.

"The night is still young," he said. "There might be enough time."

She smiled and kissed his ear. "Then what are we waiting for?"

19

Just before dawn Arielle awakened to the sound of a siren. She stirred and for an instant stared at the unfamiliar surroundings before she remembered that she lay in Carter's bed, not her own. She turned to reach for him and was momentarily shocked to find herself alone. Then she heard a noise in the hall and looked up to see Carter strolling toward her with a glass in his hand. A crazy sense of relief washed over her at the sight of him.

"I was thirsty," he explained, slipping back under the covers. He held out the glass. "Want some?"

"Yes. Thanks." She gratefully accepted the water and drank a good portion of it. Carter waited for her to finish and then put the glass on the nightstand beside him. He lay upon the pillow and turned his head toward her, smiling as she raised up on an elbow to gaze at him.

They'd made love most of the night, and had snatched only a few hours of sleep, but Carter looked alert and well-rested, his dark eyes glinting with good humor and contentment. Arielle played with his glossy black hair, letting the soft strands slip over her fingers. She brushed back the lock falling over his forehead, and was highly conscious of her nipple brushing his rib cage at the same time. Desire flashed through her. She would have thought six hours in bed with Carter would have satiated her, at least for a while, but one touch was all it took to set her off again.

"You have such gorgeous hair," she commented. "I can't imagine you with curly brown hair."

"Well, I had it, and it looked weird on me."

"You said you were ugly before. I can't imagine you being unattractive, either."

"I was butt ugly. Believe it."

"It's hard to, because you're so handsome now. You're quite dangerous, you know."

He grinned mischievously and gave her exposed flank a squeeze. "Danger is my business."

Smiling, she rested her head against his chest, listening to his heartbeat and knowing it would be difficult to imagine the world without Carter in it. Yet he might never have survived had it not been for Mack's bone marrow donation. The thought of Carter dying in a hospital alone, without her having had the chance to know him or help him, filled her with sadness. She embraced him with all her strength and turned to press a fervent kiss on the underside of his jaw.

He sighed and stroked her back with the warm flat of his hand. "What was that for?" he asked softly.

"Being thankful for your transplant."

"So you could kiss a cute guy?" he teased.

"So I could come to know you."

His hand stopped stroking her and for a minute she thought he'd even quit breathing. Was he not ready to talk about his feelings? Perhaps he didn't have as strong an attraction for her as she did for him, or maybe he was the type of man who ran from emotional commitments. Arielle drew her hand out from under him and laid it upon his chest.

"You might have died," she continued. "I've heard the success rate of bone marrow transplants is only fifty/fifty."

"It's a little higher than that now," he replied. "But not much."

"Were you really sick before the transplant?"

"Yeah. It was sudden, devastating. One day I had landed a great new job and had a good thing going with a new girlfriend, and practically the next day I was flat on my back with some doctor telling me I might have two months to live."

"Two months?" she asked, incredulous. She knew some cancers were quick and invasive, but not that extreme.

"Aplastic anemia is a pernicious little situation." Carter combed her hair with his fingers. "I'd get home from work exhausted, and sleep through my alarm until the next evening and miss a whole day of work. I thought I had mono or something. After I collapsed in a meeting, I finally went to a doctor. He knew what it was right off." Carter sighed. "My girlfriend couldn't handle it. She left when she found out."

"Some people can't deal with the trauma of a serious disease."

"Yeah, I don't blame her for leaving. But it was a blow at the time."

"So what happened? Who took care of you until the transplant? Your relatives?"

"I managed on my own."

"Through the chemotherapy?"

"Through everything."

Arielle stared at him in surprise. She was well aware that chemotherapy was one of the worst stages of cancer treatment, and one most people couldn't get through without a support system to help them face the days and nights of debilitating nausea and fatigue.

"How did you do it?" she asked. "And afterward— after the transplant—how did you get along, stuck in isolation for months?"

"I had no choice but to just get through it."

For a moment Arielle fell silent as she was reminded again just how similar Carter was to Mack. Mack had endured his island banishment and Carter had walked through a near-death experience completely on his own. Both had possessed the perseverance and the will to take on a nearly insurmountable challenge and survive.

Carter's voice interrupted her thoughts. "There was this little guy there the same time I was. In the next room. He was only nine. The nurses talked about Ben a lot, because he was such a great little kid, even though he was going through a bad time. I used to draw him stupid cartoons which the nurses would hold up to the window so he could see them."

"That probably meant a lot to him," Arielle put in.

"It did to me, too. It gave me something to do, a reason to get up every day and take all the medicine that made me wish I *had* died."

Arielle didn't say anything more, for she sensed that Carter needed to talk without interruption. He continued in a voice full of quiet tenderness. "I'd come up with some silly idea, and then I'd draw it. Sometimes I wrote stupid limericks for him. One time," he paused and stroked the back of her neck. "One time when the nurse took him one of my drawings, I heard him laugh through the wall." Carter's chest rose and fell quickly and she wasn't sure if he was chuckling or choking back a strong emotion. "That still ranks as one of the finest moments of my life."

Arielle closed her eyes and squeezed him. Somehow she could predict how this story would end, and she didn't want to hear it or make Carter repeat it.

"Even today," he whispered. "Right now, lying here with you, Ari, I can't understand how a kid like that— with great parents, lots of friends, and a whole life ahead of him—didn't make it, while some ugly prickly guy like me slipped right on by."

"The death of a child never seems fair," she said simply. It was all she could say. She held him for a long time after that, until she felt something ease in his embrace. Then his voice rumbled in his chest.

"But enough about those days. I want to know what shook you up last night."

"That's right. I never told you."

"So give, Flo."

"All right." She knew the best thing for them both would be a change of subject. Arielle snuggled into the curve of Carter's arms and told him about her awful day. She relayed the way she'd found the frog on her desk, and how it had rattled her. Carter hugged her and urged her to be extra careful until they could find Mack and clear up the goings-on at the reservation. Then she told him what had occurred in Dan Williams's office. Carter swore and threatened to exact physical damage for Dan's treatment of her, but Arielle asked that he refrain from avenging her. It would only cause more trouble, and Dan didn't actually hurt her. She would make sure that Dan wouldn't have an opportunity to bother her again.

After Carter's anger subsided, she told him about the Rolodex card that linked Dan to Reuven Jaye.

"I knew it," Carter said. "I knew there was something going on."

"What do you mean?"

"Remember those guys at Dan's Christmas party who used the private elevator to go to the basement?"

"You only assumed they were going to the basement."

"I know they were going there."

"How?"

"I just do." Carter sighed and squeezed her absently, and she glanced up to find him glaring at the wall behind her, preoccupied.

"Carter, when are you going to trust me?" she whispered.

"I don't know." He released her, rolled onto his back, and flung his arm across his face. "Maybe I'm incapable of trusting anyone."

"I don't believe that."

He remained silent, his expression hidden from view, but she knew he was listening. She moved closer and slowly drew her fingertip across the firm set of his lips. The line between his top and bottom lip formed a wide V, slightly tipped to the left, like the silhouette of a gull soaring above the sea.

"Trusting is risky," she said softly. "But without risk, there are no rewards."

"I don't expect rewards from life."

"You couldn't have come through a transplant if you hadn't believed in something. Patients without hope don't survive ordeals like that."

Carter didn't respond.

"You claim to be a loner, you pretend not to care. But I saw you with Evaline the other night. And what about that boy in the hospital? I think you have a heart the size of Texas, but you've convinced yourself to ignore what it tells you."

"Listen, Arielle," he said gruffly. "We've found some common ground that's pretty nice. Let's not ruin it by analyzing it, okay? I'm a guy with twisted dials. I admit it. But you're going to have to take me or leave me, just the way I am."

"And what *is* that way, exactly?" she asked, her frustration rising. How could he see himself in such limited terms? A man who didn't care couldn't possibly have made love to her the way he had, and couldn't have drawn cartoons for a dying boy. "I don't believe you know yourself, Carter. I don't believe you will let yourself see what you really are."

"I know what I am," he retorted. "I'm an asshole."

"Bullshit!" Arielle jerked up.

"We all learn things from our lives," he said from under his arm. "My life has taught me to depend only upon myself and to go my way alone."

"Maybe that was your life then, Carter. But things can change. People can change."

"No." He lowered his arm. "Some things go bone deep."

"And some people's bones get renewed," she answered, "with the spirit and strength of a good man. Perhaps you've changed in more ways than you realize."

Carter stared at her and she saw a shadow pass through his eyes. Had she finally gotten to him? Then he sat up and put his feet over the side of the bed. He sighed heavily and leaned his forearms on his thighs.

"That's what I've been trying to tell you, Ari. I don't know who I am. I don't know how this will all shake down in the end. I have a face that changes a little each time I look in the mirror. I hear things. See things. I can't even guarantee I'll live through the next four years."

"Did I ask for any guarantees?" She reached out to touch his shoulder, but he stood up as though to avoid her touch.

"Don't you understand?" He turned and glared at her, his eyes blazing. "I want some guarantees. I need them with you."

"Life holds no guarantees."

"So there we are, back to the trust issue." He crossed his arms over his chest.

"Carter." She rose, knowing their little bubble of isolation from the world had irrevocably burst. "You're confusing trust with guarantees. They're two separate things. Mack once told me something I've never forgotten. We were standing in the water, fishing one day, waiting for something to swim by. I grumbled and whined, complaining that there was no guarantee any fish would come and we'd stand there all morning in the cold water for nothing. Mack agreed there was no guarantee of a catch, but that if I didn't trust the fish to come, they never would. And waiting would be all that much harder. He told me to turn my thoughts from doubt to trust and see what such a change would manifest. I thought he was crazy. But I tried it for lack of anything better to do. I was flabbergasted to find out it worked."

"Mack." Carter shook his head bitterly. "He seems to have all the answers. When we find him, maybe you should pick up where you left off with him. You're half in love with the guy anyway."

Arielle felt her heart breaking at the quick return of Carter's sarcasm. She thought they'd found a place to be gentle and real with one another. But Carter had reverted to his usual defense tactics, shutting her out, just as he had many times before. She walked past him toward the door, knowing she couldn't stay with him until morning. His bitterness and her frustration invalidated all the hours of wonder and love they'd shared. Arielle turned.

"I don't think you realize how alike you and Mack are," she said quietly, leveling her eyes upon Carter's glinting ones. "But you're right. I do care for Mack in many ways. But not nearly as much or in the same way that I care for you."

She watched the first glimmer of incredulity flare in his face, and then she hurried to the bathroom to retrieve her clothes. She dressed, anxious to slip out of Carter's apartment before he had a chance to detain her, and before she succumbed to the tears of disappointment welling up inside.

Ron Bennett called just before Carter left work that evening, saying he had returned from the reservation in one piece, and would be happy to try the trip again once the weather cleared. After the phone conversation, Carter left his office and headed for the market. He was certain that if he took a brisk walk through the festive crowd and gift-laden stalls, he'd feel more like himself. He'd spent the whole day brooding about Arielle, thinking he should call her, and then decided it would be better to stay out of her life.

She expected more than what was realistic and believed in him far too much for her own good. He knew he was an asshole and that things wouldn't work out between them. She just couldn't see it—or didn't want to. Was she blind? Didn't she realize he was incapable of sustaining open communication with her, or with anyone? He was doing Arielle a favor by stepping away before he really hurt her. Yet, all he could think about was her beautiful face, her slender body, her soft voice and chestnut hair, and the way she held him, the way she seemed to understand him. How could he ever again sleep in his bed without her? He didn't want to face the prospect. So he planned to stay out late, eat dinner, see a movie—anything to keep from returning to his apartment and lying there, awake and alone.

He strolled through the market, expecting the noisy crowd and street musicians to distract him from his thoughts. But the holiday ambience barely sank in, and made him feel all the more lonely. The blind woman he often saw playing guitar by the herb shop was at her usual spot strumming Christmas carols and singing in her reedy voice, her pale eyes staring up at the cloudless black sky. Carter paused and listened, and a lump formed in his throat. The carol made him feel abysmally alone.

He thought of his childhood Christmases when he hoped something magical would happen to bring his family together, when his mother would reach out to him and his grandmother would succumb to the joys of the season, just enough to make the day special. But the magic had never descended. His mother and grandmother had remained distant and self-absorbed. What few gifts appeared beneath the tree had been perfunctory and impersonal: cologne, socks, and books, nothing to surprise or excite a child.

Carter soundlessly dropped a five-dollar bill in the blind woman's open guitar case and walked on. For some reason, he had hoped this Christmas might be different, that he might spend it in a meaningful way, with a person who found much meaning in life. Arielle. But that was just another dream never to materialize. Merry Christmases were for other people, not him.

He ate his dinner at a Cajun restaurant and then went to a spy/thriller movie that did little to take his mind off Arielle. When it ended, he walked out of the theater and headed for a coffee shop. Though it was close to ten, he wasn't tired enough to face his empty bed. He zipped up his jacket and walked down the hill toward his favorite espresso place. But he hadn't gone more than a block when he heard the wolves.

Pausing on the sidewalk, Carter turned in the direction of the sound: the parking garage near the clinic again. A shadow darted down the hill and loped across the bumpy brick road. This time Carter willingly followed the shadow wolf, determined to see what was in that crate in the storage room.

He dashed down Post Alley, unmindful of the handful of people on the street who looked after him in surprise. He sprinted past the clinic, and ran across Virginia Street to the parking garage. It was empty, except for a truck idling near the door to the storage room. For once he was glad he'd followed the wolves immediately, for they'd brought him to the garage just as the crate was being moved.

Panting, Carter ran to the passenger side of the truck and crept around the back. He could hear men talking in the room beyond, but couldn't see them. Should he chance stepping into the corridor that led to the storeroom? Or should he wait until the men carried the crate to the truck? Carter scowled. He didn't have a weapon and he'd come alone. He was sure he'd find the Wolf Clan's house post in that crate, yet he had to see it before he could prove his theory to anyone else.

Carter climbed up the ramp leaning against the back of the delivery truck and glanced around. The truck was empty except for a pile of tarps and some ropes thrown in the corner. Quietly he climbed in, burrowed into the corner, and covered himself with the tarps. He would wait until the crate was loaded, open the box en route, and then pray he could get out of the truck without anyone seeing him once the post was taken to its destination.

The treated canvas smelled musty and was considerably heavier than he would have guessed. He tried not to breathe as he scrunched down, making his body as compact as possible. After a few minutes, Carter worried that he would suffocate before the crate was ever loaded.

Then he heard voices approaching, the sounds of grunts as the men heaved the crate onto the ramp, and a scraping noise as the heavy object was pushed into the truck. The truck bed trembled under the weight. Sweating, Carter held his breath while male voices swore at each other. After a pause, he heard the back panel rolling shut, and a few moments later the truck lurched forward.

He waited a while before crawling out from under the odoriferous tarps, only to find himself in complete darkness. At least the air was less oppressive. Carter grabbed onto a metal support as the truck turned a corner. The ride though the hilly Seattle streets was rough, and he knew he wouldn't be able to stay on his feet until the truck reached more level ground. He worried that the crate would be taken to the waterfront and put on a boat before he'd have a chance to investigate. But presently, the vehicle chugged up a hill, careened around a wide curve, and then gathered speed, grinding with the effort until it reached a high gear. They must have entered the freeway.

Gratefully, Carter struggled to his feet and reached for the box for support. His eyes adjusted to the darkness so he could just make out the basic shape of the crate. With desperate hands, he felt along the wooden slats, trying to find a way to open the box. After a moment, his fingers felt the cool metal of a latch on one end. He flipped it open and moved to the other end where he expected to find the mate. He found the second latch, flipped it open, and raised the lid, his heart pounding in his chest.

In the dim light he could see the outlines of a huge animal head—a snarling wolf—and then the face of a man, and something that looked like a beak sticking out. He'd been right. Dan Williams had been storing a priceless tribal house post in his parking garage. And now that Carter knew how much the posts were worth, it made sense that Dan had hosted a party, ostensibly for Christmas but in reality for taking private bids on the piece.

Why was the post being moved from the garage? Had a buyer been found? Had a deal been struck and money changed hands? The connection to Reuven Jaye was now glaringly obvious. The elder had probably made the arrangements for the post to be stolen from the reservation. Was Reuven in a panic now, since people had started asking questions about Mack Shoalwater? Did he want the house post hidden somewhere else?

Carter lowered the lid and refastened the latches. He'd have to wait until the truck stopped before he could get out, and who knew where it was going or how long he'd be trapped in the back? He returned to the pile of tarps and sat down on them, hoping the truck wasn't going cross-country.

An hour later the truck slowed and left the freeway, crawling through winding streets with endless stoplights. There was no window in the back of the truck, so Carter had no idea where they were. Finally, the truck stopped, longer than usual. Carter climbed back under the tarps and froze in position when he heard the tailgate opening.

"Pull out the ramp," a man said.

A loud scraping noise rent the stillness of the cold night air.

"Hurry up, Chuck," another man said.

"I'm hurryin', dickhead."

"Not that end, the other one, idiot."

Carter heard heavy footsteps clump toward him. He held his breath, praying the light was poor enough to conceal his shape.

"Does the boss want the tarps, too?" a younger voice asked.

Carter nearly choked. What if they uncovered him?

"Naw," the rough voice replied. "Just the crate. Come on, push it this way."

More grunts filled the truck and Carter heard the box sliding toward the ramp. The men jostled it off the ramp and tramped away. Carter waited until their footsteps disappeared before he cautiously slipped out from under the tarps. The truck was parked in an industrial section of a big city, near a set of railroad tracks bordered by three-storied warehouses, all of them unlit. He edged his way to the end of the truck bed, looked both ways to see if the coast was clear, and then jumped to the ground.

He turned, ready to race toward the main street off to the left, when a voice stopped him.

"Hey you!"

Carter flushed and pivoted while a figure stepped into view on the driver's side of the truck. In the dark, the man's hair glowed white, like wisps of cotton candy at a ghostly carnival. Carter's stomach clenched in alarm when he saw the gun trained on his gut and the wicked smile blooming on the face of the man in front of him.

"Why, Mr. Greyson," Dan Williams drawled in his nasal tone. "What a surprise."

20

Arielle didn't hear from Carter for the remainder of that Tuesday. Even though they'd exchanged heated words early Tuesday morning, she hadn't expected him to drop out of her life altogether. Carter might be able to put aside the beautiful night they'd spent together, but she knew he wouldn't abandon the search for his bone marrow donor, and she didn't think he'd pursue Mack without her.

When the plasma truck stopped by that afternoon, Arielle asked the driver if he had any publications about donor programs. He was happy to supply her with a folder full of brochures about various programs, which were distributed to health care agencies in the hopes of enlarging their donor pool. Arielle thanked him and flipped through the brochures while she took a coffee break. At lunch she drove up to the university and perused the stacks at the Health Sciences Library for books on bone marrow disease research. She was interested in learning how Carter could have been physically transformed by a bone marrow transplant.

She didn't have time to read the library books and the brochures didn't provide much more information than that already given to her by Carter. However, she did come across an inspirational piece taken from a valedictory address written by a teenager who had survived the very same disease Carter had suffered. In the insightful words of the teenage boy, Arielle recognized the heart that Carter tried to hide from the world. Struck by the similarity in the two stories, and hoping she could somehow encourage Carter to open up to people, Arielle wrote a short note on a Post-it and stuck it to the booklet. Then she slipped it into a manila envelope to give to Carter the next time she saw him. No matter what happened, she knew they would see each other again, in some capacity.

By the time Arielle climbed into bed Tuesday night, she felt unusually alone, and wished the phone would ring just so she could hear Carter's voice. But the phone and her beeper remained silent. She fell asleep, chiding herself for waiting for a man to call her; such behavior wasn't typical for her.

Wednesday morning she put in a full day at the clinic, glad to have a busy day to keep Carter from her thoughts, and grateful that Dan Williams didn't show up for his usual morning coffee and leering session. Arielle worked until five and then popped down to the market to get some fresh fruit for dinner. On her way back up the hill, she returned to the clinic to retrieve a journal she'd forgotten on her desk.

"I thought you went home," Katie remarked, pulling on her coat as Arielle stepped into the clinic.

"I did, but I forgot something in my office."

"Well, I'm calling it a day. My better half and I are doing some last minute Christmas shopping tonight."

"Have fun." Arielle smiled as Katie rolled her eyes.

"Everyone else is gone, so be sure to lock up."

"I will. Bye." Arielle waved as she headed down the hall. She heard Katie close the front door of the clinic as she opened the door to her office. Arielle couldn't help but be reminded of the dead frog each time she entered the room, especially now that she was alone. She immediately cut off the workings of her overactive imagination. There would be many hours spent alone at the clinic in the months to come, and she couldn't allow herself to waste her valuable energy worrying about Native American voodoo. Arielle stepped boldly through the doorway, only to pause abruptly when she saw the shape of someone sitting in the gloom in a chair near her desk.

Arielle flipped on the light, her heart in her throat, and stared at the person who turned slightly to gaze at her from the side. In the chair sat an old woman, certainly a Native American, and most likely a street person judging by the look of her faded print dress, tattered old tennis shoes, and patched gray sweater. She wore her white hair in a simple braid down her back, and though she didn't appear to be dirty or ill, there was something slovenly in the set of her mouth.

Arielle kept her hand on the doorknob, wondering why the woman was in her office. Had she been a patient before? Arielle briefly inspected the woman and was sure she didn't recognize her. "May I help you?" she asked.

"I don't need help." The old woman turned in the chair to fully glance at her, and Arielle tried not to suck in a breath of surprise. The woman's mouth was deformed, with the lower lip hanging down in a slack loop, as though it had been cut, revealing the nearly toothless gums of her lower jaw. "I am here to help *you*," the old woman said. Her words came out in a muffled staccato, due to the strange lip and her lack of teeth.

Her words surprised Arielle, and she paused, trying to decide whether to step all the way into the room, or dash out of the clinic and call for help. She didn't like surprises, especially those that occurred after hours when she was alone at the clinic. Arielle studied the face of the woman more closely. Her skin was so wrinkled and dark it looked more like crazed pottery than flesh. And her eyes, once dark brown, gazed at her from behind milky blue cataracts. Arielle doubted the woman could see beyond basic shapes in light and dark, let alone find her way through the clinic unassisted.

"Did Katie tell you to wait for me here?" Arielle asked.

The woman shook her head and turned back around to face the desk. Arielle entered her office, confident now that the woman posed no physical threat. Arielle walked to her desk and picked up the forgotten journal, which she slipped into her briefcase. The old woman watched the movement of her hands and remained silent.

"You said you were here to help me." Arielle rested both her hands on the top of her briefcase. "What do you mean by that?"

"You seek the way to the island. I know of the way."

A chill raised the hairs on the back of Arielle's neck. "What island?" she asked, testing the woman.

"The island of the banishment."

Arielle ignored the way her heart beat furiously in her chest. She studied the old woman, wondering how she had found the clinic, much less her office, and how such a half-blind crone could possess the wherewithal to guide a person anywhere. Could she have been sent here by Reuven, to lead Arielle astray?

"There is not much time left," the old woman said. "The Wolf Moon rises tomorrow night."

"What do you mean, the Wolf Moon?"

"If you look at the moon tomorrow night, you will see the head of the wolf on the full moon." She drew a fingertip down an imaginary line in front of her. "This mystic moon comes only once every ten years. In the legends of my people, the Wolf Moon is a turning point, a time of separation or of joining, a time of beginnings or endings, a time of injustice or reparation."

Ten years ago, she'd been on the island with Mack. Certainly a great change had taken place then, just as the woman had said. Arielle thought of Mack and Reuven and then of Carter and herself. What was to transpire between them this time—a beginning or an ending? She couldn't make a logical guess.

"What does this mystic moon have to do with the island?"

"Everything. From tonight until tomorrow, great change can occur." The old woman struggled to her feet. "You must come with me, Leaf-on-the-Water."

Arielle froze. No one but Mack Shoalwater had ever called her Leaf-on-the-Water. She had divulged her special name to no one, not to her parents, and not even to Carter. How did this woman know her spirit name?

"What do you know about the island?" Arielle asked.

"All that needs to be known."

"Do you know of Mack Shoalwater? Is he alive?"

"Yes, but in danger. You must work to save him."

Arielle's heart leaped at the news that Mack was alive. "How can I help him?"

"You must reach him before the others. The storm has passed from the north, and now the others will seek him out and kill him."

"The others? Who?"

"You will soon see."

Arielle licked her lips. The old woman spoke more in riddles than in normal conversation. But Arielle didn't doubt the call to alarm, especially in regard to Mack. Still, she had one more question.

"What do you know about frogs with their lips sewn together?"

"It is witchcraft, used to bring death or misfortune."

"Someone left a dead frog on my desk. Do you know about that?"

"Ask Reuven Jaye," the old woman replied. "He is the one who would use witchcraft. But come, we must go."

"What do you want me to do?"

"You must get a boat. I will guide you to the island."

"Now? It's already dark."

"Yes. There is much danger."

"But how will we get there at night? The island is nearly impossible to find in the daylight."

"The path to the island is one of the heart, Leaf-on-the-Water, not of the eye."

Arielle frowned and stared at the old woman for a moment. If she hadn't already learned to trust Mack's philosophies, she would have thought the old woman was crazy. But over and over again Mack had proved to her that the mind was a weapon of unlimited strength and the heart a divining rod of unwavering accuracy. Still, she had trouble with the concept of a night trip with a half-blind woman, across a stretch of water whose depths had taken the lives of four friends and had nearly taken hers as well.

"I don't know." Arielle shook her head. "I doubt I can get a boat at this hour, or someone willing to take us." As soon as she raised the question, however, she knew whom to call: Ron Bennett. She'd put his business card in her wallet last Sunday and hadn't thrown it away yet.

"You will find a boat," the old woman said, nodding in complete confidence. "But we must hurry."

Arielle wished she shared the woman's certainty, but she couldn't allay her doubts. "I'll try a man I know," Arielle said, opening her briefcase. She retrieved Ron's card and dialed his number. To her relief, he answered. After a tense few minutes of convincing him she had a guide who could take them to the island even at night, she made arrangements to meet him in La Conner at seven o'clock. Then she dialed Carter's phone and let it ring until his answering machine kicked in. She left a message, telling him where she was headed and when she expected to return. Then she hung up the phone, wishing in more ways than one that Carter had been there. Not only would his company be welcome, she knew he would have wanted to share in Mack's rescue.

Disappointed, she grabbed her briefcase and lifted it off the desk.

"He is in danger, too," the old woman commented.

Arielle glanced at her sharply. "Who?"

"Two Wolves."

"Who is Two Wolves?"

"The man whose heart you carry inside you."

Arielle felt a flush flare across her cheeks. How did this woman know her innermost secrets? She hadn't told anyone of her newly blossoming love for Carter. And she had no way of knowing if Carter's spirit name was Two Wolves. He might not even be aware of his Indian name. But this old woman apparently saw everything with her haunting blind eyes.

"We'll take my car," Arielle said, holding open the door of her office and not about to talk any further about her relationship with Carter. "We're meeting someone with a boat at La Conner."

"Good. I knew you would go with me." The woman walked past her, her wide feet shuffling along the floor, and one gnarled hand stretched out in front of her like an antenna. Arielle watched her hobbling gait and wondered if she were foolishly endangering both their lives.

Just after eleven o'clock that night, the *Shangri-La* bucked through the current at the opening of a bay, and then pushed onward to another ring of land. Arielle stood at the wheel with the old woman and Ron Bennett, her eyes boring into the darkness, trying to locate a single landmark in the darkness that would tell her they'd reached Mack's island. She couldn't make out a thing in the gloom. Still, her heart surged into her throat and her senses roared to life as she smelled the fragrance so familiar to her—the pungent salty air laden with the sharp scent of cedar. Perhaps the old Saquinnish woman was right—this wasn't a path to be searched with the eye. Perhaps her spirit was shouting out a truth her eyes couldn't validate. Ahead of her was the island she'd left ten years ago—she was sure of it—the island and the man who had changed her life forever.

Arielle leaned forward, her hands clenched around the railing and her pulse racing. Though it was cold, she felt sweat forming beneath her parka.

"Is that it?" she asked, glancing at the old woman. "Is that the island?"

"Do you believe it is the island?"

"Yes!"

"Then it must be so."

"Don't you know?" Arielle stared at her. "I thought you knew the way."

For the first time, the woman smiled in a hideous expression, since her lower lip did nothing but hang as her upper lip raised the corners of her wide mouth. Arielle's confidence shifted at the smile.

"Oh, I know the way," the woman said. "But only through you, Leaf-on-the-Water. I have been listening to your spirit."

"As a guide?"

"Yes. Your spirit is connected to the heart of the wolf. The line between you is strong and will never be cut."

Arielle turned back to the rail, knowing the woman was correct. An unshakable familiarity tugged at her, pulling her toward the dark hump of land now directly ahead of them.

They motored through a low bank of clouds sitting on the surface of the water which concealed the shoreline. Ron commented that it was dangerous to navigate in such fog, for he couldn't see rocks sticking out of the water or deadheads that might be floating on the surface. If the boat hit either one, there'd be trouble. Arielle asked him to keep going, even if they had to continue at a slower speed, and she went forward with a walkie-talkie to watch for dangerous flotsam or reefs. Only her concern for Mack kept her from going out of her mind with fear of being in dangerous water.

A half-hour later she spotted Mack's meditation rock. Arielle jerked around. "That's it!" she shouted joyfully and then remembered to use the walkie-talkie. "That's the island!" she said into the mouthpiece. "I recognize that big rock."

Ron waved at her. Arielle returned to her post, hardly able to contain herself. She wanted to hurry, almost wanted to dive in and swim the rest of the way, but she knew the water was ice cold, too cold to withstand for more than a few minutes before hypothermia set in. She peered into the mist, straining to see evidence of Mack—a fire, a light in his shack, anything to sustain her hope that he was still on the island and still alive. But the mist roiled up the beach, shrouding the trees and rocks in grays and blacks. Besides, at this late hour Mack was probably asleep.

They dropped anchor and lowered the dinghy into the rippling waters of the bay. The old woman said she would stay behind, that she was too old to go climbing in and out of boats. Arielle clambered into the metal rowboat and sat down, while Ron took command of the oars. In the fog, their voices and the clanking noises of the oars in the locks seemed inordinately loud.

She didn't speak as Ron rowed to the shore, and she kept her hands clutched to the sides of the boat as it bobbed in the water. She'd never feel safe until her feet hit solid ground. Minutes later the dinghy scraped bottom and Ron stowed the oars. He got out and pulled the boat onto the sand as Arielle jumped out.

"Thanks, Ron," she said.

"Take the flashlight," he suggested, nodding toward the bow of the boat. "I'll be right behind you."

"Okay." Arielle scooped up the large plastic flashlight and switched it on. The beam barely penetrated the thick fog, but Arielle set out eagerly, her feet slipping in the loose sand and pebbles.

"Mack!" she called. She glanced down and saw the remains of a recent fire in the same spot where they had often eaten dinner and talked. At least someone had been here lately. With a small catch in her throat, she noticed all evidence of her lean-to was gone, as if she'd never been there. Arielle hurried past the fire and across the sand to Mack's plywood shack, which was more crooked and shabby than she remembered.

She rapped on the board wall beside his crude plywood door. "Mack, are you in there?" she asked. "It's me, Arielle!" She pounded again, louder this time. After she received no response, she glanced back at Ron, who shrugged. Arielle pushed open the door and stepped in, shining her light into the small cluttered quarters of Mack's shed, and was shocked to see Mack standing in the middle of the room with four white men. One of them, dressed in a blue ski jacket, had a gun. The other three, though seemingly unarmed, were beefy enough to pose a threat to anyone's safety. Someone turned on a powerful flashlight, blinding her.

"Mack!" she cried. After a moment, her eyes adjusted to the light, and she could see his hands were bound in front of him, and that one of the men had ahold of his bad arm. Surely, the rough hold caused Mack considerable discomfort, although the pain didn't show on his face. His hair, once raven black, was now lightly streaked with gray. He seemed to have lost a bit of weight, but his physique was still strong and straight, as virile as ever. Mack said nothing in the way of a greeting and didn't even appear surprised to see her. He just stood there, his eyes glittering at her in silence, but then she saw him give a nearly imperceptible nod.

"Who are they?" the man in the blue jacket demanded of Mack, jerking his head toward Arielle.

Mack didn't answer.

"Want another broken arm, chief?" Blue Jacket asked with a snarl. "It can be arranged."

Mack, taller than any of the men around him, stared down his nose at the man with the gun, his bearing so full of pride and so lacking in fear that he easily belittled his captor. The familiar expression made Arielle's heart surge full of love for him.

Then Arielle saw the man in blue aim his gun at Mack's good arm, and she lunged forward. "Don't you dare, you bastard!" she shouted.

Blue Jacket's glance darted her way and he whirled to point the gun at her chest, stopping her in her tracks. "Hold it right there, lady. Chief's got a little journey to take."

"Where?"

"None of your damned business." He waved the gun toward a carton of canned goods. "Get over there. You too, grandpa."

Arielle wished they'd had the foresight to bring a gun with them. But they'd never expected to run into anyone but Mack on the island. Her only choice was to do what the man said. Arielle moved to stand beside the carton while Ron stepped all the way into the shack and joined her.

"Tie 'em up," Blue Jacket commanded. One of his companions moved forward and wrapped nylon twine around her wrists and then did the same to Ron.

"You boys go easy on Dr. Scott," Ron said. "You hear me?"

"Dr. Scott?" Blue Jacket raked her with his cold gaze. "Dr. Arielle Scott?"

Arielle withstood his scrutiny, sure that the revelation of her identity wouldn't bode well for her.

"You Arielle Scott?" he questioned, putting his face too close to hers. She arched back but didn't give him an answer.

"Yank on the chief's arm, McAllen."

Arielle watched Mack's captor twist his crippled arm backward. Mack grimaced in pain but didn't cry out.

"Okay!" she retorted, her eyes blazing. "What if I am?"

"So that little froggie didn't scare you off, eh?"

"You left the frog on my desk?"

"Yeah. For the boss." Blue Jacket sidled closer. "And the boss'll be really happy to get his hands on you. Two birds with one stone as they say. And geezer makes three."

"What are you talking about?" Ron demanded.

"Shut up, grandpa!" Blue Jacket backhanded Ron with a savage slap. Arielle gasped, appalled that Ron's offer to help had plunged him into danger, and prayed they wouldn't hurt him any further. She glared at the man with the gun, while Ron recovered from the blow, his blue eyes flaring with anger.

"I'll cooperate if you let him go," she said.

Blue Jacket sized her up and then stared at Ron. "Why should I?"

"He doesn't know anything. He just brought me here in his boat."

"Innocent bystander, eh?"

"Yes. He doesn't know who you are. Please, just let him go."

"Yeah, sure, Doc." Blue Jacket turned to the man nearest him. "Tie the guy up. He's staying for a while."

"You can't just leave him here!" Arielle exclaimed.

"Why not. He'll make a good dinner for some bear," Blue Jacket replied, heading toward the door. "Come on boys."

One of the men grabbed Arielle by the arm and yanked her toward the door. She wrenched around to look at Ron Bennett, whose feet and hands were tied. They pushed him to the floor and then knocked him unconscious with a swift crack to his skull.

"Ron!" she cried.

"That's enough, Doc!" Blue Jacket shoved her in the back, sending her sprawling toward the door.

Arielle staggered out the door to the beach, wondering how to get word to the old woman still aboard the *Shangri-La*. There was a chance the woman could help Ron. But how could the crone get to shore, as old as she was and without the dinghy?

Mack came up beside her as they trudged down the beach in the opposite direction of the *Shangri-La*. Arielle glanced at his stoic expression and kept walking, wondering where they were being taken and what would happen to them. She longed to talk to Mack, to share their stories of the last ten years, to tell him about Carter and Reuven. But talking would have to wait, as would the huge hug she wanted to give him.

Then, out of the fog materialized a sleek white ship sitting in the bay, much larger than Ron's 40-foot craft, and much more modern in design. Lights blinked on, displaying high-tech radar equipment and communication dishes. It looked more like a military vessel than a pleasure craft.

She must have sucked in her breath, because the man with the gun glanced at her and smiled. "Nice little number, eh?" he commented. "That's Mr. D's hovercraft. Fastest sonofabitch on the West Coast."

Arielle made no reply, but wondered who the mysterious Mr. D. was, and what connection he had to Mack and her.

A launch waited at the edge of the water. Blue Jacket's men shoved them into the craft and told them to sit. Then the small boat took off, churning up a wake as it zipped out to the awaiting ship. As they pulled alongside, a man stepped out of the main cabin and sauntered to the rail, his form backlit by the lights behind him. His hair glowed in a wild nimbus around his large head, and without seeing his features, Arielle knew exactly who Mr. D. was.

Dan Williams.

21

Evaline drove the old Ford down the lane toward Salmon Point, careful to keep an even speed in the gravel and freezing mud, when what she really wanted to do was step on the gas and roar to the village as quickly as possible. She hoped her father wouldn't notice his car missing from the casino parking lot, but even more so, she hoped what she'd overheard him say on the phone wasn't true—that Carter Greyson was being "kept out of trouble" at the Wolf House on Salmon Point.

Around midnight, she'd gone to the casino to take her father a late-night snack of warm apple pie that she'd just baked, wishing he'd tell her what had been troubling him for the last few days. She worried about the chilly rift that had developed between them since she'd shared information with Arielle Scott, and wanted to make amends. Not having her father to talk to had

- 289 -

opened a dark hole in her life, for he was her single remaining relative.

When she'd approached his office door, she'd heard his voice oddly hushed as he talked to someone on the phone. The tone of the conversation induced her to pause at the door and listen for a moment. That's when she'd heard him mention Carter being kept out of trouble.

Kept out of trouble from what? And against his will? Apprehension and hurt clogged Evaline's throat, because she sensed that whatever her father was involved in was not honorable. She didn't want to believe her father could be involved in anything illegal, and the only way to dispel her fears was to search the village for signs of Carter and get back to the casino before closing.

In any other circumstance she would have had faith in her father, would have waited until he got home, and then talked to him about what she'd overheard. But this incident included Carter Greyson, the only other man in the world who meant something to her, and to whom she owed a debt. If by some remote chance he was at the Wolf House, suffering or being held against his will, she was honor-bound to help him.

Hating every minute of doubt that dragged by, Evaline drove toward Salmon Point, and a half-hour later rolled into the gravel lot that marked the end of the road. She parked beside a clump of sea pine, grabbed the flashlight from under the seat, and then turned off the Ford. Shining the light on the glove box, she unlocked the compartment and took out the pistol she knew her father kept there. The gun slipped comfortably into her hand, the cool curve of metal and wood familiar to her, for she had spent a considerable amount of time at target practice. Never again would she walk through the woods without a gun to defend herself—from wolf or man. She checked the safety and the rounds in the chamber and then got out of the car.

Wind plastered her jacket against her body as she faced the deserted houses. In the darkness the village was steeped in silver and shadow. As a child she had visited the village when the tribe had held rituals in the ancient clan houses. But those visits had been made during the daylight, and everyone had made certain they were long gone from the houses when the sun went down. Now, no one came out to Salmon Point, since interest in tribal rituals had waned years ago. What few rituals were practiced these days were done at the much more modern tribal center.

No one came up here anymore. Even the teenagers, who sought out places to drink and neck, avoided the village, probably for the very reason she wished she could jump back into the car and drive away. The place gave her the creeps.

Too many Saquinnish had died here. The first deaths had occurred in the 1840s when smallpox had decimated the population. Then ten years later, according to the stories of the tribe, an altercation had arisen between white fur traders and the Saquinnish. The "Boston Men" had come ashore with their guns and killed all who didn't flee into the forest. The adult males remained behind to stand and protect their families, and none of the warriors survived the massacre. With so many slaughtered, it was said their bodies bloodied the water red. After the attack, no one had lived in the winter village again, for it was considered an accursed place.

Shuddering, Evaline hurried along the beach toward the row of houses. She could barely force herself to explore the old buildings, but she kept on walking. She had to see if Carter was imprisoned in the Wolf House, although she wasn't sure what she'd do if she found him. Her father might have a good reason for keeping Carter out of the tribe's affairs, and she might be doing more harm than good by sticking her nose into the business of the elders. Still, Carter had come to her rescue at the casino, and she couldn't deny that he occupied a special but secret place in her heart. She had to know if he were safe at least, and then she'd confront her father before deciding what to do. Evaline went past the first houses, shining the light on the fronts to check the crest markings. When she got to the last house in the row, she recognized the faded wolf design painted around the door.

Carefully she walked up the stairs, wondering if the old cedar planks would hold her weight. The steps and veranda were rickety, but still intact. She ducked through the round opening at the front of the house and stepped in, shining the flashlight on the floor in front of her. Inside, she was surprised to find that part of the perimeter ledge had collapsed. She jumped down the few feet to the lower cooking level and made a complete circle with the flashlight, so she could see the entire floor of the empty lodge.

"Carter?" she called out, her voice sounding puny and ineffective in the huge cedar building. She stepped across the sandy floor. "Carter?" Evaline paused, her ears straining to hear over the wind whistling in the roof planks high above her head. She thought she heard something at the back of the lodge. Visions of ghosts rippled through her mind, and the possibility of a bear living in the old house slowed her steps. The sound seemed to have come from behind the wood screen at the back of the lodge. In order to explore the space behind the screen, she would have to slip through the round hole at its base. What if she came face to face with a bear or cougar sleeping within? Either animal would fiercely protect its den, and she of all people knew well the injuries a wild animal could inflict.

"Carter," she called, edging toward the screen. "Are you in there?" Once again she heard a faint response. Her pulse quickened and she ventured close to the hole in the screen, her imagination and fear of animals nearly getting the better of her. Five feet from the screen, she stopped and tried to train the light on the hole, but her hand shook too much to hold the flashlight steady. Her palms grew slippery with sweat, and she could feel the heat of her body simmering inside her jacket as fear immobilized her.

She remembered the snarl of the wolf ten years ago as it had leapt out of the shrubbery, knocking her to the ground, slathering and ripping at her face and neck. Evaline's vision darkened around the periphery of her eyes, and she realized she was about to faint, just as she had done in her father's office during the assault a few days ago. She couldn't faint now. She had to get hold of herself. What if Carter Greyson sat behind the screen, bound and gagged—or heaven forbid, injured? The worst thing she could do for him was to fall into a dead faint. She couldn't think of herself at a time like this; she had to concentrate on Carter.

Summoning all her courage, Evaline stepped toward the screen and trained the light as well as the pistol on the opening at the base. Her perspiration turned cold and clammy. Beyond the screen she could see an empty chamber, formed by the walls of the lodge and the back of the screen. Neither Carter nor a bear was anywhere to be seen. She ducked through the opening and stood up straight on the other side. This was the space where the leader of the clan and his wife had slept and kept their valuables—which would have been considerable, for the entire Wolf Clan had paid tribute to them, giving part of every hunt, fishing trip, or trading expedition to the chief of the clan. Nothing remained now to speak of the wealth of the ancient Saquinnish chiefs, except for the magnificent house posts and the screen behind which she stood. The only sign of a contemporary presence was a forgotten roll of duct tape sitting in the corner.

"Carter?" she repeated, wondering where he could possibly be. Other than the tape, the walls and floor around her were completely bare.

The muffled sound came again, from somewhere near her feet. Evaline glanced down at the plank floor. Could someone be hidden under the boards? She trained the light on the floor. Each plank had been cut to an exact length and fitted together snugly, leaving barely a crack between them. She moved aside, set the pistol on the floor, and tried to find a way to lift one of the boards. As soon as she moved, she noticed the plank she'd been standing upon raised a fraction, enough to grab the end. She set the flashlight on the floor and bent to lift the board, sliding the heavy cedar aside.

She was not surprised to see Carter lying on the earth below. His ankles and wrists were tightly bound, and a cloth was tied around his mouth, pulling back his lips into a maniacal smile. He must have pushed up the plank with his feet.

"Carter!" she cried, crouching down on hands and knees. With his eyes, he implored her to do something. She reached down and loosened the gag.

"Thank God!" Carter gasped, licking his lips. "Evaline!"

"What are you doing here?" she asked, grabbing the flashlight and running the beam over his body to see if he was hurt. "Who put you here?"

"Evil piano movers."

"What?"

"Some guys who stole a house post from this lodge. I found out about it and they brought me back here to get rid of me."

"Who? Who brought you here?"

"Listen, Evaline, untie me," Carter said, raising his arms toward her. "I've been here since Tuesday night."

Evaline shied back, uncertain what she should do or where her loyalties lay. She hated to refuse Carter's request, since he'd been imprisoned for over twenty-four hours and must be frozen stiff, but she didn't know if she should help him just yet.

"Evaline?" His voice cracked in disbelief at her hesitation. She thought the sound would break her heart.

"Carter, I don't know if I should untie you."

"Why in the hell not? You can't leave me here, dammit!"

"Who did this?"

"Some guys who work for a man named Dan Williams. He has something to do with your father."

"My father?"

"Yes. Do you have any reason to suspect your father is involved with the theft of the house posts?"

"Of course not!" Evaline nearly shouted the denial, she so vehemently believed in her father's innocence. Yet her protest sounded far too strident, even to her own ears. "He'd never steal from the tribe."

"Then you have nothing to worry about." He licked his lips again. "Help me get out of here, Evaline, please."

She glanced at his hands and feet, and then at his handsome face, so sharply defined by the beam of her flashlight. She would do almost anything for this man, even go behind her father's back for the first time in her life. Still, she hesitated.

"Why do you say my father has some connection to this Williams character?"

"His phone number was found in Williams's office. Somebody knew the posts were here and guided others to the village, or committed the actual theft and sold the posts to Williams afterward."

"Mack Shoalwater was the one who did the stealing."

"He's not the one I saw in the truck that brought me here last night. Mack couldn't have taken that post. He's been banished for more than a decade. And *his* name wasn't the one found in Dan Williams's Rolodex, either."

Evaline blinked and looked down, her thoughts churning and her heart in turmoil. She had never been in a position like this before, when she had to make a decision outside the aegis of her father, if not in direct conflict with him. The Saquinnish tradition was not to act alone, but to seek counsel from elders and act as a unit.

"Carter, I want to help you, but I'm not sure—"

"For Pete's sake, Evaline," Carter sputtered. "I'm freezing! Do you think I deserve to be here, tied up like this, left to die?"

"No, but—"

"Do you think I'm a criminal or involved in any way with the theft of Saquinnish artifacts?"

"No." Evaline's thoughts swirled, blotting out the voice in her head that insisted she remain loyal to her father and her people.

"I'm going to freeze to death down here," Carter added. "Do you want that to happen?"

"Of course not."

"Then help me, dammit." She glanced down at his face—the face she longed to kiss, to touch, and to gaze at more than anything in the world. She couldn't deny him. She couldn't refuse Carter Greyson anything he asked of her.

Evaline moved another plank aside and then stopped, tilting her head at the sound of a human voice outside.

"What's the matter?" Carter demanded.

"I hear someone coming." Evaline panicked, not knowing whether to help Carter scramble out of his prison or stuff the gag back in his mouth. No matter who approached the Wolf House—friend or enemy—it would be more prudent to pretend Carter hadn't been found, than to help him out the back way at the risk of him being caught and her being implicated in the escape.

"Sorry," she whispered. "I'm going to put the boards back, Carter. Don't make a sound."

"The hell I won't!"

"It might be Williams coming back. Or my father."

"Evaline!" Carter sputtered. "You've got to get me out of here!"

"I will. Trust me."

She hated to slide the plank back in place over his ashen face, but she did it anyway, averting her gaze and her thoughts from the sight of his stricken expression. Then she picked up the pistol and pivoted to shine the light on the back of the lodge. There she saw the wide plank that covered the opening hole of the back door. The voices outside grew louder and she could hear feet clumping up the stairs to the front of the lodge.

Evaline snapped off the flashlight, let her eyes adjust to the dark for a moment, moved aside the plank and then slipped through the back opening, her heart pounding out of control. She leaned against the side of the house, her small frame half-swallowed by the dried weeds growing in the sand. She'd wait near the door and listen, and if anyone threatened Carter, she'd intervene. If anyone ventured to the back of the lodge, she'd sink into the waist-high grass and disappear. No one would see her small shape in the shadows. For once, Evaline was grateful for her petite frame.

Moments later a ragged sliver of light sliced through the crooked planks at the back of the house and into the weeds beside her. Whoever had come to the lodge must have brought a heavy-duty flashlight. Cautiously, Evaline turned and peered through a crack, and was shocked to see a whole group of people standing on her side of the screen, among them Arielle Scott and a tall man she guessed was Mack Shoalwater, from what she remembered of him as a teenager. He bore an uncanny resemblance to Carter, both in his face and physique, though his hair was streaked with silver and not as thick. Arielle and Mack stood with their hands tied in front of them and gags across their mouths. Arielle's eyes flashed with suspicion and anger above her gag. Evaline gazed at her a moment, marveling at the lack of fear in the doctor's expression, and wished she had the guts to face the world head-on as Arielle seemed to do.

Evaline's gaze traveled over the rest of the group, dismayed to spot her father standing to the side of four white men, one of whom had wild blond hair and an expensive leather coat that reached past his knees. Evaline put a hand on the plank beside her, wondering what role her father played in the strange assortment of people in the clan house. Two of the men held powerful flashlights that lit up the entire lodge, and all of them carried sacks that appeared to be full of something heavy.

"Go ahead and get the two poles in the front," the man in the leather coat instructed his men. "And make it snappy. I want to be out of here in an hour."

One of the men gave a flashlight to his boss and then he and his companions ducked through the hole in the screen and trotted to the front of the lodge. Evaline could see them through the round opening of the screen, like peering through a porthole, and watched them run to a house post carved in the shape of a wolf, a man, and a frog. The men set to work on the left post, dislodging it from its corner position and struggling to lower it to its side using a block and tackle they'd thrown over the support beams above. A cold flush passed through Evaline as she witnessed the same crime for which Mack had been so long banished.

"Where's Greyson?" the blond man asked her father.

"Down there." Reuven pointed at the floor where Carter lay bound beneath the planks. "Where nobody'd look for him."

"What about these two?" the blond man said, jerking his head toward Arielle and Mack Shoalwater.

"What about them?" Reuven replied. He pushed up his glasses. "I thought you were going to take care of them."

"Me?" The blond man laughed unpleasantly. "You expect me to do all the dirty work? I've gone to enough trouble for my share. No sir, Jaye, this is your problem. You messed up, you take care of it."

"Messed up?"

"If you'd taken care of the big chief here when I told you to ten years ago, we wouldn't be having these complications."

Reuven fell silent and Evaline stared at him, her heart crying out from the words that implicated her father in the house post thefts, as well as the persecution of an innocent man, and perhaps the death of that old fisherman for which Mack had been blamed. Her father stood there, small and old, his shoulders rounded, his body spare and bent, looking ineffective and whipped in the presence of the taller white man. Had Reuven aged over the years and she just hadn't noticed? Or had the transformation occurred in the split second it had taken for her respect of her father to shatter? A sheen of tears dimmed Evaline's vision as her sheltered world—so dependent upon her seemingly loyal, upstanding father—suddenly spun off track.

"So it's up to you, Jaye," the blond man said. "But do it this time, and do it right."

"Maybe I'll just leave them here," Reuven said. "No one ever comes out here."

"I wouldn't count on it. Somebody's been here since we took that second post. They broke through the platform."

Reuven glanced at the front opening and then back. "What if I paid you, Dan?"

"Paid me?"

"To take care of them."

Dan surveyed Arielle and Mack, his eyes cold and calculating. "What do you think they're worth?"

"Everything. I just want the money for the second post. You can have my share for the ones you're taking tonight."

"Hmmm." Dan paused and rolled his eyes toward the ceiling. "That wouldn't be a bad night's work."

"I want out, Dan. I just want out."

"Getting cold feet, Jaye?"

"I'm an old man. I'm not cut out for this kind of stuff anymore. You take them. Dump them in the Sound. I don't care. I don't want to know." Reuven waved his hand toward Mack and Arielle and walked toward the circular door of the screen.

"No!" Evaline whispered, a sob in her throat. She couldn't believe her father could sentence people to death like that, with a cursory wave of his hand. She stood watching the commotion through the door of the screen, while her father and the man named Dan ducked through to oversee the theft of the posts. Evaline took the chance to slip back into the lodge.

As she darted across the floor toward the doctor, she saw Arielle's eyebrows raise in surprise. With trembling hands, she pulled the tape from Arielle's mouth.

"Get Mack's knife," Arielle whispered, nodding toward the tall man standing beside her. "It's in his front pocket."

Blushing, Evaline shoved her hand into the front pocket of Mack's jeans and found a penknife. She pulled it out and used it to cut the rope around his wrists and then turned to cut Arielle loose. Out of the corner of her eye she saw Mack pulling the tape off his mouth. Even with all the others to worry about, she was highly aware of his looming presence, as if his spirit were more powerful and imposing than anyone's in the lodge.

"Let's get Carter," Arielle said softly, kneeling on the floor. "How do we get him out?"

Carter apparently heard her, for he pushed up the plank as he had done for Evaline. Mack and Arielle lifted off the boards while Evaline stood by the door, her pistol in her hand and her divided loyalties cracking her soul in two. She should be helping her father, but instead she was assisting the white doctor and two men who looked like Saquinnish people but who were not true members of her tribe.

"Carter!" Arielle breathed as she cut his bonds and helped him out of his prison.

Evaline turned to look as Carter climbed up to join the others.

22

Arielle watched as Carter and Mack took silent measure of each other. No one could miss the resemblance between the two men, especially when they stood face-to-face. Mack's expression was a mask of inscrutable control as his dark eyes traveled over the younger man, and he neither smiled nor raised a brow in surprise. Carter, however, still hadn't regained his color. Arielle wasn't sure if he had paled in astonishment at seeing Mack or from his ordeal of being bound and gagged under the Wolf House.

She was anxious to hear what Carter and Mack would say to each other, but there was no time to talk. In fact, there was no time to do anything before Dan and Reuven headed back to the room behind the screen. Over the noise of the men taking down the house posts, she could hear Dan's voice getting louder as he and Evaline's father walked back toward the rear of the lodge.

"Might as well take the others back to the ship, since I'm going to be disposing of them." Dan's nasal tone easily carried to the four people hiding behind the wooden screen.

"What about the money?" Reuven asked.

"Come to the office in three days and I'll have the cash ready, just like last time."

"I thought you said you'd pay me tonight."

"What—and carry that amount of cash around? No way. Come down to Seattle on Friday and you'll get it then."

While they talked, Mack stole across the floor to stand beside the hole in the screen. Carter seemed to guess his intent and moved to join him on the other side. Evaline and Arielle stepped out of sight, pressing their backs against the screen so that whoever came through the hole wouldn't see them immediately.

Reuven ducked through first. Mack let him straighten and then he grabbed him with his good arm, covering his mouth and dragging him soundlessly against him. Dan was still talking about the sale of the house posts as he passed through the hole.

Carter swooped down on Dan, in the same way that Mack had pinned Reuven. And though Dan was taller than Carter, he was too surprised to react before Evaline aimed her gun at his midsection to eliminate any thoughts of resistance. Arielle picked up the discarded roll of duct tape, ripped off a piece, and pressed it over Dan's mouth, deriving a sense of satisfaction in muzzling the bastard. Then she taped Reuven's mouth and tied both men with the ends of rope that had formerly imprisoned her and Mack.

"Now what?" Evaline whispered.

"We need a phone to call the police," Arielle mused. "And I bet Dan has one."

Dan dashed toward the hole in the screen, but Carter shoved him back out of view and suggested that Arielle unbutton his coat and search for a cellular phone while Carter held him. Arielle scowled. She had no desire to make close contact with Dan, especially after her run-in with him at his office, but she had no alternative given the circumstances. She put the roll of duct tape on the floor and then straightened. She unfastened Dan's coat and soon found a slim phone tucked in the chest pocket, as well as a handgun in a holster slung around his chest. This she removed and gave to Mack, who stood near her elbow. Now there were two of them with weapons against three of Dan's men, who probably all carried guns. If it came to a standoff, they might be able to defend themselves long enough for help to arrive.

Arielle turned to Evaline. "What's the number for the tribal police?"

Evaline glanced at Arielle and then at her father, her features contorting with indecision. Reuven hung his head and didn't look at anyone, including his daughter, and gave no sign that he'd heard what they were talking about.

Shaking her head slowly, Evaline whispered the number and then tightened her grip around the handle of the gun, concentrating on a singular task so she wouldn't fall apart.

Arielle dialed the number and spoke in low tones to the dispatcher, who promised to send a unit out immediately.

Arielle turned off the phone and glanced at Dan. His eyes, cold as steel, narrowed with hate, and she knew she'd made a dangerous enemy. A dead frog with sutured lips was far less unnerving than the venomous glint she saw in Dan's eyes.

While they waited for the police, Arielle stood near the door of the screen and watched Dan's men drag the house posts across the floor to the hole in the north side of the lodge. She crouched at the screen opening, observing their progress and hoping they wouldn't finish their job before the police arrived. After about ten minutes, she heard a motor turn over and a vehicle drive toward the side of the lodge. At first she thought the police had driven up, but realized it was far too soon to expect them. Then, by piecing together snippets of comments made by the men, she deduced someone had backed a truck up to the broken north wall.

The minutes dragged by. No one spoke behind her, and she was aware of their intense gazes glued to the hole in the screen. Arielle glanced at her watch. Fifteen minutes had elapsed since the call to the police. Surely they'd be coming soon. When she'd driven out to Salmon Point a few days ago, the trip had only taken about a half-hour. Arielle forced herself to remain perfectly still and continued to watch the men working with the posts. She looked at her watch again. Only twenty minutes had gone by!

To her consternation, Arielle saw the man in the blue jacket break away from the others and stride toward the screen. She scrambled to her feet and stepped aside so he couldn't see her looking out. He stopped at the edge of the perimeter ledge.

"Hey, Mr. D," he called out. "We're all set to go."

Arielle exchanged worried glances with Carter and Mack. Carter made a pantomime of taking off the tape and Mack raised his gun to Dan's temple, while Arielle reached up to pull back the tape.

"Mr. D, you hear me?" the man asked.

Dan glared at her, refusing to answer his henchman. Then Mack jabbed him harder with the end of the gun.

"I'll be right there," Dan said through gritted teeth.

"Okay, see you at the truck."

As soon as the man in the blue jacket turned to leave, Arielle pushed the tape back on Dan's mouth.

Just then, they heard shouting at the front of the lodge.

"The cops!" somebody yelled. A moment later the man in the blue jacket barreled through the screen opening, scrambling into the chamber on his hands and knees.

"Freeze!" Mack demanded.

The man in the blue jacket paused, jerking his head up in surprise. "Boss!" he sputtered when he took in the situation. He rose to his knees, gaping at Dan and then at the others. "The cops are here!"

"Good," Arielle replied, reaching for the roll of tape. "Now shut up and sit down."

Just before three A.M., Evaline Jaye drove Arielle, Mack and Carter to the marina. Arielle had told them about Ron being left for dead on the island, and about the old woman marooned on the *Shangri-La*. Evaline, being the last of the Wolf Clan to know the secret of the currents and the way through the veil of mist, had offered to take the men out to the island. She had the spare ring of her father's keys, one of which would gain them entrance to his fishing boat.

One of the elders volunteered to give Arielle a ride to the La Conner marina, where she'd left her car. She couldn't go out to the island because she had to report to work at the Pike Place clinic in a few hours. But she promised to return after her shift to get Mack and Carter.

Arielle watched Evaline and Mack pull in the lines of the boat, and Carter climb up to the bridge. The tribal police had agreed to let Mack go, realizing he was innocent of the plot to steal the house posts, both in the past and the present. Their only request was that he stay in the area until the trial was over, in case they needed to ask him questions. After Reuven's complete confession of guilt—including his part in the house post theft, the death of the fisherman, and the framing of Mack Shoalwater—he had been taken to the tribal jail on the reservation, and Dan and his men were driven to the county seat of Bellingham where they would be held in jail until bail was set the next day.

Tired and worried that the adventure still wasn't quite over, Arielle watched Reuven's boat chug out of the small marina and into the predawn gloom. She still hadn't talked to Mack yet, and was anxious to hear what he'd been through in the last ten years. She also wanted to clear the air with Carter.

Carter waved at her from the wheel and she waved back, her heart swelling with tenderness and concern for him. What would happen between them? The search for Mack had brought her and Carter together, but now that Mack had been found, Carter might fade from her life forever. He hadn't said a word about his feelings for her, and perhaps didn't harbor strong emotions for her. Perhaps he had taken her to bed out of sheer hunger and loneliness. What their lovemaking had meant to Arielle might have meant something entirely different to Carter.

Would he come back to her after this was all over? Would he find peace within himself, enough to let him live a full life? And what of Mack? Arielle was dying to talk to her old friend. She waited until she could no longer make out Carter's shape, and then she turned to the tribal elder standing beside her.

"Ready to go, Dr. Scott?" he asked.

"Yes." Though she was weary to the bone, she gave him a quick smile and got in his pickup. Country and western Christmas carols twanged from the radio. After exchanging a few pleasantries with her companion, they both fell silent and the music swirled around her, in an irresistible lullaby. Arielle's eyelids grew heavy, until she couldn't fight off the sweetness of sleep that rose up around her in the warm cab of the truck.

Snow blanketed the reservation as Evaline brought the boat into the marina late in the afternoon. Darkness was already descending over the mid-December day, but kids on inner tubes and pieces of plastic were still sliding down the hill across from the cafe, laughing and shouting. Once the sound might have buoyed her spirits, but now all laughter seemed a mockery to her. Though she was glad that Arielle's world was in good shape—Carter was safe, Mack exonerated and Carter's friend, Ron Bennett, rescued from the island—her own world had collapsed.

Tired and depressed, Evaline watched Carter and Mack secure the boat, and then they walked together down the dock, toward the cafe where Arielle had agreed to meet them. Mack carried a bag containing his few valued possessions, and quietly took in the sight of the snow-covered reservation around him. Evaline noticed a tenseness between Mack and Carter, as if they had things to say to each other but had had no opportunity for private conversation. Neither of them had spoken more than a handful of words during the entire trip to the island and back. Perhaps at the cafe, they'd have a chance to talk. Though Carter had invited Evaline to grab a bite with them, she intended to beg off, to give them the chance to be alone. She was too distraught to be hungry anyway, and she definitely would not be good company.

She was surprised to see the green Miata on the street in front of the cafe, for she hadn't expected Arielle until later. Evaline noticed the car was still free of snow, and guessed Arielle hadn't been there long.

"She must have gotten off early," Carter remarked.

"Maybe the clinic closed early," Evaline ventured.

"Maybe."

A bell tinkled above the door when Mack held it open for the others to walk through into the cafe. Evaline glanced at the crowded room, recognizing every face. Many of the customers turned away and made no greeting to her, which led her to believe that news of her father had already traveled through the reservation. Perhaps, however, they were too busy gawking at Mack Shoalwater, whose return from the island had caused quite a stir. Blushing, Evaline stumbled through the crowd, glad to see Arielle stand up at a table near the window and smile at her.

"Thank God you're back!" Arielle exclaimed. She looked as if she wanted to throw her arms around them all and give them a hug. Instead, she motioned toward the table. "Come on in and sit down, have some coffee."

Arielle's eyes sparkled and Evaline noticed her joyful glance kept landing on Carter, who sat down beside her. Mack lowered to a chair next to Evaline.

"Did you find Ron?" Arielle asked, pouring them coffee from a plastic carafe on the table.

"Yes, we did," Carter answered, pushing a mug toward Evaline. "He was okay. A bit stiff and sore, but okay. He took off down the coastline for La Conner. I wrote him a check for his trouble, but he wouldn't take it, the bull-headed so-and-so."

"What about the old woman?"

"Funny thing, she wasn't there."

"What do you mean?"

"She vanished," Mack stated. Then he sipped his coffee and stared out the window, his silence like a black wall between Evaline's shoulder and his own. Evaline knew he probably bore a grudge against her for being the daughter of the man who had imprisoned him, and his coldness was the harbinger of what likely would come from the rest of her people. Her heart couldn't bear being shunned for a loss of honor as well as for her scarred face.

Before they had a chance to talk further, they were interrupted by a beeping noise. Arielle grimaced and checked her pager.

"Excuse me," she said, rising. "I'll be right back."

After Arielle left them to find a phone, silence descended upon the table. Carter perused the menu and Mack stared out the window, his breathing strong and steady. Evaline couldn't stand another minute of sitting in his stonelike presence.

"Mr. Shoalwater," she began, her voice quavering.

He turned and leveled his intense gaze upon her, and for a moment Evaline forgot what she was going to say. Then she swallowed and forced herself to continue.

"I just want to tell you that I'm sorry."

Mack's eyes glittered. "Sorry?" he repeated harshly.

Evaline nearly wilted at the tone in his voice, but she commanded her spirit to be brave and face the man who had suffered such a terrible wrong at the hands of her father. With Reuven in jail, it was now up to her to offer apologies. "I'm so sorry for what you've been through. If there's anything I can—"

"Evaline," Mack interrupted, putting his coffee cup down on the table. "Are you a Christian?"

His question surprised her, but she stammered out a quick reply. "Of course I am."

"Well, I'm not. I don't believe the sins of fathers are visited upon their sons and daughters."

A maelstrom of confusion and relief swept through her. "Pardon?" she choked.

"I don't hold you responsible, Evaline. And don't you shoulder guilt that doesn't belong to you."

"But my father was—"

"Your father had me banished. Not you. You have done much in the last two days to help us. And I am grateful to you."

Evaline gaped at him, unable to speak. She hadn't expected such words from Mack Shoalwater, not after what he had been through.

"We all are grateful, Evaline," Carter put in.

At that moment, Arielle returned to the table. Evaline glanced up at her and instantly knew something was wrong. Apparently, so did Carter. He stood up.

"What's the matter, Ari?" he asked.

"There's an emergency at the reservation clinic. And the physician in charge just slid off the road in the snow and sprained his arm. Somebody knew I was here and the clinic paged me. I've got to go."

"Do you want us to wait for you here?"

"If you would." Arielle reached into her purse. "I'll call as soon as I know anything." She pulled out a manila envelope and gave it to Carter. "Here's something you might want to look at while you're waiting. I've had it for a few days, hoping I'd have a chance to give it to you."

Carter looked up in surprise as he took the packet.

"It's some medical information you might find interesting," she added.

"Ari, do you want me to come with you?" Evaline asked.

Arielle smiled kindly at her. "Thanks, but no. You should go home, Evaline. You look exhausted."

Evaline tried to smile, but felt fatigue and anguish pulling down her already distorted mouth.

Arielle touched her shoulder. "Thanks for taking Mack and Carter to the island, Evaline—for everything. We owe our lives to you."

"I was glad to help."

"See you soon. On Saturday when I'm up for my regular rounds?"

Evaline nodded and watched Carter walk Arielle out of the cafe. She saw him open the door and stand there in the snow, with the light from the neon cafe sign faintly reflecting on his head and shoulders. She memorized the vision of him standing there in the glow as Arielle unlocked her car. He was so handsome, so lean and proud, she couldn't get enough of the sight. Then he reached for Arielle's elbow in a gesture of familiarity, and Evaline tore her gaze away and pushed back her chair, her heart painfully aching. No matter what she'd done for Carter, he would never take her in his arms again. He would never kiss her, never look at her with warmth streaming out from his eyes as he had gazed at her that one time at the casino. She could tell that something linked Arielle and Carter, shutting out all others. Evaline swallowed a lump in her throat, half-choking on the bleak reality of her life as it disconnected from her fantasy of Carter. She jumped to her feet.

Mack looked at her and she briefly met his glance. "I have to go," she sputtered.

"Good-bye," he said simply. "Perhaps we will meet again."

All the way home Evaline drove in a state of numb despair. Life as she knew it had completely shattered. Her father had become a stranger to her. The past she knew with him was now subject to a review she didn't care to make, and the future held nothing but sorrow and rejection. Her father would surely be sent to prison, leaving her alone in the world for the first time in her life. She couldn't imagine living without him.

Almost as bad as her father's imprisonment was the prospect of facing everyone now that they knew of Reuven's crime. Not only would they shun Reuven, they would question the part Evaline played in acting alone to rescue strangers to the reservation. Such behavior would surely elicit silent censure, turned backs, and stormy glances—more ostracism than ever before. It would be impossible for her to hold her head up among the others.

She parked the Ford, let herself into the dark, cold house, and fell into bed, crying.

Carter walked back into the cafe and stomped the snow off his shoes, taking more time than necessary for the task. He could see Mack was waiting for him at the window table, and he had no idea how to begin a conversation with him. During the trip to the island and back, he'd gone over and over what he'd say to Mack when this moment arrived, but everything sounded fake or sappy. Why was it that he had no gift for conversation?

He walked across the room toward the red-and-white checkered tablecloth, wishing just like a coward that Arielle was with him. She'd know what to say. She could set a person at ease. She could make a guy feel like a million bucks, like he could talk all night totally at ease without ever having to worry about choosing the right words. But Arielle had no place in the upcoming discussion. She'd already handled *her* meeting with Mack on that island ten years ago. This was a moment he had to face alone, and he'd have to come up with something better than worn-out bullshit clichés. With his heart pounding in his ears, he returned to the table.

"Hi. Where's Evaline?" Carter asked, pulling out a chair.

"She left." Mack poured a cup of coffee for Carter and as he did so, his sleeve crept up his arm. Carter couldn't help but notice the twisted bones above his wrist, and immediately he recalled Arielle's mention of Mack's old injury. Mack calmly continued speaking as though immune to Carter's wide-eyed gape. "How long have you known our mutual friend?"

"Evaline?" Carter sat down. "Not long, only about—"

"I meant Arielle."

Carter paused. What had Mack sensed between Arielle and him? Was he going to get a lecture about staying away from white women in general, and from Arielle in particular? Carter felt his bristles stiffening. Who did Mack think he was—Arielle's father? Then Carter felt a flush heat his ears. If Mack was anyone's father, he was Carter's. If that was true, Mack was a man who had seduced a white woman and then abandoned her and her infant son. He had no intention of taking advice from a man who could walk out on a pregnant woman. He sat back in his chair, trying to contain his anger. In the past few days he'd been reminded yet again that anger didn't get him anywhere.

"I met her a few weeks ago."

Mack nodded but didn't say anything more. He picked up the menu. "The chili looks good."

Carter could barely form a reply, he was so stunned by Mack's sudden change of subject. Where was the old man's advice he expected, the hardass warnings to steer clear of Arielle? He'd been asked a question and his response hadn't even made a dent. Shaken, he picked up the menu.

"Uh, yeah, the chili does look good." He made a pretense of studying the menu, while trying to regain his composure. He suddenly realized how clipped Mack's comments were, how they were just as rapid-fire and truncated as others probably found his own. Talking with this guy was going to be a nightmare of stilted answers to stilted questions. Carter thought of all the times Arielle had tried to draw him out and how he'd refused to budge. He realized what a difficult companion he'd been for her.

"She ever eat fish?" Mack asked.

"Shrimp."

Mack smiled, still perusing the menu. "Bet she doesn't eat salmon."

"I wouldn't know."

Mack put down the menu as the waitress arrived to take their orders. They both ordered the same thing: chili, corn bread, and milk. After the waitress left, Mack flipped one of his braids behind his shoulder. "What's your connection to Arielle?"

"Mine?" Carter held the coffee cup just inches from his mouth while he carefully considered his words. "We crossed paths as a couple of strangers looking for the same person."

"Why were you looking for me?" Mack asked, his expression blank.

The moment had arrived for Carter. He prayed he wouldn't mess up, prayed he wouldn't sound ungrateful, or worse yet, sappy and ingratiating at having received another chance at life because of this man.

"Well, Arielle has been wanting to look you up for years ever since she spent time with you on your island. And me, well, I guess I wanted to look you up for kind of the same reason. She's told me a lot about the time she spent with you, and how you ended up giving her lots of things—wisdom mostly."

Saying nothing, but with a look of kindness about his eyes, Mack motioned for Carter to continue.

"This has to sound like the most farfetched coincidence, Mr. Shoalwater, but Arielle and I discovered that we both have things to thank you for. She's really appreciative about all the things you taught her, and I—"

"Arielle has much wisdom, and she had it well before I knew her," Mack interrupted. "I was merely present when she realized this to be true."

"Well, that's not how she remembers it. I don't think I've heard her go more than an hour without quoting you or saying something in praise of you."

"I could have an equal number of good things to say about her. She became a physician without any help from me, you know."

Again Carter felt the heat from under his collar rise into his face. Wasn't there a way to offer his simple thanks without getting caught in some damn debate?

Before Carter could respond, he saw Mack lean closer. "Arielle has nothing to thank me for," Mack said softly, "and I don't understand why you do either."

"I wanted to thank you for something you gave to me when I desperately needed it. You did it selflessly and anonymously, and without any idea where your gift was going to end up."

A shadow passed through Mack's eyes. "I gave you something?"

"Yes. My life. And I want you to know that I'm grateful. I don't know one goddamn thing about how the world works, but I can watch and listen and learn from people like you and Arielle. I wouldn't have had the chance to do it without you, and there's no way you can avoid taking the credit for it."

Suddenly amazed at himself for the rush of words, Carter paused but then pressed ahead. "I have reason to believe you donated bone marrow about a year ago." Carter stopped again, keeping his gaze riveted on Mack's face. "Isn't that right?"

"A year ago?" Mack glanced up at the ceiling. "In 1994?"

"Yeah. At the Fred Hutchinson Cancer Research Center."

"Yes, I did—I had a blood test when I went in for a medical emergency and was told they were desperate for minority donors." Mack's glance traced over him skeptically, but not suspiciously. "How did you know about this?"

"From a file I found in Reuven Jaye's office." Carter leaned forward. "I was at the same facility you were, at the same time."

"You? Why?"

"I was sick. I was dying of aplastic anemia, and my only hope was a bone marrow transplant. That's when I found out I was part Native American. My mother never talked much about my father, and I never knew what kind of blood I had until the doctors said they'd matched me with a Native American donor from a tribe somewhere nearby."

Mack's eyebrows lowered almost imperceptibly. "I'll

bet you always had some suspicions about who you were though, am I right?"

Carter nodded but said nothing. Only a person who had lived through a childhood marred by loneliness and alienation could ever know what his life had been like. He wouldn't even attempt to explain, not today.

Mack continued, "And you think I supplied the bone marrow?"

"Seeing you face-to-face, Mr. Shoalwater, I'd say over ninety-nine percent sure."

"What does my appearance have to do with it?"

Carter gulped his coffee. "What I look like now is really different from what I looked like a year ago. Ever since the transplant I've been changing. It was gradual at first, but as my health improved, my appearance began to shift. It was like the anonymous stranger's bone marrow had taken over my body. I was sure this was a ridiculous idea, but one of my nurses said it isn't all that uncommon in these kinds of cases. Marrow recipients can even inherit behaviors—like food cravings—from their donors. My hair turned black, the bones in my face became a little sharper and more defined, and my beard practically quit growing."

Hoping for some reaction from Mack but receiving none, Carter was forced to continue.

"Then I began to have episodes."

"Episodes?"

"For the past few weeks I've been hearing wolves in my head. Phantom wolves."

"Phantoms?" The corners of Mack's mouth raised a fraction. "Why do you say they're phantoms?"

"No one else hears them."

"Perhaps few are meant to."

"You don't act surprised, Mr. Shoalwater."

"I'm not." Mack chuckled. "I've heard them, too. For the past few months I have heard little else. They were calling for help from the clan, but I could do nothing. I was stuck on that island, practically powerless."

Carter's heart leaped in his throat. "Did you hear the wolves last night at the clan house?"

"Of course! They were howling in distress at the house posts being stolen from the clan."

Carter stared at Mack. Relief poured over him. Maybe he wasn't going completely crazy. Maybe there was a reason for the illusions of the past few weeks, and for the hallucinations he'd had in the hospital of wolves leaping over his bed, standing guard at his door, and watching over him through the night.

"I knew you were coming, Two Wolves," Mack said in a subdued tone. "I could feel that you were near. I called to you often at night, hoping to reach you through your dreams when your spirit was more receptive."

A chill raced down Carter's back, and the restaurant clatter and bustle completely disappeared as he remembered the haunting voice of his dreams. He had attributed the voice to an entity of his nightmares, brought on by some strange lingering effect of chemotherapy. He couldn't speak now, struck mute by the possibility that this man's power might be strong enough to touch a stranger miles away. Yet *was* Mack a stranger? The other question, that he and Mack might be related, shot like a bullet to the forefront of his thoughts.

"The Wolf Clan needed help," Mack continued. "And there are so few to lend assistance. I could sense your presence, but I had no idea who you were, only that you were the warrior sent to help our people."

"And you," Carter swallowed, still a bit shocked by the revelation. "You are the shaman?"

23

"*Yes.*" *Mack sat back*, his dark eyes glinting. "And now it is I who must thank you for your gift."

"For what?"

"For choosing to pursue the cause of the wolf howls and see if you could help. You did this selflessly and anonymously, and I thank you for it."

Carter looked down at the table, too moved to allow Mack to catch a glimpse of his expression.

"I'm beginning to see there are more similarities between us than just facial features," Mack added. "And those similarities have existed for years, well before you got sick. The unfamiliar reflection you see in the mirror now is due not so much to the change in your appearance, but to the change in *how* you see yourself."

For a long moment neither of them spoke. Then the waitress arrived with their food and they set to eating their meal. Mack didn't say a word as he consumed his chili, and Carter couldn't help but remember how

Arielle had told him of the silences around the dinner campfire with Mack. Carter ate quickly, too wound up to appreciate the food.

After Mack took his last bite of chili, he put his spoon on the plate beneath the bowl and sat back in his chair. "That was damn fine chili," he remarked. "It's been a while since I ate someone else's cooking."

"It was good." Carter wiped his mouth with his napkin and pushed away his empty bowl. Then he fished out a credit card and put it on the bill before Mack could say anything about paying. He doubted the older man had a penny anyway.

Carter was surprised when Mack reached for the bank card and held it up. "Carter Greyson," he remarked. "I thought that's what I heard them say."

"Who?"

"Williams. Last night at the clan house when he asked where you were, he called you Greyson."

"Yeah." Carter felt a burning in his stomach that had nothing to do with the chili he'd just eaten. "That's my name."

"Greyson, huh?" Mack's eyes narrowed. "Where are you from?"

"Atlanta, Georgia."

Mack reached for the coffee carafe. "Want some more?"

"Sure," Carter answered, pushing his mug forward. "Why not?"

"How about some pie?"

"That sounds good."

"I'll go get us some. What kind do you like?"

"Peach or berry. I'm not real picky."

"All right." Mack rose, his good posture quickly taking hold as he walked away. His worn clothes hung on his powerful frame. Carter wondered what could be going through Mack's mind. Had he left the table so he could digest the facts Carter had just given him? Carter played with the handle of his mug and discovered that his hands were shaking. He peered out the window, wondering what Arielle was doing, if the emergency had been taken care of by now. He wished she would show up and sit down beside him.

A few minutes passed before Mack ambled back to the table. "No peach," he said. "How about blackberry?"

"Good. Thanks."

Mack put the plate in front of Carter and then sat down, concentrating on his slice of pie. Carter tried to eat his dessert, but the crust stuck in his throat. He was too nervous to choke it down.

"Did you ever know a woman named Elizabeth Greyson?" Carter asked finally, making sure his voice remained steady.

Mack studied Carter's face for a moment. "Yes."

"From Atlanta?"

"Yes. But I met her in Boston. She attended college there."

"Do you know whatever happened to her?"

"No, but I have a feeling you're going to tell me."

Carter flushed. Was he that transparent? Would Mack sense the bitterness and anger of thirty years in his voice as well? He heaved a tight, frustrated sigh. "Ah, forget it," he said, shoving the zigzag shape of the piecrust around on the plate.

"How old are you, Two Wolves?" Mack asked.

"Thirty."

"And I take it Elizabeth's your mother?"

"Yeah." Carter shot a glance at Mack, but then quickly looked away, afraid that his stare would burn a hole through the man.

"Your mother would have been about twenty when she had you."

"Yeah."

Mack fell silent and studied the dark window. Carter watched him, waiting for him to say something, anything. He could see Mack's jaw working as he clenched and unclenched his teeth. Then the older man turned back to him.

"She never told me."

"Right."

"She didn't, Carter."

"She waited for you for years!" Carter cried. "She was sure you'd come back."

"Come back? Why would I? She told me to get lost."

Carter narrowed his eyes in disbelief. "What?"

"She wrote me a letter. Called me names I was surprised she knew. Told me to leave her alone, that she'd found someone new."

"I don't think so."

"It's the truth." Mack reached out and surprised Carter by grabbing his wrist. "Do you think I would have turned my back on my own son?"

Carter stared at him, his mind in a turmoil. That's all he *had* thought for the last thirty years. But now, after meeting Mack and after hearing Arielle's tales of the man, he knew Mack wasn't the type of person to abandon a child, no matter what the circumstances. The thought of Mack shirking responsibility was ludicrous, almost laughable. Yet Carter felt far from laughing. Someone must have intervened to keep Mack and his mother apart, someone who had written the letter to Mack all those years ago, ruining the chance for happiness of a woman and a little boy. He knew instantly who was capable of such behavior: his rigid, fastidious, ever-proper southern grandmother.

Mack released his arm. "So you're my son."

Carter blinked. "Yeah. It seems so."

Mack sat back in his chair and openly stared at Carter, a half-smile of wonder on his face. The expression only served to confound Carter more. "What do you know? I gave bone marrow to my very own son."

Carter didn't know what to say. He only knew that something heavy was falling away from him.

Then Mack's smile vanished. "But your mother. What of her?"

"She died years ago."

"I'm sorry to hear that."

"I don't think she ever got over you."

Mack shook his head sadly and gazed at the table.

"I hated you," Carter ventured.

"You had every reason to."

"But I don't, now that I know what kind of man you are."

Mack looked up. For a long moment they stared directly into each other's eyes, bridging the lost years with respect and acknowledgment for the men they had become.

"I will see more of you," Mack finally said, "if you wish to, Carter."

"Yeah, I do."

"Perhaps you will join me in restoring the Wolf House."

"I would like that."

Mack nodded and rose. "I'll look forward to us working together."

"Aren't you going back to Seattle with Arielle and me?"

"No. I belong up here for now."

Carter got to his feet, surprised that Mack intended to leave the cafe. "Do you have somewhere to go, somewhere to stay?"

"I suspect the elders will assist me, seeing how I have been wronged by one of their own."

"But what about Arielle? I know she wants to talk with you."

"I will go by the clinic. It is just down the road, isn't it?"

"Yeah, but—"

"Good-bye, Carter," Mack held out his crooked right arm. "I am glad you found me."

Carter shook Mack's hand, feeling compelled to embrace his long-lost father. But there would be time for that later, when his healing wounds were not quite so raw.

"I'm glad, too," he said simply, suppressing the quaver in his voice. "See you, Mack."

He watched Mack walk out of the cafe, his gait smooth and rolling, his shoulders straight and proud, while all the heads of the customers turned to watch as well. Carter realized the people didn't stare at Mack because he was a stranger in town, or because he was once a notorious ostracized tribal member who'd just been returned to respectability. They turned to look at him because he was a man full of confidence and goodness, and his character beamed like a spotlight around him. The man everyone was staring at was his father. His dad. The man whose blood flowed through his own veins. For the first time in his life Carter's heart swelled with pride in his heritage.

Carter waited until the door shut behind Mack, and then he sank back to his chair, overwhelmed by a strange glow of joy.

"More coffee, Mr. Greyson?" the waitress asked, nodding toward the carafe.

Carter glanced at her in surprise. How did she know his name? Did everyone know everyone's business on the reservation? In the old days he would have preferred to move anonymously through the crowd, acknowledging no one and comfortable with the fact that no one was particularly aware of him. Less trouble came his way when he kept a low profile.

But he suddenly realized he didn't mind if the people on the reservation knew who he was. They didn't see him as an ugly misfit or a bitter outsider. He was Carter Greyson, the guy who'd helped save tribal artifacts from the clutches of Dan Williams. He was the one who'd helped uncover Reuven's plot that kept an innocent man imprisoned. He was proud of those successes and was proud to be the son of Mack Shoalwater.

To be connected to Dr. Arielle Scott gave him pride, too, for she was a person who truly saw the interior of a man. Suddenly it wasn't so bad to be Carter Greyson. In fact, it felt damn good.

He grinned at the waitress, and her eyes lit up in surprise. She smiled back. "Is that a yes?" she asked with a small laugh.

"You bet." He slid the carafe to her and glanced at her name tag. "Thanks, Georgia."

"Oh, and you can put that away," she said, pointing to his credit card. "The boss says the meal for you two is on the house."

"Well, thanks!" Carter slid the plastic card into his hand.

She replaced the empty carafe with a full one and left him sitting alone. Carter poured a new cup of coffee and sipped it while he watched the last of the sled-riding kids walk off the hill. Then he remembered the manila envelope Arielle had given him, and he reached down to open it.

There was a Post-it note from Arielle attached to a little blue booklet about bone marrow donations. *"See if you recognize anybody in the speech on page 8,"* she'd written. Curious, Carter turned to the page she'd indicated and began to read.

High School Valedictorian speech:

Hello. My name is Sebastian Stewart, and I am very, very grateful to be standing here tonight and addressing my class, our parents and friends, and our teachers.

As most of you know, I came down with aplastic anemia in October of my sophomore year. Nobody ever plans on getting such a serious disease, and nobody really knows all the things that are involved in helping a patient recover. I'm standing here now as a person who was fortunate enough to receive support from so many different groups of people, and I want to offer my appreciation here tonight.

To begin with, I want to thank the teachers who first noticed a change in my attitude, who saw a change in my ability to think, and noticed my stamina starting to drain. They called my parents and suggested that I see a doctor immediately.

In the County Hospital, I learned the grim truth. I was lucky to be alive for I had blood so weak it could barely support life. We left immediately for the Fred Hutchinson Cancer Research Center in Seattle.

The next day I learned there was no chance for a bone marrow transplant from my family. It was a Saturday, and it was the scariest day of my life. I looked fine and I wanted to feel fine, but I was given very little medical hope by the doctors.

I stayed in the Seattle hospital for three weeks, receiving a special drug in hopes that it would stimulate my bone marrow to grow. By mid-November, I needed blood and platelet transfusions monthly, and then it was needed weekly. I want to thank the local Red Cross and the people here tonight who came out in force and donated blood in my name.

Finally, I needed blood every day, and I entered the County Hospital to stay. My only hope was a 100,000 to 1 chance that the Hutchinson Center in Seattle could find a person with an exact match to my bone marrow, and that the person would agree to undergo a surgery where some of their bone marrow would be donated to me. The search began.

Soon I needed specific platelets every day, which were getting harder and harder to find. Once they had to be flown in from California, and I was so weak that they almost came too late. By this time, the doctor was preparing my parents for the worst because sometimes a line has to be drawn to separate hope from reality. But my story has a happy ending. The call came from the Hutchinson Center. They had found a donor. After a farewell party, we were off once more to Seattle.

The nurses say it is rare when a patient has support from his community that never lets up, month after month. But I had that support for four months in Seattle. The actual medical procedures kind of defy explanation, but be assured that I am very thankful for the doctors, research scientists, and especially the nurses, that helped me and my family through the whole process. These people have devoted their lives to saving people like myself.

Often I'm asked whether the experience changed me forever. It has.

I know I use humor more now when things get tough. I really understand much more about caring and community support. I appreciate others rather than judge them, and I know we all do the very best we can with what we have. I take life slower and more easily. I have learned to take more responsibility and to say I'm sorry when I've made a mistake. I listen more and smile more. I treat my body better, and I have learned right down to my bones the power of a positive attitude. I like to be happy and enjoy life. And I have learned to say Thank You.

Most of all, I want to say thank you to the wonderful person who donated bone marrow and helped me to live.

Carter closed the booklet and stared down at the cover. Arielle Scott knew him in ways that surprised him. Arielle had that skill which could sense the goodness inside him, the goodness that shone like a beacon in the words of a high school kid who'd stared into the same abyss Carter had. She could see into his cancerous depths, where he'd been grasping for gratitude, hope, and a desire to live a full life—but had been burning himself black with those things he held tight to his chest. Unlike Sebastian, he'd never had any support or care, and he lacked the courage to let his hopes out, if it meant they might be crushed underfoot. Yet Arielle had cared enough to help him venture into a new world where his fledgling tenderness could emerge and gather strength, and there was every indication she'd enjoy living in that world with him.

°   °   °

Arielle pulled off her scrubs and tossed them in the laundry bag. Though she had lost hours of sleep over the course of the last few days, she didn't feel as tired as she should, and the emergency birth she'd just assisted with, though difficult, had ended happily for both mother and child.

Just as she grabbed her bag and was saying good-bye to the nurse, she looked up to see Mack standing in the waiting room. She glanced around, but couldn't spot Carter anywhere, and wondered if the two men had had some kind of argument.

"Mack," she greeted, striding forward. He met her at the entrance to the ring of chairs and couches. "What are you doing here?"

"I'm here to say good-bye."

"Good-bye?" Her heart plummeted. "You're leaving?"

"No. You are. You're going back to Seattle tonight, aren't you?"

"Yes, but aren't you coming?"

"I have decided to stay behind and repair the Wolf House. The posts need to be restored to their rightful places, the wall needs to be fixed, and eventually, the other two poles must be recovered. Neither Carter nor I will have real peace from the wolves until the house is restored."

"So you'll stay on here?"

He nodded. "All I need is some camping equipment, food, and tools. The elders will probably supply those. I can stay up at Salmon Point until the job is done. Maybe take some boys with me who need to work."

"Don't you want to get out?" she asked. "And see the world after ten years of absence?"

Mack smiled and shook his head. "What's there to see? The surface may change somewhat, but things are pretty much the same as they always were."

"But I thought we might spend Christmas together—you and me and Carter."

"Christmas?" Mack waved her off. "That holiday never did much for me. Too commercial. Besides, you should spend that time with Carter, not with some cranky old man."

"You aren't old!" She chuckled. "You look just the same as ever."

"But I'm crankier."

"So who isn't?" She grinned.

They gazed at one another, until Arielle couldn't contain herself any longer. "Oh, Mack," she said. "It's so good to see you again!" She stepped forward and wrapped her arms around him, hugging him for the first time in her life. She felt his strong arms come around her and squeeze her. For a long moment they didn't speak, and then Arielle turned her head toward him.

"Mack, I never forgot you. No matter what you might have thought, I never once forgot you."

"Why would I have thought that?"

She stepped back and he released her. "Because I didn't come back to get you off that island."

"It wasn't your job to rescue me."

"Still, I would have, except that Reuven Jaye told me you had died."

"More of his lies." Mack shook his head. "Reuven. He was a decent man who made many wrong choices and got in over his head. Once he stole that first post, it was like being swept into a riptide."

"Reuven wasn't decent," she retorted. "If he hadn't been caught, he would have kept you on that island for the rest of your life."

"It wasn't so bad, Leaf-on-the-Water. You of all people know that to be true."

"Even so, there was so much I wanted to say to you in thanks. I thought my chance was lost to tell you how much you changed my life."

"Thanks aren't necessary." He reached down into his plastic sack and pulled out a small cardboard box. "Here," he held out the carton, "I brought you a Christmas present."

"What?" She glanced curiously at the box and then back at him.

"Open it and find out. It is from your place on the beach."

Arielle sank to the nearest chair, balanced the box on her knees, and opened the tattered flaps. The musky smell of the sea drifted up and she guessed what was in the box before she caught sight of its contents. Her old shell collection! Arielle's heart warmed with memories of her days on the island with Mack, and of the hours spent searching for perfect specimens of shells, while finding morsels of Mack's wisdom that she'd saved just as carefully.

Mack stood over her. "I thought you might get a kick out of seeing those shells again."

"You kept them all this time! Thank you!" She reached into the carton and picked up the round gray shell of a moon snail, and then a limpet shell whose conical shape looked like the cedar hats worn by the coastal Indians a century ago. She could still remember some of the places she'd found the shells, and the evenings spent lining up duplicates by the fire and judging which shell would stay in the collection and which would be discarded.

"This is great." She beamed. "I'm going to have these mounted and framed so I can hang them on my wall. My first piece of artwork."

"Sounds like a plan."

She closed the box and stood up. "But I don't have anything for you."

"Arielle, seeing the woman you've become is plenty enough, believe me."

"Well here," Arielle stuck her hand in her parka pocket and pulled out a business card. She offered it to Mack. "That's where I can be reached. I have a pager, too, so you can call me anytime. You'll always have a place to stay with me. You know that, don't you?"

He nodded. "But what about that cooking of yours?"

"What cooking?"

Mack laughed in the warm, chuckling rumble that she remembered so well. "See what I mean? Some things never change."

"Any time you want to come over and whip up some nettles and bark, feel free," she put in.

"I might just do that."

"I'm counting on it."

Arielle gazed at him and realized she was close to tears. She didn't know how to say good-bye to this man. She felt as if they'd barely said hello. And she hadn't even begun to tell him all the things she wanted to.

"There will be time for us to talk," he said, reading her mind. "Soon, when we are both not so tired. But right now there's a young man waiting for you at the cafe with much to tell you, and he's probably wondering if you are ever coming back to him."

"I'm the one wondering that about *him*."

"Oh, I wouldn't worry about him, Leaf-on-the-Water. That young man is quite perceptive."

"What makes you say that?"

"He knows that you consider those months on my island to be quite an important time in your life. He recognizes the value of all that you learned there, and hopes some-day he can learn such things for himself."

"He said that?"

"Yes." Mack tilted his head. "Do you know how lucky you are, Arielle, to be loved by someone who knows what is important to you, someone who will honor and defend those things?"

Arielle flushed. "Carter's never told me he loved me. Did he say so?"

"In many ways." Mack looked at the door. "But that is a subject better left for you and him to discuss. I'm going now, though. I'm beat."

"But, Mack—"

"If you need to get hold of me, I'll be staying at the tribal center until I can make arrangements for the restoration. The elders have offered me a place to stay, probably out of guilt."

"They owe you a real apology, Mack, as far as I'm con-cerned, and financial reparation at the very least."

"As long as they support the restoration, I'll be satisfied."

"Well, if you're sure you don't want to come down to Seattle, I'll see you in a couple of days then," Arielle replied. "I work here at the reservation clinic every other Saturday."

"Good. We'll talk then." He held out his straight arm and hugged her a final time. "Thank you," he said, "for coming back, Leaf-on-the-Water. For righting the wrong against me."

She nodded against his chest. She'd never felt a sense of belonging to a family quite like this moment with Mack. Having him in her life was something that was meant to be, something that made her feel complete and contented. Slowly she pulled away, a hot swell of tears welling up in her eyes.

"Bye for now," she whispered hoarsely.

"See you around," Mack replied, giving her a thumbs-up sign. "Like a doughnut."

She shook her head at his familiar habit of lacing his philosophic talk with jarring modern phrases. Then she grabbed her shell collection and hurried out of the clinic to meet Carter.

24

That night Evaline awoke and forced herself to crawl out of bed. Though she was still weary after only a few hours of sleep, she couldn't let her father spend the entire day alone in the jail. He probably needed things from home and would welcome a piece of the pie she'd baked the night before. Evaline gathered his toiletries together, put some clean clothes in a bag, placed a large wedge of the apple pie in a plastic container, and stowed it in the bag on top of his folded slacks. She got back in the car and headed for the jail.

As she drove through the snowy night, her anguish rose up like flames inside her. Evaline had to know why. What had driven her father to commit such a heinous crime? Stealing from his own clan was the worst sin he could have committed. Her father wasn't a criminal. What had made him do such a thing?

She parked in the lot next to the tribal police station and went inside. Jim Nickles, one of the guys she'd gone to high school with and who had become a policeman, checked the bag she'd brought and then took her down the hall to her father's cell. Evaline quietly walked behind him, fighting a flush of shame which she knew was the first of many she'd have to endure. When they got to Reuven's cell, Evaline glanced across the room and saw her father lying on the narrow cot, his arm flung over his eyes.

"Jaye," Jim called gruffly. "Evaline's here to see you."

Reuven stirred and slowly sat up, appearing as though the movement pained him greatly. Jim held open the metal door and Evaline brushed by him. She stood before her father, waiting before she spoke until Jim closed the door and left.

She held out the bag. "I brought you some pie and clean clothes," she said.

He didn't reach for them, so she set them on the end of the bed.

"Go home, Evaline," he said, his eyes trained on the cement floor. "Don't come back."

"Dad!"

"I don't want you here."

"Dad, why?" She fought back a wave of tears. "Why did you do it?"

His expression sharpened, and he glared at her. "I did it for our people and for you."

"Why?"

"We needed money to build the casino. I found out how much I could get for a house post and decided it would be worth far more for the Saquinnish to sell the post to a private collector than to leave it in a deserted village, rotting away."

"But, Dad, that village is part of our heritage!"

"Heritage? What use is heritage when we don't have decent schools, decent health care?"

Evaline paused, unable to argue with his line of reasoning. Then she remembered that the house posts had cost two men a great deal, one of whom was now dead and the other wrongly banished for over a decade.

"But how could you have framed Mack Shoalwater? That doesn't seem like you, Dad."

"Mack?" Reuven frowned and pushed up his glasses. "He just happened to be at the wrong place at the wrong time. If I hadn't silenced him, he would have blown the whole operation."

"But what you did was wrong!"

He shot a bleary glare at her. "Don't you think I know that?"

"And you were going to let Dan Williams kill Dr. Scott and the others!"

Reuven slumped and ran a hand through his hair. "Things got out of hand. I didn't know what to do. And I needed the money."

"Why?" Evaline stared at him. "What could be worth the lives of all those people?"

"Your future." He glanced at her, his eyes glistening. "I did it for you, Evaline. So I could pay for another operation."

Evaline felt the color draining from her face. Her father had ruined himself for her sake? He had been willing to kill people so that she could undergo more useless plastic surgery? She couldn't believe it.

Reuven rose. "I couldn't bear the thought of you going through your life without a chance for happiness, Evaline."

"But, Dad, the operations have never helped."

"I've found a specialist. He said it would be different this time—"

"No!" Evaline cried. "Not for my face. You didn't barter our heritage and the lives of other people for my face!"

"I never meant it to—"

"No!"

Reuven reached out to touch her, but she backed away, overcome with revulsion and disappointment. She bumped into the cold bars of his prison and began to cry.

"The wolf attack was meant for me," Reuven said, his face contorted with grief. "For stealing that first house post. I should have been the one to suffer the scars, not you. Not you, Evaline! Not my beautiful little girl!"

His shape shimmered and diffused as tears flooded her vision.

"I had to do something. Don't you understand?" He stepped toward her, but she edged farther away from him. "I had to fix it, to make it better for you. All your life I've looked at you and have seen my sins reflected in your face. How could I let you suffer the fate that should have been mine?"

Evaline swallowed her sobs and dashed away her tears. "You killed a man, Dad, didn't you?"

"He saw us hauling the post away. Dan Williams thought it was better to silence him."

"And here I thought you were the best father in the world. The finest man I'd ever known."

"I thought I was doing the right thing," he explained. "But it just got out of hand."

"We'll never be the same." Evaline swallowed again, trying to talk over the lump in her throat. "This has ruined us forever."

He stared at her and gradually his shoulders drooped, and he seemed to implode into himself. Stumbling backward, he collapsed upon the cot, and slumped into a beaten shape, his forearms on his thighs.

Evaline looked at him. She couldn't see her father any longer. All she could see was a weak, white-haired stranger, who now had no place in her heart, and who no longer had any real meaning in her life. Feeling faint again, she called for Jim to let her out of the cell.

She stumbled out of the police station in a daze. Jim called to her but she couldn't make out his words. The world of the reservation, the only world she'd ever known, would no longer be a haven. And the other world, that of Arielle and Carter, would never accept her. She couldn't even escape the darkness of her own thoughts. There was nowhere to go, no place of sanctuary.

Snow stuck in her lashes as she walked across the parking lot. She trudged past the Ford, barely registering it as a familiar object. Her feet continued to walk, taking her past the casino and cafe, all lit up and full of noise—blind to her pain and sorrow. Weeping silently and feeling nothing but a black void inside her, Evaline stumbled to the marina, down the dock, and past the silent boats bobbing in the bay as the tide went out. Directed by a force other than her own spirit, she walked to the end of the dock where her father's fishing boat lay moored securely in the slip. Slowly, mechanically, Evaline lowered the dinghy to the water, unmindful of the wind blowing through her hair and clothes. She stepped into the small rowboat, uncaring that the oarlocks remained empty, and sat in the bottom of the craft. The current tugged at the boat, pulling it away from the dock.

Miserable and lost, Evaline sank down and looked up at the night sky. A huge full moon stared down at her, as if it knew what her father had done, as if it, too, blamed her for the misfortunes her face had caused. Hot tears rolled out of the corners of her eyes and fell on her jeans, mingling with the snow that slowly covered her clothing with a pristine veil of white.

"My wedding gown," Evaline murmured, as the boat drifted farther and farther from shore. She lay back, offering herself to the moon and the sea and feeling curiously immune to the bone-chilling air. She thought of the Sea Wolf, the mythical creature of Saquinnish tales, who inhabited the waters at the edge of the reservation. Only a mythical being would accept her for what she was, for what she had become. Outcasts belonged to the netherworld, not to real life. Only the Sea Wolf would take her in, pulling her into the depths where darkness would hide her face and her family's dishonor forever. She closed her eyes and said a prayer with lips already stiff from the cold.

"I come to thee, Sea Wolf, as your bride. Allow me entrance to your lodge. Give me salmon to eat and a warm blanket to wrap myself in, and I will serve you for the rest of my days."

Evaline sighed. The prayer floated upward as she relinquished herself to the forces of sea and sky. Her thoughts turned to Carter, to the last time she'd seen his face outside the cafe. But soon the bittersweet vision dimmed and her thoughts grew sluggish. She was aware of the rhythm of the boat as it rocked beneath her on its sightless journey toward the open sea. And presently she felt nothing at all.

"Carter?" Arielle called out to the dark shape she saw leaning over the railing at the marina. Though he stood in silhouette, there was no mistaking his lean figure and the set of his hips. His form was indelibly inscribed in her vision, as was Mack's, and she would always recognize them no matter how brief the glance. She'd been informed by the waitress that Carter had left the cafe to take a walk, and she'd found him just minutes later, standing alone at the marina and looking down at the boats in the water.

He turned and waited for her to walk up to him.

"Hi," he greeted. "Did Mack find you?"

"Yes. He's staying here."

"That's what he told me. Are you disappointed?"

"Kind of." She hunched her shoulders. "I thought he might want to spend Christmas with me, but he had other plans."

Carter studied her, his black eyes steady and probing, and probably missing nothing in her expression.

She wanted to take him in her arms, wanted to kiss him, to touch his face, to squeeze him tightly and never let him go. Instead, she slipped her hands into the pockets of her parka. "So what are you doing out here in the freezing cold, Mr. Greyson?"

"I thought I heard something."

"Not the wolves again!"

"No." He shook his head and squinted out at the bay. "I'm not quite sure if I heard something or sensed something. I just felt compelled to come out here."

"And?"

"I didn't see a thing." He turned to face her and shrugged. "So much for my compulsions."

"I wouldn't discount all your compulsions."

"Oh?" He gazed down at her. "Such as?"

"Your bathing compulsion. I wouldn't want to see you give that up."

"You wouldn't?" A smile played at the corner of his mouth.

"No. I admire a man who can handle a wet bar of soap."

"It takes a certain amount of skill, I admit. And the more one practices, the better one gets."

"Practice does make perfect."

Arielle smiled, but her grin soon faded as she gazed into his dark eyes. An intense pause stretched between them, heating the undercurrent of their bantering. Yet he didn't reach out for her, and she wasn't sure what to do. She'd given Carter a blatant hint. If he didn't pick up on it within the next minute or so, she'd know he had no intention of continuing their relationship, at least not at the level they'd soared to on Monday night.

Each second that ticked by in silence made her doubt her effect on him, yet he didn't alter his steady regard of her. The silence made her nervous.

"So," she began at last, knowing that to gaze at Carter was dangerous, should his feelings for her be merely casual. She knew her eyes would say far too much to him if he had decided to walk out of her life. "Are you ready to fly south?"

"Yeah. All this talk about bathing reminds me that I need a shower. Bad. I haven't had one for days."

"Let's hit the road then."

"Fine with me." He took her elbow and guided her back up the sloped walk toward the cafe parking lot. Disappointed in the lack of intimacy between them, Arielle got into the Miata, waited for Carter to slip into the passenger seat, and then headed for Seattle.

During the first few miles, Carter stared out the window, going over a conversation in his head, rehearsing the things he wanted to tell Arielle but hadn't wanted to bring up in a cold dark parking lot on the reservation. Her small car wasn't the right place to hold the discussion, either. He hoped she'd understand his reluctance to talk. What he had to say was far too important to replace with idle chatter.

Then he looked at the side of her face and saw the strain showing at the corner of her eye. What had her day been like? What had the emergency at the clinic entailed? What had Mack said to her? If Carter cared about her, he would want to know what she was going through. And he *did* care about Arielle. Of that he was certain.

Carter leaned back. "So what happened at the clinic?" he asked, starting with a less personal subject and hoping he would have enough subjects to talk about during the hour drive.

Arielle shifted gears and pulled onto the freeway. "It was a mess," she replied. Then she told him about her day, about everything, and Carter found himself telling her about how he'd been kidnapped by Williams on Tuesday night and how they'd found Ron on the island. Before he knew it, they were taking the exit for downtown Seattle. The miles had whizzed by without him being aware of the time. Arielle had a way of doing that to him.

Arielle drove through the busy streets of Seattle, down Second Avenue, and pulled up in front of his building. She didn't turn off the car, and waited with her hand on the gear shift as he turned to her.

"Want to get some dinner?" Carter asked.

A look of mild surprise crossed her face. "Sure."

"Why don't you come up while I take a shower. I won't be long."

"All right." She turned off the engine and got out. He held open the door for her and let his gaze travel across her glossy brown hair and her shapely backside as she climbed the stairs ahead of him. Suddenly, he didn't feel so tired. In fact, he felt a rush of adrenaline that went straight to his loins.

Arielle stood aside as he unlocked his door. Then he motioned her in and closed it behind them.

"Want me to build a fire?" Arielle asked. "I'm good with fires."

"Practice makes perfect, eh?" he teased.

In answer she shot him a dark glance of amusement.

"Sure, go ahead." Carter peeled off his jacket. "Make yourself at home."

Carter strode to his bedroom and stripped, tossing his clothes in the laundry. Then he walked to the bathroom just down the hall. He could see Arielle kneeling at the hearth. Already she had a healthy blaze going. He liked the sight of her in his apartment, taking care of things, being her usual capable self that he had grown to appreciate. It was hard to imagine he had considered leaving her once they found Mack. But in finding Mack, he had found a part of himself that recognized Arielle for the role she had played in his life and should continue to play. She was not a woman to run from but a woman to run *toward*. Smiling, Carter glanced down at himself, realizing that other parts of him recognized her value as well.

Still, Arielle had been carefully reserved the last few hours, as if to create an insulating space between them. He wasn't sure why or for whom the space had been created—for himself or her. Maybe she'd finally realized he was just another asshole and had decided to keep their relationship on purely a friendship basis. God, he hoped not.

Carter slipped into the bathroom and turned on the water, more worried than ever that he'd turned her off for good with his silence.

He had just lathered up his hair and was backing into the spray when he felt a faint cool breeze brush his skin. He glanced to the side and saw the door of the shower slowly slide open. Carter felt his jaw go slack with surprise at the sight of Arielle on the other side of the door, stark naked. He couldn't believe she would boldly walk in on him, couldn't believe she would have disrobed and presented herself to him like this. She kept her eyes leveled upon his and never once glanced at the rest of his figure. Carter's body reacted with a surge of desire, producing the hardest, most straining erection he'd ever known.

"I thought you might like the services of a professional bathing engineer," Arielle ventured, her eyes twinkling.

"Professional?" he asked, pushing the door open so he could see all of her. Her breasts peeked up at him, begging for him to taste them. "And what kind of degree do you have, madam?"

"A certain degree of affection for you." She put her hand on the door while he flushed with pleasure at her words. Why did he doubt her feelings for him, when she had proven over and over again that she cared? "May I?"

"Of course." He helped her step into the tub and struggled to affect a cool facade that he didn't feel. The sight of her creamy thighs and slender waist set him on fire, and the possibilities of sharing an enduring relationship with her sent his heart thumping madly in his chest.

Their hands lingered together, as did their gazes, until Carter couldn't take another moment of separation. He stepped forward, drawing her into his arms at the same time, and pressed her against his chest.

"Ari!" he exclaimed.

She said nothing, but reached up with her hands to caress the sides of his face. A look of love streamed out of her eyes, rendering him speechless with wonder and gratitude. Then she stood on tiptoe and lifted her mouth to his. Their lips met in the spray, and he moved slightly to protect her from the water, slanting his mouth over hers. He wanted to kiss her until they fused as one, until they reached the space where no speech was necessary. Her body felt warm and wet and slick as she wrapped herself around him and surrendered to the kiss.

He'd never dreamed the night would come to this— holding her in his arms, kissing her, and backing her against the warm wet wall, just as he had done when they had first made love. And just like that first time, he couldn't hold back. Neither could she, it seemed, for she raised a leg to straddle him. He lifted her thighs with his hands, opening her just enough to push in.

As his hard length slid into her, they both sighed. Arielle tilted back her head and closed her eyes, and for a moment Carter stared at her rapt expression, amazed that he had the power to bring such pleasure to this wonderful woman. Her strong feminine hands swept across the muscles of his back and shoulders, caressing him as though she were memorizing by touch every rise and dip of his body. Soon his own eyes closed as he moved inside her, slowly at first, and then more urgently as her cries and his own hunger drove him to completion.

For a long time afterward, they stood together, his body still merged with hers and her lips and hands moving over him in a delightful exploration. Then he stopped up the tub and they sank together into the hot steamy water that rose around them.

"That was nice," she murmured, rising up on an elbow to gaze at him. "I like that no-nonsense approach you have."

"It's called serious lack of control."

"Uncontrolled?" She raised a brow. "You?"

"Yes." He flicked her chin playfully. "You do that to me, you know. Especially when you walk into my bathroom in your birthday suit."

"You'd prefer something else?"

He squeezed her rump. "Are you kidding?"

Arielle rested her chin on his chest and gazed up at him. "I never kid about serious things."

"And are you serious about me?"

"You know I am, Carter."

Carter's cheeks felt hot. He leaned forward at the neck and kissed her. Then he lay back and stroked her hair. "I hoped you didn't mistake my silence earlier in the week as a sign of disinterest."

"I assumed you had a lot on your mind."

"I did." He glanced down his nose at her, marveling that he had found a woman who seemed to understand him, even in his more prickly moments. "And then I was kidnapped."

"So was Mack your donor?" she inquired.

"Yes. And more."

"What do you mean?"

"He's my father."

Arielle raised up and stared at him. "Your father?"

"Yeah. Kind of a surprise, hmm?"

"Carter!"

"He didn't know my mother was pregnant. Ostensibly she wrote him a Dear John letter and he took off."

Arielle slowly shook her head, her eyes wide with astonishment. "I can't believe it! He's your father!"

"That's probably why I look like him so much—I got a double dose of his DNA."

"But wait a minute. I thought I read somewhere that parents can't be donors to their own children."

"Why not?"

"They wouldn't be a good enough match because half the blood characteristics come from the mother and half from the father."

"But Mack's antigens did match up, maybe not perfectly, but enough to save my life."

"It seems incredible."

"There might be more going on here than just modern science," Carter put in, stroking her neck. "And I'm not going to analyze it. I'm just glad to be alive."

"I'm glad you are, too, Carter." Arielle sat up and kissed him. Her breasts jiggled temptingly, and he tried not to stare at them. "But what did Mack say about being your father?" she continued. "Was he surprised?"

"As much as I was. But I think in time we'll both get used to the idea. He's a good man. I'll like having him for a father."

"Amazing!" She grinned and stared at him. "That's truly amazing!"

"No more amazing than you." He reached for the back of her neck and gently pulled her toward him, surrounding her with his arms and kissing her until he felt his body once again stirring to life. He knew a rightness in the way they fit together, in the way she lay in his arms—a feeling he hadn't experienced with any other woman. "Ari," he said, "you've changed my life forever. I don't think you know what you've done for me."

"I didn't do all that much."

"You've helped me learn to trust, to love, to believe in myself."

"Carter, those things were inside you all along."

"But buried. If it hadn't been for you, I'd still be up to my eyeballs in one kind of cancer or another."

She smiled in reply and kissed him. "I was happy to help."

"You know that booklet you gave me today about the high school kid with aplastic anemia?"

"Yes?"

"It really hit home."

"Did it?" She brushed back his wet bangs. "I thought it might."

"The article the kid wrote made me really stop and think."

"Any particular part?"

"Yeah. At the end of the piece he said people often asked him if going through a transplant changed his life, and he said that it did, that he is different having faced death. He said he understands much more about caring and community support. That he's 'learned right down to his bones the power of a positive attitude. And to say thank you.'"

"You remember all that?"

"It was easy. It's exactly how I feel—but not because I lived through a transplant."

"Then why?"

"Because of you, Ari." He touched the side of her face. "You've taught me those things, or at least you opened my eyes to the possibility that I have many decent things to offer the world."

"They were always there, those decent things. That's why I love you."

Carter gazed at her, half-believing his ears were still playing tricks on him. "You actually love a prickly guy like me?"

"Yes. I saw through that false front of yours from the very beginning."

"Did you, smarty pants?"

"They don't call me doctor for nothing."

"And are you willing to take me on as a permanent patient, Dr. Scott?"

"Not without a preliminary physical." Arielle felt his forehead with the back of her hand. "Hmm. You feel a bit feverish."

"Hot is the word, I believe." He grinned and pulled her on top of him. "And I'm going to be hot for you the rest of my life."

"Extended temperature elevations aren't healthy, Mr. Greyson."

"Some elevations are exceedingly healthy." He adjusted himself between her thighs. "Like this one."

"Hmm." She chuckled. "Have you had that swelling long?"

"For about two weeks," he replied.

"What brought it on?"

"The appearance of a woman in my life. A woman who drives me crazy. A woman I love."

He saw her flush with happiness and pulled her down for a kiss. "What do you think the treatment should be for a swelling like this, Doc?"

"Either an ice pack, or this." She rose up and slowly lowered herself on him. "It's a new treatment I'm developing. Does that feel any better, Mr. Greyson?"

"A bit." He put his hands around her waist and urged her to take in more of him. "Ah, yes, that feels much better."

"The swelling doesn't seem to be going down, though."

"I think it's serious." He caressed her flanks and drank in the sight of her slender body, knowing he would never get his fill of looking at her or sharing the bantering she seemed to enjoy as much as he did. "I think we should continue the treatment, Doc."

"I agree."

For a moment they moved together, lost in the wonderful feeling of their bodies coming together. Soon Arielle was gritting her teeth and bucking against him.

Carter arched into her again, unable to contain himself. "You've got what I call a dynamite bedside manner," he growled.

"You're lucky, mister," Arielle panted, without opening her eyes. "I don't usually make home visits like this."

"Lady, you *are* home," Carter said without a moment's hesitation. In the old days, he wouldn't have dreamed of blurting out such a bald emotional statement. But those days were gone. Thanks to his personal physician, he had finally learned to trust his heart and say what he meant.

Arielle paused, her eyes glistening. "What did you say, Carter?"

"I said you *are* home. Both of us have found where we truly belong."

"Yes," Arielle murmured. "Our place on the beach— together."

Epilogue

"You there!"

A voice in the distance called to Evaline, but she hadn't the strength or the heart to answer. Her arms and legs were too frozen and heavy to move, and she was far too drowsy to respond.

Leave me alone.

"Miss?"

She didn't know how long the dinghy had been drifting and didn't care. This was her last journey, and she intended to reach her destination without interruption.

Let me be.

"Give me your hand!"

I don't want to be rescued. Go away.

"Reach for me, dammit!"

Evaline sighed. It seemed she had no choice but to be pulled from her dream of nothingness back into the world where she had no reason to live and no place to call home.

You don't know what you're doing. Leave me alone.

Something jarred the dinghy. Evaline was aware of a loud bumping noise and the wobbling motion of the small craft. Then she felt someone lifting her up by her armpits. She hadn't the energy to protest.

"Hang on!" a male voice urged as someone dragged her backward out of the snow-filled dinghy. "You're going to be all right!"

Evaline slowly opened her eyes and her bleary vision gradually merged into focus. To her astonishment she saw two words looming in front of her frozen nose.

Sea Wolf.

A miracle had occurred. The Sea Wolf had come for her! As unbelievable as it seemed, her prayers had been answered. Evaline's frozen face cracked with awe, and she forced her stiff neck to tilt upward so she could see the being whose hands were pulling her out of the dinghy. A ruddy face topped by dark hair loomed over her in the darkness.

Wait a minute—the Sea Wolf was a man?

———

Evaline's story continues in *JUST BEFORE MIDNIGHT*, coming from HarperMonogram in 1996.

Author's Note

The Saquinnish Indians mentioned in this book are a fictitious tribe based on the culture and characteristics of the coastal Indians of Northwest Washington. The theft of house posts is an actual event, and the question of ownership of the artifacts is currently being decided in the U.S. court system. These priceless museum pieces, valued at millions of dollars, are being fought over, both by the tribes to whom they originally belonged and by the collectors who purchased them from individuals who may not have had the right to sell them in the first place.

Banishment for crimes committed by tribal members is a native tradition which has been revived by the Tlingit Nation in S.E. Alaska. At the time of this writing, two youths, found guilty of assault and robbery of a pizza delivery person, were banished to remote islands off the coast of Alaska in the hopes they could be rehabilitated without being sent to prison. This was the first time in U.S. history that the courts agreed to let tribal elders carry out their own justice. However, once the banishment period is over, the youths may still have to face jail terms in a U.S. prison.

In closing, I would like to thank a young man from Oregon whose fight with aplastic anemia was a major inspiration for this book. I am happy to report that he successfully made it through a bone marrow transplant and is now back on his beloved tennis courts and baseball fields. He kindly gave permission to use his words in Chapter 23 of this story, and I am grateful for his insights and generous heart. I would also like to recognize all those who have enrolled in the National Bone Marrow Donor Program. I encourage everyone to register, especially people of ethnic minority groups. Until autologous transplant techniques (using the patient's own marrow) are perfected for all forms of blood disease, there is a dire need for marrow from healthy donors. If you are between the ages of 21 and 50, please volunteer for HLA-typing today at your nearest blood center.

Let HarperMonogram
Sweep You Away!

Chances Are by Robin Lee Hatcher
Over 3 million copies of Hatcher's books in print. Her young daughter's illness forces traveling actress Faith Butler to take a job at the Jagged R Ranch working for Drake Rutledge. Passions rise when the beautiful thespian is drawn to her rugged employer and the forbidden pleasure of his touch.

Mystic Moon by Patricia Simpson
"One of the premier writers of supernatural romance."—Romantic Times. A brush with death changes Carter Greyson's life and irrevocably links him to an endangered Indian tribe. Dr. Arielle Scott, who is intrigued by the mysterious Carter, shares this destiny—a destiny that will lead them both to the magic of lasting love.

Just a Miracle by Zita Christian
When dashing Jake Darrow brings his medicine show to Coventry, Montana, pharmacist Brenna McAuley wants nothing to do with him. But it's only a matter of time before Brenna discovers that romance is just what the doctor ordered.

Raven's Bride by Lynn Kerstan
When Glenys Shea robbed the reclusive Earl of Ravensby, she never expected to steal his heart instead of his gold. Now the earl's prisoner, the charming thief must prove her innocence—and her love.

And in case you missed last month's selections . . .

Once a Knight by Christina Dodd
Golden Heart and RITA Award–winning Author. Though slightly rusty, once great knight Sir David Radcliffe agrees to protect Lady Alisoun for a price. His mercenary heart betrayed by passion, Sir David proves to his lady that he is still a master of love—and his sword is as swift as ever.